A
SURE
THING

E.H. Ward

Tirgearr Publishing

Published by Tirgearr Publishing
Ireland
www.tirgearrpublishing.com

ISBN 978-1-910234-08-2

A CIP catalogue record for this book is
available from the British Library.

10 9 8 7 6 5 4 3 2 1

DEDICATION

To my mother and Marine.

PROLOGUE

Dublin - November 25th, 2005

Richard McMahon swung his white Mercedes off Clontarf Road and wound slowly through the streets. He took an indirect route to his luxury apartment block, checking the mirror every time he turned. He was fairly sure he was not being followed, but in the grey half-light of a drizzly evening, all the cars looked similar in the mirror. He pulled into the parking lot and stared at the bushes and shrubs that shielded it from the road.

The streetlight was not working. A bead of sweat formed at his hairline. He lit a cigarette and devoured it. Richard's skin was grey, almost translucent, his brow was furrowed and his crow's feet were craggier than usual. An all-day meeting with his lawyer had robbed him of energy and any sense of security that he had had a few days ago.

His company was still reeling from the drugs find, and he stood to lose a fortune. Then there was the matter of the suddenly silent Italian flight steward. Still, he was glad he had left the letter for his brother, even if it was too late to make amends – he should have treated Oliver better and helped him out when he came looking for Richard's backing and support.

Slightly calmed by the nicotine, he scanned the car park, picked up his briefcase and the long, heavy torch he kept on the passenger seat. He locked the car and hurried toward the sanctuary of the building. There was a sound from the bushes. He shone the torch, but could only make out leaves and shadows.

"Come out! I, I know you're there," he called, with a quiver in his voice. Breaking into a trot, he made for the lobby door.

Swearing, he dropped his briefcase trying to pull the passkey from his pocket. He never got to turn the lock.

* * *

The hooded man checked the photograph in his hand and satisfied himself that it was Richard McMahon approaching the lobby door. Looking left and right, he silently crossed the road and came up behind his target. As he moved, the iron bar slid down the anorak's sleeve into his hand. The blow dropped Richard to the ground. He was out before he hit the floor.

The man glanced down the street, then took his victim's watch, ripped the shoes from his feet, and searched for a wallet. Pocketing the banknotes, he tossed it aside. Then he stabbed a used syringe into his victim's neck.

Richard groaned. "Please, please . . ."

The man rose to his feet and bent over Richard. "You should've kept your mouth shut," he said. Then he swung the iron bar in a long slow arc. There was a dull crack and blood spilled onto the stone tiles.

The man walked briskly down the street, turned the corner and continued through four or five cross streets. He reversed his anorak and dropped the bar down a storm drain by the kerb on an empty street. The shoes he stuffed into a bin behind a convenience store. He fondled the Rolex and considered keeping it, but reluctantly tossed it into the waters of Dublin Bay.

As he walked along the coast road, he smiled, pushed the hood off his head and made a call.

"You tell our friends, it's done," he said.

* * *

Limerick - Nine days later

The driving rain ran through Oliver McMahon's hair and down his neck, soaking his collar. The damp sensation seeped under his overcoat and spread over his shoulders. He lowered his brother's coffin into the ground, assisted by two of Richard's college friends and the brother of his girlfriend, all of whom had been pressed into being pallbearers. Genuine mourners were in short supply at the funeral service of the workaholic who had little time for people. The company had helped with the funeral arrangements and provided a guard of honour for the coffin, although none of them looked particularly grief stricken: Oliver noticed some of them glancing at their watches.

A politician had phoned his mother, Evelyn, the night before to ask if he could say a few words about this great leader of business and a creator of Irish jobs. She had been too stunned to reply and Oliver told the man that he could give the eulogy if he liked, as neither he nor his mother were up to it. The man turned out to be a cabinet minister – Oliver couldn't remember which one – and was undoubtedly looking to gain public relations points, as he arrived to the church with a photographer and a journalist in tow. When he stood at the pulpit, he spoke at length about how Richard McMahon was a visionary, and what a privilege it was to have known him and dealt with him in his quest to see home-grown Irish business succeed.

Oliver sat in the pew, with one arm around his mother's shoulders, riveted in disgust. Why do we revere guys like my brother, Rich? He wondered. Why do we portray them as geniuses and saviours? All Rich did was to figure out a way to make money; he exploited his staff and used other people to make himself wealthy. Hell, there were plenty of rumours about how he managed to get the wheels greased. The fact that he created jobs was, to him, an unfortunate and costly side-effect; he would have done without crew if only he could have somehow automated the airline. Oliver remembered his brother fantasising one Sunday that if he had contacts in the arms business, he could push to get unmanned drone technology into his planes and then fire the whinging pilots.

Meanwhile, the priest mumbled bland, generic words about a man he had never met, as Oliver's mother held his arm tightly throughout the entire service.

The silence of the meagre crowd gathered in the Limerick city graveyard was broken by Evelyn's sobbing. She had spent the last four days in a state of despair, and now she stood by the freshly-dug grave and watched her eldest son laid to rest beside her husband. Oliver felt the shiny teak box come to rest on the dirt, and let the rope drop from his hands. It made a clunk on the coffin lid and, for the first time, the reality of the past few days hit him. Hard. His mind fell into a chasm of dizzy emotion and confusion.

The Gardai had been monotone and businesslike when they had stood on his mother's doorstep and delivered their report of what had happened: "There's been a sharp rise in muggings and petty theft in the last few months." They had explained, "Drug crime, most of it. Addicts venturing into the more respectable areas of Dublin to find the means to support their habit. It's likely that your son was unfortunate to have been in the wrong place at the wrong time."

Evelyn had collapsed in hysterics, unable to stomach the details of her son's murder, and Oliver had asked one of the policemen to call their local doctor, who arrived promptly, prescribed sedatives, and helped Oliver put his mother to bed.

Later, Oliver had sat in the kitchen gulping whiskey, while the policemen looked wistfully at his glass. "Your brother had been robbed of his cash, watch and shoes," they continued. "He had been stabbed in the neck with a dirty syringe, and struck a number of times with a blunt instrument: all the hallmarks of desperate drug crime. We are very sorry for your loss," they had said to Oliver.

The next day, Oliver had driven his mother to Dublin, checked her into a hotel, then gone to formally identify the remains and make arrangements for the funeral. There were few calls or messages of condolence. He called his fiancée, Rebecca, who said she would come over from America to support them, but he insisted there was no need. After all, she was busy and had never even met Richard.

The well-oiled PR machine in his brother's company, Freefly Airlines, made formal statements to the press. However, they seemed more occupied with deflecting the recent drugs-find scandal and finding someone to take over from a man who had never appointed anyone to deputize for him.

These events replayed over and over in Oliver's mind as he huddled under the umbrella with his mother at the graveside. He put an arm around her, and for the first time felt a sense of loss. He also felt guilty for not reaching out to his brother, as his mother had wanted. People filed past and shook his hand. He was unaware of who anybody was, until the politician sidled up. Oliver reluctantly gripped his palm without looking directly at the man. He finally snapped out of his thoughts moments later when a small, clammy hand limply took his own, and he was reminded of his brother's feeble handshake. His eyes ran up the arm to the small body and thin mousey face in front of him.

"Thank you," said Oliver on autopilot; staring through the man.

"My name's Martin Forrester."

"Oh, OK."

"I worked for your brother. Anyway, I'm sorry to bring this up now, but I really need to talk to you. It's very important."

Oliver noticed the urgency in his eyes. "Well, er, OK. Why don't you come to the house for a drink after, and we'll chat there?"

Back at home, Oliver put his mother in her favourite chair by the fireplace, and made her tea. The other pallbearers had returned to have a drink and sandwiches, along with a handful of others, but most were anxious to leave again. Oliver wished they would.

A little over an hour later, Oliver sat alone with his mother on the arm of her chair, holding her hand. She stared into space. Martin Forrester appeared in the room like a ghost.

"Bloody hell," said Oliver, standing up. "Where'd you come out of?"

"Ah, sure I stayed out of the way in the kitchen, and ate some of your lovely fruit cake. I've always been able to sink into the background – a lifetime of being afraid of your brother." He tried to backtrack. "Oh, er, well, y'know. He was a tough boss."

Oliver's expression was half-grimace, half-smile.

Evelyn snapped out of her trance, "Look, I may have been the only person in the world who loved Richard, but I won't have a bad word spoken about him. Not in this house. Not today."

Martin looked like he wanted the ground to open and swallow him. Oliver felt sick.

"Mum, I wish I . . ."

His mother stood, the colour returning to her cheeks. "Please, Oliver," she gripped his hand. "We all wish for things: mostly that they were different. But they're not. So we just have to face up to it and deal with the mistakes of the past as best we can." She sighed. "I think I'll have another cup of tea and then try to sleep." She departed for the kitchen.

Martin perched himself awkwardly on the fender by the fireplace.

"What's so important?" said Oliver.

Martin took a deep breath. "I think your brother's death is a bit convenient."

Oliver stared, his mouth slightly agape.

"I'll start from the beginning, so?" said Martin.

"That'd be great."

"A few weeks ago, a pilot came to me complaining about a steward on the Opulence Service – our private jets. Staff complaints happen quite often, but this time the pilot was livid. He said he thought something dodgy was going on, and wanted me to have the guy investigated. He said he'd go to the police if I didn't. I told him to calm down and get a hold of himself. Then I reported the matter to your brother, who hated squabbles and always dealt with them swiftly and severely.

"Anyway, when I mentioned that the complaint was against the Italian he had personally hired and put on the service, Richard became very agitated. He said it was all just bullshit and that the pilot had a history of making racist remarks about cabin crew – which is true – but I could tell he was nervous. And, God knows, nerves weren't something your brother usually suffered from."

"Unless he was losing money," said Oliver.

"You've a point there. Not that he ever lost much in the years I knew him. Anyway, he told me to leave the matter to him and not tell anyone," he went on. "The next day, your brother disappeared from the office. Later, I found out that he'd had a long meeting with his lawyer. Then, over the next few days, more meetings. I never saw him so stressed." Martin let out a long sigh. "Next thing you know, one of the Opulence jets gets searched. Turns out, the pilot went to the cops himself.

"You see, most of the pilots don't like your brother. That is, they didn't; on account of the long hours he made them work. This pilot really hated Richard: he got sued for calling a black flight attendant a *coon*, your brother paid her off, but used it as an excuse to really screw the guy on his salary. He couldn't even leave, or your brother would've leaked the story to every airline and newspaper in the country. So, I think he saw this as revenge." Another deep breath. "Anyway, the cops searched the plane and the Italian crew member after a trip to Ibiza. They found two kilos of cocaine, hidden in hollowed out wooden souvenirs in his bag. Even the guards seemed delighted to get Freefly Airlines for something – you know what the begrudgers are like."

"Yeah I do, when it came to my brother, I was one of them, but that's another story."

Martin looked puzzled. "Anyway, I don't think the company'll fail because of it, but the scandal's fairly big. We'll probably have to close the Opulence Service. The cops are livid that the Italian won't tell them anything. He just sits there muttering in his own language and he won't say a word to an interpreter. Suddenly he can't speak English. So they're dying to believe that your brother was shipping drugs around on his planes."

"How'd you find all this out?"

"I, er, I've contacts in the press. And they've contacts in the guards."

The outlandish idea of Richard as a drug dealer made Oliver pause. "OK, so you think my brother was killed in some drug war?"

"Actually, no. No, I don't. You see, um, the thing is . . . I know you work for Marco Romano."

The offices of James Foster, solicitor
January 2006

Oliver took the envelope and held it in his hands for a second, he felt like a widower at a séance. He ripped the brown paper open and read the spidery handwriting.

Dear Ollie,

I'm sorry for being such an asshole. I was only focused on business.

Mother tried to make me face a few truths that day you asked me for money, but I couldn't take back what I said, because I'm not good at admitting I'm wrong and because you were so upset that you wouldn't have listened, anyway. I wanted to make up with you, but I never got round to it. Now I'm scared enough to finally do something about it. So I did some thinking, changed my will, and did the only thing I have ever been able to do: throw money at someone instead of investing emotion.

I suppose I learnt that from Dad, but I'm not just throwing my money at you: I'm giving it to you so you can live the kind of life you deserve. I had it all but never stopped to enjoy it.

Look after Mother – who am I talking to? Of course you will.

The truth is, you always looked after Mother better than I did. You were there for her; I just saw that my money was there. And I was never there for you.

It's only in the last few days I realised what I'm like. I've had to face a few truths. Ollie, I've nobody to turn to or confide in.

Now I've got myself into deep shit – and I have nobody for support.

I've done something stupid. I agreed to take on a relative of Marco's, and he's been caught smuggling drugs. I didn't think it would be a problem, because nobody knew I had been asked to employ him, but I realized the awful truth. Guys like Marco NEVER ask these kinds of favours directly, they use middlemen or messengers, but Marco DID ask me directly. Now I have to ask myself if he'll trust me, or if he'll want to break the link between us.

I can't face telling the full story to my solicitor or the police. It would be the end of the airline, and it would finish Mum, and possibly you. I'll have to wait it out and see what happens. But if you're reading this, then something has happened to me, and I want you to get out of business with this guy.

I know this letter'll be a shock, but you can handle it. Sit and get a plan straight in your head. Don't worry about James – he's been well paid to wait and do what you want. He's a good man.

Be careful, Ollie. Do better than I did. You know you can. I know you can.

Rich

Oliver's head was spinning. How had it all come to this?

PART I

Chapter 1

New York City. August 1994

Oliver McMahon strolled through the crowds on Sixth Avenue, soaking up the summer sun and lamenting the lack of adventure during the weekend. The young Irishman was trying to stay cool despite the summer heat, but not succeeding. His straggly mop of dark hair was plastered to his tanned forehead, while the green polo shirt he wore was stuck to his tall, lean frame. His jeans felt so hot he wanted to take them off right there on the street.

He had finished work at the thoroughbred horse sales in Saratoga and headed to New York alone the day before; none of the other Irish lads wanted to come with him. He was partly glad of this, as he needed some time alone to get over his girlfriend, Rebecca, who was returning to university in Colorado. They had told each other it was better to end their relationship – she was planning to stay in America after graduation, while Oliver was intent on working his way around the horseracing globe.

Oliver's first mission in New York had been to visit Giants stadium, to witness the scene of the Irish triumph over the Italians in their opening game of the World Cup campaign two months before.

After that, he had found a succession of dark bars and had a few laughs playing pool and talking to strangers, but he didn't manage to pick up a girl. He found himself unable to get Rebecca out of his head, no matter how hard he tried. He had just turned twenty-one and could have a legal drink to drown his sorrows, but now the thumping behind his eyes reminded him he had possibly overdone it. If Rebecca had been with him, he would have drunk less and had more fun.

In his hungover state, he walked all the way to Central Park Zoo to watch the animals for signs of boredom or unhappiness that most people failed to notice. Oliver sat on a bench beside a thin, sprightly old lady, fanning herself with a magazine and watching the elephants shifting their weight from one foot to another in a nervous tick. She tutted, shook her head and muttered. "Poor things, so bored."

Oliver smiled and shot the woman a sideways glance. "I bet they'd love a run in the park," he said.

The pensioner inspected him with a mischievous smile. "Gee, now that'd be a sight." She got up to walk away and dropped her sunglasses as she put the magazine in her bag. Oliver picked them up and gave them back to her.

"Why, thank you, young man."

Oliver smiled through his throbbing head. "Not a bother, you're welcome."

"That's not a New York accent. Where you from?"

"I'm Irish . . . and to be honest, I'm not really feeling the best. I think I need something to eat."

The woman smiled again and Oliver turned on his heel and headed out onto the street. He found a nearby cafe and wolfed down a burger, fries and a Coke, to kill the hangover.

Feeling renewed, he set off walking back down Sixth Avenue, headed south, with no particular plan in his head. The humidity was starting to get to him. The city seemed to generate its own heat from the sheer amount of energy created and consumed here. He put a hand up to push his hair back from his forehead, and noticed an ice-cream vendor on the sidewalk.

He bought a cone and stood eating it, when his eye was drawn to a very pretty blonde girl in a tight T-shirt and long, flowery skirt, who was desperately trying to persuade a child to hold her hand and walk calmly down the street.

The boy, who looked about nine or ten – but then Oliver was never sure how old kids were – was screaming.

"No. No!"

"God, Robert. You're not running loose in the city, OK? Too many people, too much traffic."

She looked worn out. Oliver gazed at her figure and thought she looked too young for the child to be hers, but then you could never be totally sure.

The girl spotted the ice-cream vendor, and an expression of relief replaced her frown.

"Jeez, Robert, if I buy you an ice cream, will you calm down?"

"Maybe," he replied with a grin that was part delight and part mischief.

She turned to the stall and ordered. She let go of the boy's hand to give him his cone and get money from her bag. He took the cone and bolted.

Oliver watched as the kid came straight for him. He dodged past pedestrians and tried to run away up the edge of the footpath, inches from the bustling traffic. He made one more step before his foot slipped off the edge, sending him headlong into the road, arms flailing, trying to break his fall.

The kid hit the asphalt, narrowly missing the rear of a delivery van. He lay sprawled on the road like an insect on its back, waiting to be squashed. It seemed nobody else had noticed. Oliver could see a taxi heading straight towards the boy. Instinctively, he dropped his ice cream and dived into the road. As he bent to scoop up the kid, the taxi was close enough for Oliver to see the driver in a heated exchange with the passenger.

The girl started to scream "Robert" in a panicky voice.

Oliver grabbed the kid by the neck of his T-shirt then pivoted on his heels, flinging the child onto the footpath. He overbalanced, staggered, and just knew the car would hit him even before he felt the thump of the wing mirror on his elbow. It spun him round and toppled him backwards. He hit the pavement beside the kid. The taxi didn't even slow down; the ice cream cone moulded itself into the tyre.

The boy lay in a heap, shocked and choking, his shirt tight around his neck, his breathy moans seemed to merge with the girl's frantic shrieks.

"Oh, God! Oh, God! Robert!" she dashed over to him. "You'll be the end of me! Why d'you got to keep doing this stuff?"

Robert fell into the girl's arms, sobbing and coughing.

Oliver picked himself up, then rubbed and stretched his elbow. Nothing broken, but it would probably throb like hell in a few hours.

A few onlookers had stopped to take in the scene, but for most people bustling down the avenue, it was as if nothing at all had happened. The girl, however, looked different: pale, scared and shaking.

She looked at Oliver for the first time. Her eyes were wide with fear, tears welling up, almost like someone about to face a firing squad. "Holy shit!" she said. "Are you OK?"

Oliver flexed his elbow again. "Grand. It'll probably be a bit sore later on, but I've had worse kicks from horses. Nothing a hot whiskey won't cure!"

She looked incredulous. "Did . . . did you pull him off the street?"

"Yeah, well, ah sure, I just . . . he ran past me and kind of tripped onto the road. That taxi nearly hit him . . ." Oliver trailed off as he saw the depth of fear in her eyes, and felt he should offer some consolation.

"You've got your hands full there. He's a wild one."

"You should meet his dad," she muttered. "It sucks being a nanny. Mr. R'll go nuts when he finds out about this. It's not the first time, either."

"I knew you looked too young to be his mother." Oliver gave her his best smile and turned up his Irish accent. "Hey, it can't be that bad. I can always vouch for you."

She half-smiled. Still gripping the sobbing Robert, she tilted her head to one side.

"You know what? I might take you up on that. I'm Cassie and this is Robert."

She turned the boy around to face his saviour.

"And I'm Oliver McMahon," he said to them both.

"Look, can I get your number or something? Really, I owe you, and so does he."

She looked down at the child. "Thank the nice man, Robert. He saved your life. Those cars would have hit you. D'you get that?"

The anxiety in her voice was starting to diminish.

The boy looked up, wiped the tears from his eyes and started rubbing his throat.

"Thanks, I guess, Mister," he sobbed, in an accent that Oliver could not place.

Charming, thought Oliver. Pretty girl, pity about the obnoxious brat.

"That's really not necessary, you know. I'm just here for the weekend, doing the tourist thing."

"Where're you staying?"

"At a hostel near Times Square. Not exactly the Waldorf Astoria, but it's OK."

"Then give me the name and your room number."

Oliver beamed confidently. He pictured himself in a bar with Cassie. "Well, it's the Linehouse Hostel and it's room two; more of a dorm, actually. No room service."

Cassie rooted in her bag with one hand, keeping the other firmly gripped to Robert's wrist. She drew out a pen and paper and handed them to Oliver.

"Can you write that down, please?"

He did.

"Now, we got to get back to the car. Thanks again, Oliver. I'll be in touch." She smiled and shook his hand.

"Come on, Robert, the driver'll be waiting and we've had enough excitement."

She turned away and the kid meekly went with her. Her hand latched onto his wrist.

Oliver watched her lovely figure fade into the mass of people. He smiled and thought that perhaps the weekend was not a complete loss, after all.

Chapter 2

Oliver strolled around for an hour or so. Then he went to the Museum of Modern Art, before heading back to the hostel for a nap and to be sure he would be in if Cassie called. He awoke to the shouts of the receptionist, a lively Chinese man in his forties who was also the manager, cleaner and owner of the hostel.

"Sir, Sir. You must wake up. You Irish Oliver, right? Phone call. Come now."

Oliver rubbed his eyes and looked at his watch. Eight-thirty. Excellent, the night was about to begin. His elbow was sore and slightly swollen. He popped two paracetemol as he made his way down the stairs to the front desk, thinking of Cassie.

"Well, hello there!" he drawled into the phone, in his huskiest voice.

"Oliver McMahon?" asked a male voice in a New York accent.

Definitely not Cassie.

"Er, um, er, yes."

"Good. I'm callin' for my boss. He wants to say thanks for what you did today."

"Well, er, I didn't do very much."

"In an hour, there'll be a car at your hotel. Get in it. OK?"

"Err, OK."

"Hey, lighten up. You're a goddamn hero."

The line went dead.

Bizarre, thought Oliver. So much for a chat to the lovely Cassie. All the same, he smiled as his mind filled with possibilities for the night ahead. He jumped into the shower, whistling as he got himself ready for the unknown adventure. Whatever happened, it beat spending the weekend talking the same old shite to his colleagues in the Irish bar back in Lexington, Kentucky. He was sure they were there, huddled round a table, right at this very moment.

Exactly one hour later, Oliver sat on the steps outside the hostel waiting for the car. He wondered what had happened to the kid when he got home; the nanny had said he'd be in for it. In Oliver's childhood, that would have meant a walloping from his father. But people who had nannies probably didn't do that kind of thing. It would be no TV, or grounded for two weeks, stuck inside their upmarket apartment. What a hardship.

He was so engrossed in gazing down the avenue towards the lights of Times Square that he didn't notice the sleek black Lincoln Town Car pull up silently in front of him. The driver's window cracked open. A loud, rough voice snapped him out of his thoughts.

"Hey, you the guy? Oliver, right?"

"Yeah, that's me alright." He went around to the passenger door and sat in. The driver was a tall, muscular guy in his thirties, with wavy dark hair coiffed into an elaborate bouffant. His immaculate clothing and appearance didn't quite go with his crooked smile and the sharp, taut skin on his face. He looked a little surprised.

"Usually people sit in the back, but it's OK. You can ride with me if you want. I'm Mike."

"Thanks, Mike. Where are we off to?"

"Cardinales."

"What?"

Mike looked aghast. "You haven't heard of Cardinales?"

"No. Is it good?"

"Good? It's one of the best restaurants in town. Got a great fuckin' view." He looked at Oliver and smiled.

The young tourist spent the journey downtown staring out the window at the marvellous city as it passed by. He gazed at the flashing billboards, endlessly selling products, movies and TV shows. He heard the wailing sirens, roaring engines and constant chattering of the crowds. It sounded like a riot was always in progress, somewhere, everywhere. The sheer energy of the noise and lights gave life to the residents. They drank it up. They consumed the energy of the city with an urgency that Oliver had never seen before. Perhaps this was the essence of the American Dream. The idea that everything was possible, and that here, there was enough energy to achieve anything. That was why he loved working in America.

He had run out of Ireland as soon as he could, like anyone else of his generation with any sense. The noise and madness of New York was a million miles from the serenity of the Kentucky stud farm where he worked, but the spirit and determination to build, to achieve, to get on was the same. Oliver woke every day feeling bloody lucky. He loved the racehorse breeding business, and aspired to manage or even own a stud himself one day.

Now he was travelling the globe and immersing himself in the horse-world, so that when the time came, he would be experienced enough to set up shop wherever he wanted. And it got him out of Ireland. To the dismay of his parents, he had not followed his older brother Richard's example of getting a business degree at college in Dublin. The fact that he was learning his trade from the inside out did not resonate with his folks. Where was his certificate on the wall? That was how you got on: letters after your name.

His father had struggled to farm a large tract of land in County Limerick, and had only recently found respite when he sold a substantial part of the farm for development. He disapproved of his younger son wanting to enter a rural pursuit.

Oliver was jolted back to the present by Mike, who announced that they were about to cross the Brooklyn Bridge.

"Like I said, this place has the best view of the city, my friend. It's a little out of the boss's turf, but he was on Long Island today, so he thought you'd like it."

Oliver felt excited. Long Island. Probably had a house there. Cool. Maybe he would get to meet Cassie again.

The car swept over into Brooklyn and pulled up on a street one block from the waterfront. Mike pointed to a smart-looking restaurant. "Go on in, he's waiting."

Oliver entered and the maitre'd disdainfully looked him up and down. Oliver observed the man's immaculate suit, and glanced sheepishly down at his own scruffy boots. Then it occurred to him that he didn't even know the name of the man he was to meet.

"Good evening, Sir. Mr. Romano is waiting for you. Before I show you to your table, perhaps I could offer you a jacket."

"Oh, thank you."

Oliver was led through the elegant restaurant; not one table was unoccupied – mostly business types in expensive suits and ties, indulging their wives, clients or mistresses. Everybody looked smartly dressed and full of money. He was stunned by the enormous window the length of the room and its truly breathtaking view of Manhattan. Only after staring for some time, did he notice the man sitting alone at a table right beside the window.

The maitre'd approached the table and pulled a chair back for Oliver. The seated man stood, smiled, and extended a large, powerful hand.

"Oliver! Good to meet you, I'm Marco Romano. I hope my guy got you here OK?" he smiled as he spoke in an accent that was trying to sound refined and elegant, but at the same time, possessed a warmth that might have come from an old friend. This put Oliver at ease, as he focused on the man gripping his hand like he imagined a father should do.

"Yeah, thank you. What a mad city, beats Limerick any day of the week."

Marco Romano was a tall, heavyset man in his mid-forties, with a wide face beneath thick black hair, carefully slicked back. His intense dark eyes bored into Oliver – in a way he felt could almost become uncomfortable – but Marco's still-firm handshake reassured him. His enormous hands protruded from white shirt-cuffs and a smart, well-tailored jacket, which covered his massive shoulders. The power in his physical form seemed to surge through his handshake and make Oliver tingle. They both sat, and Marco poured the young man a glass of wine.

"This your first time in New York?"

"Yeah."

"You'll like this Chianti, it's really good stuff," he said in his strange, almost bizarre accent.

Marco raised his glass and continued.

"Let our first drink be to you, the hero of the day."

"Well, thanks. But, sure, like I said to Cassie, I really didn't do very much."

They clinked their glasses together and drank.

Oliver pondered Marco's accent and speech. Something wasn't quite right about it. It reminded Oliver of his days in the boarding school on the outskirts of Limerick city that he and his brother attended. All the pupils were strictly disciplined if they failed to speak properly, with correct grammar and clear diction. After years of drilling, this rather old-fashioned speech became second nature for the pupils, in order to avoid the wrath of the monks, but they soon learned to tone it down and try to fake the city accent when they were allowed into Limerick at weekends and found themselves ridiculed by other school kids and, most crucially, the local girls, who were relentlessly cruel.

Marco, it seemed, was doing the opposite. Oliver could not think why, but he knew Marco was trying to conceal something, and in a strange way he felt this made them kindred spirits.

"Please, Oliver, don't be modest. Cassie told me that without you risking your own skin, my son would have been under a car." He paused and took another sip of wine. "Oliver, Robert is my only child. It's been tough – he's been tough – since his mother died last year. As for that Cassie, huh!" He let out a long sigh. "The fact is, I owe a very great debt to you."

"Mr. Romano, really, it all just happened so quick. Anyone would've done what I did. And I am so sorry to hear about your wife. That must be very difficult for both of you."

A downcast look came into the black eyes. "You look much too young to be married, but let me tell you: when you do take a wife, you don't want to lose her." He paused again and stared out the window with faraway eyes.

For some reason, Oliver suddenly thought that he should

defend Cassie. "Also, I think Cassie was doing her best. She was trying to reason with Robert before, well, you know..."

"She said you got hurt. You OK?"

Oliver rubbed his elbow and slowly flexed his arm. "It'll be grand. I've had worse knocks."

"You're some guy, you know that?" Marco focused his intense gaze on the young Irishman. "Oliver. I want you to fully understand what I am saying." The man spoke very deliberately and much slower than before.

"I'm a man who likes to get things done, and I attend to details. But no amount of power or money could save my wife. My family was torn apart; now my son is my only reminder of her. He's beyond precious to me. Without you today, I might have been preparing another funeral."

Marco's black eyes pierced Oliver, as if they were looking through his face, right into his head. This was all getting a bit heavy – marriage and kids, and all, never mind burying a wife or protecting a child.

"I owe you more than you can possibly imagine. If there is anything I can ever do for you, just let me know, and it'll be done. I mean that. You understand, my man?"

Of course, he did. Helping each other out, backing up a friend, was what made the world go so much easier; but there was something about the intensity of Marco's declaration and the look in his eyes that put the young man on edge.

"Yeah. Yes, yes, thanks. I really appreciate that." It seemed to be all he could say.

"You know, Oliver, in this day and age, too many people look the other way and pretend not to notice when something bad is going to happen. They just don't want to get involved." He arched his eyebrows and a smirk almost cracked his mouth. "Now, sometimes, that's a good thing. But sometimes it's not. People like you are rare in New York. In America even."

Marco then produced a card.

"This is my main business card. We have a club and a bar in Jersey, and some other interests. These numbers are my office lines." He turned the card over. There was a handwritten number. "This is my cell. Not many people know this number. Do NOT show this to ANYONE, OK? This is just for you."

Oliver took the card and placed it directly into his wallet.

"Good. Now that business is over, let's eat. And tell me about yourself."

He motioned to the waiter, who scurried over. Marco ordered for them both.

"The lobster here's amazing, Trust me, it's fresh from New England. And don't be afraid to get drunk."

Oliver enjoyed the meal and the wine flowed freely. He felt at ease once more.

Marco continued to surprise him. He would deliberately start eating his lobster, using the finger bowl and napkin constantly, then when he became engrossed in conversation, his hands would resort to ripping the crustacean apart and he would stuff a rough chunk of meat into his mouth and swill it down with a gulp of wine. The glass would hover in mid-air on the way back to the table, as if Marco had remembered something. He would swallow, clear his throat, take a deep breath and return the glass gently to the white tablecloth. Oliver found this rollercoaster ride interesting and amusing in equal part. In an effort to ignore the sideshow, he told Marco about growing up in Ireland and working in the horse business.

"Racehorses! No shit!" He leaned in over the table. "Can you give me any tips? I go to the track at Belmont or Monmouth sometimes, to meet people. It's interesting. A friend of mine has a horse. We won a couple bucks on her once. Maybe I'll have one myself. One day."

"Well, the best tip I can give you is not to bet too much unless you have inside information." Marco let out a belly laugh, "Yeah, I know, it's a crooked game."

"No, it's not so bad, but when you know horses like I do, you know what can go wrong, there's no such thing as a sure thing."

The older man smiled and looked at the young Irishman opposite him. "Now isn't that the truth! In life also." He took another sip of wine, sighed, and looked out at the lights of Manhattan.

"And what do you do, Mr. Romano? You said you have a club and other interests."

"Please, call me Marco." He turned to face Oliver again. "I'm involved in a number of business ventures, but the two most profitable are sports betting and nightclubs. So you can see why horseracing interests me."

"Well, yeah. But, like I said Marco, I find the best way is not to bet. Or else I'd end up like the poor eejits who give all their money to guys like you!" The wine was starting to loosen his tongue.

"Unless you have the inside information, right?" Marco smiled, and they both burst out laughing.

They continued talking and, despite the somewhat shaky start, after a couple of hours Oliver felt it was like talking to a mate, someone he'd known for a long time. It reminded him of the odd times his father used to take him and his brother out of school early on a Friday and treat them to lunch in a hotel. Except this evening, Oliver wasn't being scolded and told to be more like his brother. He was being spoken to like an adult; an equal.

As they ate, the restaurant gradually emptied around them, the staff tidied up, and waited patiently for them to finish. Eventually, Marco stood and announced that he was leaving.

"Mike'll take you home again. And if there's any place you want to go on the way, just ask. He knows all the good nightclubs in the tri-state area."

"Jesus, I haven't a clue."

"Don't worry about it. He'll take care of you."

Oliver stood up and followed Marco to the door. They walked out past the staff, who were lined up and seemed to look at Marco and him with a certain mixture of awe and dread.

"Well, thanks for dinner, Marco. That was really great."

As they got to the door, Marco turned and gripped the young man's hand as he had done before, but this time he patted Oliver's right shoulder with his other large palm. The gesture felt almost like a hug to Oliver and made him feel mildly embarrassed. His father had never hugged him or his brother, preferring to leave such gestures of affection to their mother.

"No, *I* thank *you*, Oliver. And I mean it. Call me or come to see me if you ever need anything. Now go on, enjoy the town."

He released his hand and gestured towards the open door, which was held patiently and reverently by the *maître'd*.

This time, there were two town cars waiting on the street. Marco strode towards the nearer and sat in gracefully. The car pulled away immediately. Oliver got into the other.

"Nice dinner?" asked Mike. "Where to now?"

"I've no idea. Marco said you knew every club around."

A crooked grin appeared. "Leave it to me."

Chapter 3

They sped across the Brooklyn Bridge, back into the city and across town. Oliver was lost. "Normally I'd take you to one of the boss's places in Jersey, but I reckon we should go to this place I know in the meat-packing district. It's getting to be a happening part of town. Business startin' to move there."

"Cool, sounds good."

The car stopped on the dark street outside a club with a long queue of people waiting to get in.

"Come on, man." Mike tapped Oliver on the shoulder.

They both stepped onto the street and the car was whisked away by a valet. When Mike approached the entrance, the doorman nodded and let them pass without a word. Once inside, a lithe young woman engaged Mike in friendly conversation and showed them upstairs to a balcony overlooking the dance floor. They were seated in a booth and a bottle of champagne appeared on the table, as if by magic.

Oliver was stunned; he had never been ushered in anywhere like a VIP. He beamed from ear to ear and looked out at the steaming mass of people, all writhing to a pumping tune. There were professional dancers in cages and men on stilts. Lexington, Kentucky, it was not.

"Yo! Oliver, my man, you like the place?" said Mike.

Oliver turned back to Mike. "This is wicked. Cool out! Spot on. Nice bubbly, too!"

Mike laughed and shook his head. "You sure are one weird guy! Anyway, you're here to have fun, so here you go." Mike flicked his wrist at Oliver and a small bag of white powder shot towards him and landed in his lap. Oliver's eyes went wide.

"Is this, is this, er . . ."

"Well, it ain't baking soda. Of course, if you don't want it."
With that, Mike stretched out his hand again.

"No, no, I'll try it! It's just that I never have before, that's all."
He held the bag in his fingers and fondled it with his thumb. The
powder inside felt fine and light. He felt nervous, but curious.

"That's serious quality stuff, man. But don't rack up out here:
that's too messy. Go to the VIP restrooms."

"Rack up? I make it into lines and snort it, right?"

"You live a sheltered life, or what?" he smiled mockingly.
"Yeah, that's right. But don't do it all at once, and chop it up a
little with your credit card." He gestured towards the back of the
club. "Now go on, have some fun. I'll wait here. In fact – fuck it
– I'm coming with you."

In the restroom, they crammed themselves into a stall. Mike
produced another bag from something strapped to his ankle, and
prepared four lines of the white dust on the toilet cistern. He then
rolled up a crisp hundred dollar bill and handed it to Oliver.

"Go for it, my man. One in each side."

Oliver inhaled deeply through his nose. He couldn't feel very
much, apart from a numbing sensation in his throat; the high
seemed to be very subtle, but as they left the restroom and the
hostess from earlier asked him if he was OK, he suddenly felt on
top of the world. He smiled and kissed her on the cheek.

"Easy, buddy." She gently pushed him back. "I'll get a friend of
mine to come drink with you."

They sat back down. He started chattering at a rate of knots,
while Mike nodded and laughed at him.

"Man, you're a good guy. But you need to calm down. It's goin'
to be a long night!"

They talked shit for about twenty minutes, shouting over the
music, before the most beautiful, tall, fit, sexy brunette Oliver had
ever seen approached and sat directly on his knee. She put an arm
around his neck and shouted into his ear, "Coke's great tonight,
huh?"

She turned her head. "Hey, Mike. Who's your buddy? He's cute."

"I'm Oliver," he roared back into her ear. "Nice to meet you and, yeah, the coke's amazing! It's my first time!"

"Oh my God, I love your accent. Where you from?"

"Ireland."

"That's so cool."

"You want to dance?"

"Sure."

As he led her by the hand down to the dance floor, he really couldn't believe his luck. And Cassie was far from his mind as they kissed amidst the seething, roaring mass of clubbers.

The night faded into a blur of cocaine, champagne, pretty girls and energetic dancing, and the best blow-job he had ever had. He couldn't quite remember the girl's name as he boarded his plane back to Kentucky the next day.

Chapter 4

When he arrived back at the stud near Lexington, his housemates were desperate for all the news of how he'd got on in New York. In the stud farm business, it was usual for many of the staff to live in shared accommodation on the farm, so his housemates were also his colleagues.

Kieran, Tom and Eamon were Irish, and all working in America on various visa programs. The four of them were in the same boat and had roughly the same aims in life. They all worked long, hard hours, and spent their evenings cracking jokes, drinking beers and waiting for the weekend when they would supplement the back-breaking work with partying.

That evening, he swept into the house, grabbed a beer from the fridge and plonked himself down on the sofa without saying a word. He sipped his beer and felt the others stare at him, desperate for information about his trip. They had returned to Lexington straight after the horse sales in Saratoga.

"Oh, for fuck sake, McMahon, did you get a ride or what?" said Eamon, the oldest of the bunch at twenty-five and the most focused on his desire to trade horses for a living.

"Yeah, c'mon, any birds?" asked Tom, chuckling. "I bet they're fuckin' beat all, up there."

Oliver sipped his beer and spread a slow, satisfied smile across his face.

"Ya dog!" said Kieran. "Ya did!"

"No, no. Sorry, lads."

"Go 'way, liar. Ya did! It's written all over your face."

Oliver shook his head. "But I did stop a kid getting run over, had dinner with some rich businessman, and got taken to a mad club by his chauffeur." He took another swig of beer and kept looking at the TV. After a moment of silence, he glanced at the three open mouths. Putting them out of their misery, he recounted the story of the weekend, leaving out the cocaine, which was considered quite a taboo amongst these guys.

They lapped it up. Kieran trotted out to the fridge to get more beers, Tom sat there laughing himself to tears, but Eamon thought about it for a moment before he opened his mouth.

"This rich lad; you should tee him up for a fuckin' cleaning. Flog him a few yokes that nobody else wants."

Oliver shot him a puzzled look.

"I'm tellin' you, this lad sounds like he doesn't know a horse from a dog. Sure, you could unload some pure shite on him and get a nice cut from the deal." He winked. "Everyone loves a new lad in the game. What was his name?"

Oliver sighed. Eamon was only interested in emptying everyone else's pockets. He never even bought beer for the house; he was well able to drink it, though. "Eamon, d'you not think it'd be better to help a man buy good horses and enjoy a bit of success? Then you'd have a client for life, instead of robbing him today."

"Ah, you're thinking too far ahead, McMahon. You shouldn't be doing that. Better you clean him today, than some other fucker tomorrow."

"Aah, Eamon, you're an awful whore. You'd take advantage of anyone. Ha! Oliver, remind me in a few years never to buy a horse from this dodgy fucker."

"Go fuck yourself, Tom. If I was helping you unload a yoke, you'd be kissin' my hole."

"In your dreams, bollix."

Oliver finished his beer and got up to leave.

Eamon shouted after him. "Hey, McMahon! Can you work instead of me next weekend? I've a mission to go on."

"Sure. No problem, Eamon," he said. "What're you up to?"

"Oh, I can't be tellin' you that."

Oliver shook his head and laughed as he slipped off to bed.

Two weeks later he sat round a table in a bar in Lexington with Ricky, a local guy from the stud farm, and a friend of Ricky's from University of Kentucky. Oliver had bought a few rounds and recounted the story of his New York trip, with Ricky and his friend hanging on every word. He had told them about the cocaine, sharing a joint earlier in Ricky's car. But something stopped him from mentioning the business card with the private numbers on it. Perhaps it was Marco's intense stare that stopped him, or maybe it was just that Oliver didn't want to disclose every detail of the story.

The other guy – a bright chemistry major called Ted – was quiet while Ricky laughed and jibed Oliver. Then he clinked glasses with Oliver and asked, "So, have you thought about what you're going to get Marco Romano to do for you?"

"Shit, I don't know." Oliver smirked. "I suppose if I need coke, girls or free entrance to a club in New York, then all I have to do is ask!" With that, he and Ricky burst out laughing again. But Ted kept looking at Oliver. When they calmed down, Ted spoke again.

"Dude, you really don't know who that guy is, do you?"

"What do you mean?"

"Man, you horse guys are too wrapped up in your world of racing and betting, and whatever. Don't you read the papers?"

"Only the *Daily Racing Form*," replied Oliver.

Ted rolled his eyes. "This Thing of Ours," he said in an Italian accent.

Oliver and Ricky stared blankly.

"This Thing of Ours – *La Cosa Nostra* – ring any bells?" he said, raising his eyebrows and cocking his head to one side.

Again, blank stares.

"Geez, you guys. It's been on the news for weeks. The Feds are really cracking down on the mob, putting guys away this time." He took another swig of beer for dramatic pause. "Marco Romano is the head of a family in New Jersey. Well, not the head exactly, he's like the deputy or some shit like that. The real boss has just been put away in prison."

Oliver's jaw hit the ground. "You're joking! What, you mean, he's like a gangster?" He started shaking his head. "No way. The mob and stuff, that's like the movies. Guys like that don't really exist anymore, do they?"

Ted gave him an incredulous look.

Oliver thought back to the events of that night, and began to feel a little nervous and defensive. "No, no. Couldn't be. I mean, he, he was like . . . well, I got on better with him than I did with my dad. We relaxed, talked for hours."

Ted rolled his eyes. "That's why he's known as Marco 'The Gent' Romano. I'm telling you, dude, you had dinner with one of the most powerful, most wanted men on the eastern seaboard and you didn't have a clue who he was. He must have thought you were either the coolest motherfucker in the world, or the dumbest asshole he ever met. Go check it out, dude, he really is a mob boss!"

Oliver thought about it and suddenly felt cold. He knew it could be true. It helped all the details make sense. What he didn't know was how he should feel about it, or what – if anything – he should do about it. His instincts told him it might be better to stop telling this story – to anyone. He felt very sober all of a sudden, and wanted to call it a night.

Chapter 5

Ten years later - Ireland
April 2004

He groaned as he lifted his arm to pivot the fork-load of steaming horse manure up in the air and into the trailer. It was sheer drudgery; brainless, mechanical work that could be done on autopilot, and Oliver had to spend hours doing it. Every day. The rain poured down all around him and on him; it collected in deep pools in the gravel of the yard outside.

Oliver finished that stable and climbed onto the tractor. The rain had flooded the seat on the old wreck. He tried to wipe it off a bit, not that it really mattered. He was soaked already from the constant, driving rain. He moved the tractor and jumped off into the next stable, glancing at one of the other guys who had stopped to send a text. Typical.

There were forty-four stables to be cleaned out every day and, although he was the manager, he had to be there to set the pace. His days were always busy, making sure all his employers' horses were attended to properly, but he knew as soon as he went into the office or off to the sales to buy fresh horses, the four guys that worked under him would all just sit around smoking and drinking tea. They were useless lazy bums, really. He would love to fire them all and hire proper horsemen who cared about the animals, but at the same time, Oliver couldn't really blame them. They were being paid the minimum wage, expected to work all hours God sent, and had no interest in the animals or the job. Not that the boss cared; he just wanted cheap labour. So the stress and drudgery continued, day in, day out.

Oliver stopped shovelling and stared out into the rain. How had it all got to this? He wondered. Life had to be better than this; it just had to. He was worn out.

All those years ago, after his New York adventure, he had moved on from Lexington. There were stints in Australia and Argentina, where he had worked and played hard, building his knowledge all the time. By the time he came home to Ireland, he was looking for a real challenge.

He thought he had found that in David Gorman, a successful businessman whose huge ego compensated for his diminutive stature. The man had made a fortune in property and hotels, and was retiring early to set up a stud farm to own and breed top class racehorses. He wanted to put together a young, dynamic team, or so he told Oliver when they had first met. He waved money at Oliver, plus the promise of glory, independence, and a chance to prove himself. Oliver had jumped at the opportunity.

Some land was bought in Cork, not far from where Oliver grew up in Limerick, and the stud farm was designed and built by Oliver. The future looked bright. Oliver devoutly believed that hard work always paid off, so he threw his heart and soul into the place. However, he began to realize that while Gorman was willing to invest – to a point – in horses, he constantly refused to invest in a team of staff or quality infrastructure, and he always wanted more than his pound of flesh. He could never understand that horses were living, breathing, athletic bundles of energy; to Gorman, they were commodities. So the more Oliver gave to his work, the more that was expected.

More, more, always more.

His phone rang, bringing him back to the present. He fished out the device.

"Morning, Boss. How are you?"

"I'm going through the accounts, the farrier bills have gone up *again*," Gorman said in his affected southside Dublin accent. "I told you about this before. I thought I ordered you to get this guy to put his prices down."

"I know," Oliver sighed, and rolled his eyes. "But as I said, he's *already* doing us a good rate. If we beat him down any more, he'll just stop coming."

"Then we'll get another one. Jesus, farriers are ten-a-penny, it's not exactly brain surgery; not that you'd know it from the bills. Besides, he should be honoured to work with my horses."

"Farriers may be ten-a-penny, but not good ones."

"Look, the bottom line *is*: he's more expensive than most."

"Sorry, Mr. Gorman, like I said before, from a horse management point of view, this guy's top class. He's worth the money. Remember that job he did last year on the colt who got his foot stuck in a gate and ripped a part of it off?"

"Hmm, the way I remember it, that was down to your fucking negligence."

"*My negligence?* I wasn't the one flying down the fenceline on a quad bike, showing off to my girlfriend."

"What the fuck is that supposed to mean?"

"Why don't you ask your nephew?"

"What? That's it! I want you in my office now."

"I can't leave the yard while the mucking out's being done, or they'll *never* get finished."

"Shit shovelling. That's all you're good at, isn't it? Get yourself to my office at four this afternoon, and don't be late."

The line went dead.

"I never am," Oliver said into the phone. He sighed, stuffed the damp handset back in his pocket, and turned to pick up his fork.

Whenever Gorman treated him like this, he wished he had someone to talk to or share his frustration, but there was nobody to come home to. In the beginning, he had shut himself away in the stud. The odd girlfriend came and went, but none would put up with his obsession with work. Before he knew it, he was alone.

When he finally opened his eyes to the reality of his job, seven years had passed. He was stuck, and had nobody to share it with. The happy-go-lucky Oliver had been trodden into the ground. He used to get an occasional respite by going out partying in Dublin with his friends, but one by one they had settled down, got married and moved on with their lives. These days, Oliver stayed in, except to take his mother shopping, or to dinner, or to one of her bridge tournaments. He sometimes considered leaving but, as bad as it was, he kept believing that his work would pay off and that Gorman would change. And part of him was afraid to take the initial step into the unknown.

Meanwhile, over the past decade, his brother Richard's ventures had gone from strength to strength. Since graduating from Trinity College with a first in his degree, he had borrowed money to set up a taxi and minibus service around an expanding provincial town in the Irish midlands, specializing in pub-runs and trips to sports matches. The vehicles were all top of the range, giving customers a feeling of luxury, and his flyers – *Pick-me-up Cabs; anytime, anywhere* – were in every pub, club and place of work within a sixty mile radius. He had swiftly annihilated the pitiful opposition by having his drivers available twenty-four-seven, and his cars outside nightclubs to entice tired, drunk customers.

By the time he had a regional monopoly in the midlands, the newly-appointed Minister for Transport announced that his department was to initiate a rural program of intensive breathalyser checkpoints as part of the war on road safety. It put the fear of God into drinkers, and ensured that this ever-expanding fleet was constantly busy. Some ugly rumours went around that Richard had resorted to bribing some of the local Gardai to be extra vigilant. This was strongly denied by the local officers, and one journalist was threatened with legal action. But years later, after a few too many brandies during dinner with his mother and Oliver, Richard had joked, "*Oh, the Guards! Gifted men! Some coincidence alright, that drink-driving war. Gifted men!*" Then he'd abruptly changed the subject, but the words stayed with Oliver.

His brother expanded the business to take in the rural northwest, and soon after that, he sold up for a handsome profit to a syndicate of local businessmen, three of whom were the sons of retired Gardai. Richard promptly used his success, money and influence to find investors to back him in his next venture. He took the then unbelievable risk of setting up an airline to provide mass-market, cheaply-priced travel, to and from Ireland.

He bought a failing regional airline for peanuts, sold off their old planes to somewhere in Africa, and was brave and charismatic enough to charm the right people to invest in new aircraft. Through hard work and a very tough business style, it paid off. There were some initial stories that he had won certain choice routes and slots a little too easily, and that some politicians enjoyed a very cosy relationship with him, but again these soon died down with the threat of legal action.

All this success, and he wasn't even a nice guy. *The fucker*, muttered Oliver, whenever he thought of him. Why did the assholes always succeed? Their father had been so proud of Richard, and never let an occasion pass to remind Oliver what a success his brother was.

"Yeah, yeah, Dad. He's brilliant, isn't he?"

"He's got the balls to get things done, unlike some around here."

Whenever he felt down, the same old ghosts came back to haunt him.

At ten to four that afternoon, Oliver crossed the yard and let himself through the gate leading to the office and his boss's house. He winced when his eyes met the sprawling modern complex that Gorman had built to deface this lovely former dairy farm. The house was a modern monument to ostentation. It looked like somebody had stuck a large blue and white mushroom in amongst the old beech trees. Some of the neighbours had even nicknamed it *The Smurf House*. It was the only part of the development that had nothing to do with Oliver, and to make matters worse, it reminded him of the monstrosity his own brother had built for himself in the midlands.

He opened the office door, kicked off his wellies onto the mat and padded into the empty reception area. The secretary had long since quit and not been replaced. Instead, the pair of beady-eyed accountants who occupied the small office next to the boss, were charged with answering the phone. When it came to horse matters, most people chose to call Oliver directly on his mobile.

He nodded to Tim and Pat, who studied him intently as he made his way into the wood-panelled cavern that was Gorman's office. Tim made a noise to get Oliver's attention, which he studiously ignored. He was not in the mood to discuss penny-pinching with the bean counter.

"The only thing that matters is the bottom line," he frequently droned at Oliver. When Oliver explained that the bottom line was producing top-class racehorses, the accountant's face would glaze over.

Oliver shut the door and was surprised to find himself alone in the huge room. He checked his watch and his eye drifted to the trophy cabinets. Memories flooded back as he scanned the silverware and photographs, but he felt slightly disconnected from them. Although he had done all the hard work selecting, raising and pre-training these elite racehorses, he had never been allowed to go to the races to see them perform. In the last five racing seasons, Oliver had bought horses which had won eighteen Group One or Classic races; the highest achievement possible on a racecourse. Other blueblooded steeds had won many of Britain and Ireland's major handicaps, not to mention the victories in ordinary everyday races.

Overall, the percentage of winners to horses bought was a staggering seventy percent – simply unheard of. Not a single individual horse had cost more than a hundred thousand Euro, and later many of them were sold on for a fortune in America or the Middle East, except for the pick of the females, who were brought back to the farm for breeding.

Much to Oliver's disgust, Gorman simply refused to pay the high fees to use the country's best stallions. Instead, he followed fashion and used the cheapest, unproven commercial horses, and many of the foals were not up to the standard they should have been. This only added to Oliver's disgruntlement.

His eye caught the picture of his boss receiving the Epsom Derby trophy from the Queen of England, after Nephew's Choice – named after Diarmuid, the so-called horse expert relation of the childless Gorman – had romped home by three lengths. Oliver had watched the race at home on TV that day, and Gorman wouldn't even answer his phone when Oliver tried to contact him afterwards.

He hissed in disgust and turned his gaze to the gable end of the room and the oil painting of the horse, which had been sold to Japan for fifteen million Euro, after adding the King George VI and Queen Elizabeth Stakes and the Irish Champion Stakes to his resume, and second place in the Prix De L'Arc De Triomphe. Oliver had desperately tried to convince Gorman to keep Nephew's Choice and stand him as a stallion at the farm, but to no avail. The lure of the money won the day.

Oliver and the staff saw not a penny of the fifteen million. Not a penny. No mention of the bottom line after that deal. He nearly vomited every time he looked at the photo of Gorman and his nephew in the parade ring at Longchamp before the Prix De L'Arc, surrounded by the Japanese.

Gorman had an unerring method of editing Oliver out of the picture at the horse sales, too. They bought weanling foals, because they were cheaper than race-ready yearlings and Oliver could feed and raise them to maximise their athletic potential. Gorman would dispatch Oliver to the foal sales with this favoured nephew, Diarmuid – a snotty, spoiled know-it-all, who gambled plenty on horses, but had never worked with them or bothered to observe them. One of his favourite pursuits was racing around the farm on his quad bike, or posing as a country gent. He had just graduated from university with a degree in Equine Science, and styled himself as a bloodstock agent. Gorman was very proud, and assigned him to work with Oliver to make the preliminary checks.

Oliver hated having to drag the lazy little shit along with him and answer his mundane, idiotic questions. On top of it all, he would inform his uncle if Oliver discussed business with anyone else at the sales. When Oliver had looked at all the horses, compiled shortlists and formed his opinions, his boss would arrive the morning of the sale, meet with him and Diarmuid in the privacy of a hotel room, and take Oliver's sale catalogue from him, containing all his notes. Gorman would then team up with

Diarmuid, and the two would buy the top selections from Oliver's list. It was Diarmuid's name that always appeared as the buyer.

Oliver was usually instructed to wait in the hotel until any foals selling later in the week arrived on the sale grounds. He was then to examine these – discreetly, of course – and give a further report. He would then be sent back to the farm. Oliver waited for the day there would be some kind of crisis on sale day, which would require his presence. But if there was one, the call never came.

Some people in the industry began to suspect that the quiet, focused guy at the sales was doing the real groundwork for Gorman and his nephew, but most people never put two and two together, especially as Oliver wasn't even listed as the Stud Manager in the industry directory. They assumed that Diarmuid really was a judge of horses. And over the years, Gorman started to believe it was all down to *his* skill and vision – nothing to do with Oliver. Just like he believed his success with property and hotels had all been down to him, and nothing to do with the Celtic Tiger opportunities or the re-zoning of land he purchased for peanuts.

After each sale, Oliver received the purchases. They would be nourished and grown into young athletes for the next twelve months or so, before being carefully and gently broken-in, pre-trained, and finally sent off to trainers that he was required to select for Gorman.

Chapter 6

"Ah, you managed to get here on time," a voice boomed behind him. David Gorman was a prissy man in his late fifties, with a thinning head of dyed hair and a deep sunbed tan. His reading glasses were perched on the end of his nose and his usual grin was plastered on.

He had crept in to stand at Oliver's shoulder, admiring the painting. "Some day that. My name forever on the Derby roll of honour." He clapped his hands together and his grin collapsed into a thunderous grimace, making him look a bit like an evil goblin. "Right, first: how dare you bring Diarmuid's name into it? He's a university graduate. He knows horses and has a degree to prove it. What formal qualification have you got?" Gorman arched his eyebrows over his reading glasses. "If you'd installed proper gates around the farm, then the animal would never have caught its foot."

Oliver's mouth hung slightly agape.

Gorman plopped himself down at the head of the large mahogany edifice he liked to call the *executive table*; though exactly where the executives and directors were in this dictatorship, was beyond Oliver. He was not invited to sit.

"But . . . But two years ago I put in a written request to have all the gates fitted with wire grills, specifically so this kind of thing would never happen, but Tim and Pat refused it."

"I don't recall that. Anyway, we've been over this before," he waved his hand dismissively. "I called you in here because I want you to change farriers *immediately*. I'm not paying another cent to that robber."

"He's one of the best in the country, he's worth every penny."

"Fire him. Today."

Oliver opened his mouth as if to retaliate, but closed it again. His words had always fallen on deaf ears, and now he simply didn't have the energy to go at it again.

Gorman glanced up at him over his reading glasses, a flicker of satisfaction in his eyes.

"I'll call him and meet him somewhere, break the news face-to-face."

"No, you'll call him and tell him over the phone. You're not wasting my fucking diesel and time going to see him. What do you care anyway? Unless you're taking a cut of his extortionate rates?"

Oliver was speechless at the accusation. Surely Gorman didn't really believe that? He wanted to rant and rave at the little fucker, but he bit his lip, turned on his heel and left. He felt like spitting on the polished glass of the trophy cabinet as he made his way out.

Chapter 7

The next day, the sun shone. It was the first glorious day in a few months, and Oliver took advantage of it to walk the paddocks and assess the yearlings running about, playing with their peers. He felt it was important to allow them as much time in their natural environment as possible, and liked to keep them in one big group where they could develop their natural herd instincts.

He started his tour with the paddocks nearest the barns, where the mares grazed. As he slowly walked among them, they glanced up from the lush, green pasture before lazily resuming their grass-picking, occasionally snorting at their baby foals frolicking in delight with the sun on their backs. Then on to the pregnant mares, who ambled around gingerly, waiting for their big day. A nice bunch – pity they were in foal to moderate stallions.

Oliver worked his way around the farm, checking the fences and water troughs, scanning the empty paddocks for weeds and rabbits, and ended up in the thirty-acre field which was overlooked by the main house.

He paused to turn his face to the sun and savour the rays. Then he switched his attention to the nine yearling colts in the paddock. He saw them over at the far end, playing about near the water trough. They were a lovely bunch; he was sure there was a classic winner amongst them.

A rabbit scurried from its hiding place in long grass, startling the young athletes. The big dark bay – almost black – horse led the group in a dash around the fence line. Oliver smiled as they passed him. He never tired of watching horses gallop around, regally displaying their magnificence. When he watched them intently, the outside world faded into oblivion. He observed everything, from the way they extended their delicate limbs, to the way their feet hit the turf underfoot, to the way they carried their heads and how fluidly they moved and breathed with each stride.

Oliver could watch horses for hours, and on long summer evenings he frequently did; it was always interesting, and helped him to understand something else about athletic potential. He had become so good at it now, he could predict without fail how each horse would train, run, and what distance they would prefer. And, of course, usually how much ability they would have. In fact, he never put a horse on his list unless it showed him sufficient athletic potential when he viewed it at the sale.

Oliver loved the big black colt and was impressed that he was not only the established leader of his peers, but also that he was so active in the paddock. The animal simply loved to run. Handy really, given his *raison d'etre*.

The familiar ringing broke his concentration. Pulling the phone out of his pocket, he glanced up at what he knew was the master bedroom window and saw the usual figure standing at the glass.

"Morning. Lovely day, isn't it?" said Oliver cheerily.

"What the fuck are you doing standing in a field with your thumb up your arsehole?" was the reply.

"I– I'm checking the paddocks and looking at the colts."

"I don't pay you to stand around. Did you tell the robber we don't want him anymore?"

"What?"

"Oh Jesus! The farrier: did you fire him?"

He sighed. "Yes."

"Good." He hung up.

That afternoon, Oliver was mixing a batch of horse feed when he heard Diarmuid's quad-bike zoom through the yard and down the lane.

Oliver stuck his head out the door. "Slow down!" he roared after him.

There was no response from the young man, or the pretty girl riding pillion. Oliver shook his head despondently.

As he swept up every last spilled morsel of feed to deny the mice a feast, Oliver heard the quad in the paddock and the colts thundering along the fenceline.

He dashed outside and saw Diarmuid chasing them, beeping the horn, showing off to his companion.

"Not again," he muttered. "I've had enough of this shit." He hurried to the paddock, vaulted over the gate, and stood in the field waving his arms.

The yearlings were galloping flat out along the far end. Diarmuid sped after them. The big black colt led the bunch and skidded as he reached the corner, almost losing his footing. Oliver put his hand to his mouth as he braced for an accident. A few other horses stumbled and slipped as they made the turn. Diarmuid seemed not to notice. He kept gunning the bike along.

The last colt of the group was panicked by the noise of the engine and the horn; sweat formed a white lather on its neck. Its front legs went from under it as it tried to turn, and the animal's eyes bulged as wide as Oliver's as it realised it would hit the fence. Four hundred kilos of galloping thoroughbred slammed into the wooden post and rail barrier. There was a loud, sickening crack, and a tangled mess of horse and fence. Diarmuid skidded the quad to a halt inches from the stricken horse.

Oliver sprinted across the field, desperately hoping the colt was unscathed. As he got closer, he could see the front legs lying at unnatural angles and the panicked snorting of a horse in terrible pain. The animal began to thrash, trying to flee from the ordeal, but it couldn't get up. Its front legs flapped about from the knees down, only held in place by skin and tendon.

The forlorn whinnying seared into Oliver's brain.

"I suppose you'd better call the vet," mumbled Diarmuid, pale, shocked.

The girl burst into tears and buried her face in her hands.

"The vet could take forty minutes to get here," said Oliver.

"This animal's in too much pain. Run to the house and get your uncle's shotgun."

Diarmuid blinked, his mouth wide open.

Oliver grabbed him by the jacket. "Get it. Now. Or I'll rip *your* fucking legs off."

Diarmuid hopped over the wrecked fence and dashed for the house.

Oliver threw his jacket over the stricken horse's head. Without sight, the animal calmed slightly and stopped thrashing.

Oliver put his arm around the sobbing girl and guided her over the fence. "Don't look at the horse. Go inside, make a cup of hot sweet tea, and sit by the fire. Try to forget this ever happened." He watched her amble toward the house, sobbing and shaking.

Oliver turned. The other colts were standing twenty metres away, their heads down, snorting. They could smell the fear. He was about to call the yard when he saw the four lads running down the lane towards him.

"Heard the crash," one said. "Jaysus, look at the state of that. You alright?"

"Fine. Get the other horses into the far paddock. I'll have to put this one down."

The horses were led slowly away and Diarmuid returned with the weapon.

Oliver grabbed it and checked both barrels. He offered the gun back to Diarmuid. "Your mess, you end the misery."

"I-I, no . . . But . . ."

"Yeah, yeah. Didn't think so," Oliver spat. He braced the butt against his shoulder and pressed the muzzle to the horse's head. Out of the corner of his eye, he saw Gorman trotting towards him, shouting.

Oliver squeezed the trigger.

Gorman arrived at the scene. He was livid. "What the fuck are you doing?"

Oliver kept his eyes on the blood seeping into the ground. "Dealing with your nephew's disaster." He glared at the young man and handed him the weapon. "You made me kill a horse.

Right now, I feel like using the other barrel on you. Clean it and put it away before I change my mind."

Gorman was speechless for once. Diarmuid skulked back the house. Oliver phoned the local fox hunt to come and remove the carcass.

"They'll be here in an hour, and I'll be gone tomorrow," he said to Gorman. Then he turned his back on the scene and walked to the yard, wiping the tears that formed in the corner of his eyes.

That evening, sitting in his house on the stud with only a bottle of wine for company, Oliver surfed the internet. He perused the usual racing websites, and even checked out the classifieds, but no decent jobs were available. He even considered logging on to a chat room, but dismissed the idea as sad, and figured what nice girl would bother with a desperate, lonely, workaholic in cyberspace? He wondered where Rebecca was. Probably married with kids by now, and a practising vet in Kentucky or Colorado.

After an hour or so, he put the name Marco Romano into a search engine, as he had done a few times over the years, especially when he felt down. The results appeared on the screen. He clicked on a site with Mafia-related stories and news cuttings. Occasionally there was an old photo of Marco posted on a site, but he was mostly unmentioned, except for a small piece a few years ago speculating about how, after the sudden death of his boss in prison, Marco was the front runner to take over the family. Since that news item, there were no updates on the Jersey family.

Oliver often thought back to that mad night. It seemed like a lifetime ago. He had never told his parents or brother about it. He just couldn't bring himself to listen to the lectures, criticism and judgments.

He turned off the computer, poured a glass of wine, and wondered just what he was going to do now. He had to do something on his own terms. What was needed was a new start, to strike out on his own. Richard had managed to find investors for his first business, so why couldn't he? He knew he could do the job; he didn't doubt his own ability. Despite the years of Gorman's bullying, Oliver knew the horse business better than all but a handful of people, and could see every single mistake that all new owners made.

It was time to stand up and make a mark. Time to be a man and start something himself. He mulled over an idea for an hour or so, then looked at his watch: nine-thirty. Richard would still be at his desk, no doubt. He found the phone and dialled.

It rang only once. "Hello," Richard blurted, quickly and sharply.

"Hi, Rich. How are things?"

"Frantic, Ollie. Mental. What's up with you?"

"Well, I need to talk. Can I come and see you tomorrow?"

"What day's tomorrow? Sunday? Yeah, sure. Come for lunch. We might even go out on the boat. That is, if your boss'll let you off the leash for a whole day."

"Huh, he won't have a choice this time. I'm tired of his shit. I'll explain everything tomorrow."

"Great, see you then. I suppose I'd better send a driver to collect Mother and get her up for the day as well."

"I'll bring her. It's on my way."

"If you want. But I can easily send my driver."

"No, I'll do it."

"OK, whatever. See you."

Oliver hung up. Great, he could tell them both at the same time. He drained his glass and went to bed.

Chapter 8

It was a beautiful, sunny morning as Oliver pulled into the long driveway of their family home. As he drove along, he could see the houses being built just behind the bordering hedgerow. The unstoppable suburban sprawl of the so-called 'Celtic Tiger' was at their doorstep.

He stopped the car in front of the large Georgian farmhouse where he had grown up. It used to be immaculate when his father had it painted every three years, but it hadn't seen a lick since he died and it was flaking badly in places.

As Oliver approached the door, his mother emerged with a smile lighting up her painfully thin face. Evelyn McMahon was a quiet, reserved woman, who had brought up both sons in the old-fashioned way – lacking in displays of affection – and who was always required to do her husband's bidding and share his points of view. When he passed away four years ago, her friends and Oliver had expected her to open up and start to live her own life. Instead, she had seemed to fade away, as if life did not really interest her anymore.

"Oliver! What a lovely dinner you made the other night; the leftovers kept me going for days!" She frowned suddenly. "You look even more tired today. Everything alright? How's work?" Evelyn was well-spoken and her sons spoke in the same clipped, though slightly old-fashioned tones. It was the one reason she had agreed to send them to the monastery boarding school, even though she had missed them desperately during term time.

"Oh, the usual. Gorman's such a shit—"

"Language, Oliver."

He smiled through the rebuke and kissed her on both cheeks. She hugged him stiffly.

"I wish you would find something more rewarding to do. Farming all but killed your father. Well, that and the cigarettes, but it was the constant slogging that broke him."

"You know I don't farm like that, Mum," he shrugged resignedly. "Still, you're right. I do need to find something better to do. In fact, I'm in the process of making some changes."

"Really?"

"Yes, really. I'll, er, I'll tell you both during lunch." Changing the subject, he gestured towards the hedge. "Those shitty, awful boxes they call houses are going to look right into your garden. It's such a pity Dad had to sell that land."

"Yes, well . . ." She looked at her feet uneasily. "At least he put the money to good use and got some pleasure from his last years."

"Sorry. I, um, I didn't mean anything by it, Mum."

She looked at her watch. "We'd better get going."

They got into the car and continued on to Richard's house. It was nearly two hours later when they drew up in front of the imposing, wrought iron security gates. Oliver opened his window and punched in the code. The bars parted and they drove up the avenue.

The car pottered up the long, meandering driveway, bordered by strips of freshly mown lawn and neat rows of daffodils. Beyond them was new post and rail fencing and lush, green paddocks where a few sheep grazed. Evelyn smiled as she took in the serenity of it all.

"I do love this place, Oliver, don't you?"

"Yes, Mum, it's beautiful. It's a bit too well kept, though, and I bet he's charging Little Bo Peep a fortune to keep her sheep here."

"Now, now, Oliver. No jealousy."

He could hear the mother's scolding tone in her voice. She was right, though. Oliver was a little jealous of his brother, but also infuriated by him. Richard had bought this beautiful, crumbling mansion by the shores of Lough Derg as a weekend retreat from the pressures of Dublin. The ruin came with eighty acres of land and Oliver had been excited at the prospect of Richard returning it to its former glory. However, he had promptly had the unlisted building demolished and replaced with a modern, steel and glass monstrosity, visible for miles. A 'concept house', as Richard liked to call it. Oliver couldn't stand 'the concept', and he suspected his mother was appalled as well, though she was too loyal to admit it.

Everybody wondered how on earth he had managed to get planning permission; it looked as if a spaceship had touched down amidst the paddocks and trees. The only old building was the stone stable yard, which was restored, but used only as storage for old files, dust and cobwebs, serving only to highlight the hideousness of the monster beside it.

They parked and walked across the gravel, as Richard appeared behind a glass panel front door. He was tall and lean, much like his brother, with tidy dark hair; striking in his own way, but the years of grind in an office and too much smoking had reduced his skin to a ghostly pallor, cracked with stress lines. Evelyn opened her arms and hugged him in the same stiff manner as she had greeted Oliver. "How are you? It's so good to be here again on such a lovely day."

He stood rigidly. "Good to see you, too, Mother."

"Hi, Rich, long time no see." Oliver stuck out his hand. Richard shook it limply.

"Really? I've been that busy, time's a blur. Was the drive OK?"

"Yeah, but you should see what used to be the west dairy fields at home. Full of little boxy houses, pity for Mum. They'll look right into the garden when they're finished."

Richard smirked. "Well, that's progress. You can't stop it, I supp–"

Their mother interrupted. "Come on, boys, I'm starving. What's for lunch?"

Richard took them through the sparsely furnished house. It really needed a woman's touch, but Richard's lifestyle did not leave time for a wife and family. Evelyn had given up being excited at seeing Richard's photo on the society pages with a glamorous blonde on his arm – eventually they all realized they would never be more than a distant second to his airline.

The sun beamed in through the conservatory and warmed the air. They sat around the large table and Richard poured the wine, as the woman who came to do the cooking appeared and began to place the food on the sideboard.

Evelyn greeted her cheerily. "Hello, Marigold. How are you?"

The spritely middle-aged spinster answered with an enthusiastic smile. "Ah, sure I'm grand, thanks. Tipping along."

"What are you treating us to today? I do like your cooking, but it's been so long since I've had the pleasure."

"I've a lovely steak and kidney pie for you, with mash and peas. Just the job!"

"Mmm, sounds delicious."

Richard shot his cook a withering glance, which she ignored and disappeared into the kitchen.

"Mother, do you have to fraternise with the staff?" he asked, standing to serve himself.

"I'm surprised at you, Richard. Marigold's a nice woman, and I hadn't seen her in so long."

He grimaced uncomfortably. "Yeah, but she should be seen and not heard. I mean, it's just so gauche to chat amiably with my employees. Familiarity breeds contempt, you know."

Evelyn's jaw hung agape. "That's an awful thing to say. I didn't raise you to be so rude."

"Hey, Rich, I'll have a plate while you're up there," said Oliver. His brother shot him a sideways glance as he sat. Oliver smirked and served himself and his mother.

They began eating in silence, which nobody felt like breaking until Oliver decided to hit them with his news.

"I've got something to tell you both," he announced.

Richard raised his eyebrow quizzically.

Oliver cleared his throat. "Well, er, look, I know I haven't ever really discussed this with you, but, well, my job hasn't exactly gone the way I thought it would. To be honest, it's a nightmare. I'm stuck being Gorman's lackey and I'm sick of it.

I need to branch out on my own, do something for myself. I told him I was quitting yesterday."

Evelyn looked at him, slightly startled. "Well, that is a shock! I thought you loved horses."

"I'm not quitting horses, Mum, just the job. It doesn't agree with me. I spent more time than I should have shovelling shit and taking abuse, then he and his bloody nephew take all the credit."

"Well done, Ollie! It's about time you grew some balls." Richard beamed his most winning smile as he slapped his hand on the table. "What's your plan, then?"

"Well, I want to buy some horses. Some foals to pinhook and some to race."

"What's *pinhooking*?" asked Evelyn.

"It's when you buy weanling foals in November or December at the public sales, with a view to re-selling them the following September. It's pretty much what I was doing for Gorman, except we – that is, he – kept them all to race. I'll sell some for a quick buck and keep the others to race. It's tough to get the right foal, but the odds for profit are good." He looked at his older brother. "Plus, the turnaround is quick, so overheads are low – unless one gets ill and sticks us with big vet bills."

"Sounds interesting, but risky. What are your margins like?" inquired the businessman.

Oliver perked up and leaned in over the table. "Rich, it's like this. Buy a number of foals and aim to double your money on re-sale. Some will do better, but some will do worse. In the end, taking into account overheads, we should aim to make 75% or more profit on the investment. Also, like I said, we'll keep some to race. I'll raise them to be athletes and they'll kick ass on the track, just like Gorman's horses. We'll have great fun at the races and, Rich, you'd be surprised at the prize funds even for average races these days. And if we buy horses with top class pedigrees, well, d'you remember how much Gorman got from the Japanese for that Derby winner we had? And he only had an average bloodline."

Richard narrowed his eyes, the wheels turning. "Hmm. Sounds exciting, Ollie. How much will your initial investment be?"

"See, Rich, that's what I wanted to talk to you about. I want to start with a million. I have forty-five grand saved. That includes the ten that Dad left me. But I was hoping you and Mum might help me out by becoming my investors."

Richard was about to take a sip of coffee, but paused with the cup almost to his lips. He placed it back down on the saucer and stared into space for a minute.

Their mother's jaw almost hit the table. She spluttered, but no words came out. As the seconds ticked away, he realised this wasn't exactly the reception he had anticipated. Surely his own family would help him out?

It was Richard who spoke first. "There's no way, Ollie. Sorry, I just can't do it at the moment."

"What?" Now it was Oliver's jaw that almost hit the table. "I . . . but, you seemed impressed by the business plan. And you know I know the horse business like the back of my hand. I've bought serious performers for Gorman. Jesus, he even won the Epsom Derby. And don't try telling me you're broke. When you floated your shares last month, you made a killing. It was all over the papers, for God's sake." He took a deep breath. "And I also thought it'd be nice for all of us to enjoy a day at the races with a runner to cheer home. I can do this for all of us. I can make it profitable." He snorted, almost in amusement. "I mean, shit, I've done it before."

Richard shot a withering look at his brother. "What? What have you done before? What is it that you claim to have done for Gorman? I've never seen your name connected with any of his purchases or victories – and I do read the papers, you know – you don't even go to the bloody races. For all I know, you *are* just the guy who sits on the farm and cleans out the shit. The stable boy. What do you know about the business, about making profit?" The last word came out in a tone that was almost religious.

Oliver was speechless. He pinched himself to be sure he wasn't dreaming.

His brother continued, "Look, Ollie, this is all confidential – I haven't announced it yet – but I'm just about to expand the business to include a private jet hire service. Everything's tied up."

Oliver masked his look of disbelief and tried a change of tack. "But that's the thing. You won't have to stress or worry. I'll be doing all of that for you. We can keep the horses here, instead of having to rent a property, or put some of them at home on the paddocks Mum still has. Come on, Rich, we'll have a lot of fun AND make money. It's just the three of us at the moment, no wives or kids. We might as well race thoroughbreds." He turned to look at his mother. "What do you think, Mum? It'd be great!"

"Oliver, I think it's a wonderful idea. I really do. I'll be so proud of you if it works, but I don't have that kind of money." She started to fiddle with her napkin as she continued, repeating herself nervously, "I would love to help you, but I really don't have the money."

"Oh, come on, Mum. Dad got a fortune for those fields and, God knows, he never spent much on anything when he was alive."

"Oliver! Your father *did* put his money to use, and I . . .'"

"That's enough, Mother," Richard cut in, hastily. "Look, Ollie, neither of us can be the soft touches you'd like us to be. I bet you thought coming to us'd be better than a bank, huh? Because, if you mess this up you can just say sorry and not pay us back. Am I wrong?"

Oliver's eyes widened with incredulity. "I can't believe you just said that. Am I really talking to my own brother? I came to you because I *know* I have a proven record and a sound business proposition, which will not only yield a return – potentially a high one – but also give you, me and Mum a bit of sport and some good days out." He turned to his mother. "And we all know it would do you good to get out of the house more often."

His mother was aghast.

"I also thought you would be the ones I could count on more than a bank manager. They'd never give a loan like that to buy *horses*."

"The answer's no. End of story."

"But why, Rich, why? You know I'm not an idiot." His tone was getting desperate.

"Do I? I mean really, Ollie, what is it that you do? Basically, you're a farmer. Killing yourself just like Dad did."

"Richard! How dare you say that about your father?"

"Why not, Mum? It's true. You know it. That's why Dad was so disappointed in Ollie. And that's why I'm not going to back you. I just don't think it's good business."

"But I'm your brother."

"I don't care who you are."

"That's enough, Richard." Evelyn was shouting in a hoarse voice. "After all your father did for you, you don't have the right to say those things. Not in front of me. Has your success made you forget?"

Oliver interrupted. "What do you mean 'after all he did for you'? What did Dad do for you, Rich?"

It was Richard who answered. "If you must know, Ollie, he gave me the money from the land to buy my cabs. He gave it to me because he knew I would make it into something and not fuck it up. And he knew I'd take care of Mum after he was gone."

Oliver felt sick. He stared at the table in stunned silence for a second before looking up at his mother. He had a questioning look in his eye, hoping that she would deny it. Hoping that she would say that Richard was lying just to hurt him. Hoping that his father was not so disappointed in him that he had given everything to his brother.

The tears welling up in her eyes gave him his answer.

"Oh, Oliver, Oliver," she wailed. "Your father didn't want you to know, and I knew that if you had known then you would've been so upset. After he died, I just couldn't tell you."

"So that was the good use he found for his money. That was the pleasure he had: seeing his favourite son succeed, while the other was treated like a fool. And why? Because I wanted to go into stud farming!"

"Oliver, I'm so sorry. I wish I could make it up to you, but he left me with very little."

"Yes, and it's me who looks after our mother now, Ollie. What do you contribute?"

"I can't believe you just said that. I go up home every week and do something with her. We have dinner together regularly. Dinner that I cook, Rich. When was the last time you cooked or went home to see Mum?"

"I'm busy doing business, Ollie, not playing with horses. Anyway, I pay for her living costs."

"Then I take her to the monthly bridge tournaments in the city."

"Bridge? When did you start playing bridge?"

"Almost a year ago, Richard," said Evelyn acidly. "I've had enough. You've become quite a monster. It's your duty to look after me. That's what your father wanted. And I think it's your duty to help your brother."

"Oh, do you now? Well, I beg to differ. And while we're on about what Dad would have wanted, I don't think he would have wanted me to waste money on Oliver – or else he would have given him a bit more than ten grand. I mean, Jesus, Ollie, you were a fucking doormat for your boss for years and you didn't have the balls to stand up to him. I have an office full of guys like you – they're very good at their little jobs, but they never amount to much in their own right."

"Well, we're not all sharks like you. I bet if Mum and I were dead in the water, you'd eat us. Wouldn't you?"

"Vultures eat dead meat, Ollie. Not sharks."

"Fuck you." With that, Oliver stood up quickly, sending his chair backwards so that it tipped over and crashed on the floor. "I'm off home. Mum, are you coming?"

"Oliver, please stay." She cleared her throat. "Come on now, boys, can't you sort this out."

"We can talk all you like, Mother, but I'll never throw away that kind of money on him. So he might as well go."

"Fine. Rich, you're an asshole."

"Ollie, look, you really shouldn't take it personally. It's just a business decision."

"Don't give me that bullshit. That's an excuse used by guys like you to justify acting like selfish pricks. How can I not take it personally? You're my brother."

Oliver stormed out through the house, towards the entrance

hall. His mother hurried after him. "Oliver, I want to stay a bit longer. Try to talk some sense into him."

"Sorry, Mum, but I'm not staying another second. I'm sure one of his minions'll drive you home."

He opened the glass door and slammed it so hard behind him that it cracked. Glancing over his shoulder, he saw what he had done and smiled.

As he got into his car, the realization dawned on him that his plans lay in ruins. Without his family's help, there was no way he could buy the kind of horses he wanted to. He also knew going back to Gorman would kill him. He started the engine and drove off, not knowing and almost not caring what he was going to do.

Evelyn went back into the conservatory and sat down. She looked at Richard, who had lit a cigar and was leaning back in his chair, nonchalantly blowing smoke rings.

"Richard, I do think you should give your brother the same chance that was given to you."

He took another puff, exhaled and shook his head. "No way, Mum. Truth is, he needs to grow up. He was looking for an easy loan. He doesn't have the killer instinct to pull off a business deal and make a profit."

"You got an easy loan; no, you got a gift. Your father never asked for a penny back. He was just so proud to see you succeed. Can't you do the same for your brother?"

"No. Because I don't think he'll succeed. He's just a farmer, for God's sake. Dad backed me because he knew that I never give up till I get what I want. Oliver's just not that tough."

"He never was as competitive as you, I'll admit that. But he's hard-working and very diligent. Now, I know I don't know anything about horses – neither do you – but your brother understands them, and he has devoted his life to studying them and working with them all over the world. And he really has had all that success for Donald Gorman, or whatever his name is. Surely that counts for something, Richard."

He stubbed out his cigar. "You may be right there, Mum,

and I'm not saying he's useless, but I'm not risking my money on him. Sorry." He stood up abruptly. "I've got a call to make. I'll get a driver to take you home. It was nice to see you both again, though." He strode out of the room, leaving his mother alone at the table. She made no attempt to hold back the tears.

Oliver's drive back to Cork calmed him and, without his mother's chat filling the car, he had time to think things through.

He stopped for petrol and noticed a mother with two daughters; the older one was eyeing a big chocolate egg. "Mam, can I have that?"

"No, dear, it's too big."

"Ah, go on, pleeeease."

"I want one, too," cried the smaller girl.

The harried woman weighed up the situation. "Christina, if I buy it, you have to share it with your sister - equally."

"But I said it first."

"You'll share or have none at all,'" their mother replied, wagging a finger.

"Okay," Christina said, with a sulky face.

The smaller girl smiled. "Yay!"

* * *

Oliver paid and ambled to his car, staring at his feet. His brother was a champion asshole for treating him like that. And, as for his father . . . He swore and pulled out into the traffic. He knew that the only way to prove them all wrong was to be a success in his own right and make his own opportunities happen. He just needed to re-think; he knew this couldn't stop him, though in hindsight, he had probably gone into his pitch a bit amateurishly.

Oliver got back to the farm and went for a walk in the paddocks as darkness set in. He cleared his head completely and considered his options as he strolled through the yearling barn and watched the big black colt munch hay sedately in his stable. The elegant steed ambled over and hung his head over the door, snorting and sniffing Oliver's sleeve. Something occurred to Oliver that suddenly seemed like the best idea he had ever had. Sure, it was a bit crazy and off the wall, but what was it people said about thinking outside the box? That night, he formed a new plan; a plan that did not involve his brother.

The next day, Oliver handed in his written resignation to Gorman. The man read the letter and burst out laughing. "I suppose you think I'm going to get on my knees, offer you a pay rise, and beg you to stay?"

"Actually, no. This isn't a ploy. I'll work out my notice," said Oliver.

"You idiot. This'll be the end of you!"

"I doubt that, but it might be the end of you." Oliver turned on his heel and started to walk out. "Get Diarmuid to run the place," he said over his shoulder.

Oliver was shaking with nerves as he walked out. He dragged his feet back to the yard and told the staff. They stood silent, apart from one who said, "Sure, you're a brave lad. Good luck to you. You've always been fair. I suppose that little shite Diarmuid'll be taking over?"

Oliver shrugged. "It's a possibility."

"God help us."

Oliver took a long walk around the farm, and his pace quickened and his back straightened as he went. By the time he returned to the yard, he was smiling. He dashed about with renewed enthusiasm.

* * *

That evening he called his mother and told her he was coming home for a while.

"You sound chirpy," she said.

"I am, Mum. I am."

One interminable month later, he had a final look at all the horses. He approached the black colt in the paddock and rubbed the animal's forehead. The horse snorted, sighed and leaned into Oliver. "Mind yourself, Bad Boy."

At precisely five o'clock, he drove through the gates and on to

Limerick. An hour later he was on his mother's doorstep, his car packed with his few belongings. He sipped tea with his mother in the large old kitchen and told her that he was going to buy horses, anyway, without Richard's help. Then he went up to his old room, set up his laptop, connected to the phone line and searched the internet for cheap flights to New York.

Chapter 9

May 2004

As the plane took off from Shannon Airport, Oliver's stomach was churning with nerves. He could not sleep during the five hour flight to Newark. He fidgeted and spent his time flicking from film to film, much to the annoyance of the old lady next to him.

He opened his wallet, took out Marco's business card, and held it like it was the Holy Grail. It was still as pristine as the day it was given to him, ten years before. He put it away and wondered what on earth he would do when the plane touched down.

He had purchased a one-week return ticket, though in truth, he did not know how much time it would take. He changed some money and went to a payphone in the arrivals hall, took out the card, placed it carefully on top of the phone, and assembled his large pile of quarters. He had brought his mobile phone with him, but having watched so many Mafia movies, he thought it better to use a public phone.

He tried the number that Marco had scrawled on the back of the card. 'I am sorry, the number you have dialled is no longer in service,' the message announced. Not really a surprise. Next, he tried the office numbers. They, too, were either out of order or had changed. No luck. In a strange way, Oliver was relieved that he did not have to explain himself over the telephone. He then picked up the phone book and checked for Shadows nightclub; it still existed, according to the listing. He took down the new number, then went to the information desk and asked about cheap hotels close to the airport. The clerk gave him details of a nearby place and he took a waiting taxi to the soulless hotel.

In his room, he flopped onto the bed and looked at his watch; it was six-thirty on a Thursday evening. He picked up the bedside phone and called the club. The phone rang out for at least a full minute before a rough male voice answered. "Yeah, Shadows."

"What time do you open tonight?"

"Uh, doors at nine."

"Thanks." Oliver hung up and considered what he would do when he got there. He thought it was best to play the mindless optimism card, to just believe that things would be okay once he made contact with Marco. He closed his eyes and drifted off.

Later that night, a taxi dropped him to the town of Elizabeth and deposited him by the small parking lot at the side of the club. It was nine-fifteen. Oliver walked around the corner to the front of the two story flat-roofed building. There was a man-mountain doorman on duty, who looked Oliver up and down as he approached.

The Irishman smiled and said hi, then paid the girl in the booth and went inside. It was a large square room with a bar down one side and a raised box for the DJ at the end. There were booths along the other side, and the dancefloor was the entire middle of the room. The place was quite dark – not much of a lightshow. It looked a lonely place without customers.

Beside the DJ box, there was a spiral staircase that led up to a balcony. The club was almost empty, apart from three guys sitting at the bar and waitresses idling about hoping for punters. The music was ambient and soothing, the kind of thing a DJ plays when he is just killing time until the crowd arrives.

Oliver made his way over to the bar and slid onto a stool. One of the waitresses approached him – a blonde with enormous breasts, who looked like she had seen better days.

"How're you doin' today?" She smiled with her mouth but not her eyes.

"Good, thanks. Can I have a beer?"

"Sure."

The other guys at the bar all stopped talking and looked directly over at Oliver. One of them wore a cheap suit and the other two both wore nasty-looking polyester slacks with loud shirts and leather jackets that were slung over their barstools. The guy in the suit was tall and thin; he had narrow, darting eyes, like a weasel. The other two were burly-looking and thuggish. Their collective gaze unsettled Oliver.

"Oh, and maybe a shot of whiskey, too," he shouted to the waitress, feeling his stomach tighten. He needed some Dutch courage. Suddenly, this was real. He didn't know who these guys were, but they seemed pretty interested in him.

He gulped down the bourbon and took a sip of beer. "I think I'll have another shot," he declared.

His heart was pounding and he hadn't even uttered a word about Marco yet. He downed the second shot, turned to the others, raised his beer, and said, "That's better. It's been a long day!"

The one in the suit cracked a sinister smile and spoke in an aggressive tone. "That ain't a Jersey accent, where you from?"

"Ireland. I just flew in."

"And how the hell you end up here? It ain't exactly for tourists." The others laughed.

Oliver cleared his throat and decided it was time to go for it. "I heard about it ten years ago . . . When I was last in New York. So now I'm back, I thought I'd come in for a pint."

The suit stopped smiling. "And how'd you hear about it then? Like I say, we don't get tourists in here."

"Well . . . The truth is, I, er, um, I met the owner and he said I should drop by if I was ever in the area. So here I am." He took another swig of beer and felt his heart thumping in his chest.

"You met some guy who said he owns this place? Ten years ago." He made a grunt that was meant to pass for a laugh. "And now, here you are? What are you – on drugs?" He turned to the others. "Can you believe this guy?" They laughed again.

"It's the truth, really. Here, he gave me this." Oliver pulled out his wallet, produced the card and slid it down the bar.

The suit reached for it, examined it, and flipped it over. His eyes took in the handwritten number on the back. Startled, he turned to the others and they huddled together. There was much gesticulating and tilting of heads in Oliver's direction.

His mind was filling with all sorts of mad images – his head in a freezer, his body in a bath of acid. Or maybe the other way around.

The guys finished their discussion and the suit addressed Oliver.

"So, you know the boss, do you? Come on, let's go up to the VIP lounge for a talk." He got off his stool, as did the other two. One of them clicked his fingers at the waitress, who was instructed to bring up a bottle of bourbon and four glasses. Oliver was a little shocked. He stayed rooted to his seat, until the suit came over and put a hand on his shoulder.

"Come, on. It's just up there." He cocked a thumb towards the balcony.

Oliver accompanied him up the stairs, while the other two followed behind Oliver. At the top, the suit crossed the balcony and led them into the lounge. It was a small room, which was really more of an office. To the left was a large window looking out over the club, which Oliver realised was actually a mirror he had seen above the dancefloor. Under the glass was a large sofa, with a coffee table set in front of it and two desks. The two thugs positioned Oliver between them on the sofa. The suit leaned on one of the desks and pressed a button, and immediately the music outside was pumped into the office at full volume. The waitress served the drinks and hurried out.

The suit stood over Oliver. "Where the fuck did you get this card?" He had to lean close to talk through the music. Oliver could smell his foul breath. "Who gave it to you? And when? These numbers are old."

"Yes, I know. I tried calling them." Oliver took a large gulp of bourbon. "This was given to me by Marco Romano. I had dinner with him in New York a long time ago. He wanted to thank me for saving his son from getting run over."

The suit grinned. "I gotta tell you, I hear some wild shit every day, but that's the best fuckin' story I've ever heard! So, even if you are tellin' the truth, why you show up here, now, acting like a tourist?"

"Well, he said that I could come and see him anytime I wanted."

The suit glanced down at the club, then he returned his narrow-eyed gaze to the Irishman. "Take off your fuckin' shirt."

Oliver's eyes widened, he shook his head in a gesture of incomprehension. "Excuse me?" "You heard me! Take off your shirt, then your pants. You can either do it yourself, or Sal and Vinny'll do it for you."

Immediately Oliver got to his feet, shrugged off his jacket, and started undoing buttons. In seconds, he stood before them bare-chested with his jeans around his ankles, his lean frame on display for all to see. The colour had drained from his face; his heart felt as if it would start to make a whirring sound, it was pumping so quickly.

"And your underwear," said the suit, "down to your bare fuckin' ass."

Oliver did as he was told.

The others looked at him, then at each other, and burst out laughing.

"Goddamn, he's white," roared the suit. "You ever see the sun?"

"Don't get me started on the Irish weather."

"OK, needledick, put your clothes back on. Sal, get the scanner."

The taller and fatter of the sidekicks stood and went to a desk drawer. Oliver was doing up his belt and about to sit down.

"Not so fast," said Sal. He had a small black device in his hand that looked like a metal detector wand. He passed it over Oliver from head to toe. "Now turn around."

Oliver did so and Sal repeated the procedure. "He's clean."

The suit seemed to relax, but only a bit. "So, if you're not wired or chipped, then I can assume, for the time being, you're not law enforcement. But I still need to know how you got that card."

Oliver told them of the events on that hot August day ten years ago. He told them everything he could remember, which was everything. From the colour of Cassie's T-shirt to what they had for dinner.

When he had finished, the suit made a call.

"Yeah, it's me," he barked into the microphone. "You gotta come down to Shads. Like, as soon as you can. We got a guy here, says he met you ten years ago. You're not goin' to believe this shit."

The voice on the phone spoke. Then the call was over.

"OK, my friend," he crooked his lips in a hideous smile at Oliver. "You wait here. Have a drink. Sal and Vinny'll keep you company. Someone's coming to see you. So if you're bullshitting, now would be the time to speak up."

"It's all true. I promise you."

"Whatever." He turned to Sal and Vinny. "You guys stay here, I gotta go. Don't get him too drunk." And with that, he marched down the stairs, across the floor and out.

Sal and Vinny moved to sit at the desks, leaving Oliver alone on the sofa. All three sat in silence for over an hour, by which time the bottle of bourbon had been demolished. Sal and Vinny looked at Oliver with equal parts curiosity, jealousy, and awe. For if his story was true, this was a very interesting situation. And if it wasn't, well, no doubt they would receive their orders.

Oliver hoped desperately that Marco would remember him and take the time to listen to his proposal. The truth was, however, that none of them knew how the night was going to pan out.

A trickle of revellers came in and the music cranked up a notch. If he turned his head, Oliver could see through the glass down to the main floor and even to the entrance. He scanned everybody that arrived, hoping to recognize Marco's impressive bulk.

An imposing, plump man in an expensive shirt and trousers appeared through the door of the club. As he crossed the floor, Sal and Vinny stood up and tried to look like soldiers on parade. The man climbed the staircase and, as the door opened and his head appeared, it occurred to Oliver that there was something familiar about his elaborately coiffed, thinning hair. Sal and Vinny both shook his hand and patted him on the back respectfully, then the new arrival focused his gaze on Oliver. A large smile spread across his face, bearing some crooked teeth.

"Well, fuck me! If it isn't the cocaine kid from Ireland."

Oliver put the voice together with the remnants of the bouffant, and instantly knew the man. "Mike! I'm glad you remember. I was getting a little worried. I know it's a bit weird, me turning up after all these years."

"Damn right. So, how you doing?"

"Er, yeah. Good."

"So, what brings you here?"

"Er, I wanted to meet Marco."

He arched an eyebrow. "Yeah, and why's that?"

"I have a business proposition for him."

Mike laughed loud and hard. Sal and Vinny joined in because they thought they should.

Mike stared at Sal and Vinny and opened the door. They left. He sat on the sofa beside the Irishman.

"OK. Oliver, isn't it?" He didn't wait for a reply. "I'm going to assume that you're not as fuckin' green and wet behind the ears as you were back then. I'll also assume that you realize our mutual friend has other businesses besides Shadows. Are you following me?"

"Yeah, I know what you mean."

"Good, then we can dispense with the bullshit. So what does a guy like you have, business-wise, that would interest him?"

"I was hoping to have that conversation directly with him."

"Yeah, I'm sure you were, and you might yet, but you've gotta to run it by me first."

Oliver took a deep breath and prepared to pitch his future at Mike. A feeling of confidence swept over him. He suddenly felt that this was all going to fall into place. He started to speak with assertiveness. "Marco said that he would do me a favour anytime I wanted it. That he owed me for saving his son. Now, I'm not going to ask for a handout, but I do want him to invest in me, in my proposal."

Mike nodded. "Go on."

"I want to buy racehorses."

"Get the fuck outta here."

"No, wait. For him; I mean, for us." He took a deep breath.

"What I mean is, I want him to front me some cash to buy racehorses for him. He *will* make a profit from the venture."

"And what makes you think he wants to own racehorses?"

"He said so, during dinner that night. I was hoping that instead of asking for an outright favour, he might be interested in helping me set up a business for him."

Mike had an amused look on his face. "You're just full of surprises, my man." He rose to his feet and looked at his watch. "It's late. Where are you staying?"

"The Best Western Hotel near the airport."

"OK, I'll drop you back there. I gotta do some things. You got a cell?"

"What?"

"A cell phone. Do you have one?"

"Oh, right. Not on me. Are we going to see Marco?"

"Chill out, my man. Be patient. Give me your number and I'll call you tomorrow. Get some sleep. Relax, OK?"

"Sure. Grand. OK." He gave Mike his number. "It's an Irish phone."

Mike shrugged. "Let's go!"

They got into Mike's white Cadillac and he drove Oliver back to his hotel. They pulled up by the front door and Oliver jumped out. Mike watched him disappear inside, before flipping open his phone and making a call.

Oliver got to his room, turned on his phone, and put it to charge. Then he flopped onto the bed and was instantly asleep – the stress and adrenaline of the evening had finally left his body.

* * *

There was an old blue Chevy in the parking lot opposite Shadows. The man in it scribbled notes on a pad, then he eased out onto the road and followed the white Cadillac to the Best Western. He waited half an hour before he went inside and asked for details of the man who had just been dropped off. He returned to his car, then jotted something down before taking out his phone.

Chapter 10

May 2004. Dublin

Richard McMahon emerged from his meeting with a smile on his face. Even the stress lines on his forehead were gone. He was allowing himself a rare moment of delight, having just secured two executive jets for his new venture, at an unbelievable price – a steal, really.

Both jets would begin flying out of a small airfield near Dublin and would mark Richard's initial foray into luxury travel. He would start by ferrying businessmen to and from meetings around Europe, and Ireland's new rich to exotic holiday destinations. The planes also had the range to make Trans-Atlantic flights. He knew that his proposed price rates were borderline lunacy, but he also knew it would be achievable.

In Ireland these days, it was all about one-upmanship and flaunting wealth. Richard had made his fortune by providing low cost flights all around Europe for the many, but he knew that the country's *nouveau riche* were not yet very discerning about price. There was a kind of prestige in being able to afford something, whether it was value for money or not. However, that said, he did plan to undercut the prices offered by several continental-based private jet leasing companies, because sometimes even the rich liked to make a saving.

Oh yes, he was going to make a killing. Clicking his fingers, he walked across the hallway to his office and sat in his leather chair. Now he needed to figure out how to run the private jets as cheaply as possible to maximise his margins. He picked up the phone, and barked at his efficient, harried secretary.

"Janine, get the whole accounts posse in here. I want ideas for the new jet service."

He hung up without waiting for a reply.

An hour later, he was asking stern questions of the assembled team and not getting many fresh ideas.

He stood at the table, gesticulating wildly. "What the fuck am I paying you for? Apart from the usual – cheap labour, overworking the flight attendants, etc., you mean to tell me you came up with nothing new? Fucking useless, the lot of you!"

Martin Forrester, a limp, timid man who usually sat at the end of the table as far from the torrent of abuse as possible, summoned up his courage. "Well, er, excuse me, Boss, but I, well . . ."

"Oh, spit it out, Martin, before we all get bored to death."

The man cleared his throat. "Well, I think we have to have some celebrity clients. We could photo them and leak the odd shot to the press, like you know, so-and-so boarding with our tailfin and logo in the background. Just one or two in the right magazines and we'll have 'em rushing to fly with us."

"Hmm . . . that's more like it. Grow a pair of balls and open your mouth more often, Martin. Put yourself in charge of making that happen."

"Alright so, Boss."

Richard started smiling again, and everyone in the room sat back a fraction.

Chapter 11

New Jersey

It was nearly noon when Oliver woke to the ringing of his phone. He fumbled it open. "Hello?" he said, groggily.

"You sound like shit." It was Mike. "Get yourself together. I'll be there in twenty minutes."

"OK."

Oliver hauled himself into the shower. He was dressed and down in the lobby as the white Cadillac eased to a halt outside the revolving front door.

When Oliver sat in, Mike wore a crooked smile and extended a meaty hand.

"Hope you slept well, my friend. The boss wants a sit-down with you at his place. Now." He wagged his finger in Oliver's face. "You should be honoured. He never does that."

"Great, but, could we, er, stop for something on the way? I'm starving."

"No. We're eating there."

"Even better," said Oliver, as a large grin spread across his face.

They drove for about thirty minutes, leaving urban Jersey for the leafy suburbs that sprawled over so much of the garden state. Oliver stared out of the window and marvelled at the huge expanse of suburbia. Everybody had their picket-fence houses with half an acre of landscaped garden. Welcome to the American dream. Oliver's thoughts turned back to the little box dwellings being thrown up next to his childhood home.

The car stopped outside a large set of solid wooden gates,

73

flanked by a three metre high wall that stretched down the road in either direction. There was a camera mounted on the wall, to the right. Mike leaned out of his window, pressed the intercom and waved at the camera. The gates opened slowly, revealing a large stone house behind them. It was an enormous mansion, with a fountain as the center piece of the forecourt. The water shot into the air from a lion's mouth, and cascaded down with a crashing roar. To the left of the house there was a garage containing four identical black Lincoln Town Cars, and to the right was a tennis court set amongst some bushes. Immaculate, clipped lawns, dotted with trees and shrubs, covered every other inch of the three-acre compound, save for one building covered in creeper, tucked behind the tennis court. Mike nodded at the swarthy man carrying an automatic weapon, who skulked by a tree just inside the main gate. Oliver stared with his mouth open.

They got out and approached the heavy oak front door. It was opened by an elderly man wearing an immaculate black suit, unremarkable except for a scar running across his throat. The old man simply nodded at Mike, who led Oliver across the entrance hall. They entered a wood panelled library with a huge mahogany writing desk, and a fireplace flanked by a matching pair of sofas. Marco was seated on one, throwing biscuits to a black and tan Jack Russell terrier jumping about at his feet. The dog advanced towards the guests and began to sniff Oliver's shoes and trouser legs.

"He just wants to check you out," said Marco, as he rose from his seat.

"I love terriers, my father used to breed them." Oliver patted his thighs and the dog jumped up at him in pure delight.

"Yeah, he's better security than some of the clowns outside." Marco laughed and Mike joined in.

Marco got up and shook Oliver's hand warmly as he had done in the restaurant all those years ago. He was wearing an expensively cut tweed jacket, crisp white shirt, and a navy blue cravat. His grey trousers were pressed to within an inch of their lives. The whole ensemble gave him the appearance of an English aristocrat. The intervening decade had been kinder to him than it had to Mike, for Marco still had all of his hair, though touches of grey were now evident at the temples.

His dark eyes once again pierced Oliver. "Good to see you again. Really. It's a pity Robert's not here. He's in California – at art school!"

"Oh wow, good for him," said Oliver.

"Can you believe it? I wanted him to do business or law; he got the grades, you know. But no, he wants to be a sculptor. I guess he gets it from his mother. She used to paint when I met her." He looked solemnly into the fireplace for a moment. "Anyway, I thought you were never going to call. Most people wouldn't, you know. They'd be too afraid." He looked into Oliver's eyes and half-smiled. "But you're not afraid, are you?"

"Well, I was a bit nervous last night, till I met Mike."

Marco laughed mischievously. "Yeah, I heard Jimmy and the guys checked you out. He was right; you do look pasty and white."

"Ah, that's the soft Irish climate for you. We get a week's sunshine about once a decade."

"Jesus," snorted Mike. "Must be depressing."

"It is."

"Come on, let's eat," said Marco. They followed him across the hall into the dining room. Oliver admired the long antique table, but Marco led them over to the bay window where there was a small round table laid for three. Marco poured some wine.

"Oliver, if I remember, you like Chianti."

"Oh yeah."

"So, tell me about your life. How are things? You married?"

"No, not married. And to tell you the truth, I'm feeling pretty disillusioned at the moment."

"Really, why?"

Oliver threw his eyes skywards. "Oh, work shit, family shit."

"Aah, work shit – we all got that, but family? What's up?"

"My brother. He's an arsehole. He was given a free start in business, but when I pitched him an investment proposal – a sound one – he shot me down. He flatly refused to help me get on the first rung of the ladder and . . ." Oliver hesitated. "He reckons I don't deserve a chance."

"Who gave him a free start?"

"I'd rather not get into all that."

Marco shrugged. "Hmm, he sounds like he's forgotten his roots. I gotta say: I think it's his duty to help you. He needs to understand that."

Marco shrugged and glanced at Mike, who stifled a smile.

"Yeah well, you might think that, but Rich is a 'my way or the highway' kind of guy."

Again Marco shrugged.

Oliver continued, "But, you know, I really don't want his help. Let him keep his millions, I don't want a thing from him."

Marco took another sip of wine. He thought for a second, then spoke. "So tell me, what is it that I can do for you, exactly?"

Oliver took a deep breath. Here goes. Close the deal.

"Well, I want to buy some racehorses and purchase some others to sell on in a few months for a fast profit. The plan is to buy eight to ten horses. Half would be resold inside a year, with the aim being to double the money. But in reality, allowing for expenses and the odd veterinarian bill, I believe the profit would be seventy-five percent. The others would be kept to race, win prize money and of course, to place bets on.

"I know the horse business like the back of my hand, I've a proven record of buying good animals, the only problem is most people don't know it."

Marco arched his eyebrows. "Really? Why's that?"

"Oh . . ." Oliver paused to choose his words; he didn't want to sound like a doormat. "Nepotism and politics," he said with a dismissive wave of his hand.

"Ha, politics! I hear you. So what horses have you bought?"

"Do you follow European racing? Would the names sound familiar if I went through the list?"

Marco shook his head. "Probably not."

"Then all you need to know is this: in eight years, my ex-boss never made a loss. And one year we sold a horse for fifteen million

Euro to the Japanese." He let the figure sink in for a second. "He cost us ninety-two grand and before we sold him, he won nearly two million on the track."

Marco's face remained stoic. "Go on."

"Anyway, the only thing I lack is funding. I was thinking this: If you front me the money, I buy the horses for you. That is, they'll run in your name, or a company name, or whatever. I handle everything else about the business. When we re-sell the first batch, I take a forty percent share of any profit we make on them. I would also take twenty-five percent of any prize money won by the racehorses, after they recoup their purchase prices. The training fees come out of the initial sum, until the horses break into the black. We would both have the option to re-invest a large chunk each year to buy more horses.

"You said you would do anything for me if I asked, but I don't want a direct handout, just a bit of faith – backed up with cash, which you'll see returned with profit. What do you think?"

Marco let out a belly laugh, slamming his hand on the table. "I think you're the gutsiest, strangest guy I've ever come across, and believe me, I come across all types. Guys like you are a rare breed – I think I told you that last time we met. You come over here all by yourself, turn up at my club saying you want to do business with me! Ha, I love it! Most people are scared shitless of me, isn't that right, Mike?"

"Either that or in complete awe, Boss."

"Tell me, Oliver, just how much money did you have in mind to start up this little venture?"

"A million Euro."

Chapter 12

Marco didn't flinch. "And you think I'm just going to give you that kind of money to mess around with?"

"No. Not to mess around with. Look, Marco, I'm going to invest it. You once said to me that you liked horse racing, and that you and some friends won a few bucks on a horse. Well, I'm giving you the chance to have your own horses to win money with, because I'll buy us the right kind of horses. You can even come to the sales with me, so you can see what I'll buy, and I'll explain why I want to buy a particular horse. I *will* make you money. And by giving you success, I'll also create success for myself. Nobody loses."

"I thought you told me there's no such thing as a sure thing? Now you're saying it's easy?"

"I said that about betting on races as a punter, or casual observer. Here I'm talking about an investment, which will tip the odds in your favour. You'll control more of the variables than a street gambler. It's more of a calculated risk."

Oliver couldn't believe it. He had never sold himself like this before, he felt confident. Perhaps this was what his brother meant by killer instinct.

At that moment, the butler placed three plates of home-cooked lasagna on the table. Marco shifted his bulk and took another drink of wine. He placed the glass down very carefully. When he looked up, the dark eyes pierced Oliver as they had done ten years earlier.

"I tell you what. I'll give you the money. And I'll trust you to set up the business. But I want to do this in my son's name. The horses'll be *his*. That clear? You won't own anything on paper. And I think twenty-five percent of resale profit for you is more realistic than forty. That's my position. And I'll come to these horse sales, see what goes on."

Oliver grinned broadly. "That's great, excellent. You won't regret this, Marco."

The steely gaze remained on him. "Oh, I know I won't. I never regret anything Oliver," he winced slightly. "Except letting my son go to California."

Oliver was floating. He was sure this was the same feeling his brother got when he closed a deal. Sheer ecstasy. The worries and nervousness had melted away. The old Oliver was returning. "I do have one more small request."

"Oh, you do?" Marco raised his eyebrows and a smile crept across his face. "Well, go ahead, what more can I do for you?"

"Well, the thing is, I . . . How can I put this?"

"Just spit it out."

"OK. I don't want to be answerable to, or vulnerable to, the whims or agendas of other guys who . . . work for you. I need to be sure that I'll work for you, and only you."

The big man did not flinch. "In my absence, Mike'll be the guy you will deal with. Nobody else. That clear enough for you?"

"That's perfect." Oliver smiled at Mike.

"I've got to tell you, Oliver, you intrigue me. You're different."

"Different? From who?"

"From anyone I've ever dealt with, different from my son, too – you guys've got to meet again. I wish he had some of your drive and guts. I love him and all – he's like his mother, but I wish he was more of a go-getter."

"Yeah, er, it'd be great to meet again. Well, I say again, but we didn't really meet the last time. You said he's studying art in California?"

"Yeah. Unbelievable." Marco rolled his eyes.

"Is he any good at it?"

"His grades are great. They seem to think he has talent. His mother used to paint weird stuff, abstract she called it, so I guess it's possible. What do I know?"

"Well, if he's passionate about it, it could be a good career for him."

Marco fiddled with his fork. "We'll see. He may get tired of it soon."

They began to eat lunch. Marco poured more wine for Oliver.

"This really is an amazing house," said Oliver.

"Thanks, it came into my family several years ago." He gestured up to the beamed ceiling.

"My son likes it more than me. Apparently it was built a hundred years ago. That kind of stuff doesn't really interest me. I just want somewhere secluded to call home. What was it like where you grew up?"

"It was nice, we lived on a farm. Peaceful, you could say. Ireland has changed, though. The country's so wealthy. Everything moves faster, people are more stressed. Don't get me wrong, we're better off; there are plenty of jobs, lots of construction going on – too much, in fact. Cities are growing rapidly, so's the population. It's sad to see the country swamped in concrete and housing estates."

"But you guys must be happier," said Mike. "I mean, you haven't gotta get on the boat to come here anymore." He grunted and looked at Marco, expecting a laugh.

Oliver pondered this for a second. "That's true, I suppose. But you've got to set your sights a bit further afield, don't you? I mean, I want to." He shrugged. "Ah, sure it'll all be there to come home to."

"Man, you guys are weird. Now you got it all, but you're not happy," said Mike.

"That's the price you pay for economic success," said Marco. "I know my life changed as I got more successful in business. You don't have as much time to enjoy life. The stress of staying on top takes its toll. But what are you going to do? That's life. We should be thankful for what we have and for our families."

"Never a truer word, Boss," said Mike.

"Huh, I don't know," replied Oliver.

"You just need to get married, settle down to make your

own family, my friend." Mike patted him on the shoulder encouragingly.

"Are you married, Mike?"

"Yeah sure; wife, two kids, steady mistress," he chuckled.

Marco shot him a sideways glance.

"Aah, enough about me," said Mike hastily.

Marco finished eating and wiped his mouth with his napkin. "OK. So, how long are you going to be in Jersey?"

"I bought a one-week return ticket."

"OK, here's the deal. My driver'll take you back to your hotel. Do what you want tonight. Tomorrow, check out and come stay here. Mike'll pick you up at the hotel. I'm going to get my son home for a few days, you guys can get to know each other, and we'll thrash out the details of this horse deal. Then you can go back to Ireland and get started."

"Wow, cool. That's very kind of you. I'd love to stay here, are you sure it's no trouble?"

"It's all arranged. Now off you go. Wait outside the front door and I'll have the car sent."

Marco stood and extended his hand. Oliver placed his own into the iron grip.

"I'll call you tomorrow. Keep your phone on," said Mike.

With that, Oliver left the room and was taken back to his hotel.

* * *

Marco stared out the window for a few minutes. Then his dark eyes fixed on Mike.

"When you pick him up tomorrow, make sure he understands about discretion. I've got a good feeling about the kid. I think he's basically honest, but there's no harm in giving him a little briefing. Tell him to expect the Feds. When it all comes out that he's buying horses for my family, they'll try to get him and use him, that's for sure. Fuckin' assholes are low enough to do it. He needs to know exactly what talking to them would mean."

81

"Sure thing, Boss. Do you want me to arrange a little entertainment for him tonight?"

"Yeah, but don't go out with him yourself. Send Candy with a full pocket. Make sure she gets him totally off his head. Then, see if he'll sing about us. That'll be his first test."

"OK, done." Mike walked out to his car.

Marco dialled Robert's number in California.

Chapter 13

That evening, Oliver was about to go out for a drink when the bedside phone rang. "Sir, there's a young woman at the front desk to see you."

"What? Eh . . . OK. I'll be right down."

When he arrived in the sparse lobby, the receptionist motioned to one of the sofas. Oliver saw a beautiful girl of no more than twenty-five, sitting with her legs crossed, flicking through a magazine. Her long black hair cascaded over her shoulders. She had flawless, ivory skin, large brown eyes and luscious lips, highlighted by a shock of crimson lip-gloss. She was dressed in a tight-fitting 1950s-style black dress. She looked like a package of pure burlesque sex. He was almost drooling as she looked up at him and smiled.

"Hi there, you Oliver?" she said in a chirpy voice. "I'm Candy!"

I bet you are. "Oh, that'd be me," he said with a smile. "And what can I do for you?"

She stood up and he took in the full length of her allure.

"I was kinda thinking we could have a glass of champagne and see what happens."

"Sounds great! But I don't know anywhere round here."

"See . . ." She put a hand on his shoulder and whispered into his ear. "I figured we could stay here and order room service."

Oliver's eyes stood out on stalks. He turned to the bemused receptionist.

"Is it possible to have a bottle of champagne sent to room 407?"

"Yes, sir. Right away," he said, with a knowing smirk.

When they got to the room, Oliver said, "Candy, you look

far too lovely to have appeared out of thin air. I take it we have a mutual friend who arranged this?"

"You talk funny! But your accent's cute." She kissed him on the cheek. "Yeah, I'm gonna show you a good time."

She sat on the bed and took a small ziplock bag of cocaine out of her handbag. She tossed it onto the bedside table. "Rack up, will you?"

Oliver knelt on the floor and began chopping the fine white dust on the bedside table with a plastic do not disturb card. This had never happened in his last job! His confidence was at an all-time high even before the first line.

There was a knock at the door, and Oliver retrieved the champagne and signed for it. When he turned around, Candy was already down to her expensive lingerie, lounging on the bed and snorting away greedily. She looked up at him and flashed a seductive grin. "Hey, have some more, I'm getting a head start."

He needed no further encouragement. Two hours later, they were into their second bottle of champagne and third gram of cocaine. He blurted out his best anecdotes in a torrent of words, while she smiled seductively. Two hours after that, Oliver was high on sex, stimulants, and the sense that he was finally on the way.

They lay together on the bed, sipping bubbly. Oliver was smiling inside and out. He felt like the King, and his new life was only just beginning. A new leaf well and truly turned over. He congratulated himself with another line of powder.

Candy caressed his arm. "So, how does a guy like you end up in Jersey with friends like you got?"

"Well, it's a long story."

"We've got all night."

"We do? Great! Then I don't want to waste any more of it talking shite!" He leaned in to kiss her.

She giggled and pushed him back playfully. "No, seriously. I want to know. What did you do to deserve a visit from me? I mean, you just got here a day ago, right?"

"I'm the . . ." With all the stimulants in his system, Oliver's brain was racing and he suddenly had a vision of himself in a police cell, being beaten with a hosepipe, then another of himself bundled up, in the boot of a car. "I'm just lucky, I s'pose. Right place. Right time. And that's it, really. Now can we either change the subject, or get back to what we were doing?"

"Why, sure! No problem at all." Her tongue went to work on him.

* * *

Mike pulled into the dark laneway behind the row of suburban houses. He pulled on the latex gloves and a second pair over them. He checked the contents of the holdall one last time, grabbed the bag, and set off down the lane. He casually walked to the fifth house on the row, glanced over his shoulder and slipped through the gate, up the garden path and into the shadow of the back porch.

Peering through the tattered screendoor, he could see Freddie and Tony snorting cocaine off the countertop. "Dumbfucks," he muttered, pulling a nylon swimming cap over his hair. He knocked on the door.

As the last nail slammed home, Mike put the nailgun in his bag and stood back to take in his handiwork. He looked from one man to the other. They were trying to scream through their taped-up mouths. Panicked breaths flared their nostrils. Mike sighed. He needed to work faster before they passed out from the shock. He placed the boxcutter on the table. The muffled screams became more desperate.

Mike stared at the man to his left. "Freddie, what the fuck you need to see a lawyer for?"

Freddie's breathing slowed.

"Yeah, I know about that. Should've kept your mouth shut. Planning a little *kiss and tell*, were we?" Mike ripped the tape off his mouth.

Freddie gulped air. "Oh God, it hurts! Please, Mikey, I didn't tell him anything, I swear. I got scared. We, we both did . . . Right, Tony?"

Tony's eyes bulged as he shook his head violently.

Mike glanced at him and returned his attention to Freddie. "Don't call me Mikey. Now, what the fuck you got to be scared about? I told you to chill out and everything'd be OK. I told you not to fuck things up. I told you to do your *fuckin' job!*"

"Yeah, I know." Tears began to form in his eyes. "Look, Mike, I started seeing cars around; guys I didn't know. We were being watched, I'm sure of it. I . . ."

"You're paranoid. I told you that shit'll fuck you up if you do enough of it. Nobody's watching you."

"Mike, that's some dodgy stuff you got us to do, I mean, we're not wiseguys. That shit's out of our league."

Mike taped up Freddie's mouth again, slowly picked up the boxcutter and stood behind him, his head down beside Freddie's ear. "I suppose you think you got guts, huh?"

Freddie looked confused, unsure whether to nod or shake his head.

"Let's have a look," said Mike. He reached down and slashed the man from navel to chest.

Just before Freddie passed out, he saw his own intestines spill over his knees and onto the floor.

Mike looked at Tony, who was redfaced, hyperventilating. He ripped the tape off his mouth.

Tony started babbling, "I swear, Mike, I wasn't worried. I told him not to go to that lawyer. He was stupid. That's why I called you. I don't give a shit if this is your thing on the side or if it comes from Marco Romano himself. I don't wanna know. Makes no difference to me, man. Please, Mike, pull the nails out. I'll do whatever you want."

Mike raised the boxcutter and let the duct tape drop into the bag.

* * *

The next morning Mike sat alone in a diner, reading the city section of the paper. There was no mention of last night's work, but he did not really expect there would be – not for a while, anyway. His phone rang. "Yeah?"

"Mike, it's Candy. It's done. I asked him, but nothing; absolutely nothing. I'll tell you something, though, he loves to party," she whispered.

"Thanks, Candy. Tricky as always."

"Gee thanks. This one was fun, too. He's a good guy. It's none of my business, but don't be too hard on him."

"That's right. It's none of your business." He pocketed the device and took a sip of coffee.

"Another fuckin' lamb to the slaughter," he muttered.

Chapter 14

It was early afternoon by the time Oliver got into Mike's car, nursing a massive hangover. He was not expecting serious conversation.

Mike drove a few miles to a quiet, wooded area, and stopped the car. He turned to Oliver and smiled.

"So listen, my man. I need to make you aware of a few things."

Oliver nodded and wished his head didn't hurt so much.

"OK, as you know, the boss values discretion, honesty. He has no time for people who betray confidences, give away information. You understand me?"

Again, Oliver nodded. This sounded rehearsed.

"Good. Now, if he ever does business with anyone, that implies a level of trust from him, and he expects that trust to be honoured with the respect it deserves, capiche?"

"Sure. That makes sense."

"You know what I like about you, my friend?"

Oliver shook his head.

"You're discreet, honest, loyal, a real stand-up guy. You'd never do anything stupid."

"Absolutely. I don't like others to know my business."

"Right, your business, or anyone else's."

Oliver was sobering up now. The conversation was beginning to register. He stared at Mike's lips as they moved.

Mike continued, "Stupid people fuck things up for everyone, but especially themselves. And we don't want that, do we?"

"No, Mike, we definitely do not want that."

"Good. Then we understand each other. Oh, there's one more thing."

"What's that?"

"It's like this: I guess you've figured that once your business becomes public knowledge, certain people are going to want to take an interest in you."

"Certain people?"

"The Feds."

"The Feds?"

"What are you, a parrot? The FBI. Don't tell me that hadn't occurred to you."

"Um, er, sure it had. Yeah."

Mike raised his eyebrows. "Well, you'd better *start* thinking about it, 'cause it'll happen. They're a bit distracted these days, trying to catch terrorists and shit, but you can still count on them taking an interest in you. They'll try to make you piss your pants, get you to wear a wire, and do all kinds of degrading shit. But they won't have anything they can pin on you." Mike jabbed his finger at him. "Your start-up money'll be legal. Our friend won't even own the horses on paper; everything'll be above board. They'll never be able to touch you, long as you don't get stupid. Is that clear?"

"Crystal."

He was fully alert now. The pain in his head had vanished.

"Good. So don't worry about a thing. Keep your cool, and when they make contact, you tell me. OK?"

"OK, Mike. No problem. No problem at all."

And it wasn't a problem, he said to himself. After all, he was only buying horses. It was of no concern to him what his patron did for a living. Mike was right: they couldn't touch him.

Later that afternoon, Oliver sat in the spring sunshine on a large wooden armchair in the garden of Marco's mansion, with a whiskey in his hand. The terrier raced around his chair, mad for action. He sipped the drink, savouring the strong taste. This life, he could get used to.

Oliver shrugged and cast his mind back to the ecstasy of the previous night and onto Mike's talk in the car. He downed the remainder of the drink. He was doing nothing wrong. Keep quiet, enjoy life, buy good horses, and watch the money roll in.

Marco appeared and sat opposite him. The butler brought refills.

"You been settling in? How many of these d'you have?"

"This is my second. And yes, thanks, I've been enjoying the serenity here."

"Good." Marco picked up his glass. "Here's to fast horses!"

They clinked glasses.

"Robert'll be here tonight. I want him to help you out with the business."

Oliver smiled. "Great!"

Marco nodded enigmatically. "And I want you to stay here for the rest of the week. Hang out with him, see New York again."

"Cool. Sounds good." He cleared his throat. "Er, you're very kind to invite me in like this."

Marco swirled the ice in his drink. "I'd like you and Robert to be friends, and I know I can trust you not to take advantage of that." He took a large gulp of bourbon. "Anyway, let's get down to business. When do you need the money?"

"Not till late August. I'll buy yearlings in Kentucky in September, then maybe some in Ireland in October. Then I'll buy what we call *weanling* foals in November or December in Ireland."

"OK. Here's what I'll do. Robert will get the money; he'll be like your business partner. I'll put an accountant on it, but when you need to pay for a horse, Robert'll do it. That makes the money matters simpler. Bills will be paid in his name. That way he can go with you and learn your business as well. It also means we don't have to worry about anybody trying to steal the money. I know you want a million Euro, but if you intend to buy in Kentucky first, we'll see how much you spend there before I convert the rest to take to the sales in Ireland. I'm sure you'll agree, what with the weak dollar and all that."

"Sounds fine to me. But I, er, I thought you said Robert wanted to be an artist?"

"He does, but . . . we'll discuss it tonight, all three of us." He downed the rest of his drink and motioned for another. "What're you going to do with these horses after you buy them?"

"The American purchases will need to be kept at a boarding farm in Kentucky, till I find trainers for them. As for the Irish ones: I'll keep some at my mother's place, but depending on how many we buy, I may have to see my brother about renting his land."

"Renting? From your brother? You serious? You can't just use his land?"

"What, free of charge? No chance."

"Some piece of work! I mean, don't get me wrong, I like to make a buck as much as the next guy, but when it comes to family, some things should be done on faith. You know: family should just do things for each other. No questions asked." He shook his head. "I'd like to meet this guy someday."

"I'm sure I can arrange that." A smile began to creep across Oliver's face, which he promptly buried in his glass.

The expression was not lost on Marco. "You kids these days. You think everybody's *Vito Corleone* or *Tony Soprano*. That wasn't what I meant. And don't start trying to get smart with me." He wagged his finger at Oliver.

"Sorry, Marco."

Oliver sheepishly looked up at Marco, who burst out laughing. Oliver laughed nervously.

After a few more drinks and more chat about race horses, Oliver was feeling a bit drunk and he could see that Marco was a bit tipsy and loosened up. The terrier was lying in his lap now.

"You know," said Marco, as he ran his fingers through the terrier's smooth hair. "People think they're small, soft dogs, but let me tell you, they're real hunters. Vicious little fuckers when they want to be. But you probably know that, right?"

"Yeah, my dad used to breed them. They dispatch rats for sport."

"Now that's useful," said Marco, with a glint in his eye. "There's always a rat around."

Oliver thought he got the point, but was unsure whether to

laugh or remain serious. "We even used to put them into foxes' earths to flush them out. Dad used to wait outside with a shotgun, but sometimes the dogs would fight the fox, one-on-one."

"I can believe it." Marco took another gulp of bourbon.

There was a pause of nearly a minute as Oliver decided to broach another subject.

"Marco, can I ask you a question?"

"This sounds serious! Sure you can." He gave Oliver a direct look.

"Is it stressful? Your life, I mean, running your business and having to watch out for people trying to get you."

Marco looked surprised by the question. "Let me tell you something, Oliver. Running any business successfully and staying out of trouble, is stressful. And my line of work is no different. In some ways it's better, but in many ways it's worse. Take the Feds, for example. They'd love to put my head on a platter. Not just mine, either; a lot of my friends are in the same situation. They make us out to be the evil core of America, then along comes a bigger threat, and they want us to be their buddies."

Oliver frowned. "What do you mean?"

"9/11, my friend. Before that, we were Public Enemy Number One. Now they want us to report to them about dodgy Arabs in our unions." Marco put on a whiny voice, *"Anything unusual at all. We really appreciate it,* they say to some of my guys, all in the name of patriotism. It's not the first time they've used us, either."

"You mean informers and stuff."

"No, I mean when the country was at war with Hitler and Japan, they came to us for help."

Oliver's face was blank.

"Oh, come on. You're a smart guy, don't tell me you don't know about this – don't you read?"

"Yeah, but only horseracing books."

Marco shot him a sideways glance. "FDR was President. He did a deal with Luciano, who was in jail. Got our friends back in the Old Country to pave the way in Sicily, and guys here to protect the shipyards. Then after the war, it all gets forgotten about. Well, fuck 'em, is what I say. Bin Laden did us all a favour." He wagged a finger at Oliver. "That don't mean it was right; killing all those people – women, children, families. But he sure took the heat off us."

"I never thought of it like that."

"Aah, why would you? It has nothing to do with you."

Oliver shrugged. "Did you ever re-marry?"

Marco sighed. "No, never did. I didn't feel like taking another wife. I had plenty of offers, mind you, but they just wanted to be my wife and not Robert's mother. So I figured we're both better off without anyone else." He nodded his head towards the trees. "This place is big and empty these days, with just me here. Still, I suppose Robert'll get married one day and come to live here."

"I admire your family values, Marco. And I can't believe the way you treat me. I mean, even all those years ago, you took me to dinner without knowing anything about me, except that I'd helped your son."

Marco smiled wryly and looked directly at Oliver. "Oh, don't worry, I had you checked out."

"You did?" Oliver's eyes bulged. "But how? I mean, you didn't know me."

"You gave the nanny your full name and told her you were Irish. I have some friends in Immigration so I had your passport checked out. Your J1 visa led me to the Kentucky stud farm you worked at. I knew you were who you said you were. Then, when we met, it was obvious you didn't know me. So I had nothing to worry about."

Oliver was astounded by this revelation, but at the same time he was in awe of the man's efficiency: simple, discreet, and thorough. The Irishman was excited at the prospect of working with, and learning from, such a man.

"It's a bit like making a bet, I suppose," said Oliver. "You need to get all your ducks in a row before you put the money down."

Marco looked at Oliver with an expression of approval and respect. "Now we're on the same wavelength. Good."

He looked at his watch and pushed the dog off his lap. "I got things to do. You make yourself at home. Robert gets here in an hour or two."

Later, Oliver put his bag in a large bedroom with an adjoining bathroom at the top of the mansion. He splashed water on his face, wandered downstairs, and found himself in Marco's office. He was drawn to the leather-bound tomes on the shelves near the fireplace.

All of a sudden his ears twitched, and he heard the front door opening. Startled, he replaced the book and sat on a sofa.

A few minutes later, Marco entered the library with a young man the spitting image of him. Robert Romano was tall and stocky like his father, but it was all muscle. He had a crazy mop of black hair that sat around his head like a lion's mane, and the same piercing dark eyes of his father. He wore a slim-fitting T-shirt and baggy jeans.

Oliver stood when they entered.

"Robert, Oliver." Marco thrust his hand in Oliver's direction. "I'm sure you guys'll get on. Hard to believe this is the screaming kid you grabbed, eh?"

"You've certainly changed." Oliver offered his hand. "Good to see you again."

Robert shook it warmly. "Yeah, man, nice to meet you, too. Like, properly. Dad told me a lot about you."

"I don't think you could grab him by the shirt now, huh?" said Marco, with a smirk.

"Well, I could, but I don't think I'd stop him."

"I try not to run out in front of cars anymore," said Robert, with a smirk like his father's.

The clock on the mantelpiece chimed seven. Marco announced they would eat in an hour. The room was beginning to darken as the sun dipped behind the trees.

They flopped onto the sofas; Marco and Robert on one, Oliver alone on the other. A bottle of champagne and three glasses appeared as the butler turned on the lights.

Marco proposed a toast. "Here's to winning races and making money."

He looked at Oliver as they all clinked glasses. Robert cast a glance at his father.

"So," continued Marco. "We discussed everything on the way from the airport. He's up for it, and things'll proceed like I told you earlier."

"That's great," said Oliver. "Can't wait to get cracking on this."

"Yeah, man," said Robert. "It sounds like a blast. Totally like something out of a novel. Horse racing's a bit crooked, huh?"

"Ah, not so bad, but it's not perfect, either."

"As long as it's imperfect or perfect enough to let us profit," said Marco. "After that, I really don't care."

They all laughed. Oliver laid out the plans for Robert, but he seemed only vaguely interested and asked Oliver few questions. Marco was mostly silent, content to just sit there, nodding approvingly from time to time.

Over dinner, they laughed and joked about the random events which led to them all meeting, and ultimately, to this dinner table.

The next day, Oliver struggled down to the kitchen around midday. He poured himself a coffee from the pot, opened a newspaper, and turned to the sports pages. The sun blazed through the large window, onto his back. He did not hear Robert enter.

"Hey. How's it going?" said Robert.

Oliver looked up. "Good, slept like a log. Feels like a holiday."

"Hey, I was thinking. We should take off into the city. We could hang out, or go to see something – whatever you want. Then go to a bar and party. I know some places."

Oliver nodded, smiling. "Sounds like a plan."

"So, where you want to go?"

The visitor took a second to consider the many options in a city like New York, before deciding on a place that he had already been. "Well, I went to the Museum of Modern Art the last time I was here. The day I met you, in fact. I hear it's all renovated and redesigned now. Might be good to take a look."

"OK, cool, and I was thinking I'd like, take you to Ground Zero. You been?" he asked.

"No, what's it like?"

"Strange. You'll see." He drummed his fingers on the marble surface and considered the logistics. "OK. So Dad'll give me a car. No driver. That way we can park in midtown, take the subway, and stay in the city for the night. No driver to keep an eye on us."

"When do you want to leave?"

"When you finish that coffee."

Less than an hour later, they cruised through the Lincoln Tunnel and into Manhattan. Oliver was astounded once again by the energy of the city. People dashed urgently along the streets, and the advertising billboards flickered constantly: enticing, seducing.

They deposited the car and walked the few blocks to the Museum, then spent almost four hours slowly progressing from room to room, staring at great length at the pieces they liked. Both of them took turns to mock several pretentious people who were walking around the gallery with an air of self-importance and apparent looks of disdain on their faces.

"That guy's so full of shit," whispered Robert, nodding towards an expensively dressed man in his mid-forties, who was talking loudly about symbolism to a much younger and very beautiful girl. She looked like she wanted a cocktail and to go to Bloomingdales with his credit card.

"If he's not careful, he might disappear up his own arsehole, at any second," said Oliver. Robert burst out laughing. "Man, your accent's cool. It's like the whole tomayto/tomahto thing – asshole/arsehole. Man, chicks must love you here."

"A foreign accent in America's like being Superman – I'm different – but Ireland's my Kryptonite." They laughed.

They moved on downtown by subway, and toured Ground Zero. It was now fairly orderly, with the construction of the memorial just getting underway. Neither of them spoke much as they wandered, stopping only to take in the various shrines, statues, bronzes and other messages.

By evening they found themselves propped against the bar in a dark joint in SoHo. They knocked back imported beers and grazed on overly-salted pretzels; they had worked up a thirst.

Oliver considered how well they had been getting on. The guy sitting opposite him didn't seem like the spoilt brat who had nearly got himself run over ten years ago.

"Robert, you're not twenty-one yet, are you?"

"Will be in October. Why?"

"How come you didn't get carded when we came in here?"

"Nobody cards me where they know me, but even if they do, I have a fake ID." He smirked. "Well, it's real, just has the wrong date of birth – present from Mike for my eighteenth."

"Isn't it great to have connections?"

They grinned at each other, clinked glasses and drank. They sat in silence for a moment, until Oliver broke it.

"What happened to your nanny that day? Cassie, wasn't it? She looked shit scared when you ran off. You were quite a handful."

"Can't remember." He shook his head slowly. "Man, I had so many nannies. They never lasted long. Dad told me the Feds were always trying to get to them for info on him, or whatever . . ." His voice trailed off.

"It brought it all home for me earlier, to actually see the trade centre site," Oliver said. "Your father and I had a conversation about the attack and how it made things easier for his line of business." He was testing the water now.

Robert took another sip of beer and stared at the wall for a second. "Everyone in his line of work thinks the same," he said finally. "But I don't think that makes them bad people. Everyone has their reasons." Another sip. "I mean, I bet the fucking government were delighted to be handed an excuse to do whatever they want all over the world."

Oliver chewed his lip. He reckoned that sounded like Marco, not his son.

"What was your mother like?"

"I don't remember her as much as I want to. That kind of scares me, you know, in case I forget her completely. She was great, always played with me, let me make hand-prints on the walls of her studio. My dad . . . He, uh, like . . . After she died, he just spent all his time on work."

"When did you first know that your father's business was, er, unusual?"

Robert shrugged and ordered two more beers. "I don't know. I knew we weren't like other families. At school everyone was, like, afraid *and* in awe of me. I suppose I knew my dad was someone who scared people." He took a large gulp of the ice-cold liquid. "Anyway, I don't know much detail about what he does. I just know we're never short of cash. And I like that. He's good to me."

"He's a generous man. I mean, he's helping me out more than my own family ever have." Oliver told Robert about his brother.

"I guess I'm lucky I don't have brothers or sisters. I used to be lonely when I was a kid, though. It was difficult having friends over. I guess their parents worried they'd turn into little hoodlums, or some shit like that. That's kind of why I wanted to study in California, to get away from all that," he sighed. "Only problem is, I like my lifestyle and the money and the way things just seem to happen, doors open for me. Know what I mean?"

Oliver thought about it. That was the second time in a few minutes that Robert had sounded mature; maybe there was more to him than the rich party animal. Oliver said, "I do. And I understand. I mean, I'd say I'd feel the same way if I was you."

"Hey, Dad'll look after you, too. Don't worry." Robert shrugged. "Well, enough of that shit. Drink up!" He nudged Oliver's elbow and motioned towards his beer glass. "Let's move on, the night is young! You sure an old fella like you can keep up?"

"Not so old, you cheeky bastard. Only thirty-two. I'll keep up."

They left the bar and visited a succession of others in the district, each one darker and more crowded than the last. They were starting to feel quite drunk. Robert decided cocaine was the remedy. They packed themselves into a tiny toilet cubicle and greedily consumed the white powder. By the time they got out of a taxi in the meatpacking district, they were floating. They walked round a corner and saw a huge line of people on the street, all vying for the attentions of the nightclub doormen guarding the velvet ropes.

Oliver was having flashbacks to the time he had come to a

place just like this with Mike. Maybe it was the same place? What difference did it make? As long as they got in and the girls were as good as the coke.

Robert scanned the line. "Follow me," he said.

He approached the doormen; they nodded, opened the rope and let him through. When he passed between them, each shot out a meaty arm to block Oliver.

"It's cool guys, he's with me," said Robert.

Oliver grinned at them. Nice one: straight in the door. They strolled into the booming mass of people and Robert made straight for the bar. Oliver followed him, checking out women writhing suggestively on the dance floor. At the bar, Robert pushed a drunken guy out of his way so he could order. The guy, who was as big as Robert, reacted by shouting and making threats. Without a word, the young Romano looked the guy up and down and walked away, then jerked his head for Oliver to follow.

The guy shouted, "Pussies!"

They headed back to the door, where Robert whispered to one of the gorillas. The guy spoke into his headset and nodded.

"Watch this," said Robert, making his way back inside.

Two bouncers appeared and stealthily attached themselves to the arms of the drunk. He was swiftly escorted towards the door in a state of bewilderment. As the guards dragged him out, Robert could not resist smirking at him.

Oliver, in his cocaine haze, didn't know whether to laugh or be shocked. "I can't believe you got him kicked out," he said.

"Fuck him, he's an asshole – or should I say, arsehole?"

They both cracked up into fits of laughter.

After that, they were taken up to a secluded balcony, where there were two busty, sweaty- looking girls drinking cocktails and sniffling. Oliver was getting that déjà vu feeling. They sat and chatted. And drank. And snorted. The night passed in a blur of drugs and girls.

In the early hours, they had finished the cocaine and the high had come crashing down. They stumbled into the lightening day and took a taxi to their rooms at the Marriot in mid-town. As

Oliver drifted off to sleep, he thought to himself just how lucky he was.

They spent the rest of the week the same way that: drinking in some bar in Jersey or New York, snorting coke and playing pool. Oliver didn't see Marco again. He got a message from Mike that he was away on business, which relieved the Irishman, considering how hard he and Robert had been partying.

Before he left for the airport, Robert and Oliver exchanged numbers and agreed to keep in touch. Mike whisked Oliver away, but dropped him back at the Best Western. Oliver, slightly puzzled, looked at him with raised eyebrows.

"You take a cab from here," said Mike.

"Sure. It's safer, I suppose?"

"Something like that. Open your cell phone, save my number. Under Mike, just Mike. Gotit?"

"Got it."

"OK. Take care of yourself, tell me when you're coming over again and remember everything we discussed. If you need anything, I'm just a phone call away."

They shook hands and Mike clapped a hand onto the Irishman's shoulder.

"Thanks for everything, Mike. Really, you and Marco've been great."

"Aah, that's what family's for. We help each other out. Now go on, get outta here."

Oliver sat in the departure lounge and allowed himself a satisfied smile. Job well done. Now he just had to buy the horses. Who needed a family when he had friends like these?

* * *

Agent Huntley picked up his phone. "Yeah?"

"It's Rosen."

"What've you got?"

"Do you want this Irish guy questioned before he gets on his plane?"

"No. It's too early, I want to see where this goes. But make sure the system flags us if he comes back."

"OK. They must like him, they got him an expensive hooker, then he stayed the week at Romano's house."

"At his house? You're shitting me?"

"No."

"Christ, nobody ever goes in there, I mean *nobody*. Except Mike, that old servant and Luigi, the security chief. This is huge." Huntley flipped the device shut and pondered an idea as he stared out the car window at the police cars and forensics van. He watched an officer running crime scene tape around the clapboard suburban house.

He sighed and got out, flashed his ID to the cop on the door, and was let inside.

"Thanks for calling, Jim," said Huntley.

The grizzled, burly cop turned and half-smiled. "Yeah, well, once I figured it was Mike the Nail's work, I knew you'd want to see. Jesus, Huntley, you look like shit – you ever sleep? Or you just lie awake counting the ways you'd like to get Romano?"

Huntley rubbed his temples. "Save the wisecracks, Jim. Tell me what you got."

Jim led him into the kitchen. Huntley saw two men, probably late twenties, early thirties, slumped over each end of the table.

"How long they been like this?"

"Bout a week, I guess. Neighbours complained about the smell, we sent a unit to investigate. Nice surprise, huh?"

Both men were stripped to the waist and gagged. They had their hands spread out in front of them and nailed to the table. Their knees were nailed to the chairs and their feet to the floor. Their bellies had been slashed open, and intestines spilled out over their knees and onto the linoleum. The floor was covered in a pool of dried blood. The stench of decay was unbearable.

Two forensics officers were taking photos and swearing. "Mind your goddamn step," barked one.

"Any cash or drugs in the place?" asked Huntley.

"No, but our guys reckon that's cocaine residue on the countertop," said Jim.

"Who were they?"

"Two fuckin' idiots. Thought they could get involved with your friend and the Nail, and it wouldn't bite them in the ass."

"So what went down?"

Jim shrugged. "Who the fuck knows? Who cares?"

Huntley jabbed his finger at the cop's barrel chest. "I fucking care, Jimbo. Answer my goddamn questions or I'll have your badge."

Jim looked furious. One of the forensics guys stifled a smirk.

"Jesus Christ, Huntley, give it a rest. You'll wreck your life trying to get these guys. We got two more bodies with nails in them and fuck all else. And I'll *bet* you my badge we don't get a print or a hair in the place from anyone except these two." He shook his head. "Why don't you go after Colombians or terrorists instead?"

Huntley ignored him. "I'll call you in forty-eight hours. You can give me the full report then."

Jim grunted as Huntley spun on his heel.

Back in his office, he summoned Rosen. Karl Rosen was stocky and shorter than the thin, gaunt Huntley. Rosen knew that people called them Herman and Uncle Fester, after the characters in the *Munsters'* films, and even he thought Huntley was a grey as a vampire.

"What now?" he said, plonking himself on the sofa with a sigh.

"I've had enough of the Gent."

Rosen rolled his eyes. "What happened now?"

"They nailed two more guys."

"Shit. Worse than before?"

"The same."

"Any evidence?"

"The usual: fuck all. Anyway, this Irish guy could be our biggest break yet. I've been thinking. We'll need a few more guys and a couple of girls, too . . . Yeah, two girls: young, straight out of Quantico, if possible. And good-looking, too."

"Shit, Pete, you don't ask for much. We'll never get approval for that unless you can link it to terrorism."

"Fuck terrorists. The Gent's worse. You leave approval to me.

You just start going through personnel files and keep an eye on the Irishman when he comes back."

"You sure we'll see him again?"

"He's been to the Gent's house. You know that never fucking happens, right?"

Rosen sighed again. "If you say so."

"I know so. He'll be back. He'll get in with the Gent, and he'll probably end up nailed to a table. Unless we put Romano away first."

Chapter 15

The next morning, Oliver was sitting in the cosy kitchen of his mother's house, sipping coffee and trying to stave off jet lag.

Evelyn appeared and was both startled yet delighted to see him. "Oliver, what a lovely surprise." She gave him a peck on the cheek and sat beside him at the large oak table. "I didn't hear you get in."

Oliver rubbed his bleary eyes. "My flight got in at five-thirty; I didn't want to wake you. God, I'm knackered; running on adrenalin."

"How did it go? You left in such secrecy, and I didn't hear a word from you. I was getting worried."

"Yeah, sorry, Mum. I should have called, but it was a mad week. Feels like a dream. Or a scene from a movie." He yawned and stretched. "The good news is, I found myself an investor and we worked out a deal. I'm going to start buying horses in a few months."

Evelyn lit up. Her whole face erupted into a smile of pure joy. "Oh, my dear Oliver, that's wonderful news." She couldn't help but embrace him. "Tell me all about it. I knew you could do it."

Oliver raised his eyebrows and cocked his head at her. "Did you? Really? Huh, you might have let me know."

"Oh, Oliver, don't be like that. I prayed for you every night and lit candles for you at church last Sunday."

"I'm sure that made all the difference."

"Don't be sarcastic, Oliver, and don't mock my beliefs."

"Sorry, Mum, it's the jet lag. Thanks, really."

"That's OK, I'm just happy you've found an investor. Now,

this calls for a celebration. I'll make you a nice fried breakfast while you give me all the details."

She went to the fridge and started to prepare bacon rashers, sausages, eggs, tomatoes, black pudding, and lots of tea and toast. The smell wafted around the kitchen.

Oliver drooled with hunger. "Mum, you're a star. I love your breakfasts. But as far as giving you all the details, there isn't much to tell. It's someone I knew from when I worked in America ten years ago, and he trusts me enough to back me. And for that, I am very grateful."

"Yes yes, Oliver. But who is he?"

"Oh, he's new to the horse business. Wants to keep a low profile. I'll be working mostly with his son, but he may come to the sales."

"It all sounds very mysterious. Are you sure he'll give you the money?"

"Positive, Mum. Cash up front. No empty promises with this guy, I'm sure of that." He shuddered as he had a flashback of the conversation with Mike in the car.

"You should tell your brother the good news, he'd be delighted for you as well."

Oliver stiffened and made a grunting sound.

"Oh, come on Oliver, he's not as bad as all that. He just lets business rule his heart sometimes."

"Sometimes? Huh. That's what business is to him, Mum: heartless. I really *do not* want to talk to him."

"I hate to see you boys fighting. I think he would be proud of what you've done this week. You really should call him." She sighed and placed a sizzling plate of breakfast in front of her younger son. "His new business with the private jets is starting this week. He has some pop stars booked on the inaugural flight; they're off to Germany on tour. It's been all over the news. Quite exciting, really."

Oliver didn't reply, but tucked into his breakfast. Evelyn sat at the table with a mug of tea and some toast. The smile slid away from her face.

Chapter 16

Oliver held his head high as he strode purposefully around the large cluster of barns that was the Keeneland Thoroughbred Horse Sales complex. It was a balmy September day in the heart of Kentucky's picturesque Bluegrass Country. The humid heat of summer still covered the area like a blanket, and sweat dripped from Oliver's brow.

Since they flew into Lexington three days ago, Oliver had looked at almost four hundred yearling horses and the week was only beginning. He was hot and tired, his shirt and khaki shorts stuck to him, but he shrugged it off. Nothing mattered except finding the right horses. He was in his element.

The forty-two barns in the complex were full. Over the next twelve days, nearly five thousand thoroughbred yearlings would change hands. It was a mammoth auction for potential racehorses. Buyers would assemble from all over the world. Everybody thought they would be the ones to spot a champion in amongst all the others.

Robert was doing his best to keep up, but was unable to match Oliver's enthusiasm for the long days of endless walking and standing. To him, all the horses looked the same. Oliver did plenty of explaining, but it was as if he was speaking another language.

Oliver had met several old friends and spent time catching up over drinks or dinner. All were happy to see him, and everyone wanted to know whom he was buying for. They all did their best to pry information out of him and his new friend, but to no avail. Robert found all this curiosity amusing and couldn't quite believe that not one person knew who he was, although whenever Oliver introduced him to anyone, it was simply as Robert – no surname. Oliver, in particular, enjoyed the bit of mystery. He loved to keep them guessing. After all, they would find out on sale day, when Marco was due to make his appearance.

They stopped under the central arch of barn eleven, to let Oliver check his list and gather his thoughts.

Robert leaned against the wall. "Goddamn, I'd murder a cold beer." There was a chiming from his pocket, and he pulled out the phone.

"Hi, Dad. What's up?"

Oliver looked up from his catalogue.

"I can't tell one from the other. I'll put you on to Oliver." He handed the phone over and said, "Dad says he'll be here today, at four."

Oliver clutched the handset to his ear. "Hi, Marco. That's great you'll be here early." He started chattering excitedly. "Things are going well, I've a list of about thirty for a second look. Quality stock. I'll show them to you–"

Marco cut in. "Good. See you later, my friend." The line went dead.

Oliver handed the phone back. "Well, if your Dad's going to be here in a few hours, we might as well have lunch."

"Cool. Shit, I thought I was going to have to hit you over the head to stop you looking at horses." Robert ran a hand through his sweaty mop of hair. "Man, I'm thirsty. Let's go!"

They walked out of the maze of barns, past the auditorium where the horses would be auctioned, and made their way towards a restaurant in the grandstand of the adjacent racetrack.

"This place is far out, man. You kinda *know* big deals have been done here."

Oliver smirked. "Just you wait till tomorrow when the bidding starts. The air'll be thick with money."

They went up to the panoramic restaurant and took in the view of the oval racetrack. It was two tracks, really; the dirt track outside a grass one, with another line of tall oaks set behind, obstructing the noise of the highway. Oliver felt warm and nostalgic, thinking back to the time he'd spent here.

A pretty brunette sitting at another table noticed them. She excused herself, left the two men she was dining with, and made her way towards Robert and Oliver. She was petite in height and build, but moved with cat-like grace and athleticism. Her cropped hair sat in a spiky mess on her head, and her dazzling turquoise eyes stunned everyone she met.

Robert nudged Oliver under the table. "Hot chick at two o'clock," he muttered through closed teeth.

Oliver casually looked in her direction. He stood, smiled broadly and threw his arms out wide as she neared the table. She flashed her perfect white teeth at him. They embraced and he kissed her on the cheek.

"Dr. Liddell, I presume! What are you doing here? Are you practising here?"

"Right here in Lexington; enough horses here to keep an army of us busy. I specialize in reproductive work, but I'm starting to do some surgeries at the clinic. It's a good job. The hours suck, though." She eyed Oliver up and down. "You look great, it's good to see you again. It's been what? Ten, eleven years?"

Oliver shrugged. "Something like that. You look stunning." Her sparkling eyes and tanned skin still mesmerized him. She was that rare thing: a hard-working vet who knew her stuff, who could pull off attractive even whilst knee-deep in blood and manure. Hell, in just a T-shirt and jeans she was a knockout.

She glanced at Robert, who stood reluctantly.

"Rebecca, forgive me, I'm rude. This is Robert. Robert; Rebecca Liddell, an old friend of mine."

Extending a well-toned arm to shake his hand, she said in her clipped, Ivy League accent, "Nice to meet you Robert. You have a surname, or has he forgotten it?"

Robert smirked. "Maybe he has. It's Romano."

"Will you join us for lunch, or do you need to get back to your companions?" asked Oliver.

She glanced back; the two men were paying the bill and

getting up. They waved at her.

"They're colleagues, they've been here all week x-raying and doing pre-sale examinations. We've already eaten, but I'll join you to talk and catch up."

They sat and ordered. Oliver couldn't help himself but look at her. "It really is good to see you. You haven't changed a bit."

"Oh, you're too kind." She winked at him. "So, what brings you back to Kentucky after all this time?"

He took a deep breath. "I'm here to buy horses for a new partnership. Robert's father is my backer. It's very exciting."

"Is your father in the business?"

"Horses? No. He's interested to see what the game is like, but he kinda wants to keep a low profile."

"People round here love gossip. He won't stay underground for long," she prompted.

Oliver interrupted on behalf of an uncomfortable-looking Robert. "He'll be here in a few hours, so that should take the mystery out of it."

The drinks arrived and Robert downed his first beer as if it was the elixir of life. Oliver and Rebecca stuck to juice and water. Robert looked at Oliver's glass with astonishment.

"You not having a beer?"

"Need to keep a clear head. But don't worry, I'll be going mad once we buy the horses." He thought for a second and asked Rebecca, "Do you do sale exams?"

"Sometimes, but most of the locals prefer the senior partners to do it."

"Well, if I give you a list of horses, can you check them for me this afternoon?"

She flashed that smile again. "Sure, love to. How many?"

"Thirty."

"I can do that."

He produced his catalogue, tore a blank page from the back and scribbled lot numbers on it. "They're for days one and two. I put my cell number on it, too."

She folded the paper and stuck it into her pocket. "Great. OK,

I've got to run back to the clinic quickly, but I should have them all done by five or six this evening. How's that sound?"

"Excellent! You can meet up with us after, and we'll discuss things. Call me when you're done."

She looked at her watch. "Later." She kissed him on the cheek and left with a spring in her step.

"What's the story?" asked Robert. "You guys used to date, or what?"

"Yeah," Oliver replied with a downcast voice.

"And you're still crazy about her, huh?"

"Was it that obvious?"

"Yeah, but don't worry, I didn't see any rings on her fingers."

Oliver looked at him with raised eyebrows. "I noticed the wedding finger alright." A smile

crept across his face. "She's cool."

"Why'd you break up with a chick like that, anyway?"

"Our lives went different ways." Oliver let out a long sigh. "We had an intense summer romance, she was doing holiday work at a vet clinic here in Lexington, then she went back to University in Colorado. Come to think of it," he paused for thought, "it all happened just before I pulled you out of the street."

"I guess you can thank me later."

"Thank you?"

"Sure! Like, if I hadn't run onto the road, we wouldn't be here right now. And you'd still be in Ireland."

"Probably. OK, so I'll thank you if I get her out on a date."

Robert made a mock toast with his beer glass. They grinned at each other.

Chapter 17

At four pm, they were waiting outside the front doors to the sale auditorium. Oliver was pacing, tapping his pen off his catalogue, and smiling. Robert wanted another beer.

The black Lincoln pulled up in front of them. A small, wiry-looking man in a suit jacket and jeans leapt from the front passenger seat, pushed back the valet, and opened the rear door. Marco got out gracefully and stood to take off his tweed jacket and tie, exposing an immaculate white shirt, with black stone cufflinks.

"It's warm. Why didn't you tell me?"

"Sorry, Dad. Didn't think of it."

Marco embraced his son and then Oliver. "You guys get in any trouble down here? What's the local skirt like?"

Oliver blushed and shot a sideways glance at Robert.

"Don't look at me, I didn't say anything."

"What's this?" Marco said. "You been getting some action?"

"Hot vet chick; old flame," said Robert.

Again Oliver blushed. "I, um, I'd rather get on with business, but you'll meet her later, Marco."

Marco slapped Oliver on the back as they turned towards the doors of the auditorium. The swarthy guard brought up the rear.

They walked into the corridor which circled the auction ring. It was theatre-like: a semi-circle of seating for 500 looking onto a small stage, with the auctioneer's rostrum set behind and above it.

Marco let out a whistle. "This place is something. I was expecting some kind of shed, or an old tobacco barn."

"Wait till you see it tomorrow," said Oliver.

111

Twenty minutes later, they stood under a tree in front of barn seven: Oliver, Marco, Robert and the guard, whom Marco introduced as Joey. An elegant thoroughbred yearling was being paraded by a groom, back and forth before them. Oliver gazed at it, concentrating hard. The horse came to a halt in front of him.

"This one's at the top of my list," he said, in a low voice that was almost a murmur. "There'll be quite a bit of interest. He's the first foal of a very good racemare, but the pedigree's not fashionable. Neither is his father, so that might help keep the price down."

Marco was staring at the animal. "Tell me why you like him."

"He's very well made, physically. His legs are straight and correct, he's muscular, and he walks with a long, graceful stride – he looks like an athlete." He threw a glance at the groom. "Give him another walk, please.

"You see, Marco, look at that. He eats ground with every stride, but more than that, he's nimble, light-footed."

The groom finished the lap with his charge and brought it to a halt again.

Oliver continued, "But what really turns me on about this horse is the elegance of his body – we call it quality – and the look in his eye. He stands there with his big ears pricked and a bold look about him, like he wants to run and battle. Like he won't give up easily. I love this horse. He looks like he'll race at a classic distance." The animal whinnied nervously, making his veins stand out. "He might be a bit highly-strung, but that shouldn't matter as long as he's trained right. We have to get this guy."

Marco switched his steely gaze from the horse to Oliver, his skepticism was evident. "And you can tell all that just by looking at him? Jesus. He looks like any other horse to me."

"If I'm sure of one thing, it's this: he is not just any horse," said Oliver, fixing his eyes directly on Marco's. Then, out of the corner of his vision, he noticed the vendor of the horse approaching. "OK, Marco, here's the seller. Poker faces." He glanced at Robert, too. "We don't want to show our hand."

Pat O'Malley was a small, round, balding man in his fifties, who had landed in Kentucky straight from Ireland more than a quarter of a century earlier. He had a shrewd brain for horses and deals, but he relied on his affable exterior to persuade clients to part with more hard cash than they ever dreamed possible.

"Well, lads, how're you doing? He's a beauty, isn't he?" he said, pointing to the horse.

"Not bad. I daresay there's been some interest in him," said Oliver. "Even with the pedigree."

"Jaysus, he's been flat out with lookers and vets." Pat eyed Oliver up and down. "Have we met before?"

"About ten years ago, Pat, you were just starting your new farm here, and I was a student over at Harleston Way Farm. We used to drink in the same bar. Oliver McMahon."

"Oh, Jaysus, I remember now! You were going out with that vet student."

"Er, that's right."

Marco smiled. "I'd say he's chasing her again," he said to Pat.

Pat turned to face Marco. "Well is that right? Ah, sure why not? She was a good-looking bird!" He let out a cackle, which made Oliver blush and Marco and Robert smirk. "Who are you fellas, anyway?" he asked Marco.

"My man here's going to buy us a few winners."

Instantly, there was a twinkle in his eye. "Pat O'Malley," he said, as he thrust out his hand to grip Marco's. "Nice to meet you."

"Marco Romano."

"You should look at my three other horses; they're all beauties. You fellas'd do well to buy 'em all."

"Thanks, Pat, we'll come back later. We've others to look at now," said Oliver.

"Not at all, sure you're here now. I'll have 'em pulled out for you in a second." He looked back at the barn and whistled to two members of his staff.

"Really, Pat, we've a lot to do before dark," Oliver objected.

"It'll only take you five minutes," insisted Pat.

"He says he don't want to see them, I don't want to see them," said Marco. He fixed his dark eyes on the small round man. The gaze did its job.

"Oh, um, I'll leave you fellas to it, then." He hurried away back to the shadows of the barn.

"Thanks for that. He's a slimy little shit. A good horseman, but he wants everybody's money," said Oliver. "Still, he could be useful."

"How?"

"If we buy his horse, he'll have to do us a discount rate for board and keep when I ask him if he can look after him for a month or two, until I get him broken."

Marco gave Oliver a look of admiration. "You impress me more and more each day, my friend."

"Thanks, Marco. I'll continue to impress you," he said. "Right, now on to the next one."

As the group passed through the complex, a few heads turned, some people did double-takes as they passed Marco. There seemed to be an air of gossip and rumour flying around. Oliver loved it. He felt like some of Marco's presence was rubbing off on him. When they asked to see the next horse, the vendor – an American – took one look at Marco and dropped his cup of water.

"Could we see lot two-five-seven, please?" repeated Oliver.

"What? Oh sure. Right away, sir."

Oliver's face was a mixture of surprise and amusement. He shot a look at Robert, who sported a satisfied grin.

The horse was produced and Oliver began to absorb every detail of its physique. He was so lost in the horse and explaining the regal beast in hushed tones to Marco, he did not notice the vendor peering out at them from the shadows of the barn.

The man stood with two other people. All three were having a rapid but quiet discussion about the large man with the slicked back hair and immaculate shirt. They decided Marco was indeed the spitting image of a Mafia boss who had been in the news several years ago, but that there was no way it could be him. That is, until somebody pointed out the seedy-looking man in the jacket and jeans who kept close, but discreetly so, and who paid as much attention to the comings and goings of everyone around as he did to his charge.

Oliver asked for the equine athlete to be walked again and put away. He then led the group onto the next horse, and so it went until late afternoon. As they made their rounds, assessing every potential racehorse on Oliver's shortlist, the gossip followed. Robert and Oliver could sense the constant whispering that floated behind them. If Marco picked up on it, he made no indication of it.

Oliver felt a rush of adrenaline; a powerful sense of authority came over him. His client was the centre of attention in Keeneland, and tomorrow when Oliver started bidding on Marco's behalf, that would make him one of the most talked about buyers at the sale. It would instantly raise his profile in the business.

It was six-thirty that evening when they finished looking, and went to the bar in the complex to meet Rebecca.

It was half-full, with about sixty people standing around in small groups, all engrossed in discussion and only about horses. There were stud owners from Kentucky, dressed in LL Bean shirts and shorts, pressing their wares onto potential buyers; bloodstock agents from Europe on the phone to their clients; trainers from all over the country and the world; and the entourage of two Arab sheiks, taking up five tables and drinking only mineral water.

Into this buzzing mélange of cultures, strode Marco, Oliver and Robert. Joey entered a few paces after them and loitered by the door, watching everyone. Marco dispatched his son to the bar for drinks.

Rebecca was sitting alone in a corner, checking her catalogue and the findings of her examinations. Oliver pointed her out to Marco and they made their way over.

"Ma'am, are these seats taken?" Oliver said in a fake Southern accent.

She looked up, surprised. "What? Oh hi! It's you." Her face brightened. "How was your afternoon?"

"Interesting, good. I'd like you to meet someone." He said,

turning to usher Marco towards the table. "Rebecca, this is Marco. Marco, this is Dr. Rebecca Liddell."

From her seated position, Marco was like a giant. His face softened into a warm smile and he extended his hand.

"Marco Romano. The pleasure is mine. You're the vet, right?"

"That's right."

"You're as gorgeous as he says."

"Am I now? Why, thank you, sir." She glanced at Oliver, who looked embarrassed.

They sat and Robert appeared with the drinks. "Hi, Rebecca," he said, as he placed the glasses on the table. "I got you an OJ, you want something in it?"

"Vodka, please."

"Now that's more like it," he said, returning to the bar.

"Right," said Oliver. "Business first. Did you find anything strange or startling?"

"I found–" she began.

"Excuse me," Marco interrupted. "But what do you look for? I ask because, well, I'm interested, and it seems like my man here can see into their souls."

"Oh, sorry. I start by making routine physical exams on all of them. Lameness, general wellbeing, etc. I listen to their hearts and check their vision. Then I go to the x-ray repository at the back of this building and check their shots. All horses have a full set on file, these days. Which reminds me," she looked at Oliver. "Do you want me to get any heart scanning done, to grade them for size and strength?"

"No. It's a waste of time, if you ask me."

"Okaay," said Rebecca, her nose slightly out of joint.

"Why?" asked Marco.

"Because I can tell you that at least one Breeder's Cup Classic winner of the last ten years was failed at this very sale by a vet who scanned his heart, claiming it was small and weak."

"Really?" said Rebecca. "Which horse? Which vet?"

"I can't tell you that, but suffice to say that the vet in question has given up scanning hearts."

Rebecca started racking her brains.

"And how do you know this?" said Marco.

"Grapevine. I know someone who worked for the lady who wanted to buy the horse, but she didn't because of the vet report."

Marco wagged a finger at Rebecca. "He's putting pressure on you."

She winked. "Oh, I can handle it."

"I bet you can," said Marco.

Robert returned with the vodka, which he poured directly into Rebecca's juice.

"Thanks." She took a sip. "So, where was I? OK, of the thirty I looked at, all were clean of heart, lungs, limbs, and were all sound at a walk. Except for lot 433, he had a grade one heart murmur."

"Bad?" said Oliver.

"No, grade one's my lowest. But, still, I wouldn't recommend buying into that kind of problem."

"I agree. Next."

Marco and Robert sat back in their chairs and watched the two horse people dissect the animals on Oliver's list.

"Lot 287 has had operations to remove bone chips on both knees. Not a good start in life."

"His legs are correct, though. Might not matter to him. He comes from the Weinstein's farm in Midway. D'you know it?"

"They're not my clients, why?"

"Do they have a lot of these kinds of problems?"

"No more than anyone else, far as I know."

"OK, next."

They continued like this for another twenty minutes. Marco's gaze darted between them like a scanner.

Finally, Oliver came to the last horse on his list. "Now, what about 687, the big colt of Pat O'Malley's, anything there?"

"No, clean as a whistle. Nice horse, too."

"Good, and you're right, he is."

"I had to endure Pat's tirade of smutty questions while I was doing the exam." She rolled her eyes.

"We had to put up with him earlier. Till Marco shut him up."

She turned to Marco. "I'm impressed. How'd you manage that?"

Marco shrugged, a mischievous twinkle in his eye. "I deal with guys like him, in my line of work. They usually take the hint."

"And what is your line of work?" she asked.

Oliver stopped writing notes and looked up at Marco, searching his face for a displeased reaction or *that look*. But the big man's expression remained affable. He smiled at Rebecca.

"I have nightclubs, bars, and a sports betting business. Your guy here persuaded me to see what life is like when you're not just taking the bets. You horse people amaze me – really."

"How's that?" said Rebecca.

"You guys are talking about animals, right? But you take them apart like they're machines."

"That's because we want to find the ones who are going to run like race cars. We – that's everybody you see here – are all looking for racing machines. Right, Oliver?"

"Absolutely." He looked deep into her eyes; she returned the gaze.

"But," she began again, "because they're living things, we need to try to cover as many of the variables as possible, to try to shorten the odds of actually buying a good horse."

"I couldn't have said it better myself." Oliver turned to Marco. "Now, here's my revised list."

He moved his catalogue so it was facing Marco. "It's down to twenty, all listed in Lot order. The stars beside some indicate priority, and the figures, their approximate value, and bidding limit. I'll get Robert to mark it into your catalogue tonight."

Robert looked less than enthused about this.

"OK," said Marco. "Now, let's all go have dinner? I'm getting hungry. Rebecca, you'll join us?"

She thought for a second. "Sure. I'd love to. Where and when?" she said, looking at her watch.

"Nine. The Marriot," said Marco.

Chapter 18

Over dinner, Marco ordered lavishly from the final pages of the wine list, and listened intently to the horse stories that Oliver and Rebecca regaled him with. Nonetheless, Oliver found it difficult to relax. His mind was split between the sales, getting the results Marco expected, and the distraction Rebecca posed as she sat listening to Marco's anecdotes or holding the table's attention with some of her own.

Sensing Oliver's preoccupation, Marco interjected, "Hey, relax, my man. Things're going well." He gave the Irishman a reassuring pat on the shoulder. "Chill out, enjoy the evening."

Afterwards, Robert tried to hasten his father's departure upstairs, so the three of them could have some fun, but Marco insisted that his son join him in the room. Robert rolled his eyes at Oliver as he reluctantly followed his father to the elevators.

Oliver and Rebecca moved themselves to an empty corner of the bar, with half a bottle of wine to finish, far from the crooner and his piano.

"He's under his father's thumb, isn't he?" she said.

"A bit, but he's a good guy, really. It's weird; sometimes he says things you wouldn't expect. I reckon he hasn't had it as easy as you'd think, even aside from his mother's death. We should go out for a night with him after the sale. He knows how to have fun."

Rebecca looked sullen and stared into her glass.

"What's up, Bec?"

They both sat looking at each other for a minute, both realizing that this was the moment to say things, but neither knowing what to say. It was Rebecca who took the plunge.

"I'm so glad I saw you in the restaurant today," she said. "But . . . if you hadn't seen me at the sales, would you have looked me up?"

Oliver stared into his wine glass; words almost failed him. "I don't know, Rebecca. I wanted to, but I, well it's been a long time. To be honest, I figured you'd be married with kids."

"Oh, come on. You know me: work, work, work. Do you really think anyone wants to marry a woman like me?"

"I'd imagine the list is endless." He looked at her. "I know I'm on it."

"That's the nicest thing I've heard in a long time." Her whole face broke into a huge smile. "That mean you're going to ask me out on a date?"

His confidence returned, he gave her a winning smile. "Well, possibly."

She grinned back. "Asshole."

"Here's to new beginnings." They clinked glasses.

"New beginnings." Those stunning turquoise eyes sparkled, and he hoped that another part of his life was falling into place.

"Speaking of new things," she said. "Your business has got off to quite the flying start. Your client is – well he's striking; unusual. Very courteous, but scary at the same time."

Oliver smiled. "Now, you said it. Do you recognize him at all?"

"No. Should I?"

"You didn't hear the gossip today?"

"No." She paused for thought. "But come to think of it, before I left the complex, a farm owner outside the bar asked me who Marco was, and what he did. I told him exactly what Marco told me."

Oliver thought for a few seconds, drained his glass, glanced around to make sure there was nobody within earshot and said, "I have a secret, and I need you to keep this to yourself."

"OK, sure." She looked both concerned and curious. "This sounds juicy. I like a good secret." She huddled closer to Oliver, conspiratorially.

"Oh, you won't believe it," he said. "I hardly can myself."

He poured more wine and started from the beginning.

Rebecca was shocked. "Jesus. I can't believe you work for him."

"Well, it's all true. But I work with him, not for him"

"You sure there's a difference?" She leaned in closer still, and took his hand in hers. "Do you really know what you're doing?"

"Yeah." He frowned. "Come on, Bec, you know me. This is just the chance I needed. I was squandering years working for that wanker Gorman. Now I've got some decent cash behind me and the chance to get my name on the buyers' list, I'll show the bloody lot of them. And I'm not going to let you go this time, either." He kissed her passionately.

"Oh, I'm not going anywhere. And I do think you'll buy good runners, but that wasn't what I meant." She sighed. "Oh, Oliver, you haven't changed. I always loved the way you persevere in seeing the best in anyone." She paused. "Are you sure this guy means what he says? He's not going to shaft you, is he? I mean, he is a criminal. Why get involved with him, at all?"

"Like I said: success and glory. It'll be worth it."

"You sure?"

"Yeah, I won't fuck it up."

"It's not all down to you."

Oliver wished she could see the good in his situation; he so wanted her to trust him and to see what a future he had ahead of him. "Listen, you've seen the way he is with me. He knows I know my stuff – and he treats me with respect. He thinks I'm worth listening to. Sure, it doesn't hurt that he owes me a favour. That's why we're doing business together. He needs me as much as I need him. That's how business works."

"Wow. That doesn't sound like the Oliver I knew. You've become a bit cynical during the last decade."

He sat back in his chair and stared at the ceiling. "Yeah, well, I got tired of catching all the horseshit at the bottom of the pile. I figure if I'm going to be used, then I want to get as much as I can out of the situation. I'll deliver for him, alright; he'll have no reason to fuck me." He shrugged and looked at her again. "I mean, he wants to win races and make money, right?"

"Right, I guess."

"And you'll get paid for all the exams and any other work you do on our horses."

"Oh, I wasn't referring to that," she said. "You'll get a bill from the practice, anyway."

"So there you have it." He waved his hand dismissively. "Don't worry so much, Bec. Things'll be OK."

"I like the new you. You were always ambitious, but a bit soft. Now, you're a bad ass!" She smiled, got up, and sat on his lap, kissing him again, long and hard.

"I suppose I'd better be going," she said eventually. "We both have an early start."

"When the sale's over, we'll take a day for ourselves," Oliver said.

They stood and hugged. Walking her to the door, he added almost absentmindedly, "So how're your parents doing? They still in Maine? Your dad still golfing every spare minute?"

Her face paled for an instant and she couldn't look at him. Oliver gently touched her on the arm, breaking her reverie.

"They're dead," she blurted out. "Three years ago. Car accident. It's just me now," she said in an attempt at bravado.

"Holy shit, Bec! I'm sorry. Er, I . . ."

"Shit happens. Car was totalled, a truck hit them. They reckon my dad fell asleep at the wheel, but I can't imagine that . . ."

"Jesus, Bec, I . . . I'm so sorry."

He kissed her lightly on the forehead and pushed through the doors into the night air.

"Thanks," she said.

"How come you didn't go back to Maine?"

"I had to sell the house and cash it all in to pay my student loans, because Dad had been helping me with them. Now it's just me and my apartment here. I miss them. I even miss my dad's golf obsession."

"God, that's awful." He had only met her parents Hunter and Ashley once. Hunter had insisted he try golf and had kept smiling, no matter how many balls Oliver lost in the rough. Ashley had fresh cookies on the table when they returned, and he couldn't forget their rib-crushing hugs when they dropped him and Bec back to the airport.

She wiped the corner of her eye. "Yeah, well, like I said: shit happens. Then you try to get on with life. I should go."

He hailed a cab from the rank and watched her speed off into the night.

Chapter 19

The auditorium crackled with energy. It was packed full of people, their hopes, dreams, and money. Marco nodded thoughtfully as he scanned the crowd. There were the Arab sheiks, whose massive spending power was only matched by their massive entourages. Although they all wore Western dress, they had that tough, steely-eyed look of the Bedouin desert tribes. Billionaire businessmen from all over America engaged in serious conversation with their trainers and bloodstock agents. Huddles of shrewd Irishmen and Englishmen were figuring out the angles. There were at least two groups of Japanese, trying to remain unnoticed, but not succeeding; and a swarm of Koreans, blending in with the Japanese. The atmosphere oozed with optimism and money.

One at a time, horses appeared on the small stage, led in by a groom and passed to the sales company handler, who was immaculately dressed in green blazer, black slacks and leather gloves. The auctioneer rattled through the lots, selling each one in a matter of minutes. There was no time to ponder the merits of the individual horse here; you just had to bid until you reached your limit. Oliver found the seats he had reserved for himself, Robert and Marco, and they took their places towards the back of the auditorium, directly to stage left. Joey stood behind the back row, surveying the crowd.

"We'll get a good view of the action and can see who's bidding from here," said Oliver. "Our first lot's coming through soon. But the next one in is something special. I wanted you to see this animal being sold."

Marco opened his catalogue. "What's so special?"

With that, the auctioneer's hammer went down with a bang and the previous horse was led out. A new one took its place.

"Watch this," said Oliver quietly into Marco's ear.

The auctioneer launched into his heavy drone of preliminaries: a quick summary of the animal's pedigree and relatives, followed by a starting price. His individual words were almost inaudible. A shout went out, indicating that one of the bid spotters patrolling the aisles had found an eager client. Heads turned; the board lit up with a starting price of five hundred thousand dollars. Immediately another shout came.

"Over there," Oliver whispered into Marco's ear. "In the red shirt, Sheik Ahmed of Qatar. He started, and his opposition is Mel Stone, the Florida orange magnate, sitting in row seven."

"Where?" said Marco.

"Over there, Dad," said Robert, indicating with an extended finger.

"For God's sake, don't point," said Oliver. "You might end up making a bid."

"What? Oh, sorry." Robert looked a bit sheepish. "So, I guess we don't want this one, then?"

"No. Now watch the price board."

Robert watched the figures change. Marco switched his eyes between the two bidders as they traded turns to buy the equine blueblood that graced the stage. It was like watching a bizarre game of tennis; shots were fired back and forth between the two parties desperately trying to out-do each other, hoping every new bid would be the decisive one.

The bids were climbing in increments of one hundred thousand dollars. It was less than a minute before the one million mark was reached and breached. With each bid, the noise level in the auditorium decreased. At three million, it was very quiet; at four, you could hear a pin drop.

Marco let out an awestruck whistle. "That's incredible," he said to Oliver in a hushed tone. The bidding began to slow after four-and-a-half million. Mel Stone was faltering. Oliver noticed his trainer sitting beside him, subtly shaking his head. Nonetheless, he fought on with two more bids before calling it quits. The only sound was a nervous whinny from the prize, oblivious to the price now on its head.

The hammer was about to drop, when another hand went up. It belonged to a middle-aged Korean man standing at the back, with a walking stick and a long ponytail, looking like something out of a Hollywood movie. His bid topped five million. All heads turned. Marco wanted to stand up and shout, like a man watching a boxing match, but he held his tongue. Oliver enjoyed the theatrics of the occasion.

The sheik immediately upped the bid to six million, the Korean to six-and-a-half; the sheik to seven. The Asian bidder turned his back and walked out. The hammer went down. A cheer went up.

"You've just seen the sale topper being sold," Oliver said with a flourish. "Now, imagine you were the seller."

He left the thought hanging in the air as he marked his catalogue.

Robert spoke first. "Hold on, like, you're saying the horses we buy in November and December, could make *this* kind of money on resale?" His eyes lit up. So did Marco's.

"Well, not this kind of money, but I hope we'll be in high six figures, and if we get lucky, maybe a million for a horse that'll have cost us much less. You see the potential?"

Robert whistled.

"Yeah, well it's not that easy. In this business, you always need a bit of luck."

"You got to make your own luck in this world," said Marco.

"Yeah, but when you're dealing with animals, you need a rub of the green, because they don't have to conform to our plans and dreams."

"Whatever. Let me tell you, my friend, that's the kind of profit I like."

In hushed tones, they discussed the dynamics and tactics of bidding at auction for a while, until the first horse on Oliver's list came in. It was a handsome individual. Oliver made a few bids but was swiftly blown out of the water by a Texan oilman. The hammer went down: Nine hundred and eighty thousand.

Oliver shrugged. "On to the next."

Marco said, "Jesus, I can't believe how much people pay for an unraced horse. Maybe my million Euro won't go far enough."

"That's why I set my limits before the sale. Otherwise, the temptation is to get carried away. Look, I want to buy four horses here for about half the budget – give or take ten grand. If we're priced out of it on everything I want, then we start again in Europe next month."

"And what if it's the same thing there? Do we just settle for any old horse?"

"No, we do not. But don't worry. It won't come to that. We won't go home empty-handed here, there's too much to choose from."

They bid on eighteen horses that day and failed to buy any. Their dinner that night was rather

more subdued. Oliver went to his room early and pored over the catalogue for days three and four.

The next morning, he dragged Robert out of bed at five. They were at Keeneland, looking at horses by six.

"Man, this is like, totally cruel."

"No rest for the wicked. If we're empty-handed today, we need to have a list ready for day three."

They got through a hundred and ten horses before the sale started. They then dashed to the auditorium to meet Marco and bid on two more horses, neither of which they got. Then back to the barns and more looking. Oliver drummed his pen on his catalogue, the pressure was mounting. Halfway through day two, and still nothing.

By three in the afternoon, they had looked at everything for day three, made a list of twenty, arranged the vet exams, and trotted back to the sale ring for the final lots.

They took their seats next to Marco, who had been content to sit and watch the action all day.

"How'd you guys do?" he said.

"Good, twenty on the list for tomorrow. Rebecca's doing the exams."

"I watched seven horses sell for over a million dollars today. These people are crazy."

"Well buckle up, Marco. Because in the next hour, there are three coming through that I really want so we may get a little crazy ourselves. Not million dollar crazy, though. Don't worry. I won't blow it all on one horse."

"Damn right you won't," he said, giving Oliver a sideways look.

That evening they did buy two horses. The first was a female with a very good pedigree, but slightly small in build. She cost $210,000. One of the well-dressed bid spotters brought the sale docket to Oliver, who smiled and his hand shook as he signed for the horse. His heart was pounding.

Marco clapped him on the back. "Well done. At last we have a horse."

The next on the list was Oliver's favourite, Pat O'Malley's colt. It pranced about as it entered the ring, looking fractious. Oliver started the bidding; Mel Stone bid against him, but Oliver kept his eye on a syndicate of shrewd Irishmen who sat behind Stone. If they wanted this horse, they would have the financial muscle to blow Oliver and Stone out of the water. Oliver reminded himself that the colt was by an unfashionable stallion whose first crops of runners had never performed on the undulating turf of European racetracks. That should put the syndicate off. They only wanted horses they could turn into turf performers and, ultimately, European stallions.

Stone and Oliver traded bids of fifty grand apiece until the price was half a million. Marco just kept staring at Stone, willing him to stop bidding. At six hundred thousand, in Oliver's favour, Mel's trainer whispered into his ear. Then both men stared at Marco. Marco stared back. Stone and his man shook their heads, and the hammer dropped. Oliver's joy was incredible: this was the one he really wanted. Adrenaline coursed through his veins. He started chattering excitedly. "That wasn't cheap, but I'm glad we have him. He'll be a serious machine, I can feel it."

His euphoria didn't last long. Pat slithered up to Marco's chair to congratulate them all.

"You got some balls," said Marco, raising his eyebrows at Pat. "We just gave you six hundred grand and you congratulate *us*. Ha! That's a good one."

Pat was stunned at the outburst. "Oh, well, ah, to be sure I do, you just bought yourselves a classic winner, no doubt at all."

"For what it's worth, Pat, I think you're right," said Oliver. "That's why I wanted him. I'm just glad you used an unfashionable stallion to father him."

Pat was wrong-footed by the remark; he wasn't sure if Oliver was serious or mocking him. "Ah, sure, glad to be of service."

"One more thing, Pat," said Oliver. "Can you look after him until I get him broken in and off to a trainer?"

"I can indeed. No problem at all."

"And I'm sure I don't need to say that I expect a discount on the board. Especially as I'll send you any other horses we buy here. Deal?" Oliver stared at the rotund man, in his own impersonation of Marco's gaze.

Pat shifted his eyes to the floor. "Discount? Oh, ah, well, sure, we'll talk."

With that, he thanked them again and dashed off.

"Tight bastard," muttered Robert.

"Like blood from a stone," Oliver replied. "But he looks after his stock well and he'll do the same for ours."

They bid on one more horse, but failed to get it. The evening was a frantic dash round the barns to view the horses on the new shortlist. The following day, they secured the first horse on Oliver's list – a strong, masculine male by a new stallion. Oliver considered him a bargain at $75,000. He was a dashing beast that had caught Oliver's eye quite by accident as he made his rounds of the barns that early morning with Robert. It was also lucky that he was for sale early in the day, in a half-empty auditorium.

At this stage, Oliver opted to call it quits. They had paid $885,000 for three. He marched Robert to the accounts office, where the younger man provided the necessary details for the company to receive the money transfer. They would then take their commission, before paying out to the vendors.

When they met Marco later in the bar, he was seated, looking at the catalogue pages for the purchases and their prices. "I thought you said you were going to buy ten horses?" he said with a frown.

"Well, five here, but that's the trouble with auctions. Demand is high for the nice ones," said Oliver. "It's true we've spent a bit more than I thought, but we have three dream horses. And with the exchange rates, we still have some 400,000 Euro to go to battle in Ireland in November."

"OK, my friend. You don't think we might be putting all our eggs in one basket."

Oliver looked at Marco earnestly. "I know what I'm doing."

"I hope so." He slapped Oliver on the back as he said it, and told his son to get a bottle of champagne. Robert scurried away to the counter and returned with a laden tray.

"By the way, I never did tell you. I admired the way you pitched the deal to me, for a million Euro. Still, it means we need to make more dollars to break even."

Oliver nodded hastily. "We'll do it."

As they toasted to future success, Oliver outlined the plans for the horses.

"So, I'll come back here in October to break them in and place them with a trainer. Then we just have to wait and hope," he said. "I'll buy three or four weanling foals in Ireland in November, for resale next autumn. I want to keep some money in the pot to cover vet bills and running costs." He paused for a second. "I think that's it. Oh yeah, Marco, will you come to the sales in Ireland?"

The big man thought for a moment. "You know what? Yeah, I will. I've never been, but I guess I should see where you live." He smiled playfully. "And see how the place has become a European success story." He sighed. "And I want to meet your brother."

"Er, great. I'll see if I can persuade him to send a plane over. I wonder if he'll give me a discount." Oliver grinned at his own joke. Marco smiled back.

Robert piped up. "I can't wait to see Ireland. Hey, man, you've got to take me clubbing."

"Oh, I'm sure I can arrange that."

Marco's eyes darted around, scanning the activity in the bar. Everyone was talking deals and searching for the right horse. Eventually, he stood and announced that he and Robert would leave on the next flight to Jersey. The news seemed to be a surprise to Robert, but he did not object.

"I guess we'll have to go out another time," he said to Oliver, as they shook hands. Marco was already out the door, whispering into his phone. A few people stared at him as he departed. Robert hurried after him.

Oliver sat down heavily and allowed himself a smile of delight. Phase one complete. He finished his drink and called Pat.

The rotund Irishman answered in a jovial tone. "My favourite client, how're you doing?"

Oliver resisted the urge to vomit, "Er, good Pat. Listen, I've two more horses that I'd like you to look after, can I send them over?"

"Not a bother. Colts or fillies?"

"One of each."

"Fine."

"Oh, one more thing. Vets from Watson and Hollenbach do your farm visits, don't they?"

"That's correct," Pat said warily.

"Well, I want Dr. Liddell to do all of the work on my three. Understood?"

"Grand, not a bother." He let out a smutty giggle. "She'll be nicer to look at than the other fella."

"Easy, Pat. You'll have a heart attack," said Oliver. "I'll come back in October to break them in and get them off to trainers."

"I'll keep them in good order till then."

"Do that, Pat. Or else the owner'll be upset – and so will I."

"He's a funny one. Kind of a nice fella, but kind of strange, wouldn't you say?"

Oliver smiled into the receiver. "Got to go, Pat. Thanks for everything."

"No, no, thank you."

Oliver snapped the phone shut and went through his checklist of things to do before he left Kentucky. The horses were now in order. He had one more thing to take care of. He grinned as he punched the number and felt his heart quicken.

"Hi there," she answered in a lively tone.

"How's your day, Bec?" he said, still smiling.

"Pretty good. I saw you guys bought some more."

"Yep, all done. I told Pat I want you to do all the work on them. That cool with you?"

"No problem."

"That way you can keep an eye on them for me."

"My pleasure."

"Now, more importantly, I'm free till my flight tomorrow. I was hoping to wine and dine you tonight."

"And take advantage of me, I suppose?"

"Well, er, if you insist."

She laughed. "Tell you what: come by my place tonight. We'll eat and catch up on lost time."

"Sounds like a plan."

"See you at eight. I've a place off Harrodsburg Road. Call me when your cab passes the mall." She hung up. He could not stop smiling.

* * *

"Yeah, it's me. The Irish guy came back. He flew to Kentucky. Romano joined him there. It looks like they bought horses."

"Horses? What the fuck is that about?"

* * *

To Oliver's surprise, they never made it out the door. She jumped into his arms when he appeared at the door of her compact, comfortable apartment. They made love right there on the floor. They cooked pasta and ate it cross-legged on the sofa with a bottle of wine, and talked about their lives.

"After college, I got in here straight away – those summer jobs paid off," she explained. "The work's interesting, but it's basically slavery. I mean, there's a shortage of vets in the States, but instead of recruiting from overseas like other practices, they just push us harder. Like, why pay more salaries, when you can squeeze every last drop out of the vets you have? And to make matters worse, Doug Hollenbach's a sexist motherfucker."

"Whoa, you've changed, too, Bec."

"Shit, I'm sorry, hon, must be the wine. I usually never talk about it. Truth is, I don't have anyone I can talk to. All work and no play makes Bec a dull, frustrated girl."

Oliver sighed. "I know exactly what you mean." He told her about the Gorman years. "Nobody cares anymore. It's all about getting the pound of flesh – and more."

"Ain't that the truth." She rubbed her temples. "I love my work and all, but it never ends. There's always another call-out, or hospital case. It wears me down."

Oliver pulled her towards him, and she rested her head on his chest. "The other day, I started wondering if I could have made more of an effort to get home to my folks before . . . I mean, I'd hardly seen them since I qualified, apart from their trips here. And afterwards . . . I just worked to numb the pain. Before you know it, three years passed and I'm permanently at work." She caressed his stomach. "You know the funny thing? I never gave it a thought till you showed up. Weird, huh?"

"It takes a jolt to see things in a new light."

"I hear you," she stifled a huge yawn.

"I know what you need," said Oliver.

She arched an eyebrow. "Oh, you do?"

Without a word, he picked her up and carried her to the bed. He gently laid her on the soft duvet, undressed her, and massaged her shoulders and back. She whimpered in delight before falling into a deep sleep. Oliver whipped off his clothes and jumped in beside her.

They awoke entwined in each other, and Oliver found it nearly impossible to tear himself away to make his flight. Before he left, they decided he would move in when he returned in October.

The next day, Oliver sat in the kitchen window of his mother's house, watching the rain pelt against the glass. He decided to swallow his pride and anger. He phoned his brother.

"Hello."

"Hi, Rich, it's Ollie. How're things?"

"Good. Frantic, but good. The new opulence service is raking it in; I'm thinking of expanding. I hear things are moving for you, too."

"Yeah. In fact, things have never looked better, Rich." Oliver couldn't hide a tone of enormous satisfaction.

"That's great, bro, really. I always knew you could do it if you got serious enough."

"What? I don't . . . Let's not get into that now. I called because I want to talk business."

"OK, I'm listening."

"I need one of your jets for a trip in mid-November. I'll already be in the States. I want to come back to Ireland with my client, and bring him to the sales in Kildare. Then about a week later, you can drop him back to Newark. Can you do it?"

"I can swing that, but I warn you, it's not cheap. I mean, it's cheaper than anywhere else you could go for the same, but still, you sure you can afford it?"

"I suppose a discount is out of the question?"

"This is a business, not a charity, my brother. I thought you'd changed with your newfound drive, but you're still begging for favours."

Oliver grunted, "Didn't really expect anything, but I had to ask."

Richard laughed into the receiver. "No discount, but I'll have a plane ready whenever you want it. Call Janine with the dates. As a gesture of good faith, I'll even throw in two bottles of champagne to impress your new client."

"Oh, you're too kind."

"I know." Richard added seriously, "Listen, got to go. Talk soon. OK?"

The line went dead. Oliver shook his head and thought about how leopards never change their spots.

Back in the serenity of his compound in Jersey, Marco sat on a bench in the garden with Mike. They leaned together and spoke in whispers.

"I'm going to Ireland in a couple of months. You'll be in charge, OK?"

"You don't gotta worry, Boss," said Mike, trying to conceal his delight.

"I know, I know. I'll take Robert with me. He'll have to sign for the horses."

Marco cocked his head to one side pensively. "Besides, he could be useful in other ways."

"Boss, if you don't mind me asking, you just buying racehorses?"

Marco looked at Mike; a smirk crept across his face. "Call it research. See if we can expand," he said slowly.

"You wanna take Joey, or one of the Terriers for muscle?"

"*One* of the Terriers? I thought those two little pricks were joined at the hip."

"Nah, they can be persuaded, besides, they'd do anything for you."

"That a fact," he said, filing the information away in his brain. "Call Italy, send someone from their end, it'll draw less attention. I'll let you know exactly when and where I'll be, closer to the time, but get it lined up." He wagged his finger at Mike. "And make sure this one speaks proper English."

"It's done, Boss." Mike got up to leave and the two men embraced.

Chapter 20

Kentucky. October 2004

Oliver woke to the alarm and rubbed his eyes. Six am, a dark
damp autumn morning in Lexington. He stretched out an arm
and found Rebecca's soft skin. He caressed her hip and kissed her
gently. She smiled; eyes still closed, and pulled his arm around her.
"Don't leave. It's not fair, my only day off," she whispered, groggy
with sleep.

"Got to, unfortunately. I've the horses ready to ride, and Pat's
going to help."

"Pat? Help? That'll cost you." Her eyes were still closed.

"No it won't. I can be persuasive when I want to. Besides, I
think he knows who Marco is. He never says anything, but he's a
little too eager to please all of a sudden." He sighed and dragged
himself out of the bed. "Enjoy your morning off, they're rare
enough. Have a lie-in and I'll swing by after lunch, take you to
the track to meet Claude Duvall."

He pulled into the tree-lined avenue of Four Oaks Farm just
before seven am. A small property by Kentucky standards, it was
only a hundred and fifty acres or so. The paddock railings were
immaculately white and the two old tobacco barns had been
transformed into modern stables fit for the finest blue-blood
thoroughbreds. Pat had completely transformed the place from
the dilapidated old farm it was, when he'd risked every penny he
had to purchase it. He had bought a mobile home and lived in
it for a year while the work was being completed. Pat now lived

in the small bungalow, but the caravan still remained and was now home to the staff Pat recruited from Ireland or Mexico — whichever cost him less.

Oliver parked beside the barn and went to the tack-room to start preparing the gear. Pat appeared behind him.

"Well? How's things?" he said, in his usual jovial tone.

Oliver turned. "Morning, Pat. Good, thanks. They all eat up?"

"Oh, yeah. Not a bother."

"Good. I was thinking, we'd start the filly first, then tackle the colts."

"Grand. Who'll ride them?"

"Me," said Oliver.

Pat started to cackle. "You're a big man to be riding small fillies. But, sure, I suppose, if you're riding one at night, you might as well do it in the morning, too."

Oliver rolled his eyes. "Seriously, though. I know I'm not a jockey's weight, but I'll only ride them for a week or two, before I send them off."

"Have you any trainers in mind?"

"I'd like to send them to Claude Duvall. He gets results and has teams all over the country."

"Jaysus, but you're thinking big time."

"They're big time horses, Pat."

Oliver handed him a saddle and they made their way to the stable, got the filly ready, and brought it to the covered, circular enclosure. Oliver sent the athletic animal around in circles for fifteen minutes at a trot and a canter before drawing her to a halt and handing the lead rein to Pat. Then, very carefully, he slid onto the horse's back. When he was in place, he asked the animal to move off at a trot. It did so without any fuss, and calmly made circles, all the time twitching its eyes, ears and muscles to take in the new sensation.

Pat was astounded. "Jaysus, the best breaking-in job I've seen in a while. Your three weeks of groundwork paid off. Fair play to you, you're a horseman."

Oliver acknowledged the compliment with a gracious thank

you. He knew he was a horseman, and a damn good one at that, but to hear Pat actually concede the fact, filled him with satisfaction.

They worked the other two horses in the same manner.

A couple of hours later, they sat drinking tea in the sparse kitchen of Pat's house.

"Listen," said Pat, "I think these horses, particularly the other two you bought, could use a drop of juice. Give them a head start."

Oliver put his cup down and stared at Pat. "Steroids? You've got to be joking. That'll mess them up long term."

"Not at all," he said, shaking his head. "And, listen, you can be sure they'll be getting plenty when they go into training."

"I don't believe that. People know the long term effects are harmful."

Pat cackled loudly. "Ah, will you wake up and smell the manure boy! Everybody's at it, nearly every horse runs on some kind of medication, and steroids are legal here, so what's the problem? Most people don't care about the long term effects, they want winners now."

"I'll tell you what the problem is, I don't want these horses on juice, and I'll tell the trainer that."

"Oh, you can tell away, and I'm sure he'll agree with you, but mark my words, he'll give anything he can get away with to win races."

Oliver had always known that American racing was more relaxed in its attitudes to certain medications, but he had trouble getting his head around this one. He drove away from Four Oaks that day in a bit of a daze. When he picked up Rebecca and mentioned it to her, she simply gave him a funny look.

"Hon, everybody's trying to get an edge. You know that. Do you really think they draw the line at steroids? To be honest, I'm sure there are vets and trainers giving a lot worse to horses." She shrugged. "I mean, hell, Oliver. If I could come up with some kind of wonder drug which would increase performance without showing on a dope test, I would give it to a horse if an owner asked me to. That's how some vets make their names. It's like sports doctors and chemists." She looked at him sweetly. "Don't you realize how this game is played?"

He stared at the road ahead and sighed. "I guess not," he muttered.

They pulled into the Keeneland racetrack car park for their meeting with the trainer Claude Duvall. When they arrived at barn thirty, Oliver was impressed by the personal touches that had transformed the standard trackside barn into a private trainer's domain for the duration of the race meeting. The walls had been painted a warm cream colour, and there were flowers in large tubs lining the walls and more in hanging baskets from beams outside the stable doors. Seats and a table had been placed on the grass for visitors and clients, and one stable had been converted into a kind of bar and catering area for light refreshments. *Claude Duvall Racing Stables – Success Breeds Success*, was written on an enormous and slightly gaudy wooden sign, screwed into the high crossbeam in the archway, along with a list of the ninety-five Classic and Grade One winners that Claude had trained; an impressive achievement in today's competitive world.

Oliver caught sight of a smartly dressed man in his late twenties, with a hungry, ambitious look in his eye.

Oliver approached and noticed the guy didn't look at him at all. He was too busy casting a lustful eye over Rebecca, examining her as if she were a racehorse.

"How're you doin', Ma'am," he drawled. "Ricky Metcalfe, assistant trainer, what can I do for you?"

He stuck out his hand, she shook it, and shot a glance at Oliver. He winked back.

"Rebecca Liddell. Hi. And this is Oliver McMahon, he has an appointment with your boss."

His eyes and his hand switched to Oliver. "Oh, you're the guy. OK, Claude'll be here in about ten minutes. Please, take a seat. Can I get you coffee, doughnuts?"

"No thanks," said Oliver.

They sat and Ricky scurried away.

Exactly ten minutes later, Claude Duvall strode up to them with his arm out. He was a tall powerful man, who had played college football while studying veterinary medicine. After graduation, instead of practicing, he had focused on learning the skill and art of training racehorses. A huge shock of wavy brown hair was partially hidden under a baseball cap. Inside his open windcheater he wore a tailored shirt with his initials on it, and his jet-black jeans slid over an expensive pair of cowboy boots. He had a natural charisma, every inch the salesman.

In just his third year as a trainer, he had broken into the big time by training the first Triple Crown winner that America had seen for twenty years. In the ten years since then, he had been unstoppable. The only blemish on his name had come six months ago, courtesy of his younger brother, Eddie – a graduate student at Massachusetts Institute of Technology – who was arrested and put on probation for hacking into the computers of the Boston City Municipality, messing up the traffic lights, and causing a massive jam. Claude had stepped in to pay the fifty thousand dollar fine. The papers and horse industry gossips had a field day.

"Oliver, nice to meet you." He shook Oliver's hand firmly, before turning his attention to Rebecca. "I've seen you around. You're a vet, right?"

"Yes, with Watson and Hollenbach. Rebecca Liddell."

Claude nodded thoughtfully. They sat around the small table and discussed business. Claude agreed to train the horses, and they would ship to his winter base in Florida in a week. As he and Oliver shook on the deal, Claude said, "Hey, listen, can we talk in private?" he glanced at Rebecca.

"You can say whatever you want in front of Rebecca," said Oliver.

"OK then. Let's cut to the chase. I know who was with you when you bought the horses and I bet he's the money behind you. So I can understand if you're under pressure to succeed." He clapped his hand on Oliver's back. "But don't worry, if they have any ability at all, I'll get a result. But if things do go wrong, I don't expect to wake up with one of their heads in my bed, or any shit like that. Make sure your boss understands that when you work with animals, the unexpected can happen."

Oliver narrowed his eyes and smiled. "Don't worry. Like you say, you'll get a result."

Claude looked a bit stunned. They shook hands again, though this time, Oliver's grip was firmer.

"Oh, and Claude? I don't want these horses' futures ruined by a program of steroids. If you know what I mean."

"My horses all run clean and stay healthy. You don't have a thing to worry about. Just leave it to me. If *you* know what I mean."

Later, in the car, Rebecca had a mischievous sparkle in her eye as she thumped him playfully on the shoulder. "You little shit," she said. "That was a cryptic answer you gave him. Be careful with that, I don't want you thinking you're a gangster, 'cause you're not, you know." She looked at him with raised eyebrows.

"I know, Bec, I know. I just was just messing around, keeping Claude on his toes."

"You don't need to play that game."

"You're right, but if I'm learning one thing from Marco, it's that I need to be a bit tougher, more assertive," he grinned. "Besides, it's fun!"

She shot him a scolding look. "Hon, you're a go-getter now. You're making things happen, but don't go too far, OK?"

"Ah, I'm just having a laugh."

Chapter 21

Two weeks later, Oliver felt his heart thumping as he watched the truck roll down the driveway of Four Oaks Farm, transporting his prized animals to Florida. His phone rang.

"Hey man!" It was Robert. "How's it going?"

"Ah great, just shipped the horses to Florida. Time to relax till I head to Ireland. What're you up to?"

He laughed. "That's why I called! Dad's away for a few days, so I was kinda thinking I'd come on down and party with you guys. That's if you're not like an old couple, staying in and shit."

"Cheeky bastard. We can party with the best of them."

"Cool. I'll see you tomorrow."

Next evening Oliver and Rebecca were lounging at home, drinking mojitos and watching a movie when Robert arrived. He politely kissed Rebecca on the cheek, flopped onto the sofa and tossed three small bags of white powder onto the table.

Oliver's eyes lit up. "How the fuck did you manage to bring that here on a plane?" he said.

"Ask no questions, get told no lies," he grinned. "Present from Mike."

"Which? The coke, or the method of smuggling?" said Rebecca.

"Both."

"You didn't stick it up your ass, did you?" she said, gingerly picking up the bag with her thumb and forefinger.

"Fuck, no!"

They all laughed.

Robert pushed the veterinary books off the glass coffee table and started chopping up the white powder. "Hey, pity you guys missed my twenty-first. It was far out. We took the VIP lounge at Scream, in the city. It was off the hook."

"You have a big crowd?" asked Oliver.

"Nah, only six of us . . . But Mike got us girls and some great blow; this is the last of it." He readied three lines and offered a crisp rolled dollar bill to Rebecca. "Ladies first."

She looked at the table apprehensively. "Gee, I don't know. I haven't done drugs since I graduated. Too many gossips in the horse scene. I'd get fired if anyone found out."

"Go on!" said Robert. "Who's gonna know? Besides, I bet guys you work with do shit like this. Man, drugs are everywhere."

Oliver eyed him. That sounded like Mike. Or his father.

She chewed her lip. "Hmm, I don't know."

"You don't have to Bec," said Oliver.

"Yeah, I know . . . Oh fuck it. It'll loosen me up. I could do with a buzz. But we have to clean up when we're finished, OK?"

"Yes, Ma'am!" said Robert.

She inhaled deeply. "Damn, that's good. Better than the crap we got in college."

Oliver and Rebecca, both sniffling, each tried to blurt out something at the same time. This reduced them to a fit of laughter.

"No, but seriously," she said eventually. "I bet you're right, Rob. Can I call you Rob?"

"Sure."

"You're right about drugs being everywhere, too," said Oliver. "Ireland's riddled with pills and all kinds of stuff. Lots of coke."

"No shit," said Robert.

"People have the money now. They want cocaine, it's chic compared to hash. One thing's for sure, though," he said, pointing to the lines of dust on the table. "You can't get stuff like that in Ireland. It's all shite that tastes of petrol. Not that I got out much, the last few years." He greedily took another line.

Robert hissed. "Nasty! So they like, need better suppliers, I guess?"

"Do I give out your number when I get home?"

They all burst out laughing. Over the next few hours, they drank two more jugs of mojito and inhaled another bag of coke. Rebecca put on some music; they were buzzing. She fixed her turquoise gaze on Robert, sniffed her nose, and asked him, "So what's your deal? I mean, Oliver said you're at an art school in California. You want to paint, or what?"

"Yeah, I did, and sculpt as well, but I, like, dropped out to help my dad with this horse thing." His eyes seemed to lose their spark.

"So you want to be out there studying?" she said.

Robert shrugged. "It was cool, I guess, but this horse thing could be good, too. Right?"

"That's the plan, anyway," said Oliver.

"You think you'll go back to school someday?" asked Rebecca.

"Yeah, I want to. But Dad doesn't seem to care if I do, so I don't know. Maybe. Anyway, at the moment I've got pretty much all I need in Jersey." He stared at the floor.

"Does he want you to go into his business?" asked Oliver.

Robert chewed his lip. "Like, he's never said that. To be honest man, I really don't know . . . and I'm kinda afraid to ask."

There was a brief silence. Oliver asked the question that hung in the air. "Would you want to?"

"I, um, I don't know. I mean, he makes a lot of money, but I wouldn't want to end up in jail. No way. Fuck, that's scary." He put his head in his hands and stared at the carpet.

"Look," said Rebecca, sniffling again. "All you have to ask yourself is, would you be capable of violence as a business method?"

Robert looked up, startled. "Hey, fuck you! What're you trying to say? Well, fuck you! He's my dad, OK!"

"Ah come on, easy now, both of you. Let's not spoil the night. Enough about family shit," said Oliver. "Rob, you're lucky you don't have a brother, that's all I have to say. Bec, where do we go to shoot some pool?"

"Gee look, I'm sorry if I crossed the line, Rob. Really. I . . ." She searched for something to say.

He waved his hand dismissively and re-rolled a dollar bill. "Don't worry about it. It's cool." He finished off the coke and wiped the table with his finger, before licking the remains off it. They headed out into the night, staying clear of any mention of Marco.

* * *

A week later, Oliver was sitting with Robert and Marco in one of Richard's jets, perched on the tarmac at Newark airport, waiting for take-off. Marco looked around at the plush carpeting, leather seats, and fine walnut panelling. There was seating for ten, and a large bathroom and galley area.

"I gotta admit," he said, "this is a nice plane. I usually go to Vegas on one of these. The casino sends one. But this one I like. It's smaller; a little less in-your-face. Know what I mean?"

The solitary steward informed them, in a thick Polish accent, that they would be taking off in two minutes. He was a burly guy in his mid-twenties, who looked at the floor as he spoke and seemed uncomfortable in his surroundings.

Marco watched him buckle himself into his jumpseat. "Where the hell they dig him up?"

"Lots of immigrants in Ireland now. Rich loves to work them hard. He says it costs less to train them from scratch than to pay someone with experience."

Marco grinned. "He looks like the kind of guy I'd want on my side in a fight, but I'm not sure I want him serving my lunch."

They braced themselves for take-off, and five hours later they touched down in driving rain at a small airfield near Dublin. The steward opened the door and let down the steps. A Customs agent hurried inside, and glanced at his rain-drenched clipboard. Water dripped off him onto the carpet.

"Alright then. How're ye doing? Three passengers. Passports, please."

They handed them over, gave them a cursory glance, then asked about luggage. The steward grunted and opened a locker to show three small cases.

"OK, grand job, lads. Welcome to Ireland. Hope you brought your wellies." A little chuckle escaped through his teeth, and he raced back across the tarmac to the small building that served as a terminal.

Marco sat with a look of shock and astonishment plastered onto his face. He remained like this until they were on the motorway to Kildare. Eventually, he raised the screen between them and the driver, fixed his dark eyes on Oliver and said, "I can't believe it. I mean, I can't fuckin' believe it. We just arrived in from America. A country whose law enforcement spends a fair amount of time and energy trying to piss me off, and we stroll in here with a welcome."

Oliver looked puzzled. He had no idea if it was unusual or not. "I suppose everything checked out, I mean we're coming on business and nobody needs a visa, and he checked the plane out, too. He did his job – we're not exactly terrorists. Anyway, we're famous for welcoming visitors. *Céad Míle Fáilte* and all that!"

"What?" said Marco.

Oliver grinned. "Welcome to Ireland!"

"I love this country already. Man, the Feds would shit if they knew."

Oliver looked out at the rain with a puzzled look on his face.

Chapter 22

The rain lashed down for three days, as Oliver and Robert trudged the sales complex in Kildare. Marco spent his days with them and his nights in the hotel bar, taking in what he saw of the Celtic Tiger economy. The muscular tanned and well-dressed Italian who shadowed him went unnoticed amidst the horse crowd. He looked like just another foreigner trying to find an Irish horse.

Oliver was impressed by the organization and discretion with which Marco and his associates operated.

"Man, fuck this weather," said Robert, as rain dripped down his collar.

"Ah, it's only a shower," said Oliver. "You'll be fine this evening after a hot whiskey."

Robert smiled. "Yeah cool, man." He playfully thumped Oliver on the arm. "Hey, those Irish coffees are the best."

Oliver chuckled, "You're some man to down four after dinner."

"That's the best thing ever, man. You got me addicted – shit, it's nearly better than Mike's coke."

"Nearly?" said Oliver, with a raised eyebrow.

"Yeah, nearly."

They both laughed.

They spent the rest of the day looking at the weanling horses, a full year younger than those he had purchased in Kentucky. Oliver met many old friends, all of whom had read in the industry papers that he had bought some expensive horses at Keeneland. He endured the usual questions, though nobody over here seemed to have a clue who Marco was. This came as almost a disappointment to Oliver and Robert, who had quite enjoyed the spectacle a few months before.

Every now and then, Oliver's thoughts would flood with images of Rebecca. He missed her, and his feelings surprised him; usually at a sale, he focused on horses to the exclusion of everything else. At night alone in his room, he resolved to marry her when he had made his money from this venture. His love for her calmed him, and he felt as if life was finally progressing, convinced he was on the cusp of enormous success.

At the end of the third day, Oliver was sitting in their hotel bar, going through his notes, when Marco arrived.

"Hi. OK, I've looked at two hundred foals, and got it down to twenty. I had them vetted by a guy who used to do the work for my old boss. We've about four hundred grand in Euro left. I intend to buy three horses, but for no more than three hundred, total. That leaves money in the pot for emergencies."

"Sounds good to me."

"There'll be competition, so we may find it tough to buy, but on the plus side, there are plenty of horses on offer."

"So, we take our places and do like we did in Kentucky?" said Marco.

"Exactly." Oliver flicked his catalogue shut and briefly wondered why he hadn't seen Gorman or Diarmuid ambling around the complex looking at horses.

* * *

In the offices of Richard McMahon's Freefly Airlines, Martin Forrester was perusing the week's photographs of Opulence Service passengers. He sat in his spartan office with an inventory of names, and was ticking off those who might be worth a leak to the press. When he finished, he usually had to run it past the boss, before contacting a friend in one of the tabloids. He was flicking through shots of a society wife, flying with seven dogs; a dishevelled 1990s pop star, returning from his latest stint in rehab in Arizona; and a film director's five children coming back from a trip to Euro-Disney with their nannies.

The pop star would definitely get a front page. As he sorted the other photos into a discard pile, he thought he recognized a face in the rain. It was poor quality, due to the weather, but when he checked the passenger list, his heart nearly stopped. He gathered everything and trotted to Richard's office. "Janine, is he in?"

"Yes, but he's not expecting you yet. You'll . . ."

Martin burst into the plush sanctuary. Richard was at his desk, poring over documents. "You're early," he said, without looking up.

"Excuse me, but I thought this photograph might interest you." He tossed him the photograph.

Richard glanced at it. "Yeah, so? That's a bad shot of my brother."

"Do you recognize the man with him?"

Richard looked again. "No. I suppose he's the guy backing him, but apart from that, I haven't a clue."

"Look, I know it's a bad shot, but I'm sure this guy's a Mafia boss called Marco Romano. He even flew here under his own name." Martin indicated the name beside Oliver's on the list.

Richard picked up the photo and stared at it. "A Mafia boss? I don't think so, Martin. My brother wouldn't know anyone like that. Get your facts straight."

Emboldened by the success of his stealth publicity campaign, Martin took a deep breath and spoke his mind. "With respect, I know what I'm talking about, Richard. I, well, I'm a bit of an organized crime buff. I recognize this guy. I'm telling you, your brother flew into the country with a Mafia boss and another guy, a Robert Romano, who could be his son, or nephew, or something."

Richard raised his eyebrows at Martin. "OK, you've made your point. If it's true, what do you propose to do about it?"

Martin looked puzzled. "Well, I don't know. I just thought you'd want to know."

He narrowed his eyes and paused for a moment. "So now I know. Do you have shots of anyone we can use?" he said, changing the subject.

Martin went through the list of possibilities. Richard ticked his approval and dismissed the accountant. He kept the shot of his brother in his hand.

"Oh, one more thing, Martin. Destroy any copies of this. Negatives, too, OK?"

"Yes, Boss." He trotted out, closing the door behind him.

Richard sat alone and looked at the grainy image on his desk: his brother and a mafioso. He was full of admiration and just a touch of jealousy, then a sudden wave of curiosity swept over him. He wanted to meet this guy. He stood at the window and flipped open his mobile, gazing out over a grey Dublin evening.

Oliver fished the phone out of his pocket and looked at the screen in surprise. "My brother," he said, in an irritated tone.

"Put him on speaker," said Marco. "I want to hear this guy."

Oliver set the phone on the coffee table. The tinny voice echoed. "Ollie! How are things?"

"D'you know what, Rich? Things are good. All I need now is a few more horses. How're you?"

"Great, business is booming. Did you have a good flight?"

"Yeah . . . apart from the wrestler who served our drinks. My friends were dying to know where you dig these guys up. I told them you go for slave labour."

Richard ignored the dig. "Speaking of your friends, I was thinking it'd be nice to have you all up for dinner, before you head back. I'll get Mother up, too. What do you think?"

Oliver's eyes narrowed as he stared at the phone. "Er, no thanks, Rich, we've too much to do and not enough time. Plane's already booked, remember?"

"Don't worry about that, I can change your flight plan. Come on, it'd be great to see you."

Oliver shook his head, looking at Marco, who shrugged. Richard was overdoing it a bit, and a family dinner was definitely something to be avoided.

"I thought you didn't do changes or refunds?" said Oliver eventually.

"We don't, but I can bend a few rules if I want to. Come on, Mother'd love to see you, and I'd love to meet this investor of yours."

"Sorry, we just can't make it."

There was a pause on the line. "OK, well, er, why don't I meet you guys tomorrow for a quick drink in your hotel? It's not so far, I can be there whatever time suits."

Marco suddenly clicked his fingers and nodded to Oliver.

"Er, that would work, I suppose. Call me after lunch, I'll let you know."

"Looking forward to it," said Richard, ending the call.

He sat at his desk, staring at the photo once more, tapping his fingers on the polished wood. After a few minutes, he summoned Martin, invited him to sit down, and ordered them both coffee in an unprecedented show of civility.

"Martin, you mentioned you're a Mafia fan."

He looked a bit embarrassed. "Oh, ah, I've a passing interest in it. I've read a few books about the Mob. It's intriguing. Why?"

"What's the deal with this Marco guy?"

Martin took a deep breath, "Not so much is known about him, really. He keeps himself low profile. He's known as 'The Gent', supposedly because of his cool, calm, polite persona. He took over the family when his boss was killed in prison. They reckon Marco did it, in case the old guy talked to the police to avoid dying in jail. They say he makes plenty of money in gambling and there are rumours of drugs.

"Apparently, he's unusual inasmuch as he lets his soldiers and capos keep a slightly higher percentage than normal, to keep them loyal. If it's true, it seems to be working. There's no public bloodshed and his people keep their mouths shut, even if they're put away, which is rare nowadays – according to the books I've read." He sipped his coffee and shook his head. "He must be some operator to stay out of trouble like he has." Martin had an awestruck look on his face. "A guy like that'd probably be successful at whatever he did . . . Um, bit like yourself, really."

Richard smiled and took the remark to heart. *A bit like me.* Surely there was something to be learned or gained from talking to a leader like this Marco Romano. Probably no different to an

Army General, or a Prime Minister, and he had met one of each in the last few years.

Eventually Richard snapped out of his reverie. "That's quite a summary, for a passing interest. Thanks, Martin, that'll be all."

Oliver stared at his mobile dumbfounded.

Marco was opposite him, grinning widely. "He's some piece of work."

"That was bizarre; he's never usually that nice. I bet he knows who you are, somehow."

"I bet you're right," said Marco. "Anyway, it'll be interesting."

There was a loud cheer behind them, as a group of people popped a bottle of champagne and began celebrating loudly. Oliver looked up. There were about fifteen revellers standing in a group, and they consumed the champagne urgently. Their raucous chatter was frenzied and a bit too loud, like they really wanted to be noticed. Marco cast his sharp eyes around the bar and turned back to Oliver.

"You guys have plenty of cash now. You love to flash it about, huh? The last three nights this bar's been packed, the restaurant, too."

"We've come a long way from leprechauns and the famine," said Oliver.

Marco leaned in close. "So, tell me: I bet there's a shitload of drugs being done here, huh?" He winked at Oliver.

"You're right about the quantity, but as far as I know, the quality's shite."

"Is that a fact? Interesting." He shrugged. "Anyway, I gotta say, I'm looking forward to meeting this brother of yours."

Oliver smiled.

Chapter 23

The next day, after viewing their prospective purchases again, Oliver found a place on an upper level balcony inside the circular auditorium. From this elevated position they had a clear view of everyone, but only the few others on their level could see them. The place was alive with horse dealers, who traded potential racehorses like commodities and bid hard and fast to get what they wanted. They packed themselves into every seat, corridor and viewing area available below. This was a sharper, hungrier crowd than Kentucky. They knew the angles and did their homework. Now, everybody waited for the duelling to commence, fingers on triggers like cowboy gunfighters.

"This isn't going to be easy," said Oliver. "In Kentucky, we were mostly bidding against rich guys flashing their cash. Here, we're playing poker with professional gamblers."

Marco's eyes lit up. "That a fact? Sounds like a lot more fun." He scanned the faces closely.

Oliver watched Marco out of the corner of his eye, and noticed how the man seemed to be far more tuned in than he had been in Kentucky, despite all the money they spent there.

The first horse came into the ring and was led out unsold, without fanfare, a few minutes later. Nobody even bothered to bid on it.

"What was wrong with that one?" asked Robert.

"Everything," said Oliver. "Looks like it couldn't run fast enough to warm itself, and it has an offset knee."

Marco listened intently; Robert frowned at the horse as it left the auditorium. Directly behind it, another entered. Immediately, a buzz went through the crowd. The auctioneer announced a starting price and it was met, swiftly followed by another bid. The battle was joined; fierce bidding began, though the almost imperceptible way heads nodded or wrists twitched, made it nearly impossible to discern who was raising the price.

They stood on the same spot for the next three hours and bid on twelve without managing to buy one.

"Tough work," said Oliver. He shot a glance at Marco, who looked enthralled.

"This is great – like Vegas," he said.

"Except these guys are all counting cards and playing the percentages."

As they ate sandwiches standing at their position, Oliver bought a horse: a colt foal, for exactly 100,000 Euro. Before the day was out, he had filled their order with two other colts: one for 90,000, and one for 10,000.

"Why was the last one so cheap?" asked Robert.

"He was too thin; that made him look unhealthy. But yesterday I asked some questions and found out he was ill before the sale. We'll feed him well and he'll blossom into a lovely horse next year. He's a lovely mover. The vendor was foolish to let him go, if you ask me."

"I hope you're right, my friend," uttered Marco.

"When it comes to horses, I usually am," said Oliver. "Right, that's it then. I reckon we go have a drink. I'll call Rich."

"Let's go," said Marco, slapping him on the back as they turned away from the viewing area.

Two hours later, Richard entered the hotel bar and scanned around for his brother. Oliver hoisted himself out of his soft armchair and waved. Richard moved – almost scurried – towards them.

"Hi, Ollie. Good to see you. And you must be Marco Romano. What a pleasure." He thrust out his hand and Marco nearly shook it off his wrist. Richard winced before greeting Robert.

"You must be Marco's, er, son? Nephew? Again, a pleasure." He didn't offer his hand, but turned to pull up a chair.

"Son."

Marco broke into a wide smile and nudged Oliver with his elbow.

"D'you want a glass of wine," said Oliver, pouring him one.

Richard took it. "Thanks, well, here's to your horses. Marco, I hope you enjoyed the flight. Was the plane up to standard?"

"Plane was great, but the service was a little rough. Don't you usually house-train gorillas before you let them near planes?"

"I'm sorry, you've lost me," said Richard, startled.

"The guy on the plane, your trolley-dolly, he kind of lets the image down, know what I mean?" Marco grinned. "It's like this, when I go to Vegas on a casino plane, I have strippers serving me, or proper waitresses, who look and act the part. Your guy looked like he could plough a field with his bare hands."

Richard thought for a second. "Thanks for the feedback. I'll make a note of it. But I have to say, none of our other clients have complained."

"Well, I think you should look into it." He clapped his hand onto Oliver's back. "So, your brother's quite the guy at buying horses. You should join us on this little thing."

"No thanks, horses aren't really my thing, Marco, but I wish you success. I'm sure Ollie knows what he's doing." He took a nervous sip of his drink. "So what's your line of business?"

Marco pierced him with that stare. "Gambling. And nightclubs. I guess you could add horse trading to that."

"Hey, man, like, how many planes d'you have?" asked Robert.

"Well . . ." Richard lit up and started into a lengthy summary of his business.

Oliver rolled his eyes; he had heard all this shit before.

Marco stared at Richard and asked him plenty of questions about the private jets: flight routes, flexibility, range, and capability to land at small airfields.

Some time later, when he had finished blowing his own trumpet, the elder McMahon stood and announced he had to leave.

"It was really great to meet you, Marco. You, too, Robert. If there's ever anything you need, you can get me through Ollie, and I'll see what I can do."

Marco stood as well. "Let me walk you to the door, I gotta use the restroom, anyway."

Oliver watched them walk away. Marco put a hand on Richard's shoulder as the two men proceeded towards the exit.

* * *

Marco returned to his chair. "Interesting guy, your brother."

"He's probably more interesting when you're not his brother. I thought I was going to vomit, watching him suck up to you."

"That's the thing with family. Disagreements run deeper and get more fucked up than most other things. If you ask me, your brother's problem is he thinks like a businessman all the time." Marco let out a long sigh. "But I guess he's not the only one." Another pause. "Maybe you should let it go?"

This time, Oliver stared at Marco. "Maybe someday, but not yet." He changed the subject. "So we have about two hundred grand left in the kitty after today. Might as well send it back to the States to pay the training fees. I'll keep thirty grand here for expenses and trips over to see Claude and the horses. How does that sound?"

"Could work, long as you don't disappear." A smile broke out on Marco's broad face. "And it's funny how your horse trips turn into trips to see your girlfriend. Ah, as long as you make business your priority, I'll let that one slide. Just get me a damn good margin next year."

"I will, Marco. I will." Oliver drained his glass in an effort to get the lump out of his throat.

* * *

Three days later, Marco and Mike sat in the office in Shadows. Music blared all around them. They sat together on the sofa and conversed in hushed tones. Marco started to outline his plan, while Mike listened intently, committing everything to memory.

"OK, get onto the Old Country," said the boss. "Tell 'em we

need someone young and trustworthy to go and work in Ireland. He needs to be responsible. But don't rush: let him work for a while to suss shit out, and give our friends time to get a contact. See if the gangs in Ireland'll work with us. We'll charge 'em extra, but, I mean, fuck, if we can get them a cleaner product, delivered to the doorstep, with no risk to them, what the fuck do they care? Once people realise the quality, they'll be able to charge extra, too."

He waved his hand dismissively. "Ah, we'll probably get busted eventually on ground level, unless the Irish cops and Customs are complete fucking idiots." He laughed. "By then, we'll know the network and we can figure out another way to work together. Then everybody wins: us, our friends, and the local gangs. Later on, we could use this as a new gateway to Europe, who knows? Once the relationships are in place, it'll be easy to find trade routes."

Mike nodded and smiled. "I'll see what they come up with."

"Oh, and one more thing. Make sure the details for the plane guy are fake. None of this comes back to us, or our friends. And if anything does go wrong, either we get the guy outta there or he shuts up and takes the time. Or he gets tidied up. Make sure he understands that."

"Sure thing, Boss."

They stood and embraced. Mike shut the door behind him. Marco sat at the desk, lit a cigarillo, and considered his options amidst the thumping bassline.

* * *

Huntley and Rosen sat at one side of the table in the windowless basement room.

The young recruit sat opposite them. "Like I said, I want to see some action, be a part of a big bust, and I'll do whatever it takes."

Huntley smiled. "Thanks, Mitch, I can use a guy like you. We'll be in touch."

As he got up to leave, Rosen called after him, "Tell the next one to knock on the door in five minutes."

"I like him," said Huntley. "He's hungry."

Rosen smirked. "That makes two of you."

"OK, so assuming we take him and the guy yesterday, I'll get the house sorted, then you tell them to get everything installed."

"Are you sure you have clearance for this?"

Huntley pinched the bridge of his nose. "Leave it to me."

"If you say so."

"Who's next?"

Rosen looked at the file. "Monica Kimble. Young, attractive, tough as nails."

There was a knock, and Agent Kimble entered and perched herself opposite the two men. She was a striking, fit young woman. Her flame-coloured hair was scraped back in a ponytail. Rosen had vetted her background and qualifications carefully. He thought she was too good-looking to be an agent, but that's what Huntley wanted. On the plus side, he knew she was straight as an arrow, almost antisocial, and spent most of her spare time in a gym, training to compete in triathlons.

"Kimble, I'm Huntley. Rosen you've already met."

Monica nodded.

"What do you want to do in the Bureau?"

"I want to put away scumbags. I want to make my big bust and get ahead of all the politics and bullshit. And I want to do it ASAP."

Huntley looked startled. He gestured towards Rosen "He said you were tough. That's what I need." He produced six crime scene photos of the two men nailed to the table. "You ready for this, Kimble?"

Monica studied them all in turn, with a matter-of-fact expression. "I've heard about a mob guy who likes to nail people to things." She paused, wracking her brains. "Michelangelo Cassoto?"

"Spot on, Kimble. I'm getting ready to take down a major mob figure. How does that grab you?"

Monica almost let herself smile. "When do I start?"

Huntley narrowed his eyes. "Who says you got the job?"

Monica shot him a deadpan look.

Rosen smirked. He was going to enjoy watching her spar with Huntley. "Relax," he said. "You got the job. We'll be in touch. That'll be all, thanks."

Huntley gave Rosen a sideways glance. He opened his mouth as if to say something, but stopped. Then he said, "Kimble, send in the last one on your way out."

"Thank you," said Monica, looking at Rosen as she stood.

"I think she's great," said Rosen, as the door clicked shut.

"You're probably right. Needs to lose the attitude, though."

That's her best attribute, thought Rosen.

There was a knock and a petite, shapely girl sashayed into the room. Long blonde hair bounced on her shoulders. She had large Bambi eyes, long nails and looked alert, but soft and spoiled.

Huntley looked astounded, he glanced at Rosen, who shrugged and wrote *she's what you wanted* on his pad.

"OK, Wilkins. You're still at the academy, right?"

"Yeah, I graduate next month."

"Says here, you've applied to be a data analyst or lab admin assistant."

"Yeah, I don't really see myself as a field agent. I'm more of a behind-the-scenes type."

"What if I said I could get you any placement you wanted, if you do a small task for me?"

She looked directly at Huntley. "Anything I want?"

"That's what I said."

"So what's the task? Must be a crappy job."

"A few months of undercover work. Then a lifetime behind a desk."

She chewed her lip and stared at the table. "Anything else you can tell me about the job?"

"Everything, if you agree to do it."

"A few months: like three, right?"

"Tops. Probably less. It depends on how soon you get a result."

Wilkins cocked her head to one side and narrowed her eyes. "I want the deal in writing."

Huntley smiled. "You got it. Welcome to the team. Rosen'll be in touch soon. You'll start when you graduate."

"Excellent, thanks."

As she left the room, Huntley stared at her backside. "She's some piece of ass." He closed his file and turned to Rosen. "Anyway, what's your take on The Gent going to Ireland?" He didn't wait for an answer. "What the fuck is he up to? That's the first time he's left the States since he went to Naples six years ago."

"You want me to talk to the Irish cops?"

"Hell, no! This is my baby." He rubbed his hands together.

Chapter 24

Winter in Limerick passed slowly for Oliver; 2004 inched into 2005. He spent his time at his mother's farm, looking after the three horses he had bought at *Goffs*, and doing plenty of work around the place, even finding time to paint the kitchen, bedrooms, and repair all the fencing. He attacked the work with enthusiasm, whistling as he went.

At the end of each job, he loved to see the smile on his mother's face, her pride in the place returned. She even took an interest in Oliver's horses, to the extent that she offered to feed them sometimes, when he took an evening off. She was used to feeding calves and chickens in her youth, so Oliver explained the horses' routines to her and she happily went about the job.

Oliver spoke to Claude every week; the American horses were progressing well in sunny Florida. He called Rebecca nearly every day. In springtime he planned to go out to see her and the horses. Until then, they both immersed themselves in their jobs.

Life felt both strange and wonderful. He was working for himself now, so he was fairly sure it would pay off. This kept him in good spirits, but he missed the excitement and travelling of the last few months; he missed hanging around with Marco and Robert, and people whispering about them; he missed falling into Rebecca's arms and her bed each night; and he missed the attention he got when he bought horses. Most of all, he was desperate for the horses to win, turn a profit, and for the good times to roll.

In early April, Oliver asked a local farmer to help his mother with the horses, and made a trip to Florida. He stayed there less than twelve hours, watched the horses complete a morning

161

workout, then flew up to Kentucky to spend a weekend with Rebecca. The time flew by and before he knew it, he was on the return flight to Shannon with a throbbing in his heart.

He counted the days until his next trip in early summer, when he would spend longer with Rebecca and see the horses run their first races.

* * *

As the tyres thudded onto the runway at Bluegrass Airport in the June sunshine, he felt like a schoolkid returning home for Christmas. Rebecca was waiting for him when he burst out into the Arrivals lobby. She looked a vision. Her sparkling eyes slew him again, and he hugged her, lifting her off the ground and feeling her fit frame through her linen top. He kissed her and nuzzled her tan neck.

"Good to see you, cowboy," she said, with the giddy excitement of a teenager. "I was beginning to forget your touch."

"I couldn't sleep on the plane, thinking about you."

"Well, you're here now." She eyed his pale arms. "Hmm, we need to work on your tan."

Oliver looked at his white skin, next to her honeyed tone. "Irish summers."

They chuckled and hastily made for the car park.

Lying in bed that night, he told her of his travel plans and begged her to take time off to accompany him to New York to assess the horses.

"I really want you there with me. I can feel something big's going to happen. Marco and Robert'll be there, too. Come on! Take some holidays."

She thought for a minute, then a smile crept across her face. "Hell, why not! The busy season's ending at work and I haven't taken a break for eighteen months." She kissed him. "Fuck it! It'll be fun to dress up and go to the races as a spectator."

"Spectator? You're part of the team."

The following weekend, they stood on the backstretch of New York's Belmont Park racetrack in the early morning mist, outside the barn where Claude had taken up residence for the summer season. Ricky Metcalfe was on his best behaviour, dutifully having the horses paraded for Oliver and answering his questions. He even refrained from leering at Rebecca.

Two of the horses looked in peak athletic condition. They had changed dramatically from the raw material of the previous autumn. Now they were lean, taut, alert and businesslike. Ready for action, they were going to run in a few hours. They had since been named Painter Girl and Shadows of Jersey. Marco had personally christened them and couldn't resist advertising his club, though Oliver felt the name might have a double meaning.

The big colt purchased from Pat O'Malley was slower to develop; he ambled around like a sulky teenager, though Claude was convinced that when he matured mentally, he would be a talented racehorse, such was the ease with which he completed his workouts. He was named Concrete Boot, and the name was worth it just to see the shiver it sent up Claude's spine every time he uttered it.

Oliver loved Marco's sense of mischief.

"Like I said on the phone, this guy's a serious horse," said Claude, as he followed the animal out of the barn. "He'll win a classic. I tell you that now."

"That's a big statement. Let's not get our hopes up." But Oliver longed for it to be true.

"Oh, I guarantee it, bar an accident. I've never trained a horse with such raw, unchannelled ability before. It's kinda scary." He tapped the heels of his snakeskin boots together and made a clicking sound with his mouth. "Kentucky Derby, here we come."

Oliver let his poker face slip and broke into a huge smile.

"Easy now, tigers," said Rebecca. "Don't count your chickens. It's nearly a year between now and next May."

Claude shot her a sideways glance, and Oliver reined in his smile. Neither liked to dwell on what could go wrong with such a fragile beast.

The horse was put away, they thanked Claude, and took a train back to Manhattan.

That afternoon, Marco's car picked them up and returned them to Belmont to see Painter Girl prepare for race number three. On the way, Oliver filled him in on the horses. Marco nodded and absorbed the information.

Later, Marco stood in the beautiful, tree-dotted parade ring, soaking up the timeless atmosphere of the sport of kings. He was dressed in an immaculate linen suit with a dark blue tie, and looked every inch the suave racehorse owner. Oliver, Rebecca and Robert flanked him, each dressed up for the occasion and chatting about where they might go out – hopefully to celebrate – that evening.

The fourteen runners circled the parade paddock; their owners, trainers and jockeys dotted the central grass area in small groups, the low buzz of tactical discussions occasionally punctuated by a whinny from one of the equine athletes. The wind rustled the leaves and churned the air to give respite from the warm day. Marco was soothed by the horses, and by the fact that he currently shared space with the genteel old moneyed families who also owned racehorses. He took a long puff on his cigar and smiled to himself.

He was pulled out of his thoughts by a tap on the arm from Oliver.

* * *

"Marco, this is Claude Duvall, your trainer."

"My trainer?" said Marco, still smiling.

Claude shot Oliver a sideways glance, which Marco caught as he extended his powerful arm in greeting. The two men shook hands firmly, neither wanting to end it first.

"Marco, good to finally meet you," said Claude, extracting his hand. "I'm not going to tell you the usual shit about how good your horses are, I'm sure he's filled you in. Let me just say, your filly'll win if the jockey can settle her early on, preserve her speed."

He smiled. "So, if you want to bet, get stuck in."

"You know what, Claude? I might do that," Marco replied, nodding.

Claude lit a cigarette and sucked on it hungrily, while he scanned around for his jockey. Pablo Velasquez, the pint-sized Brazilian, appeared in the paddock wearing Robert's racing colours of black, white and grey hoops. It almost looked like an old-fashioned prison uniform and made Marco smile when he saw the jockey trotting towards them. Pablo shook hands with everybody, eyed Rebecca up and down, and kept glancing at Marco as Claude gave him his riding instructions before legging him up.

"He looked at Dad kinda weird," Robert whispered to Oliver, as they left the paddock.

"Pablo's a hell of a jockey: great hands, and he rides the pace like he has a clock in his head. He'll be alright. Besides, I noticed a few owners and trainers giving us strange looks as we walked in here. I have to say, it gives me a buzz."

"I know what you mean, man."

The runners made their way onto the track and the spectators filed into the grandstand to take up their viewing positions. Claude escorted Marco and his entourage up to the owners' and trainers' viewing area. They were on the top level of the stand, with a commanding view of the winning post. Claude announced he would leave them and watch the race on the screen in the paddock. Marco handed Robert a large wad of notes and dispatched him to the nearest betting window.

"You guys betting?" he said to Oliver and Rebecca.

"I made my bet when I bought these horses," said Oliver. "I rarely bet on the actual outcome of a race."

"And I never bet. Period," said Rebecca.

Marco shrugged. "If Claude's right, this gives me an extra piece of interest. I'll take his word for it, this time. You keep telling me he's some kind of genius." He took a puff from his cigar and leaned in close to Oliver's ear, putting his hand on the Irishman's shoulder "Next time, I want to know in advance if I should bet, understand?"

"Er, sure. I'll let you know."

"Call Robert when you get the news."

"Done."

The runners trotted down to the starting gates, accompanied by lead ponies. Within a few minutes, they were loaded. The bell rang and the gates snapped open, releasing the runners in a mass of energy, 1200 frantic metres to be covered. They thundered down the backstretch, dirt flying in kickback from the powerful hooves.

Painter Girl was settled into sixth, four or five horse-lengths back from the leader, who set a furious pace. They rounded the home turn and she was striding comfortably, Pablo had yet to move his hands to ask for a gear change.

Marco, Robert and Rebecca all followed the action on the large TV screen hanging from the grandstand awning.

Oliver was glued to the action using his binoculars: he found it gave him a closer, more intimate account of the race. His heart started pounding.

Painter Girl entered the home straight two lengths behind the lead horse. Pablo switched her to the outside and urged her on, pumping his arms in sync with the movement of her neck. She shot forward with a burst of speed that sent her past the leader in a matter of strides. Her muscles rippled and her nostrils flared, as she sucked in huge gulps of air.

Marco was roaring, willing her on to win; the veins in his neck stood out, his skin was turning a shade of crimson. Oliver could barely contain himself, his heart was pumping like the first time he saw Rebecca all those years ago.

Dirt flew in a hail of athletic frenzy. Other jockeys flailed their whips and pushed their mounts on with hands and heels, in a vain effort to catch her.

As the gallant little filly flashed past the winning post, Marco shot his arm in the air and allowed himself a whoop of delight. Robert jumped in the air and embraced his father. Marco kissed his son on the cheek and said, "That's the way to do it! Now go and collect!"

Oliver let his binoculars hang around his neck by the strap, as he fumbled for his sunglasses to cover the tears welling up in his eyes.

Rebecca was dumbfounded. She turned to Oliver, took his hand in hers and squeezed it hard, then kissed him and announced to everybody, "That was awesome! You guys know how lucky you are?"

Marco released his son and looked at her, "Lucky maybe, but I tell you something, my man's true to his word. So far, anyway." He looked at Oliver. "Keep this up and you're going to be a great little earner." With that, he embraced Oliver warmly, as he had Robert. Oliver felt another rush of emotion and fought to hold his composure.

"Just the beginning," he croaked. "Tip of the iceberg, I'm sure of it. Now, I've got to go get the post-mortem from Claude."

"Tell him thanks, and remember what I said."

"Will do, Marco." He kissed Rebecca again, then trotted off to the elevator, sporting an enormous grin.

Down in the winner's enclosure, Claude was chatting to Pablo and the horse was being led in small circles; her lungs were heaving for oxygen and sweat dripped down her legs. Her eyes stood out on stalks.

Oliver eyed her up and down, waited until the jockey jogged off to weigh in, and said to Claude, "She's a bit stressed for a horse that won so easily."

"What? Don't worry about that. She'll calm down soon enough. It's a warm day, after all."

Claude narrowed his eyes. "Would you have preferred she lost?"

Oliver glanced over both shoulders, leaned close to Claude and said, "What the fuck is that supposed to mean?"

The trainer put his hands up, "Easy, fella, don't get your knickers in a knot. I'm just doing the best I can for all of us. You don't have a problem with that?"

"Of course not, Claude. Just remember what I told you. No juice, OK?"

"Don't worry about it," he said with a smirk.

Oliver looked sceptical, but offered his hand to Claude by way of agreement and congratulations.

"Now, may I suggest," said Claude, "that you relax, have a drink, sit out the next race, and get ready to cheer on Shadows. He'll do us proud as well."

"Two for two? Unbelievable." He was smiling again. "Hey, Claude, Marco wants to know in advance if he should bet, so if you can let me know the day before, or raceday morning at the latest."

"Not a problem. After all, got to keep the boss happy, right?"

"Right."

Oliver left the paddock and decided to take Claude's advice. He waded through the crowds and jumped into the elevator. Just as the doors slid closed, a hand was thrust in between, causing them to jerk open again. Two men in grey suits entered and smiled at Oliver. One was short and chubby, with a cheery look on his face; the other was stick thin with a gaunt hungry appearance, like somebody who did too much jogging and not enough eating.

As the lift climbed slowly, the skinny man said casually, while staring at the ceiling, "Must be nice to have a winner. A boss like yours wouldn't like to be disappointed."

Chapter 25

Oliver shot him a sideways look of sheer astonishment, then glanced at his stubby partner, who was smiling pleasantly.

"What's that supposed to mean?" said Oliver.

The man spoke soothingly. "Please remain calm, Sir. We're Federal Agents."

He flashed an ID. Oliver bristled at the sight of it. The conversation with Mike shot through his brain.

"We know who you are, and what you appear to do for Marco Romano."

"What I appear to do?" said Oliver, now suddenly feeling harassed. "I buy and sell horses for a living. My client could be the man you just referred to. So what?"

"So," continued the man, offering Oliver a business card. "If you ever feel uncomfortable about your client or your business, and if you ever need anyone to talk to, you can contact me at any time."

Oliver could feel his mouth go dry and his palms clam up. The agent stuck the card in his hand. Oliver read the name on it and said, "Leave me alone, Agent Huntley."

The doors opened. Agent Huntley said, "Good day to you, Sir." Then he and his partner hurried out into the crowds.

Oliver continued to the top floor, the card fixed in his hand and his mind racing. He wrestled over whether to tell Marco everything at the first opportunity and to give him the card as proof, or to simply ignore the whole episode. Again, he cast his mind back to Mike's instructions.

He stashed the card in his wallet and forced a smile onto his face as he located the others at a table overlooking the track. "Cheeky little shit," said Huntley, as he and Rosen pushed through the turnstiles to the car park. "He's way out of his depth. He'll go down with his boss, that's for damn sure."

The champagne calmed Oliver's nerves, and he put everything out of his mind as he discussed racing tactics with a riveted Marco. They watched the next race from their table, before descending to the paddock.

Shadows pranced about nervously, snorting and sweating. Claude was not happy. "I was afraid of this," he said to the assembled group. "He doesn't like the crowds or the noise. I hope he doesn't use up too much nervous energy in here."

"He looks wired to me," said Marco.

"What? Oh no, he'll calm down once he gets onto the track and down to business. He's just a little giddy, is all. Pablo has a knack of switching them off."

Oliver and Rebecca exchanged sceptical glances. Marco shrugged. Robert was unconcerned by the horse, and far more interested in a pretty girl standing near them. Claude gave Pablo his instructions and legged him up onto Shadows.

As they pushed through the crowds towards the elevator, Rebecca said quietly to Oliver, "That horse is more than just nervous, if you ask me."

Oliver sighed heavily. "Hmm. You should've seen Painter after the race. She was on another planet."

"Weird for a horse that won so easily."

"That's what I thought."

They took the elevator to the top.

Shadows of Jersey bolted from the starting gates like his tail was on fire. He covered the 1000 metres in pole position from pillar to post, winning by three horse-lengths. The other runners simply could not keep up with him. Marco and Robert roared their lungs out as he darted over the finish line. Robert darted off to the betting windows to collect. Rebecca whooped with delight and hugged Oliver, who was hiding behind his sunglasses again. Claude slapped Marco on the back.

"Congratulations, Sir. And let me tell you, this is only the beginning. We're going to kick some ass with this horse."

Marco shook his hand warmly. "I guess my man here was right about you. First day's racing, I'm two for two and up by a wad."

Claude read the race time from the TV screen, he let out a whistle. "Goddamn!"

"What is it?" said Marco.

"Your horse just won his debut within two seconds of the track record. That's incredible."

Oliver read the screen and checked the statistics in his race program. He raised his eyebrows and shook his head in disbelief.

"Incredible is right," he said, a smile beginning to creep across his face. "Claude, this guy could be a top class sprinter."

"Damn right," said Claude.

Marco raised his eyebrows and cocked his head to one side. "Top class, you say? You mean money in the bank, right?"

Oliver began to open his mouth, but Claude cut him off. "Oh, if he's a champion and you guys sell him as a stallion, then you're talking eight figures."

"My man!" said Marco, wrapping an arm around Oliver's shoulder.

The Irishman smiled as the gesture warmed his heart. Agent Huntley was far from his thoughts. After a second, he returned to reality and said, "Look, lads, let's not get carried away. He's only just won his maiden, and remember, if he's going to be a champion, then he has to stay fit and sound."

Claude smirked at him. "You leave all that to me." He checked his watch. "I gotta run. You guys celebrate." He stuck out an arm at Marco, who shook it hard.

"Thanks, Claude," he said.

"Catch you all later," said Claude, as he spun around and walked off.

They had one more drink before Marco decided they should all go back into Manhattan. Later on, as the car sped across the Brooklyn Bridge, Marco dished out more praise to Oliver and pulled a roll of notes out of his pocket.

"Here," he said, tossing the wad onto Oliver's lap. "We had a good day. You guys stay at the hotel and enjoy yourselves. I'm going back to Jersey." He looked deep into Oliver's eyes. "You've earned it."

"Well, I, er, thanks very much." Oliver was pleased, yet startled by the large roll of notes. He stuffed them into his pocket, trying to imagine how much Marco had given him. Rebecca's mouth hung slightly ajar.

"Some day at the races," said Rebecca, as they passed through the revolving door, into the lobby.

"Yeah, man. I gotta hand it to you. All that shit you told us at the sales last year, right on so far," said Robert, smiling. "Dad won a packet today and had a good time. I haven't seen him that relaxed in . . . Well, never."

"Glad I could help. I . . ." Oliver heard a police siren outside, and the meeting with Agent Huntley flooded into his mind. He stood stock still, ashen-faced.

The others stared at him. "What's up?" they asked in unison.

"Well, I, I, suddenly don't feel well. Think I'll go lie down for a few minutes."

"Aw, come on man. Bottle of bubbly'll do the trick," said Robert, punching his arm.

"No, really, I um . . ."

Rebecca looked concerned. "I'll take you up, hon. I guess it's all the excitement."

"Thanks. Yeah, something like that."

"Get started on those drinks, Rob, we'll be down later," said Rebecca.

"You bet." Robert made a beeline for the lounge.

In their room, Oliver sat on the window ledge while Rebecca kicked off her shoes and flopped onto the bed.

"OK. What's up? You thinking what I'm thinking about Claude?" she said.

Oliver stared out the window into the grey chaos of the city.

"Well, if you're thinking that Claude has some kind of wonder potion to give his horses, then yes. But like you said, if he doesn't get caught, then who cares? Right? Except, it can't be good for the horses." He sighed. "I've kind of resigned myself to the fact that he gives them something, or many things. I don't know. As long as he doesn't fuck them all up."

"Look, if he uses anything other than skilful training, it must work. I mean he's been champion trainer here for years."

"I suppose you're right. Anyway, that's not why I wanted to come up here." He took a deep breath and spat it out. "Truth is, two FBI guys cornered me in an elevator today. They told me I could talk to them anytime I felt I needed to."

"Holy shit! You're kidding?"

He looked right into her lovely eyes. "No. I was on such high after the first win that I kind of told them to piss off."

"You didn't! Cheeky bastard."

"Yeah, maybe." He paused with a frown furrowing his brow. "Look, I've done nothing wrong and Mike told me something like this might happen."

"He did?"

"Yes. Well, anyway, with all the excitement, I completely forgot to tell Marco. And now he's gone to Jersey."

"You sure you should tell him?"

"Jesus, yes! If I don't and he finds out, he'll . . . Well, I don't think he'll be very pleased." Oliver thought for a minute. "You know what, I'll call Mike."

"You're right, I guess. Best to be up-front straight away." She stared at the wall pensively. "It's a bit like a movie, all this cops and gangsters shit. We should plan our getaway."

Oliver looked downcast. "Yeah, I was thinking about that. Pity. Things were just starting to go my way . . . I'll get him a stallion deal for Shadows or Boot, and politely bid him goodbye."

"You make it sound so easy."

"It could just be that easy – as long as the horses deliver."

"Be careful, hon, OK?"

He nodded.

"Right, I'm going to grab a quick shower." She kissed him on the cheek and padded into the bathroom as he dialled Mike.

The call was answered immediately. "Got any hot tips?"

"So you heard about the winners?" said Oliver.

"Sure did. Next time I want to know if I should bet, know what I mean?"

Oliver sighed. "I do indeed. Look, Mike, you said to let you know if I had a visit from some guys, remember?"

"Course I remember. And?"

"Today, at the track."

"OK, stop there. I'll come see you, where you guys goin' tonight?"

"No idea. Robert knows."

"Wherever it is, I'll see you there." The line went dead.

Oliver smiled. That wasn't so bad, after all. Then he flung off his clothes and joined Rebecca in the shower.

Chapter 26

By the time they made it down to the lounge, Robert was reclining on a large sofa, chatting to a pretty girl in a skimpy blue dress that displayed her physical assets. They had nearly finished a bottle.

He tore his eyes away from the Bambi-eyed blonde. "What kept you guys? Resting, huh?"

"Yeah, yeah. Whatever," said Rebecca, inspecting the champagne bottle. "Looks like you've been busy, too."

He looked back to the blonde. "This is Sherry. Like the drink."

Sherry giggled in a way that seemed forced. Oliver shot her a puzzled look, which broke into a smile. "I can't believe you've downed all this already. We'd better start catching up."

And start they did. Oliver ordered, sat back, and relived the races in his head. Unbelievable. So far so good: as long as Claude didn't get too clever, and the cops didn't hassle him too much.

A little later, Sherry went to the toilet. Robert leaned over and said quietly, "Mike called, he's coming over."

Oliver nodded.

An hour later, they were all buzzing. Robert was desperately trying to convince Sherry to stay with them, but she seemed determined to leave as soon as the champagne ran out, so he kept ordering. This made Rebecca smile. "I was a bit like that at college, you know," she whispered to Oliver. "It's how to get drunk for free. The key is knowing how and when to make an exit!"

Oliver feigned an exasperated look, rolling his eyes comically.

"You know, now that I think of it," he said, "I can't remember you getting many rounds back in the old days in Lexington. Crafty little thing, aren't you?" He kissed her. "So I guess you're only after me for my money."

"Sorry, hon, but you don't have any. Remember? Except for that wad in your pocket."

"You know, after . . ." Out of the corner of his eye, he noticed Mike standing by the archway separating the lobby from the lounge. He was observing them; Oliver had no idea how long he had been there. When he made eye contact, Mike flicked his head and walked to the toilets.

When Oliver pushed open the restroom door, he saw Mike standing over the attendant. "Get the fuck out," he said, throwing a crumpled banknote at him. "And don't let nobody else in."

The elderly coloured man shuffled out nonchalantly, like it was a perfectly reasonable request. When the door closed, Mike went to the sinks and turned on all the taps.

"Tell me how those fucks harassed you."

Oliver took a deep breath and told Mike everything, except for Huntley's business card.

"I tore the bloody thing up and threw it at his feet," he added for dramatic effect.

Mike clamped one hand on his shoulder and jabbed his other index finger at Oliver's face. "You sure that's everything?"

"Yeah, Mike. What else would there be?"

"Good man! Sounds like you know the fuckin' deal." Mike slapped him lightly on the cheek. "You must've some Italian in you, my friend."

Oliver, bizarrely, felt emotional, relieved.

Mike guided him towards the door with an arm around his shoulder. "OK, you're leaving tomorrow, right?"

"The day after."

"I'll go see the boss. Wait for a minute before you follow me out." With that, he gave Oliver a mock punch on the chin. "Go fuckin' nuts tonight, OK?"

He slipped out. Oliver turned off the taps before leaving.

Rejoining the others, he shot Rebecca a huge grin. "OK," he announced. "Let's kick on out of here. Where to, Rob?"

Robert replied without taking his eyes off the curvaceous, smiley Sherry. "I was kinda thinking we'd head straight to the meatpacking district. It's kinda early, but I know a cool place we can chill. You wanna come?" he said to her.

Before she answered, he shot a glance at Oliver. "Oh shit, don't we have to wait for . . ."

"Relax, it's done."

"Cool," said Robert with a smile.

"I'll totally come with you guys," said Sherry, then looked up at Oliver and batted her false eyelashes. "So, that big dude with the weird hair who, like, stood over there." She pointed towards the archway. "He's like your dealer, or something?"

Oliver and Robert exchanged glances.

"He's a friend of my dad."

"Yeah, he just wanted some betting advice," said Oliver.

She paused for a second with a look that could have been confusion. "OK, let's go. I'm tired of waiting for my friend to show up. I wanna party with you guys!" She pecked Robert on the cheek.

As they left the lobby and passed out into the sticky heat of the city at night, Oliver grinned at Rebecca and cocked his head towards Robert and Sherry.

"Someone's going to get lucky tonight," he whispered to Rebecca.

She smirked back. "I doubt it. You know, I think Sherry's not as dumb as she looks."

"You might be right there, Bec."

They hailed a cab and journeyed into the dark revelry of clubs, cocaine and alcohol.

The following afternoon, Oliver and Rebecca were in the hotel dining room when Robert appeared. They were glad to see he looked worse than they felt.

"You look like shit," said Rebecca.

"You don't look too healthy yourself." He rubbed his eyes. "Oh man, I didn't sleep a wink," he sighed. "I think I'm in love."

"Don't confuse sex and drugs with love, Rob," said Rebecca, rolling her eyes.

"I wish . . ." He looked at Oliver. "Man, she wouldn't even let me sleep with her."

"Then she must like you," said Rebecca.

"I hope so. She's an art major, I think. I invited her home next weekend. We'll hang out. I'll show her my mom's paintings and stuff."

"Where is she now?" asked Oliver.

"I put her in a cab; she has to study." He looked at his watch. "We have to be home by five. Dad called, he wants to see you, talk racing tactics."

Oliver looked surprised. "I thought we were going to stay here? I fly back to Ireland from JFK."

Robert shrugged as he picked up a menu. "Plan's changed, I guess."

Oliver felt his stomach churn.

Chapter 27

At precisely five pm, they sat in Marco's library, drinking Coke. Marco smirked when he walked in and saw them sipping the sodas.

"Got any bourbon in that?" They grimaced at the mention of whiskey.

"Looks like you guys had a big one," he said. "And who was the bit of tail my son had latched onto him?" he asked Oliver.

Robert almost choked with surprise and shot Oliver a dirty look.

"Relax. Mike told me," said his father.

"Dad, she's an art major," he blurted out. "I want to bring her here next week, hang out and stuff. Show her Mom's paintings."

"First, get to know her better. What's her name?"

"Sherry."

Marco burst out laughing. "What, just Sherry? You sure she's not a hooker?" He winked at Oliver.

"No, Dad, she's a student, I told you. Come on, guys," he said to Oliver and Rebecca. "Back me up!"

"She seemed pretty switched on to me."

Marco took in what Rebecca said. "You're shitting me, my boy! You found an art student with blonde hair, big tits, and a name like Sherry? Unfuckin' believable. Now this girl, I've gotta meet – when you get to know her better." He winked at Oliver. "Come with me."

Oliver followed the big man across the marble tiled hall and into another wood panelled room, with a large pool table as its centerpiece. Marco leaned against it and picked up two balls,

179

twirling them together in his left hand. Oliver stood in front of him and folded his arms.

"Mike told me what happened at the races, but I'd like to hear it from you." The dark eyes were set on full beam.

Oliver wondered if he said nothing, would Marco simply read his mind? He took a deep breath and told him exactly what he had told Mike. As he spoke, he could hear the rhythmic whirring of the balls rotating in Marco's hand.

When Oliver had finished, Marco flicked the balls from his grip out onto the table; they flew the length of it and crashed around like a loose cannon shot. A satisfied look came over the Mafia man's wide face. He got up and embraced Oliver fully, kissing him on both cheeks.

Oliver was stunned by the gesture. In an instant, he felt warm, wanted and successful. He felt a bond with Marco that he wished he had had with his own cold, hard father – or even his brother.

Marco released him, brought up his left hand, and patted Oliver on the cheek. "Keep up the good work, and remember, those fuckheads don't have a thing to hassle you about." He held his index finger aloft. "There's just a small change of plan."

"What's that?" asked Oliver obediently.

"I won't go racing anymore if it's going to draw that kind of heat. I'll send Robert; after all, they're his horses on paper. You just make sure I get told when the bet's on."

"Definitely. But I probably won't go to every race, either. Just certain ones."

"That's OK, long as you get me the info in advance."

"No problem, Marco."

"And do me a favour: relax. You're doing well. Forget about the cops, and look after that girl of yours. She's a stunner. Keep her happy and she'll keep you happy, know what I mean?" He smiled a mischievous grin at Oliver. "Come, on."

Marco left the room. Oliver stood there for a minute, then shrugged. Forget the cops. Everything's going well. He almost skipped across the hall to rejoin the others.

Chapter 28

Jonathon Coleman strode across the tarmac at the small windswept airport in the west of Ireland, dragging his bags behind him, their wheels rumbling on the smooth runway. His mind was full of flight details – a hop to southern Spain with the family of a famous golfer on board. He hopped up the steps, stowed his bags in the tiny cabin, and was dismayed to see an oversized duffel taking up most of the locker. He turned to his co-pilot, who was already seated and starting his pre-flight checks. "Don't tell me we've got Pietro again."

Pat O'Connell shrugged. "I never remember their names, but if you mean the Italian Stallion, then yes."

"Greasy little dago. There's something fucking dodgy about him, and his huge bloody bag. He's always fucking buying loads of tatty stuff, whenever we go to the sun."

Pat looked puzzled. "What?"

"You know, souvenirs and shit. Fills that fucking bag."

Pat looked up at his flying partner. "Sure, at least he speaks decent English and treats the passengers well – not like some of 'em."

"He's up to something, I'm sure of it. Little fucker."

"Well, you can whinge all you like: rumour has it he was put on by the boss man himself. So you might as well piss into the wind as complain. Anyway, I reckon you're just jealous 'cause all the women love him."

With that, a deeply tanned face appeared behind them in the cockpit.

"So 'ow you doin' today, Capitani?" said Pietro. With his olive oil voice, thick dark hair and chiseled features, he was very popular amongst the female employees and clients of Freefly Airlines. His darting eyes shot from Pat to Jonathon, like he knew he had been the topic of discussion. He glanced down at his bag and returned to the cabin without waiting for a reply.

"I'm going to keep a better eye on that fucker, and have a chat to the boss next time I'm in HQ," said Jonathon.

Pat rolled his eyes. "Oh, but you're a glutton for punishment," he said, while flicking a switch.

He paused for a second and continued, "But if you're really sick of him, you'd be better off having a chat to Forrester. He's the golden boy at the moment. Not as bloody scared of the boss man as he used to be, either."

As the passengers boarded, the pilots could hear Pietro filling their glasses and seducing them with his accent and banter.

* * *

Sherry sat curled up on the large sofa, gazing around the room. It was quite the bachelor's party den: big sofas, wall-to-wall carpeting, large TV screen, music system, soft lighting and a huge, well stocked bar. She reached out for the bottle of wine on the coffee table, refilled Robert's glass, and served herself very little. "Come back here, have another drink. You're like, totally falling behind," she said.

Robert was on his feet, swaying beside the large hi-fi system, struggling to adjust the playlists on his iPod.

"Me, fall behind? In your dreams, baby!" He staggered back towards her, grabbed his glass, downed it in one gulp, and flopped down hard on the sofa. He leaned in to kiss her, but she hesitated.

"You sure we're alone? Like, no one's going to disturb us doing bad things?" she asked in a seductive whisper.

"Yeah, babe. It's cool. Dad won't be back 'fore dawn, 'n' the butler's in bed. We'r'll alone," he slurred.

Sherry sneaked a glance at the wall-mounted clock and hoped to God that Robert was going to pass out. She was beginning to worry that she might have to sleep with him to get the job done.

She kissed him, filled both their glasses, and prayed his stamina would give out.

He tried to get up, but decided against it. Sherry gave him his glass, and he clung to it with both hands.

"Y'know, Sherry, can't believe how trashed I feel. I don't drink wed rine. I, I . . . You're a really cool chick." His head rolled back and melted into the cushion, the glass of wine tipped all over his shirt, but he was already unconscious.

Sherry waited for a few minutes until he started snoring. Then she rubbed her eyes and slapped herself on the cheeks with both hands. "Focus," she muttered.

She grabbed her handbag and padded out of the room. Creeping across the hallway and into the library, she squinted in the dark and took a black device about three centimetres in diameter, with a thin wire extending from it, out of a zipped pocket in her bag.

Glancing out of the windows, Sherry grabbed a chair and placed it at the bookshelves. Reaching the top shelf, and selecting the thickest book, she opened the weighty tome and slipped the small black device into the space between the spine and cover.

With the book and chair replaced, she went into the ground level bathroom and slipped a similar device under the back of the washbasin. She relieved herself, washed her face, and took a deep breath. Her heart was pounding. Tonight had been surreal. In the last few hours she had finally met Marco, The Gent, and was now planting bugs in his holy of holies – his private house.

Sherry steeled herself for battle and returned to the party room. She chose to put the last device behind the revolting piece of abstract art hanging above the fireplace. Robert had been so eager to show her it earlier.

Finished, she perched beside Robert and used her phone to send a blank message to a number not in her contact list. Then she sat back and gulped down a glass of wine. After a few more minutes, she drained the bottle, removed her dress, Robert's damp shirt, jeans and the empty glass from his lap, and lay rigidly beside him.

Eventually, her heart stopped pounding enough to let her drift off to sleep.

The following morning, she awoke nursing a minor hangover and a foreboding feeling. She desperately hoped that the small but powerful listening devices would operate as they were supposed to. Then she could quietly slip out of Robert's life. After two months, she was sick of being Sherry, the twenty-four-year-old airhead student. The stress threatened to crack her up at any second.

Beside her, Robert groaned to life and put his arm around her hips. Her skin crawled.

* * *

Martin put down the phone and trotted along the corridor to Richard's office.

"Is he free, Janine?"

She glanced at the switchboard. "Yes, I'll let . . ."

Martin opened the door before she could finish.

Richard looked up from a thick file. "Don't you knock any more, Martin?"

"Sorry, but this is important."

Richard sighed and tapped his pen off the file. "Spit it out then."

"I just got off the phone with John Coleman. He's complaining about the new Italian, Pietro. You know, the one you hired."

The pen stopped tapping. "Look, er, Coleman's on record as a racist. What's he saying?"

"That the guy's acting suspiciously. Carries a big bag on all the trips to the sun, especially Spain. He always fills it up with souvenirs and he hates people asking him questions."

"So what? He likes tacky shite and hates the pilots – he's not alone on that score. Anyway, he's the best steward on the Opulence Service; you said yourself, all the clients love him."

"Yes but, I have to say, it sounds a bit weird to me. I told him to come in for a chat tomorrow. I thought you'd want to get to the bottom of this."

The colour drained from Richard's face. He coughed and took a long drink of water. "I'm not going to meet with a racist pilot

I should've fired years ago, just because he's complaining about a flight attendant. Tell him to shut the fuck up. Nobody's interested in his bullshit."

"But I–"

"But nothing."

"We should at least hear him out."

Richard jabbed his pen at Martin. "No! Right, if that's all you have to say, you can get back to work."

Martin knew better than to persist. He retreated and closed the door behind him.

Richard took another drink. "Fuckitty fuck," he muttered. He flipped his Rolodex and started to dial his lawyer's number. Then he cradled the receiver as he walked to the window and gazed out over Dublin. He shifted his weight from one foot to the other, a bead of sweat forming at his hairline.

Chapter 29

Oliver and Rebecca stood sipping soup from paper cups to keep the breezy Irish autumn out of their bones. They were leaning against a wall at the horse sales complex in Kildare, watching the throngs mill about between the stable blocks. Rebecca had a cap pulled down low on her head, her turquoise eyes beaming out from under it, mesmerizing many of the people who came to assess Oliver's horses.

Oliver sprang to life as he noticed a successful trainer approaching with a rich Russian owner in tow. "Another looker Bec," he said, dashing to the stable door, tossing his soup into a bin.

They showed all three horses to the trainer and his client, who were visibly impressed. Each of the colts had matured into stunning-looking athletes. Oliver had spent every day with them for the last two months. He had walked them miles around his mother's fields, and lunged them with side reins to build up their necks. And, of course, he had given them the best feed he could buy, and an hour of grooming each afternoon. They had been taught to stand still whilst being inspected, and to pose in a certain way, not fidget like hyperactive teenagers. The result was that they looked and behaved like professional catwalk models or bodybuilders.

Putting the last horse away, Oliver thanked the trainer and the Russian, while Rebecca threw the stable rug onto its back.

"Hon, I'll say it again, they look amazing. A kick-ass job you did preparing them. We've been flat out showing them to people. They'll make megabucks. Especially this one, the way his full brother raced this year." She smiled at Oliver. "Y'know, I'm glad I'm here. Best holiday in years, despite the lack of beaches and sunshine. You're some horseman, you know." She finished clipping the rug straps together. "But I'm not going to blow anymore sunshine up your ass – it'll go to your head."

He laughed. "Some chance of a swollen head with you around. Still, I'll be over the moon when they've sold. Then we'll catch up on beaches and sunshine."

They closed the stable door and Oliver scanned the complex, gauging the crowd. "It's getting late; almost six," he said, looking at his watch. "People'll stop looking soon. Let's feed up and call it a day."

"Great. Then we should go drag Rob out of his room. I can't believe he hasn't appeared since we got here."

"Poor guy's still lovesick. He hasn't said it directly, but I reckon Sherry dumped him just before Marco sent him here."

"I can't believe it lasted this long. Don't tell me he didn't see it coming?"

"I guess he didn't. Blinded by her eyelashes, no doubt."

"Oh, he was blinded by something alright, but I doubt it was her eyelashes."

They both chuckled.

"I'd say you might be right there," Oliver said, filling a bucket with water.

Rebecca went into the small tack room and filled three buckets with feed. They made sure the horses had enough hay and bedding for the night, then shut them into their equine hotel rooms and made their way to the bar beside the auditorium.

Oliver pushed through the owners, trainers and agents who had come from all over the world to buy Ireland's finest thoroughbred yearlings. There was a healthy crowd of Irish, English, Italians, Germans, and the ubiquitous Arab sheiks.

"Excellent," he beamed to Rebecca. "Plenty of deep pockets with money burning holes in them. Rock on!" He fought his way to the bar and bought hot whiskeys. They found a corner and stood while scanning the crowd.

"Well, Oliver. How's it going, Boss?" said a loud voice. Oliver saw a small, skinny, red-faced man out of the corner of his eye. He took in the man's narrow eyes and copper red hair, and recognized him as Mickey Lansdowne – a trainer based on the plains of the Curragh, Ireland's racing and training headquarters. Oliver couldn't remember ever talking to the man before.

"Not bad, thanks, Mickey. Trying to keep the cold out," he said, raising his glass.

"I thought you'd be on the champagne full time, with the year you're having. You and yer man from America came up out of nowhere; fair play to you, boy. Listen, if you ever want a horse in training over here or if you need anything, give me a shout. I spent two years running Claude's stable in California before I got homesick and came back to strike out on my own."

"Is that a fact?" said Oliver thoughtfully. He shot a wink at Rebecca. "Thanks, Mickey, but I'm just selling this week. Come to think of it, why haven't you been to look at my steeds? They'd be right up your alley."

"Oh, right. Yeah. A client of mine seen 'em alright, says he wants the brother to Wolf Spider." He started shaking his head in a disbelieving fashion. "There's no doubt about it, but you're steeped in luck. You buy a cheapish sort last winter, and then his brother comes out of the blue to win three Group races as a two-year-old. Sure, he'll go for a fortune tomorrow."

"Hey, Mickey. It's not all luck, you know. I do my homework. And I'm due my turn in the spotlight. I want plenty of zeroes on the prices. So dig deep if you want them."

"Sure, I suppose I'll have to." He looked at his watch. "I'd better be off. I'd wish you luck, only I reckon you've enough already."

"You can never have too much luck," said Rebecca.

"In fairness, the harder you work, the luckier you get," said Mickey.

"Not in my book," replied Oliver. "I spent years slaving for fuck-all. Now I'm not married to a farm anymore and actually getting more in return. Like I said, I'm due my luck."

"What farm was that?"

"David Gorman's place."

"Oh, you were running the show there?"

"Mmm."

"And holding his hand, too, I'd say. He's been a bit quiet this year. Haven't seen him at the sales, either."

"No, come to think of it, neither have I."

"Right you are, then," said Mickey. "Better move on. See ya." Then he made his way out of the bar, shaking hands, smiling at clients and prospective clients as he went. Rebecca and Oliver watched him work the crowd.

"Those guys are like politicians, always on the lookout for more horses and clients," she said.

Oliver had a look on his face like he had eaten something rotten. "He only wants mushroom owners."

"Say what now?"

"Mushrooms: keep them in the dark and feed them shit. Drain their wallets at the same time. Then, when a good horse comes along, its performance is all down to the trainer's genius."

Rebecca smiled. "They're all like that, even in the States. Except maybe Claude."

"Claude? Huh! Sure, he hates giving me the info, only he knows he can't bullshit me. And he's afraid of Marco. That's why I don't want a horse in training over here. Marco isn't known in the Irish horse world." He smirked. "We can't use fear to them to keep them sharp!"

Rebecca rolled her eyes. "Stop with that gangster shit. It doesn't suit you."

"Relax, Bec! It's a bit of a laugh." He paused. "Seriously, though, it works on Claude. I mean, there's no way he'd bother to make such a fuss of someone with only three horses. Not when he has two hundred to oversee, and not when he trains for the Krepner family."

"Still, you play with fire."

"It'll be grand. Sure, we're kicking arse."

"If it all goes wrong and these horses go for a loss, we'll see how your Italian friend reacts."

"It'll be grand, Bec. I thought you said they'd go like hot cakes."

She shot him a sideways glance that softened into a smile.

They finished the hot drinks and went to find the lovelorn Robert, still moping in his room. They dragged him out for dinner and cheered him up with talks of the sales and hopes for serious profit.

Next morning, they all arrived at the complex in the blustery grey dawn. Oliver was hyperactive, his body electrified with excitement. He meticulously groomed each horse, smoothing out their coats, and shining their muzzles with baby oil. He cleaned and oiled their hooves and applied hair gel to their manes and tails. Rebecca held them for him, while Robert looked on in awe.

"Man, I can't believe it. It's like you're doing their make-up for a fashion show or something," he said.

"Details count. If I don't shine them up, they'll look dull under the sale ring lights. And I want every penny I can squeeze out of the bidders. OK, it'll go like this: we have twenty lots between each horse, just enough time to get one sold, return it to the stable, and get the next one up to the pre-sale area. Rebecca's leading them through the ring, I'll be on the balcony to see who's bidding, and watch the game unfold. You stay with me."

"And pretty soon we'll be kicking back, counting cash," said Robert, grinning.

"That's the plan, anyway," said Oliver. "By the way, good to see you smiling again."

"What? Oh, yeah. Well, I've been a . . ."

"Listen," Rebecca cut in. "You're too young to realize there'll be a million Sherrys. Have fun, move on, and make sure the next one buys you the odd drink."

Robert looked stunned. "What? I can't believe, I mean, it's like totally . . . How the fuck did you know that? It's like she only liked me so she could party, and get to meet my dad. Like, as soon as I brought her home, that was it. Fuck. She said she was quitting school, then she just, like, stopped taking my calls. Bitch." He looked downcast. "I really liked her."

"Forget about her, Rob. Start thinking about the money we're going to make," said Oliver, punching him playfully on the shoulder.

Rebecca led the first horse into the bright auditorium. It gleamed under the glare of the lights and the crowd. Its summer coat had remained, despite the changing seasons, due to the thick rugs it wore every night.

Oliver and Robert took their places.

"Right," said Oliver. "Open your catalogue at the first page I marked."

Robert flicked the weighty book open.

"Right, this one we bought for 100,000. He's a very nice type; with any luck, we'll double our money."

"Cool!" Robert's eyes lit up.

The auctioneer called the crowd to attention and asked for an opening bid of 300,000 Euro. It was not taken, but the bidding started at 50,000, and rapidly climbed to 150,000. Oliver scanned the crowds, but there was so much activity he failed to find all the faces involved in the rapid-fire bidding. It was only when the price reached 280,000 and the hammer cracked down as the auctioneer bellowed 'Sold' with a flourish, that Oliver could see who was presented with the buyer's slip.

"Fucking nice one!" said Robert, slapping Oliver on the back. "Who bought him?"

Oliver scribbled the price in his catalogue. "Jim Clifton, English bloodstock agent. That tall red-faced man beside him is his best client, a banker who used to only have jump racers, but now he's investing in the flat." He pulled a roll of banknotes from his pocket and thrust them at Robert. "Here, dash over, shake his hand, and give him the money."

"You're kidding, right?"

"No. It's luck money – an Irish thing. Now hurry, before you lose him in the crowd. I'm going back to the stables for the changeover."

Robert walked towards the two Englishmen, shaking his head in bewilderment.

An hour later, the second horse – bought for 10,000 – was sold for 80,000. "That's like eight times what we paid," said Robert in disbelief.

"He was the one who looked skinny and sick, remember?"

"Um." He thought for a moment. "Oh yeah. Fuck, man, you were right. Nice one."

An hour later, Rebecca led the last of the trio into the sale ring. The auditorium was packed to capacity and Oliver had butterflies in his stomach.

"Tell me again why this guy's a big deal?" asked Robert.

"You see that name in bold type in the catalogue: Wolf Spider?" Robert nodded.

"Well, this season it looks like he'll be crowned champion juvenile colt in Europe, he's won a Group Three, and two Group Twos already."

"Wow, cool. And how the hell did you know that was going to happen?"

Oliver, grinning, slapped him on the back. "I didn't. Blind luck, my friend. But it never hurts to let them think I've a crystal ball!" They both laughed.

"OK, concentrate," said Oliver, wiping the smile from his face.

The horse marched around calmly, gently flicking his ears at the crowds staring from their seats. Rebecca kept him going at a military pace, to show off his athletic stride. There was a hum of anticipation as the auctioneer asked for an opening bid. The style of selling was slower and more formal in Europe, and the auctioneer spoke in measured, succinct tones; it was more like a persuasive conversation, than the impersonal business drone in Kentucky.

"Ladies and gentlemen, who will start me at one hundred thousand Euro?" he called in a theatrical voice.

The asking price was immediately met. Heads turned. Oliver's heart skipped a beat. Rebecca glanced up into the crowd and grinned.

Crown Prince Marwalla – the beady-eyed and painfully thin scion of the ruling family of an oil-rich Gulf state – was the bidder. His bid was swiftly countered by Brendan Reilly, the flamboyantly dressed Irish telecommunications tycoon whose enormous bulk was matched both by his passion for racehorses and his spending power.

"The battle's on," whispered Oliver.

The Syndicate members sat in a huddle, poker-faced, waiting to see how things would unfold.

"Rob, see those guys?"

"Yeah."

"In Kentucky, I was praying they wouldn't bid against me for 'Boot, but if they decide they want this guy, anything could happen."

"D'you think they will?"

"Don't know, but they own his father, so they might want him. Anyway, we'll soon find out."

A third bidder nodded his head at the auctioneer. The price shot up to 160,000. Oliver poked Robert in the arm in his excitement. "That's Mark Pilkington, trainer of Wolf Spider. Tiny in stature, huge in ego – bloody good trainer, though. Some people call him Napoleon, but not to his face. I've never seen him at a sale before."

The three-way duel progressed, the fighters trading blows of 20,000 each until 300,000 in favour of Prince Marwalla; Pilkington shook his head and turned away. The Syndicate sat motionless.

"Sorry to lose you, Sir," said the auctioneer. "Now, who'll give me three-twenty? It's against you now, Sir." He pointed his gavel at Brendan Reilly.

The rotund man winked at the auctioneer and raised his left hand, palm forward, fingers spread.

"Three-fifty, I have. Over to you, Sir." He looked at the Prince, who nodded and mouthed the word "four".

"Four hundred thousand I have," said the auctioneer with a flourish.

The crowd murmured in excitement and many whispered their predictions of the final price. "Four-fifty; five," roared the auctioneer, as he took the rapid bids.

At half a million Euro, Brendan Reilly took stock of the situation, glanced at his catalogue and listened to his advisor whispering into his ear. He faltered for a second, then winked again. The six members of the Syndicate vacated their seats. Oliver cursed under his breath.

"Five-fifty I have."

The Prince nodded immediately.

"Six."

Reilly looked at his agent, who shook his head. Both men turned away and walked out of the auditorium. The crowd moaned, deflated.

The auctioneer stood for a second with his mouth slightly agape, then recovered his composure and banged down the gavel. "Sold. 600,000 Euro, to Crown Prince Marwalla."

The Prince's entourage swarmed around him as he disappeared into the office behind the rostrum, to sign the purchase slip in privacy.

Chapter 30

Rebecca let out a whoop and patted the horse on the neck as she led him out, and an official slapped a sold sticker on the animal's rump. The horse left the sale ring as it had entered – a little bewildered by the spectacle, and blissfully unaware of the value now on its head.

"Hoo-haa!" said Robert. "Good return on a ninety grand buy."

"Shit," muttered Oliver. "I thought we were on for a million, with those three battling. Still, not bad, I suppose."

"Not bad? Not bad?" said Robert, as he did the maths. "Those three cost 200 grand and we just sold them for nine-sixty." He looked at Oliver. "Not bad? That's unbelievable."

Oliver beamed as he realized that they had recouped a large chunk of Marco's investment. "Come on, let's get Bec, say goodbye to the horses, and celebrate!"

"Oh yeah! Can't wait to call Dad when we're somewhere private."

"First, run into the office and give the Prince his luck money, if you can get near him."

Rebecca was just closing the latch on the stable door as Oliver rounded the corner. They looked at each other, and their smiles said it all. She ran towards him and jumped into his outstretched arms. He held her feet off the ground.

"Congratulations, cowboy," she said, gripping him. "Knew you'd do it."

"Holy shit, Bec. I thought we'd make money, but seven-sixty profit! Marco'll never believe it. I hardly can myself."

"You deserve it, hon."

He beamed momentarily, then turned it into a frown. "You know, the funny thing is: I was disappointed when the Prince and Reilly stopped battling. I thought they'd go further. I suppose you never can tell."

"Don't get greedy on me now!" she scolded him. "Hey, what was the deal with Napoleon? He didn't last long."

Oliver chuckled. "Pilkington likes to train good horses, but he considers it beneath him to have to bid at public auction to get them. In fact, I don't think I've ever seen him bid at a sale before." A thought crossed his mind. "He must *love* Wolf Spider."

A voice behind them shouted, "Get a room!" It was Robert.

"Did the Prince take the money?" asked Oliver.

"No chance. His minder wouldn't even let me near him." He handed the roll back to Oliver.

"Then it looks like the drinks are courtesy of the Prince," said Rebecca, with a glint in her eye.

"Hang on a sec," said Oliver. He went into each stable in turn, rubbed the horses on the neck and whispered thanks in their ears.

Robert watched him in astonishment.

"You're a big softy," said Rebecca.

Oliver blushed. "Come on, I need a drink," he said.

They walked through the auditorium. This time all heads turned for Oliver; people watched him as he strode along. They whispered about him. A few of the guys he nudged past called his name and congratulated him in a mixture of jealousy, curiosity and newfound respect, but this respect had little to do with his backer. This was a case of his peers acknowledging what he was doing with just a small team of horses. Oliver was making a name for himself in the business, where the ability to select the right horses was seen as the ultimate talent: the Holy Grail of the bloodstock world.

* * *

They went to the top floor restaurant; it was quiet in the post-lunch lull. A few groups of people sat at tables, some scanning the results on the monitor. Oliver ordered a bottle at the bar, while the others found an isolated table in a corner.

Robert sat, flipped open his phone, and dialled. "Dad, you sitting down?" he said.

"Why?" was the suspicious response.

"We just sold all three for seven-sixty profit. Euro."

"You're kidding, right?"

"No, Dad. We totally did it. We're having a drink to celebrate."

"Pass him the phone."

Robert did as he was told.

* * *

Oliver, still standing, pressed the device to his ear and walked away from everyone. "Hello?" he said.

"The sale was good?"

"It was."

"Well done, my friend. Turns out you were right again. When do we collect?"

"In a couple of months, usually. It'll go into the account over here. We were helped by the health of the market. Trade's strong, but to be honest, I thought we might get a million for the last colt, but they just stopped bidding."

"Couldn't you twist their arms?" Marco said with a chuckle.

"I wish."

"OK. I gotta go. Take your cut, then send the rest back. Nice work." The line went dead.

Oliver sat down with the others. Robert took the phone and went to the toilet.

"Congratulations, hon." She smiled mischievously. "So, now I am with you for your money."

"I knew it," he said drily.

They both laughed.

"You're right, though, Bec. I've been so drunk with success. I haven't stopped to think about my cut till Marco mentioned it just now." He took a deep breath and stared at her. "A hundred and ninety grand." He sat silent for a moment to let it sink in. "Fuck yeah! I did it. In fact, I should call Mum and let her know. And my asshole brother."

"Good idea, but don't gloat when you call him, OK? Be the better man."

Oliver pondered this for a second. "Better yet, I won't tell him. Besides, Mum'll let him know."

He punched the numbers.

"Hello?" said Evelyn, sounding frail.

"Mum, we did it! We sold all three for a serious touch."

Her voice perked up. "Oh, well done, Oliver! I'm so proud of you. You deserve it. That's wonderful."

"Thanks, Mum."

"If you're finished, come back here and bring that lovely girl with you. I hardly had a chance to say hello before you whisked her away with the horses."

Oliver looked at Rebecca as he spoke. "You should've come up here with us, like I wanted you to. You'd have loved it. They were like your horses, too, you know."

"It was nice having a bit of life about the farm, but I'd have felt out of place up there. Will you please come for a few days?"

He smiled. "Love to. We need a few days off. I'll get the outside of the house painted, too. My treat, and the rest of the inside. How's that sound?"

"Lovely!" she said. "And Oliver?" There was a pause. "Your father would have been proud, too."

"Please, Mum, don't."

"Try to understand, Oliver."

"Understand what? That he thought I was an eejit?"

There was another brief silence. "So I'll expect you both tomorrow, then?"

"Yes, Mum. Bye."

"Don't be too hard on her," said Rebecca.

He sighed and rubbed his temples. "Shit, you're right . . . It's not her I want to be hard on. Besides, more I think back, I reckon she never had a say in anything when he was alive."

Robert reappeared and plonked himself down. They all clinked glasses.

"Here's to the Prince!" said Oliver.

He let the stress and pressure flow out of his system. Success was beginning to sink in and he threw his mind forward to the autumn racing in America and their three runners. He was glad Rebecca would get to meet his mother properly. After that, he would figure out when and how he would ask her to marry him.

He was rudely dragged back to reality by his phone displaying his brother's name on the screen.

"Well, that didn't take long," said Oliver. "I suppose you want to invest now?"

"No, Ollie, like I said, not really my thing. I wanted to congratulate you. Mother just called me so I checked the results on the web. Nice one, brother. Dad would have been proud."

Oliver frowned. "Wait, back up a sec – you checked the results after Mum called you?"

"Yeah, wanted to see it for myself."

"Just in case I was making it all up, to look like the big man. Fuck, Rich, you don't change, do you?"

"Ollie, I'm delighted for you, and surprised – it was such a surprise that I wanted to see it in black and white."

"Because my word – or Mum's – isn't good enough?"

"Not statistically, no."

"Fuck off, Rich," he said, ending the call.

Oliver sat shaking his head. "The nerve – what a dickhead," he said to nobody in particular.

Robert and Rebecca sat in silence, searching for a way to change the subject.

Oliver's phone chimed with a message. It read: *Am happy for you. Sorry for doubting you. You did well. Hope you get fair share profit. Mind yourself. Take care. Rich.*

"Too little, too late," muttered Oliver, draining his glass.

Chapter 31

Dressed in a new tailored suit, and with his hair slicked back, Oliver stood with Rebecca, Robert and Claude, in the tree-lined parade paddock of Belmont Park racetrack in the cool November breeze.

Every seat, terrace, balcony and viewing area was packed to capacity. The crowd numbered easily one hundred thousand, not just New Yorkers, but people from all over the racing world. This was the annual Breeders Cup Thoroughbred World Championships. Held at a track in America or Canada every autumn, it was the supreme challenge for horses from all over the world and the finale of the northern hemisphere flat racing season.

Oliver had never attended the event before. Every year he had watched the thrilling races on television. To be here with a runner was a dream come true.

Painter Girl looked magnificent as she strode confidently around the paddock with the other runners for the next race: the Juvenile Fillies Championship, worth half a million dollars to the winner. Since that incredible day in June, she had won twice more very impressively, including a Grade Three contest. Then Oliver and Claude had thought it was best to give her a small break to freshen her up.

She was usually a relaxed filly, but became anxious and sweated profusely whenever Pablo mounted and took her down to the start. Today was no exception; she started to jog on her toes and her eyes bulged as soon as Claude legged Pablo onto her back. Many punters groaned at this display of nerves, taking it as a sign of energy being squandered. Others knew that it was normal behaviour for this talented filly. Pablo ignored her antics, he sat with a relaxed posture, but his face was a taut study in concentration, focused on the race ahead.

Despite the nervousness, she was still sent off favourite, with a price of 2/1, because of her unbeaten record and her trainer's uncanny knack of having his horses spot-on for the big days.

The air was thick with anticipation and expectation. Claude was unusually quiet and he chain-smoked hungrily. Oliver soaked up the moment, feeling truly privileged to be standing there. He quietly wondered how much Marco was wagering, or if he was holding his own betting pool. All Oliver knew for sure was that Claude had told him to pass on the message that today, she was unbeatable. He hoped Claude was right, having put 10,000 dollars of his own money on her. He planned to use some of the winnings to buy an enormous diamond engagement ring for Rebecca, who stood gripping his arm in support, unaware of the large bet he had placed. He would tell her if they won.

Robert kept scanning the groups of owners and trainers, looking for the next pretty girl in his life. He had grown quite accustomed to being his father's representative at the races and also began making an effort to dress up in suits. There had been little media interest in him.

They took the elevator up to the owners and trainers viewing area when the runners filed out onto the track. Oliver fleetingly thought of Agent Huntley, who hadn't bothered any of them ever since – as far as he knew.

In the packed viewing area, Oliver fought to get a space and raised his binoculars. He could see Painter Girl at the start, circling, dripping with sweat and shaking her head. He cast a glance at Claude, who was watching a TV monitor with Robert and Rebecca. Claude was sweating nearly as much as the horse, and devouring cigarettes. Now was not the time for anything to go wrong.

After several frantic minutes, the cream of America's two-year-old fillies were loaded and ready to burst into action. The bell rang and they erupted onto the track. Oliver's heart was beating in rhythm with their hooves, as they thundered along, kicking up dirt in their wake. He calmed himself as Pablo settled Painter Girl into an even rhythm about seven lengths off the suicidal pace.

The runners rounded the first turn and galloped onto the back stretch of the track. The hypnotic drone of the commentator punctuated the excited din of the crowd. As they thundered along the backstretch, Painter Girl appeared perfectly at ease, head down, poised to strike. The lead horse showed signs of tiring as she led the field into the final turn, and she dropped back and towards the outside of the track, allowing another to take the rail position as the race stepped up a gear.

Pablo changed his hands on the reins and, as they straightened into the home stretch, he nudged Painter Girl with his heels and asked her to extend her stride. The crowd began to cheer. In a matter of strides, almost in the blink of an eye, she was alongside the leader. Oliver exploded in a torrent of shouting, he willed her on. "Go, Painter! Go, Painter!"

Even Claude dropped his cigarette and pumped his fist in the air. "Get on with it, Pablo," he roared.

Robert and Rebecca were bouncing up and down, screaming their lungs out. Pablo raised his whip hand, he twirled the stick like a baton before bringing it down once firmly on Painter Girl's rear, and she darted into the lead. Pablo pumped both his arms on the reins, his whip stuck up in the air above his crouched body like a periscope. The stands erupted; Oliver's screams were drowned by the roar of 80,000 people. Painter Girl ate up the remaining 300 metres with Pablo clamped to her neck, driving her on for all he was worth.

Behind her, jockeys urged their mounts on, pumping their arms, flailing their whips, desperately trying to squeeze out every last ounce of effort and energy, but to no avail. Painter Girl was across the line. Pablo stood up in his stirrups and waved his whip at the crowd.

Oliver jumped up and down shouting, then grabbed Rebecca. "We did it, Bec! We did it!" he yelped. They leapt about as one, knocking into Claude, who looked visibly relieved. Robert was howling and punching the air like he had just scored the winning touchdown at the Superbowl. Oliver embraced Robert and Claude.

They dashed to an elevator. People parted and let them pass. Everyone recognized Claude and there were shouts of congratulations, pats on the back and whoops of delight. On ground level, they pushed their way towards the winner's circle to greet the exhausted athlete and her ecstatic rider, who flung his goggles into the adoring crowd.

Pablo leapt clean off the animal's back, flying into the air to the delight of the crowd, then he jumped on Robert and kissed him on both cheeks. "Well done. Thanks! She's amazing," he said in a thick accent. Robert looked a bit shocked by the gesture.

The heaving, blowing horse was un-tacked, covered with a sweat-sheet, and led away to the stables. The masses clapped her as she passed in front of the stands.

Oliver, Claude, Rebecca and Robert were ushered to the presentation area, to receive the trophy. Claude and Robert mounted the podium to collect their prizes as trainer and owner from the Governor of New York, who gave Robert a warm handshake and some rather nervous, obsequious banter: all but ignoring Claude.

After the brief ceremony, a television reporter accosted Claude for an interview.

"What can I say? Hell of a filly – talent to burn," he bellowed, as Robert and the others retreated away from the cameras.

"Future plans?" drawled the reporter.

"She'll go for the Kentucky Oaks next May, after a winter break. That's all, thanks, buddy."

Oliver stood beside the podium and gazed up at the rapturous crowd. His eyes scanned the faces. He noticed the flags and banners many brought to cheer on their favourites, he saw a huge gathering of Japanese, here to support their runner in the afternoon's last race, the Classic. A warm, hazy feeling came over him: could it really get any better than this? Suddenly he realized there was something he just had to do – immediately.

He turned to Rebecca, flung his arm around her shoulder and whispered in her ear, "Will you marry me?"

Her dazzling eyes stood out on stalks, then the shock passed and she looked at her man. "Well, gee, honey, I don't know. I'm kinda holding out for a bigshot racehorse owner."

"Oh well, pity . . ." Oliver cocked his head, raising his eyebrows, pretending to ponder her words. "Wait a second, that would be me!"

She placed her hands on his cheeks and said, "It sure would, and I sure will." They kissed and, for a moment, the noise of the racetrack faded into oblivion.

* * *

Oliver couldn't see agents Huntley and Rosen gazing at him through binoculars from the press balcony at the top of the grandstand.

"Looks like it's all still peachy-fucking-creamy for Romano's Irishman," said Rosen.

Huntley shook his head despondently. "Guys like that never see it coming till it's too goddamn late."

Chapter 32

A week later, Oliver was sprawled on a sofa in Marco's study, waiting for him to arrive. The events at the Breeders Cup had finally sunk in, and the shock of it all had turned into a euphoric sense of satisfaction and a greater feeling of self-confidence. His daydreams of winning more big races and marrying Rebecca were interrupted by Marco's large hand clapped on his shoulder. He stood over him, wearing a broad grin which spread up into the dark eyes and softened them. Oliver stood and Marco embraced him warmly.

"Well done, my friend," said Marco, releasing him. "You've delivered."

Oliver blushed. "Thanks, but it's a team effort, really."

"Don't be modest," he said, wagging a finger. "You had the balls to pitch the idea to me. So you might as well enjoy it."

"Oh, don't worry. I am!"

"Good." He sat and patted the sofa. Oliver sat beside him.

Marco pulled a fat brown envelope from his back pocket. He tossed it onto Oliver's lap, in much the same way that Mike had tossed the little bag of cocaine at him all those years ago.

"What's this?" said Oliver.

"Your cut of the prize money'll go to your account, but that's a little extra taste." He tapped his fist gently on Oliver's knee. "You've earned it."

Oliver fondled the bulging envelope as he stuffed it into his jacket pocket. I've earned it, he thought. Indeed I did. A warm feeling engulfed him. He cleared his mind to prevent tears welling up. "Look, Marco. Thanks, really – for everything. You put faith in me and that gave me confidence, and it all grew from there. And we're not done yet. You've got most of your investment back from the sales and we've three good horses to go into battle next year."

"Some battle!" he cackled. "I gotta tell you, Oliver. I like to do new things, take chances – calculated risks. I like you and I took a chance. You came through. You're safe. You're with me now."

Oliver felt a surge of emotion. His hands started to shake; he swallowed, and found himself on the verge of tears. He felt like he finally belonged.

"Horses are quite the little earners. Like taking candy from babies: you win on the betting and you win the prize money." He slapped Oliver on the knee.

Oliver felt a warning bell sound in his brain, and he shot Marco a sideways glance. "Look, Marco, horseracing's a rollercoaster. We've kicked ass so far, but they could just as easily get injured. Nothing's guaranteed when you deal with animals."

Marco thought for a second, then dismissed the idea with a wave of his hand. "Don't worry so much. They're good horses and when I'm on, they win. So relax, enjoy the ride."

Oliver nodded in agreement and decided to do exactly that.

"You know, Oliver, I got something else to thank you for."

He looked at Marco, whose face wore an expression that could have been sheepishness.

"The thing is, since you came along, it's like Robert actually wants to spend more time here. So that part of the plan worked, too."

Oliver was astonished and speechless.

"OK, let's celebrate," said Marco, changing the subject.

They spent the evening talking horses and plans for the coming spring; there was even talk of the Kentucky Derby for Concrete Boot and the Kentucky Oaks for Painter Girl. Shadows would stay sprinting, and challenge for the top races after a winter break. They also discussed insurance for the horses.

Robert appeared for dinner and they laughed and toasted success.

Oliver felt at home, surrounded by people who shared a common goal and who were thankful for his talents and abilities. He had brought success to them all.

A couple of days later, Oliver sat in the reception area of Watson and Hollenbach veterinary clinic.

Oliver sat on a bench flicking through veterinary magazines. He looked at his watch and said to the young, gum-chewing brunette behind the desk, "Linda, is she going to be much longer?"

She glanced at the work schedule in front of her. "I don't rightly know," she drawled. "Not much on her chart, but I did see a truck come in before you got here: probably an emergency."

So much for our lunch date, he thought, and resumed flicking through the crumpled magazines.

The entrance door was pushed open and a pretty girl in her mid-twenties with striking flame-red hair swept past him.

"Hey there, Linda! How's it going? God, it's cold out," she said in a bubbly voice.

"Hey! I'm good, but, aw shoot! Are you here for the interview?"

"I sure am. We'll run the piece about y'all in next week's issue."

"Well, I got bad news. Dr. Watson's been in colic surgery the last three hours, so either you come back tomorrow or wait and see if he's up to doing it afterwards."

"I'll wait, I guess," she sighed. "There goes my day."

She pivoted on her heels, and found a seat opposite Oliver, staring at him as she sat.

"Say, you're the Painter Girl guy, right?"

He looked up from an article about uterine infections. "I'm sorry?"

"Painter Girl: Juvenile Fillies winner. You bought her?"

"Guilty as charged," he smiled.

"Emmy Harris," she stood and offered him a business card. "I write for Trackspeed magazine. Y'know, I'd love to do a piece about y'all. You bought three horses and they're all winning."

"Well sure, I've been lucky. And we've a good team looking after them. So fingers crossed we'll win a big race or two next year."

"Uhuh," she scribbled on her notepad. "God, I love your

accent, by the way. Who do you work for? I've heard rumours."

Oliver dearly wanted to get his name in this magazine, which was the bible for American race fans and breeders alike. An article would be the perfect advertisement for his talents, but that churning feeling in his stomach returned. He thought for almost a minute, and just as Emmy was beginning to look at him strangely, he said. "I'd love to sit and talk, but not right now."

"Okay," she said, nodding slowly with a knowing look in her eye.

"But you can quote me about luck and a team effort."

"I'll put a few lines in a side column, but I'll need meat to do a full piece." She sighed again. "You should consider it: people love rags to riches stories. It keeps the dream alive."

"Oh, the dream's alive alright," he said with a chuckle.

Rebecca appeared from the corridor behind Linda, wearing a green medical smock and drying antiseptic scrub from her hands. "Giving interviews to the press, are we?" she joked.

Oliver stood and kissed her. He wrinkled his nose. "I love the smell of iodine at lunchtime!"

"Sexy, huh?" She tossed the paper towel into the bin and glanced at Emmy. "Hi."

"Dr. Liddell. I'm here to interview your boss for the piece on the practice."

"Oh, yeah. Don't hold your breath. He's up to his neck in intestines right now."

Emmy looked disappointed. "I'd better call the office." She pulled a phone out of her pocket and stepped outside.

"What kept you, Bec?" asked Oliver.

She rolled her eyes. "Oh God, don't. Had a mare come in that was pregnant, due January tenth, aborting. Smelly and messy. Had to evacuate the foetus, treat the mare, and prep samples for necropsy."

"You get all the glamorous jobs."

"Tell me about it. Smelled like the thing had been dead inside her for some time. God knows how she didn't get toxic and die."

"Will she make it?"

"Should do. I've got her stuffed full of antibiotics and painkillers. Have to quarantine her till the results come in." She smiled and held his hand. "Enough shop talk. I don't have rounds till two. Where're we going for lunch?"

"Well, I know this greasy truckstop . . ."

"Smartass," she laughed. "Let's go before I get called back to assist with the colic."

At a nearby café, Rebecca asked, "Did you guys give any thought to insuring the horses?"

"Yeah, I told Claude to get the exams done and we'll pay the premiums out of the winnings. But Marco only wants to insure Painter, says it's not worth insuring the other two until they prove their worth – no big wins yet.

"Risky. Concrete Boot cost a lot of money," she said, munching on her salad.

"I know, I know." Oliver looked uneasy. "Still, Marco has his money back with bells on. We'll be alright."

A phone chimed and Rebecca jumped. "Mine or yours? Shit, I should go."

"Relax, Bec, it's me." He pulled the device from his jacket pocket and frowned when he saw his brother's number. "Fuck him," he muttered, rejecting the call and tossing the phone on the table.

"You really should talk, hon."

"You sound like my mother!"

"He's still your brother. Give him a chance."

Moments later, it beeped with an incoming message. *PLEASE CALL. Something big might go down. Need to talk. Please, Ollie.*

"Probably wants to announce the latest deal he's done," said Oliver in disgust. "Later, bro," he said, turning off the phone.

Chapter 33

The Freefly Airlines executive jet coasted to a halt, and the engines powered down on the tarmac of the airstrip on the outskirts of Dublin. Pietro was sprawled out, fast asleep on one of the recliners. He loved these return journeys when they didn't have passengers; it was like he had his own plane. He slowly rubbed his eyes and stretched.

Pat O'Connell appeared in the cabin. "Jesus, lad, make yourself at home, anyway," he said, putting on his jacket.

Pietro shrugged dismissively. "Hey, the hours I work, it is my home, Capitano." He knew the pilots didn't like his casual attitude, but he didn't care. He glanced out the window to check the weather, and his mood instantly changed. It was a bright, blustery day, but there were Customs agents and Garda Siochana approaching the plane with an eager-looking Labrador. Jonathon Coleman joined his colleague in the cabin.

He glanced out the window and then at Pietro. "What's wrong? Seen a ghost, have we?"

"Vaffanculo," said Pietro in a jovial tone, with a huge smile.

Jonathon gave him a look of disgust, then muttered, "Pat, open the door and let's give that little fucker a pain in his hole."

"What?" said Pat.

Pietro's eyes darted about.

"Just open the door," said Jonathon.

Pat shrugged and pulled the levers, flipping the door open and extending the steps. Pietro composed himself.

The Customs officer skipped up the steps, ducked to enter the cabin, and announced, "How're ye, lads? Have to hold you up a bit. We're doing checks of all traffic today," he said, giving a quick wink to Jonathon.

"Be my guest," said Jonathon, waving his arm about the cabin.

The officer beckoned the dog handler on board with his charge. The animal began sniffing the carpet, seats and eventually – to Pietro's horror – his hands.

"Oo's a good boy then?" he said, trying to remain calm.

The dog lost interest in him and followed its nose directly to the flight deck. He then sat down at the back of the cockpit beside the small locker for the crew bags. There was an exchange of glances between the two officers. One of them asked Pat to open it. The dog sniffed Pietro's bag, then sat down.

"Whose bag is this?" said the dog handler, pointing at the large duffel.

"His," said Jonathon, pointing at the Italian.

Pietro nodded, resigned.

The Customs officer beckoned the two Gardai on board and asked them to apprehend Pietro on suspicion of having a controlled substance in his luggage.

Pietro stood and remained mute. He was whisked across the tarmac to the waiting police car.

Jonathon and Pat were escorted to the terminal by the Customs officers as two more Gardai arrived to seal off the plane.

"Listen, lads," said the officer. "Thanks for the tip off, the dog makes it easier to get the job done, otherwise we'd have to go over every inch of the plane."

"Ah sure, just trying to do my bit," said Jonathon.

"The Guards'll still want to question you, though, so you'll have to stay till they get someone over. You'd better call your families."

"What about the company?" said Pat. "Who'll tell them?"

"The Guards'll take care of that."

"Jesus," said Pat, laughing, "but I'd give anything to see the boss man's face when he hears this."

"Priceless," said Jonathon, sporting a satisfied smile. "Priceless."

Pat frowned. It occurred to him that the airline's future might not look so rosy all of a sudden. Jobs might be lost.

Chapter 34

A week after the message from his brother, Oliver returned from America. He wanted to spend December and Christmas with his mother, and though Rebecca had to work over the festive period, she planned to join him in early January. They decided to keep their engagement a secret until then. During the journey, the excitement of America began to leave his system and he felt exhausted.

When he got in the door, he saw his mother at the top of the stairs. She looked gaunt and frail. "Oliver! I was worried sick. You haven't called since you won your race. What on earth have you been doing? I tried to reach you a couple of days ago."

"Relax, Mum. I mean, sorry. I turned the phone off and took some time out to be with Bec."

"Relax? So you're having a grand old time while your brother's business is involved in a scandal."

"What?"

"Oh, don't tell me you didn't hear," she said, slowly descending the staircase. "You really must drag yourself out of the horse world once in a while."

"Mum, what're you on about? What scandal?"

"It hit the papers three days ago. Your brother is distraught. They're saying that drugs were found on one of his private jets. It's too awful."

"Drugs? How? I mean, what's the story?"

"Oh, I don't know. They probably fell out of the pocket of one of those seedy musicians he always carts about the continent. Dreadful types." She sighed. "Aren't you going to give your mother a kiss?"

"Sorry, Mum." He hugged her and kissed both cheeks.

"I could do with your support, and I want you to ring your brother. He's in an awful state."

Oliver looked at her; he knew he would have to do it sooner or later. "OK, Mum. I'll call him tomorrow morning. I'm too tired now."

"Good boy. Bury the hatchet."

"Yes, Mum," he said.

Oliver went to his room, dropped his bags, showered, and flopped onto his bed. Thoughts of his brother's predicament were fuzzy at the back of his brain.

He woke, bleary-eyed, six hours later, to the sun shining onto him through the window and a terrible wail coming from the ground floor. He jumped out of bed and bounded downstairs. He arrived into the hall to see two stunned-looking policemen standing at the front door and his mother collapsed in a heap on a chair. She was bawling and convulsing. Oliver dashed to support her.

"Oh, my boy, my boy," she wailed.

"Jesus, what's going on?" he asked the policemen.

"Are you a relative, sir?"

"Yes, I'm her son. For the love of God, what's the matter?"

"Sir, I'm afraid it's my sad duty to inform you that your brother, Richard, was found dead on the street outside his apartment in the early hours of this morning."

PART II

Chapter 35

"Actually, no. No, I don't," said Martin. "You see, um, the thing is, I know you work for Marco Romano."

"What?" said Oliver, stunned.

Martin explained about the photos of Marco and Oliver, and how he had shown them to Richard.

"I also know that he went to the horse sales last year to meet you and Marco, and just after that, your brother took the Italian on as a flight attendant."

"So you think Marco had something to do with Richard's death?" said Oliver, eyebrows raised.

"Yes, I do. Look, I'm, um, interested in organized crime – the Mafia. Your brother's death seems too convenient. I mean, it happened at just the right time."

"What do you mean?"

"Think about it, if you were using somebody's planes to transport drugs and there was a bust, you'd want to cover your tracks, wouldn't you?"

Oliver remained silent, his mind whirring. He wanted to say that Marco was an old-fashioned gangster and that they didn't get involved in drugs, but he kept thinking of all the cocaine he had seen and been given. A terrible feeling came over him. "So you're saying that Richard and Marco were in business together?"

Martin sucked air through his teeth, wincing as he did it. "I wouldn't say that, exactly. The last few months I'd been working closely with your brother, and for years before I'd worked under him, so I kind of know his style. And I don't think drug smuggling was it."

Oliver shrugged. "He loved his money, though."

"He did," Martin nodded. "He did indeed, but he was more of a man to bend the rules, not shatter them."

"That day he came to the sales to see me, he was all Marco, talking shite and trying to impress." He cast his mind back. "Come to think of it, he did disappear with Marco for a few minutes."

"Anyway," Martin cut in. "I'm not sure what happened, but with all the meetings and stuff, it's possible he was going to go to the police. And then he ends up dead."

"I don't know, I mean the cops said these kinds of crimes are fairly common."

"Not in the area your brother lived in, and anyway, what does it matter what the Guards said? If it was a professional job, then it would fool them; that's how these guys work."

Oliver found himself wondering if his brother had possibly got what he deserved. Then he felt sick for thinking such a thing, but surely it didn't matter too much, as long as he never said it out loud?

"So why are you telling me all this? Shouldn't you be giving a statement to the police?"

"Oh, I tried. They all but laughed at me. Said that I read too many books." He sighed. "I've no proof, you see. I gave the only photos of you guys to Richard. Anyway, they're only photos. They proved nothing except that you had flown here with somebody who looked like Marco Romano, and he's virtually unheard of over here. So I wanted to tell you. To mark your card, like."

"So, basically you're putting two and two together and getting five?" Oliver shook his head.

"I don't know, Martin, I really don't. I mean, it all sounds a bit far-fetched."

"I know, but I don't think it is. Look, you've a lot on your plate right now, I'm sorry to throw this at you, too, but I wanted you to know and I had to tell someone who'd listen." He stood, produced a business card from his pocket and thrust it at Oliver. "Here, if you ever want to talk, or if there's any help I can give you, give me a shout. Right, grand. Well, I'll be off." He slipped out as imperceptibly as he had slipped in.

Chapter 36

In the build-up to Christmas, Oliver and his mother made small talk and tried to avoid mentioning Richard. Oliver wanted it all to be over, and for Rebecca to join him on January second.

Richard's solicitor called to explain that Richard had asked him to be the executor of his will and that the reading of the testament would take place on January ninth.

Oliver thought about Richard's attempt to contact him before the terrible events. He spent a lot of time thinking, and on Christmas Eve, he plucked up the courage to talk to his mother properly.

"Mum, I have to come clean with you," he said one evening.

She looked up at him, startled. "Go on, then."

"Look, Mum. I've been doing a lot of thinking since Richard . . . passed away." He took a long breath. "I'm sorry for not contacting him to make peace. I know it would probably have been too late, even when I got home. But, well, oh God . . ." Tears formed in the corners of his eyes. "He tried to contact me when I was in Kentucky and I ignored the call. He even sent me a message, but I didn't care. But I should have. I should've been there for him, to listen or to help or whatever, because he was my brother."

"Oh, Oliver, Oliver," she said.

He held up his hand. "Please, Mum, let me finish. It's like, well, I know I lost him without ever making peace, but I was so pissed off by how he rejected me the day I went to him with my idea. It just stuck in my throat, Mum. So when I actually succeeded myself, I decided he didn't have the right to share in it, or even acknowledge it. I mean, when he called me after we sold

220

those yearlings, he even admitted he had to check the sales figures on the net – just to be sure. So I shut him out. But I shouldn't have, because we grew up in this house and we were friends – well, at least till he went to college. Oh Mum, I wish I could take it all back."

Tears were streaming down Evelyn's cheeks and her voice quivered as she spoke. "Please, Oliver, sit beside me. I have things to tell you."

He sat, and his mother put her arm through his in an unusually affectionate gesture.

"I know Richard always thought you were a bit soft and lacking in the 'killer instinct', as he called it. If truth be told, it was probably your father who instilled that into him." She paused. "I know I was never very good at heart-to-heart chats – that was how we were raised in my day; chin up and keep your feelings to yourself – but I'm sorry that I never encouraged you more. Your father always said that it was a man's job to deal with his sons' coming of age. He didn't mean to belittle you, it was just his way of trying to rile you up." She smiled. "But you were always unflappable. He just didn't want either of you to slave all your lives on a farm the way he did. I believe that's why he gave most of the money to Richard. I think if you had got out of horses and come to him with a business idea, he'd have given you a share, too, or made Richard help you out."

"Why on earth are you telling me this now? Isn't it a bit late?"

"It is, dear. It is. That is what I wish I could change. Perhaps then, at the very least, you two would have ended up as friends. I tried to say this to Richard after you stormed out the day you asked him for money, but he wouldn't hear it." Another pause. "And now look at the mess we're in. It's just us now."

They both sat drying their eyes for nearly half an hour, without saying another word.

"That reminds me," said Evelyn at last. "When are you going to make an honest woman out of the lovely Rebecca? It's about time you did."

Oliver threw her a sideways glance. "It's funny you should say that, Mum." He paused to think for a second. "We were going to wait till she came over to tell you, but I suppose we need a lift before Christmas. We, er, got engaged at the Breeders Cup."

His mother's face lit up, and she threw her arms around him. "That's wonderful news! She's the best thing that's happened to you."

"Yeah, she is." His mind suddenly filled with Martin's theory. He excused himself, went up to his room, and lay on his bed, staring at the ceiling and trying to come to terms with the fact that he was in business and out of his depth with a ruthless thug.

Rebecca arrived on January second. On the journey from Shannon Airport, Oliver told her all about his mother's confessions about the past and his regrets over Richard. He decided not to ruin the moment by telling her about his meeting with Martin. He just couldn't bring himself to do it. He tried to convince himself that it wasn't real until he shared it with her.

His mother opened the front door with a flourish as their car pulled up. Oliver, smiling, guessed that she had been sitting by the window waiting for them to arrive.

Evelyn hugged Rebecca warmly on the threshold of the house. "My dear, it's so good to see you again. I'm delighted that you're going to be a part of this family, or at least what's left of it."

Rebecca was taken aback by her words. She looked at Evelyn awkwardly.

"Oh, don't worry, my dear. I'm trying to focus on the future, not the past. It's 2006 now. New year, new start."

"All the same, I was so shocked by what happened and, well, I don't know what to say . . ."

Evelyn rubbed Rebecca's shoulders. "I know, my dear, I know. You don't need to say anything. Now, don't feel you have to be in the least bit formal here. Relax and enjoy your hard-earned break. You and Oliver are my future."

"I hope so, ma'am."

"Please, how many times did I tell you to call me Evelyn on your last visit? Ma'am makes me feel old!"

"We can't have you feeling old. Evelyn it is, then."

"That's much better. Now, what about a cup of tea?"

Oliver stood by the car watching this exchange. A wave of calm and relief engulfed him. For the first time, he felt like he had brought genuine happiness into his mother's life. He smiled. Now he just had to make enough money to secure everybody's future.

That evening over dinner and two bottles of rich red wine, Evelyn – overcome with festive cheer – blurted out, "I do hope you two will provide me with some long overdue grandchildren."

Oliver nearly choked, but Rebecca took it all in her stride. "I'm sure we will, Evelyn, but in our own time," she said, winking at Oliver.

Normally the thought of children would have prompted Oliver to dive headlong into depressed thoughts of a boring life, shackled to a brood of screaming brats and wasted time. And this in turn would have sent him to dive headlong into a rebellion of alcohol. For a second, he didn't know whether to smile or finish the bottle. In a break from past form, the smile won. He gazed across the table at Rebecca, and he felt nothing but love and serenity. Maybe it was the wine, but he could even picture himself taking a small child by the hand to lead them across the street.

* * *

Huntley snapped the laptop shut and swivelled in his chair. He phoned his partner. "Rosen, any result on the bugs?"

"Nah, mundane shit so far. That's when they actually work. My guys are bored to death."

"Something big's going to happen, I can sense it."

"Yeah, yeah. You've been saying that for ages."

"Get a load of this. The Irish cops are trying to question an Italian after he was caught smuggling coke on a plane belonging to the Irishman's brother."

"You're shitting me?""

"Oh no," said Huntley. A smile cracked his gaunt face.

Chapter 37

A few days later, the three of them sat in the comfortable office of Richard's solicitor and executor of his estate. James Foster was a senior partner at leading firm, O'Brien, Rooney and Clarke. A tall, distinguished man in his fifties with a razor-sharp mind, he had played rugby for Ireland in his youth and still cut a dash with his impressive physique, despite his advancing years.

Before graduating top of his class at Trinity, he had broadened his horizons by taking off to the Philippines each summer to work with an Irish religious mission, building houses for the poor. After graduation, his philanthropic streak had been quashed by the lure of an offer from Dublin's top law firm, where he stayed burning the midnight oil until he became the youngest partner in the firm; though he and his wife still did charity fundraising. He and his team specialized in inheritance and helping the rich to hide their money from the Government. Today, though, he looked haggard and pale.

"Let's begin then," said James, pinching the bridge of his nose. "I understand that Miss Liddell is attending these proceedings at your request." He looked quizzically from Oliver to Evelyn.

"Yes," said Oliver.

"That's correct," said Evelyn. "She is virtually family."

"Very well then. This won't take long; it's a straightforward testament." He took a deep breath and scanned the notes on his legal pad. "First, let me bring you up-to-date on the police investigation." He checked off the first item on the list. "Richard's death has been ruled as manslaughter by an, as yet, unknown assailant; presumably a drug addict. It seems highly unlikely that the culprit will ever be found, barring a lucky break. The CCTV cameras in the area did not manage to positively identify the perpetrator. The police are also inclined to believe that Richard did not have any part in the smuggling of narcotics aboard his planes."

Foster looked at them with sympathetic eyes. "I can say with absolute certainly that he had no

idea what was going on. He gave a formal statement to the police, in my presence, the day before he died. He stated that he hired Pietro Busoni because he applied directly to Richard via e-mail. Your brother was apparently impressed by Pietro's resourcefulness and CV, and he knew he needed someone a bit 'smooth and sexy', as he put it, to work on the Opulence Service. The police were happy with this statement, though they would certainly have required your brother to testify in court had he not died. It seems that Pietro was indeed resourceful, though now he is proving to be silent, and this is making the police very frustrated. His documents are all forgeries – very expensive ones – and they have no other information to go on."

Oliver sat in uncomfortable silence; Martin's theory began to seem a little more real.

Evelyn stared out the window.

Rebecca sat between them like an anchor.

"Now for the testament." He checked another item off the list. "The will is very simple and was amended last week. It simply states that everything is to be left to 'my brother, Oliver'. The assets include his house in Tipperary, the apartment in Dublin, the contents of the residences, and shares in Freefly Airlines. The shares are to be sold on the market and the proceeds are to be given you." He looked up from the document, directly at Oliver, whose jaw hung open. "There is one condition."

"What's that?" said Oliver, barely able to get the words out.

"You have to provide fully for your mother from now on."

"I would have thought that went without saying," muttered Oliver.

Foster paused.

Rebecca shot Oliver a dirty look; he grimaced. "Er, well, I'm sure Rich was just being thorough."

"Indeed he was." Foster nodded. "OK, moving on. As well as the properties, there are significant monies in various accounts and investment schemes. There is also a large amount of gold held in a bank in Switzerland. The current value of the estate, excluding the remaining shares, is in the region of fifty to sixty million Euro." He paused for a moment to let that sink in, but they couldn't fully appreciate the figure. He cleared his throat. "I'm afraid your brother liquidated a large chunk of his shares into gold and cash a few years ago. He had a theory that the economy would soon cycle into a bust." Foster shook his head with an uncomprehending expression. "I don't know. Sure, things have never been better and don't look like they're going to slow down. Anyway, the remaining stock is potentially worth another twenty, but with the scandal and the lack of an apparent successor to your brother, the value could diminish considerably, I'm afraid. And the testament does leave instructions for the stocks to be sold not more than one week after the reading."

"Jesus," said Oliver, with a whistle. "Who cares if it loses a bit? That's a lot of money. If the stock drops by 50 per cent, it's still a huge windfall. Go ahead, do what you have to do." He rubbed his eyes then looked at Foster. "Look, are you sure this was what he wanted? It just . . . I just . . . I can't . . . that is, I don't get it."

"Which brings me to the next point." Another flick of pen on pad. "I'm afraid I must ask you two ladies to leave the room for this final section." He looked sympathetically at Evelyn. Before his mother could get up, Oliver cut in. "Whatever has to be said, can be said in front of them."

James shook his head. "No, I'm afraid it can't. I have specific instructions."

"Don't worry, dear," said Evelyn, getting up.

Rebecca opened the door for her and they left.

Foster listened to the latch close and the footsteps disappear before he produced a plain brown manila envelope sealed with wax, and handed it to Oliver. "It's from your brother. Read it in full, then feel free to ask me anything."

Oliver took the envelope. He held it in his hands for a second, feeling like a superstitious widower waiting at a séance. He ripped the brown paper open and read the spidery handwriting.

Chapter 38

Oliver read it a second time, then a third. When he had finally got his head around the words and wiped the tears from his cheeks, he asked Foster, "Do you know what's in this?"

"No. However, your brother did come to see me about a week before he died. He was deeply troubled by the incident with Pietro. We discussed his position and options. As I said, he made a full statement to the police."

James tossed his pen on the desk and clasped his hands. "Your brother made sure that I was paid an advance to provide legal advice to you for a period of two years. If you wish to retain my services after that time, then we can discuss fees, should the need arise. So if there's anything I can do for you, either in terms of organizing your affairs or anything else, just let me know, but I should also inform you that I'm considering retirement, or at least seriously cutting back on my workload in a few years."

"OK."

Oliver's mind was galloping: time to take hold of the reins and control the beast. His brother's change of heart was sinking in, but he felt that he had already punished himself enough for not burying the hatchet. The more pressing issue was the realization that he was possibly on the periphery of a bizarre and deadly situation. Could Marco really have had Rich killed? He's over in America trying to keep a low profile; it didn't make sense. He still doubted it – wanted to doubt it – but his brother's words rattled around in his brain: *Marco asked me directly . . . Break the link . . .* "Jesus, if it's true?" he mouthed.

"I'm sorry?" said Foster.

"What? Oh, nothing." Oliver didn't even look up; he kept thinking. After ten minutes of frantic cogitation, Oliver counted silently to ten, took a deep breath, cleared his throat and spoke in a tone not dissimilar to the way Marco spoke when he gave orders.

"First, get me a new envelope and some wax to seal this letter. Then I want you to open a safety deposit box for me in whichever bank you think is best, put the letter in it, along with half a million in cash. Buy another half million in diamonds and gold coins and put it with them. Then, sell his apartment near Clontarf. It must be worth something; I never want to set foot there. Sell the contents, too, pay all taxes and give the proceeds to Mum."

Foster blinked in surprise and hurriedly scribbled a few notes.

"These matters will remain confidential, I take it?"

"Absolutely, you are my client."

"Good. Is there anything else?"

"Er . . . No," he said, scanning his pad. "That's all for today. There'll be papers to sign, but I'll have someone bring them to you in Limerick."

"Great. Thanks for everything, James." They shook hands warmly and firmly.

Late that night, Oliver and Rebecca lay together on the sofa in front of a roaring fire. His mother had long since gone to bed, but they were in no hurry. Evelyn had never permitted them to sleep together under her roof.

"Hey, Bec, remember when I told you about Agent Huntley, that day at the races? You said that it was like a movie."

"Yeah."

"Wait till you hear this." Oliver told her about the letter and Martin.

"Holy shit!" She sat up straight, trying to make sense of it all. "You reckon he's behind it *all*?"

"I don't want to believe it, but it has to be true. I can feel it. I'm in the shit this time."

"Hmm." She played with the loose threads on the sleeve of her jumper. "I don't think you should do anything rash, like confronting him."

"I've no intention of confronting him with the opinions of one of my brother's accountants."

"Hon, what I really meant was, even if you get *proof* that Marco had your brother killed, you need to think of yourself. Get yourself away from him quietly and leave it at that. I'm sorry your brother's dead and all, but like he said in the letter, look after yourself and your mum."

"And my fiancée," he said.

"Damn right! But seriously, promise me you won't do anything rash."

"OK."

"I mean it, hon. Grief and guilt can do strange things."

"I don't feel guilty." Oliver knew it wasn't entirely true, as he said it. He told himself he was doing a good job, making good money for everyone, and Marco was like a father figure to him. He pulled Rebecca on top of him and told her it would all work out right. He wanted to believe it as he said the words.

Oliver stared at the ceiling for a while. Rebecca lay with her head on his chest. All of a sudden he said, "I think I'll call Claude, get the progress report, and tell him about Rich. Then when I call Robert with the updates, I'll break it to him, too. It'll look a bit weird if I don't say a thing, even if it means I won't have the chance to gauge Marco's reaction."

"Can't you wait till you go over to see him?"

"I don't think I'll go till the spring. You'll be flat out with a breeding season, and Claude wants to give the horses an easy build-up for Kentucky in May. Besides, there'll be things to take care of here."

"That's a long wait. I'll miss you."

"I'll miss you, but you won't have time to miss me. The delights of another frantic breeding season await you."

"Gee, hon, you're such a romantic."

"Yeah, I know," he said with a grin.

"Smartass!"

"Smartass, is it? Whatever happened to successful owner?"

"Hopefully he'll make a comeback in the spring. Now, do we make the most of this cosy fire before the desolation of separate bedrooms?" she said, with a twinkle in her eye.

* * *

Huntley sat in the empty diner, sipping coffee and biting his nails. Rosen ambled in, slid into the booth, and ordered a burger and fries.

""Any progress?" said Huntley.

"Mitch and Jerry're like zombies, they need more guys to go through all the footage. It's a fucking nightmare."

"What about Kimble?"

"We can't have her for another two months. Besides, if I shut her in that house with those two, she'll kill them."

"Well, we can't have more guys until we get a warrant."

"We don't have jack shit to get a warrant."

"Yet. Please tell me you were going to say, yet?"

Rosen shrugged and looked doubtful.

"Fuck. Jesus H. Christ. Something's going on, I know it. Something really big. We have got to get on it before we run out of time and funding, or before the bodies start piling up."

Rosen tucked into his burger. Huntley grimaced at the sight. "You don't give a fuck, do you?"

"Sure I do," he said, chewing. "I want to get him, but I'm not goin' to lose sleep over it or drive myself into an early grave." He took another large bite.

Chapter 39

"We're going to kill 'em all! Blow 'em right away. I've never been more sure of anything in my life."

"That's, er, great news," said Oliver a little shakily. His palm started to sweat as he held the receiver to his ear, suddenly unsure of whom he was talking to.

"Goddamnit man, you could sound excited! I'm telling you, first weekend in May we're going to win the Kentucky Derby *and* the Oaks – a double whammy. It's almost unheard of. Well, not exactly. I did it the year I had Pop Up Piston, but seeing as he went on to win the Triple Crown, everyone kinda forgot I won the Oaks with Cactus Queen." Claude bellowed down the line. "Thing is, though, The Boot, as I call him, is a difficult horse. Freakish ability, but he's a bit of a loon. I've got to race him lightly. He'll get two runs, then blow 'em off the track in the Derby."

"Great, but . . . Yeah look, sorry. I'm a little distracted."

"Well focus, man. This could be a big year."

"Claude, I guess you haven't heard. My, my brother died."

There was a lengthy silence on the other end. "Christ, I'm sorry. Don't know what to say. Guess I was too wrapped up in my horses."

"Don't worry about it, Claude, I get tunnel vision myself." He sighed. "I probably won't come over for a while, though. Maybe not until you ship north from Florida in April. What's the program?"

"Well . . ." Claude's voice was quieter this time. "Painter'll have a run down here at Gulfstream, then I'll send her to

Keeneland for the Ashland Stakes, then the Oaks. The Boot'll do the Florida Derby, the Bluegrass at Keeneland, then the Run for the Roses."

"Jesus! Are you sure? He's only had one run as a two-year-old."

"One run?" Claude cut in. "He won the fuckin' Remsen stakes by twelve lengths on his racecourse debut – *that's* never been done before!"

"I know, but are you sure you can get a horse to win the Kentucky Derby with so little experience? It's a huge ask."

"Like I said, this guy don't have many miles on the clock. Physically he's the most magnificent athlete I've ever seen, but he never really matured mentally. He leaps about all over the fucking place and works himself like his life depends on it. If he has too much racing, he'll explode, and if he ever got loose from his groom or jockey, he'd run so hard and fast he'd probably kill himself – or shatter a leg."

Oliver was stunned. "Are you serious?"

"As a heart attack."

"Then if he wins the Derby, we should secure a stallion deal as soon as possible."

"That's just what I was thinking." He paused. "You sure you're OK?"

"Yeah, I'll be alright, I'm kind of over the shock. So, what about Shadows?"

"He caught some kind of viral infection, got over it OK, but training had to stop. Anyway, there's not that many classy opportunities for three-year-old sprinters till the summer."

"Why don't you try him over a mile?"

"Oliver, this horse is pure speed, but he won't last a yard over six eighths of a mile, that's a fact."

"OK, I'll let Marco know. I suppose I'd better convince him to insure Concrete Boot."

"Forget half a mill. Insure him for two at least."

"Steady there, Claude. D'you know how much the premiums are?"

"Just get him covered by Mob mutual insurance – you hit us, we hit you." He started chuckling at his own lame joke.

Oliver felt his stomach churn. "Well, thanks, Claude. Talk soon, good luck."

"Yeah, you too, man. And Oliver?"

"Yeah."

"Take care of yourself."

"Thanks, Claude, I'll try."

Oliver put the receiver down and stared at Rebecca, but his mind was spinning with Claude's feeble attempt at bonding humour. "One down, one to go. Do I have to call Rob now? I think I need to psyche myself up for it."

"No you don't, hon, but hey – aren't you forgetting something?"

"What?" Oliver had a glazed look in his eye.

"The race plans." She gently placed her palm on his cheek. "Are you OK?"

He closed his eyes and leaned into her touch. "Yeah. Claude just made a crappy Mafia joke." "And you don't find them so funny now, huh?"

He shook his head. "The good news is, he thinks we'll kick ass with Concrete Boot and Painter. He even told me he'll do the Derby/Oaks double. Can you imagine?"

"I can. He did it before, you know."

"That's what he said. I'd forgotten." He glanced out the window at the rain lashing down onto the green fields. "OK, here goes." He picked up the receiver.

"Hey! What's up, man? Long time no hear. Bet you're all loved up in the Emerald Isle?"

"Well, yeah. Bec's here now, but . . . well I . . . I guess you didn't hear?"

"Hear what, man?"

"My brother was killed a few weeks back."

There was a slight pause. "Holy fuck! You're shitting me. Killed? Fuck man, I'm sorry. I, what happened?"

Oliver took a deep breath and told him the story, or at least, the official story.

"I am so sorry, Oliver. That's some fucked-up shit, man. I know you didn't like him much, but I guess he was still your brother, right?"

"Er, right. To be honest, I don't really know how to feel. So, you didn't hear about it at all?"

"No. Should I have?"

"Well, it's been in the papers here and on the TV, but I suppose it's not really international news."

"I guess not. Look, um, I don't, it's like . . . We'll have to have a beer in his honour when we see each other, if you want to."

"Yeah, I'd like that. OK, so about the horses and the plans for racing domination."

"Like the sound of that, man."

Oliver recounted his conversation with Claude, and asked Robert to get his father to think about the insurance for Concrete Boot. Oliver's enthusiasm about the horses put a spark in their conversation. Oliver was fairly sure the young guy knew nothing of Richard's death. Time to wait and see, he thought, hanging up the receiver.

"You did that well," said Rebecca, planting an encouraging kiss on his cheek. "Hang in there."

"I don't want to hang in there at all. I want out, and if Claude's program goes to plan, we'll sell the horses for big bucks, Marco'll make a fortune, and I'll bow out gracefully, keeping my mouth shut."

Chapter 40

Stuck to his seat, Oliver felt as nervous now as he had when he first made the blind journey to Newark almost two years before. It seemed like a lifetime had passed since. He clutched the armrest as the plane touched down in the early April sunshine, and the old lady sitting next to him assumed it was a symptom of a fear of flying.

"There, there. It's all over now," she said soothingly.

He shot her a sideways glance and managed a grimace of a smile. If she only knew.

Business-wise, everything was sailing along according to plan. Concrete Boot was to be insured, but only if he won the Florida Derby. The horse duly obliged by four lengths and was installed as a red-hot favourite for the Kentucky Bluegrass Stakes in ten days' time. Painter Girl had also won her race in Florida, though less impressively than her stablemate. There was some value to be had in betting on her run this weekend. Claude was bullish about their chances and Marco was happy.

Oliver was dreading the meeting. It worried him that Marco had not spoken to him on the phone since last year. Originally, he had promised Oliver full access, and although the Agent Huntley affair had changed things slightly, Marco seemed to use the phone less and less.

Later, when he stood on the threshold of his house and greeted Oliver with a warm embrace and a smile, the visitor relaxed a bit.

"So, how you been?" asked Marco, as he led the way to his study. "You see those Florida races? We kicked ass, my friend."

"Yeah, I suppose we did. Fingers crossed it all goes to plan.

Claude's doing some job keeping Concrete Boot sane."

"Long as he keeps winning."

"Yeah." Oliver sat on the sofa and felt his heart trying to thump its way out of his chest. He gritted his teeth. "Marco, I suppose Robert told you, things've been tough at home. My brother was killed and, and . . . There was a scandal connected with his company."

"What?" Marco looked puzzled. "Oh, yeah. Robert told me he died and I heard about some kind of bad business going down – the airline, right?"

"Yeah, I can hardly believe it; they say he was smuggling drugs, then just like that, he's found dead on the street. It's incredible," he sobbed.

Marco cocked his head to one side, raised his eyebrows, and said in a soft but firm voice, "Look, I'm sorry for your loss, but if he got himself into something that blew up in his face then that's his problem." He wagged his finger at a stunned Oliver. "It'll do you no good to dwell on it."

"But he was my brother."

"I thought you didn't even like the guy, anyway."

"Well, I didn't, but . . ."

"I mean it," the big man interrupted. "You need to move on and concentrate on your mother, your fiancée – yeah, I heard about that, too – and your horses. Shit happens—get on with your life. Just make sure that kind of shit never happens to you."

A wave of panic crept up Oliver's spine. A few months ago, he might have failed to see the meaning of these words, but now he felt more awake and alert. Perhaps Martin was right. He peeled his eyes away from Marco's, looked at the floor, silently counted to ten, shrugged his shoulders, and returned his gaze to Marco.

"Fuck it, I suppose you're right. What's done is done, and like you said, I didn't even really like him, anyway. What did he do for me?" He forced a smirk onto his face. "To be quite honest, all I really want is to win the Kentucky Derby, then we'll sell the horse as a stallion."

"Now that's more like it!" bellowed Marco, clapping his hand onto Oliver's shoulder. "Let's have a mint julep for luck." He shouted for the drinks.

"Starting to feel like springtime in Kentucky already," lied Oliver, sipping the strong sharp bourbon. Now was not the time to tell Marco that he planned to use the profit from the stallion deal as the excuse to get out.

He decided he would not, ever, utter a word about his inheritance to Marco or Robert. Maybe Marco had the means to find out, but if he was involved in the events in Ireland, he would not want to have any of his people caught snooping around asking questions in law firms. Anyway, Marco had no reason to suspect Richard would ever leave a penny to his younger brother – not even Oliver had expected it.

It was essential that Concrete Boot won the Run for the Roses on the first Saturday in May, and Oliver would have a reasonable excuse to extricate himself from the deal.

Oliver flew to Lexington the next day and told Rebecca about Marco's reaction.

"Holy shit, hon," she said, stunned. "Like I said, you got to keep your head down and get out – don't even think about trying to get even with the guy."

"Don't worry, Bec, I don't think I could if I wanted to. After all, I've no proof of anything, and if I make one call to the police, I'll end up like Rich. Or worse." There was an unnerving calmness in his voice. Rebecca hugged him.

"You're taking this all very well. Maybe too well. You sure you don't want to tell me anything?"

He chewed his lip. "As they say, nothing like a crisis to focus the mind. We'll get through this together. We just need the horse to win."

Chapter 41

A week later, the plan was still on track. Painter Girl won the Ashland Stakes, making it look more difficult than it actually was. It had poured with rain before the race and although she galloped through the sloppy track without a problem, Pablo got her boxed in and couldn't find a gap. The fractious filly appeared to sulk under the onslaught of wet dirt pelting her head and chest, and when Pablo asked her to dart for the line, she grudgingly gave him the effort required and won by a neck. "A neck's a good as a mile," said Claude.

The following Saturday, Concrete Boot duly obliged in the Bluegrass Stakes. Though he got home by only half a length – nearly stopping Oliver's heart in the process – he appeared to merely be out for an afternoon stroll around the track. Claude had told everyone before the race that the important thing was to win in as calm a fashion as possible, to give the horse the illusion that this was only a training gallop. After the race, he jumped, kicked and bucked in the winner's enclosure, scattering Claude, Oliver, Rebecca and Robert.

"Fuck it, every time we race, he gets more and more wound up. Does all kinds of stupid shit like this," said Claude, pinned to the rail with the others.

"Wouldn't it be better if he was more tired?" said Robert.

"Are you fucking mad?" snapped Claude, forgetting himself. "I mean, no. He's like a timebomb. I have to get him to use himself as little as possible, to waste as little energy and ability as possible, so we can get him to Churchill Downs in a couple weeks. Otherwise, he'll boil over."

"Can't you give him something to calm him down, like a shot of bourbon or a joint or something?" said Robert, only half-joking.

Claude looked at him straight in the eye. "I need to channel his ability, not suppress it. Understand?"

"Yeah, I guess."

"Besides, Rob," Oliver chipped in. "That would be against the rules. Right, Claude?"

"Yeah, kinda. I mean, they can run on certain painkillers and diuretics, and some other stuff."

"Shit, really?" said Robert.

"Yep," said Rebecca.

"Yeah, really . . ." Claude was cut short by another flailing kick from the horse, which punched the air inches from where he stood. "Goddamn it, Ricky, get him back to the stable!" he bellowed.

His assistant hurriedly signalled to the groom and they accompanied the distraught athlete back to the quiet sanctuary of his stall. All eyes were on Boot as he left the arena. He had just been installed as favourite for the Derby in two weeks' time. The pressure was mounting on Claude and Oliver.

Chapter 42

At the beginning of May every year, Louisville, Kentucky transforms itself from a quiet provincial town into a carnival city and the focus of a nation. The streets fill with banners and an expectant buzz runs through the residents; even waitresses and university students discuss what might win the big race at the weekend. For a frantic few days, Derby fever grips everyone in the area.

The day before the great race, Friday, is Oaks Day. Churchill Downs does a dress rehearsal for the big event; good racing and great festivities, but without the seething masses that flock to the track for the Derby. Oliver took his place in the grandstand, scanned the crowd, and reflected that this was the purist's race-day. Only diehard race fans and those involved in the business were there.

Oliver couldn't bear to be in the paddock. He had a chat with Claude while he saddled Painter, then scurried away from the gaze of the TV cameras. Robert followed him up to the owners' viewing area. Oliver found Rebecca leaning on a rail, looking down at the immaculately prepared track and the winner's circle opposite the finishing line. She gave her widest smile as she saw him approach.

"I was just thinking how cool it'd be to stand over there in a few minutes."

Oliver grimaced. "Don't, please. If I do any more thinking, I'll either burst into tears or throw up, I'm so nervous."

"And what'll you do if she wins, hon?"

"Both, probably." He took her hand in his as Painter Girl was ponied onto the track and down to the starting gates. He nearly squeezed the blood from Rebecca's hand as the horses were loaded then ejected. Oliver's heart started pounding in rhythm with the hoof-beats as the horses thundered along the dirt track. When Painter Girl rounded the final turn in third position, the tears welled up in his eyes. He roared at the top of his lungs when Pablo switched her to the outside and dashed for the line. Oliver daren't believe it as she tussled in a titanic battle with Jig Dance. With neither giving in, the two animals covered the dying strides of the race locked together. When they crossed the line, Oliver had lost his voice, and not even the commentator could call the winner.

Rebecca hugged her man and said, "She got there, hon. I can feel it."

Oliver was ashen-faced and unable to speak. He looked behind for Claude, hoping to get a nerve-killing cigarette from him while the photo-finish shot was examined. The trainer passed over the packet when he saw the look in Oliver's eye, then he replaced the butt in his own mouth with a fresh one and inhaled deeply.

"I fuckin' hate photo finishes. Never had much luck with 'em."

"Now you tell me," croaked Oliver.

For five minutes, Churchill Downs racetrack held its breath. Oliver and Claude paced around in small circles, too afraid to go to the winner's circle or to the unsaddling enclosure. Both Painter Girl and Jig Dance were being led about on the track by their grooms; not even the jockeys could call the result. Neither wanted to claim the winner's circle for fear of having to exit in a few minutes.

Finally, there was a crackle as the announcement was made over the public address system. When they heard, "First: Number seven", Oliver and Claude embraced and felt the stress drain from their bodies.

Oliver turned to kiss Rebecca and she jumped into his arms. "You're the man. And you're my man."

Robert stood behind them with a beer in one hand, talking

into his phone. He flipped it shut. A broad grin swept across his face. "You guys like to give us all heart attacks," he said, grabbing Oliver's hand and shaking it vigorously. "Dad was in a sweat, too. Shit, I think he aged a year in ten minutes."

"I think we all did, Rob," said Oliver.

Claude pulled out another cigarette. "I'm still fuckin' ageing," he muttered.

Oliver glanced at him, and thought how much could change on the nod of a horse's head at the line, of how many fortunes have been won and lost on the running of a race. He threw his eyes skywards and thanked his lucky stars.

That evening, Marco called him. "That was close, my friend, I nearly gave myself an ulcer waiting for the result. Tell Claude I like to win by more than an inch."

Oliver smiled. "You know, I think I prefer that myself. And with any luck, we'll do just that tomorrow. Oh, the other thing is, if he wins tomorrow we . . ."

"What's this if? I don't want to hear about if!"

"Neither do I. You see, this horse probably only has a few races in him, so I want a stallion deal sorted as soon as possible. That way, we have our return guaranteed."

"OK."

"I'll put the word about that he's for sale and see who bites. We'll have interest, alright. It just depends on the figure."

"Give me a ballpark."

"With his looks, race record and his mother's pedigree, could be anything. He's not by the most fashionable stallion in the world, but I reckon we'll get away with that. The most important thing is that his temperament remains a secret, which isn't easy in this business," said Oliver, hedging.

"Yeah, yeah. So what's the figure?" snapped Marco.

"The stallion business is hot right now, so I reckon it'll be seven to ten, if he wins."

Marco let out a satisfied whistle. "Then you'd better hope he does. Tell Claude I said that, too."

"I'll pass it on, but it might give him a heart attack. He's nervous enough already. In fact, we all are."

"What did I tell you before? Relax, you'll get the job done. It's gone to plan so far."

An image of Richard flashed through his brain. "It sure has," he said, without much enthusiasm.

Chapter 43

Derby day was bedlam. The infield of the track was a drunken, roaring mass of people; mostly students or locals who weren't prepared to pay the high ticket prices to gain access to the grandstand enclosures. The stands themselves were packed to capacity with every kind of person. For those involved in the business, it was *de rigueur* to attend the Derby. Alongside the race fans, there were celebrities flown in from all over the country, most of them more interested in the free champagne in the corporate boxes than the racing.

Buried in this manic cross-section of humanity, there were horses. The runners for the Derby circled the small parade paddock. Owners, trainers and jockeys fought for space on the little patch of grass in the middle, while the rails appeared to strain under the weight of thousands of spectators, all pushing and clamouring for a view of the nation's best three-year-old colts. It gave the paddock a fish bowl effect, which did nothing for the nerves of Concrete Boot, or his trainer.

The horse was slightly placated by earplugs, which Ricky had inserted and Pablo would remove when the horse was at the start. The trainer was eating cigarettes, which would continue until after the finish. Oliver, Rebecca and Robert flanked Claude, as usual. Oliver got a fright when he saw Agent Huntley leaning on the paddock railing, and the two men stared at each other for a second. Huntley smiled under his sunglasses and turned away. Oliver tried to remain calm, and took another cigarette from Claude.

The bell rang and the runners filed out of the paddock,

through the tunnel under the grandstands, and onto the track. The outriders paired up with their assigned steeds to pony them the short distance to the start. All except for Concrete Boot. Ricky and the groom led him down the track. The trick worked, instead of feeding off the energy of another horse, Boot strolled along beside his regular handlers and stared at the crowds, though he couldn't hear them. Oliver, high in the stands, watched intently through his binoculars, nodding in approval.

The horse circled around behind the stalls and was the last to be loaded. As the barrier snapped shut behind him, Pablo tugged the twine linking the earplugs and tossed them away. The noise invaded the animal's brain. He would have started to sweat, but the buzzer sounded and the gates flew open to tremendous applause. Pablo was thankful for his wide draw, which gave the horses nearest the inside rail a starting advantage. Boot broke like his tail was on fire, but still found himself behind the leaders. Pablo settled him in near the rail, surrounded by horses. With no open track in front of him, Boot went at an even tempo and kept his head down.

There was a blistering early pace as the runners thundered past the stands. Pablo was eleventh of twenty and, though he was one horse off the rail, he had two outside him and was completely covered up.

"Damn, he's a good pilot," muttered Oliver to Claude. "I'd swear the horse is almost relaxing."

"Pablo's a genius on a horse, but a disaster in life," said Claude, without moving his eyes from the big screen.

Oliver shot him a glance.

"I'll tell you later. Watch the race."

The horses hurtled along the back stretch, the pace unrelenting. The leader had had enough and began to drop back.

"First casualty," mumbled Claude.

As the field veered into the final turn, another two front runners began to drop back and others took their places. This gave the impression that the pace was quickening again, but it was an optical illusion. In reality, the leaders were slowing and the others simply maintaining their speed. When they swung into the home straight, the first three were digging deep into stamina reserves as their jockeys started to knuckle down hard and push for the line.

Pablo was sitting in sixth and had yet to move. He had plenty of horse underneath him. He changed his hands on the reins, cocked a glance over his shoulder and moved Boot away from the rail to get a clear run. The horse quickened up automatically, and simply devoured the ground. This was no optical illusion; he really was quickening and using the energy he had saved. Pablo was completely focused on his mount, unaware of the roar of the crowd or the significance of the race. He changed hands again and waved his whip; he daren't actually hit the horse.

The effect was dramatic, Boot found another gear. By the sixteenth pole, he was level with the leader – a huge grey colt, owned, trained and bred by New Yorkers, whose jockey was flailing his arms, legs and whip for all he was worth. Boot sailed into the lead and was alone in front. With nothing to obstruct his view, for the first time the horse seemed to notice the assembled masses in the infield, and his left ear flicked towards the crowds straining the barriers.

Before Pablo could react, Boot veered sharply away from the rail, towards the middle of the track. The head-on shot would later reveal that Boot appeared to be moving sideways. The horse's action became unbalanced and he faltered. The sinewy Brazilian adjusted his hands and dragged on the left rein, but to no avail. Boot was spooked and continued to stray from his course. He passed the line closer to the outside grandstand rail, and a few yards after it, he was on that rail; now his attention turned to the people there and he bolted as if to round the track again.

Pablo eventually got him down to a trot and turned him back towards the winner's circle. The exhausted jockey saw Claude, Ricky, the groom, and Oliver, burst through the barriers onto the track. The other runners were being greeted and consoled by their grooms and led back under the stands to the unsaddling enclosure. Only the winner remained on the dirt. The barriers were opened to let the victorious horse and its connections enter the winner's circle, which was surrounded by the crowd in the infield.

As the groom snapped his lead rope onto Boot's bridle, Pablo had caught his breath enough to notice the aghast expressions and deathly pallour of Claude, Ricky and Oliver. Then out of the corner of his eye, he noticed the ghostly form of the New York colt circling around to his left. The 140,000 people in the stands and infield were eerily silent.

The penny began to drop. "Did we get beat?" he blurted to Claude.

"I'm fucked if I know," he replied, between drags. "What the fuck happened out there? I told you not to hit the front too soon."

"Couldn't help it . . . Just took off . . . Others dead from the pace," he said breathlessly.

The regal beast's breathing had nearly returned to normal, but the wild look in his eyes remained, and his ears flicked nervously forwards and back. His groom kept him walking in a circle and whispered calmly into his ear.

"Well, I . . ." The judge's announcement stopped Oliver in his tracks, and his stomach started to churn as he absorbed the result. He could feel the bile trying to rise into his mouth.

* * *

Up in the grandstand, the crowd erupted. Robert answered his phone.

"Hi, Dad."

Rebecca cocked her ear towards the young man.

"Yeah, they just announced it. Everyone seemed kinda stunned for a second. I dunno, he's on the track with Claude."

"OK, Dad, I'll tell him." He snapped the phone shut.

Rebecca looked at him quizzically.

"Dad seems kinda pissed. He wants Oliver back to Jersey tonight."

"Pissed? Second in the Kentucky Derby's a big deal. Nice purse to collect."

Robert shrugged. "He's not happy."

Chapter 44

Claude and Oliver tried to conceal their despair as they walked through the tunnel with the vanquished horse. An official trotted after them and informed Claude that the animal would still be required to give a urine or blood sample for analysis. The trainer motioned for Ricky to escort Boot to the examination stable.

They took the elevator to the top floor and found Rebecca and Robert looking equally stunned.

"Dad wants us to get back home ASAP," Robert chewed on his lip. "He seems kinda pissed."

"Pissed?" Oliver's jaw dropped open. "Disappointment I get, but we still came second in the Kentucky Derby. That's a big deal."

"You guys made out we only had to turn up to win, so I guess it's a let down," said Rebecca.

"What happens to the stallion value now?" asked Robert.

Oliver didn't reply.

Claude vanished to deal with a runner he had in the next race. While the prize giving was taking place and a state of general euphoria gripped Churchill Downs, Oliver, Rebecca and Robert slipped away from the track and made their way to the airport.

Rebecca dropped them off and hugged Oliver intensely, as if he was taking off on a long journey. "It'll be OK, hon," she whispered in his ear. "Marco's just disappointed, that's all. You'll still get a stallion deal."

"I hope you're right."

* * *

Oliver and Robert were sitting in Marco's office at noon the

249

next day, waiting. They had left Louisville on the red-eye, after drowning their sorrows in the airport bar while watching the TV post-mortem of the race. All anyone could talk about was Concrete Boot, much to the annoyance of the winning New Yorkers, who said as much in an interview.

Oliver felt awful. It wasn't the alcohol or lack of sleep, but the uneasy feeling he had in his gut. Images of his brother flooded through his mind. Robert sat beside him, sending text messages. They heard the front door slam and heavy footsteps crossing the hall. Oliver jumped. Robert looked up at him and laughed.

"Chill, man! It's only Dad."

Marco strode into the room with his jaw cocked and the eyes on full beam. He glanced from Oliver to Robert. "Go see Luigi, he's got a new phone for you," he barked at his son.

"What, now?"

"Yeah now."

"OK," he muttered, slouching out of the room.

Marco sat opposite Oliver and leaned towards him. "What the fuck happened out there?"

Oliver had thought he knew Marco, but he could not fathom the look on the man's face right now: was it rage, curiosity, pity, or all three? He cleared his mind and concentrated. "The horse spooked and bolted across the track. It was too quick and too late for the jockey to do anything about it."

"But his job is to win the goddamn race," he roared.

Oliver's brain was suddenly filled with an image of Pablo's violent death. He gritted his teeth, determined to put up a fight and not let Marco walk all over him. "Look, Marco, I know it's disappointing, but first of all, if it wasn't for Pablo, the horse would have taken off with the early pace and finished like a snail. Second, the whole country saw that Boot was the best horse in the race. He ate up the ground with his finishing speed. People know he's the unluckiest loser in maybe forty years. When the media circus dies down, we'll still get that stallion deal. We just need to bypass the Preakness – which won't matter because he can't win the triple crown now anyway – settle him back down and win the

Belmont. Then we take the money and run. But don't worry, the deal will happen."

Marco took all this in, nodding with a slight grin. His eyes burnt into Oliver. Without blinking, he said, "Do you have any idea how much money I lost on the book?"

There was a pause, but Oliver felt compelled to answer. "No, haven't a clue." A bead of sweat was beginning to form on his forehead. Marco glanced at the droplet and smirked.

"Relax, my man. I know you don't, but it's like this: I gotta make that money back, and fast. So you tell Claude to get the horse ready for the Preakness in two weeks. I don't want to hear any arguments, OK?"

"OK, but it could ruin our chances to maximize the stallion deal. You see, I reckon he'll either lose the Preakness or the Belmont, or both, if we run him in both. He'll just cave in under the pressure."

"Here's the thing. I *want* him to lose the Preakness. Make sure he does, OK? Make sure he finishes second or third. Then he can win the Belmont and we'll get the deal."

"But, Marco, it's not as simple as that. He's not a machine, you know. He's talented, but if he was a human, he'd be officially insane."

"Just get it done, OK? No more fuck-ups." His gaze was darkening. "I won't sit on this loss for more than two weeks. Oh, and one more thing, I gotta keep all the Derby prize money for myself. Understand?"

Oliver weighed the situation in his brain. "I'm sure the Preakness result won't be a problem, but depending on how he pulls out of the race mentally, the Belmont could go either way."

Marco looked at the fireplace, seemingly bored of the conversation. "There's a lot of things go either way in this world. Profit – loss. Credit – debt. Life – death."

Oliver was dismayed that after only one real setback, Marco was reacting badly and changing the deal to suit himself. Didn't seem fair. It reminded him of several past events in his life. Got to win the Belmont, do the deal and get out.

Marco clicked his fingers. "Don't dwell on it, my man. The past is the past. Concentrate on the future. You thirsty? Let's have a drink, then you'd better get some sleep. You're going back to Kentucky to tell Claude the plan."

If the past really was the past, then shouldn't the loss on the books be taken on the chin? Surely the bigger picture was more important?

Marco got up and slapped Oliver on the knee. "Come on. I got some good wine in last week, we'll open a bottle."

Oliver followed him across the hall to the kitchen. Maybe, he's not so pissed off after all.

* * *

The following afternoon, Oliver was part of the masses at Newark Airport. He fought his way to the check-in desk and offered his passport and ticket to the bubbly brunette behind the counter, who asked him all the usual questions and tapped his details into her computer. She frowned and picked up a phone.

"Hi," she said. "Yes, that's correct . . . OK . . . I'll wait. Thank you."

Oliver looked at her quizzically.

"OK, sir, nothing to be alarmed about. If you can just bear with me for a second, there's something odd about your reservation."

"There shouldn't be. I mean, it's a return flight."

She glanced over Oliver's shoulder, raised her eyebrows, and cocked her head back. Oliver turned and saw two policemen approaching, with fake smiles on their faces.

"What the . . ." muttered Oliver. Resignedly, he picked up his small case and moved out of the queue.

"Sir, could you follow us, please."

He mustered a smile. "What's this about, guys?"

"Please come with us, sir."

The officers flanked Oliver and led him through a security door into the bowels of the airport.

As they walked down a long empty corridor, Oliver repeated the question.

There was no answer. They stopped at a door, knocked and entered. It was a small room with grey walls. A thin, greying man was sitting at a table, with a laptop computer bag on the floor by his feet and a file placed on the table. Oliver recognized him immediately.

"I was wondering when you were going to show up again," he said with a sigh.

"Good weekend at the races?" Agent Huntley smirked and gestured to the empty chair. "This won't take long, then we'll have you on your flight."

Oliver looked at his watch.

"Don't worry, we can delay the plane for a few minutes."

Oliver sat warily. "So what do you want this time?"

Huntley drummed his fingers on the manila file under his hand. "Right, let's cut to the chase. I have reason to believe that your cosy little business arrangement is getting out of control."

Oliver stared at the file and told himself to remain composed. "It's true, we were unlucky on Saturday. But I don't see why this interests you. I've done nothing wrong," he said in a measured voice. His heart was thumping.

"Look at me," said Huntley. Oliver raised his eyes and looked into the agent's pale, sunken sockets. "I don't think you really, I mean *really*, understand who your buddy is, do you?"

"I know about all the rumours. But, as far as I know, he's just another hard-nosed businessman."

Huntley snorted in amusement. "And what do you know about Michelangelo Cassoto?"

Oliver knitted his brow. "Who?"

"Mike the Nail – your buddy, Mike."

"I really don't have much to do with him, but I've met him a few times."

Huntley shook his head in dismay and flipped open the file. "Marco Romano and Mike Cassoto have been close since before Marco took control. They've been a team for nearly sixteen years. Marco has always been the brain, Mike does the dirty work. Before Marco became head of the family, he and Mike were the guys who got things done; they made more money for the family than anyone else. Marco became known as The Gent, not just because of his affectations of grandeur and a lordly lifestyle, but among other things, he has a way of putting people at ease, of getting them to lower their guard and warm to him. Any of this sounding familiar?" He didn't wait for a reply. "Mike became known as The Nail 'cause he had a habit of nailing people to things." He could see that Oliver looked sceptical. "See for yourself."

He carefully placed a line of four photographs on the table. Oliver studied the images. The first was of a man nailed to a door with about twenty large, rivet-type nails. He was covered in small cuts and his stomach had been sliced open. His intestines spilled out and hung from him. There was blood everywhere. The second photo showed dismembered arms and a penis nailed to a wall above a body in a pool of blood.

Oliver felt ill and pushed the other images away without looking at them. "Jesus, I've only seen stuff like that in a movie."

"The first guy was someone they suspected of stealing from the family. They nailed him to the door and sliced him with a boxcutter. They finished him with the belly slash after he gave up the goods. The coroner reckoned he was alive like this for six hours. The other one was some poor guy who couldn't pay for his bets or his hookers. They did this to him for ten thousand dollars. After they put word of this on the street, they rarely had a problem with debtors."

A bead of sweat was forming on Oliver's hairline, and he wiped it with his hand. "They could be photos of any guys. You could be making all this up to scare me."

Huntley's exasperation was beginning to show. "Jesus H Christ. Wake up! Marco is extremely cunning, we don't have concrete proof he did this, but we know he did. Now, I know you think everything's gonna be hunky dory and you're only buying horses and whatever, but I'm telling you to wake up and smell the horse manure, boy. This guy is not some client you can keep on a leash. He's a parasite, who'll keep taking from you until there's nothing left." He leaned closer to Oliver.

"Marco Romano doesn't give a shit about anyone except himself, but his other great talent is that he can convince people he *does* care. *That's* why he's called The Gent. Are you with me?"

Oliver put a stunned look on his face, but fear focused his brain. His head whirled with Huntley's information, but he had to keep his eye on the ball. He did not want to end up as a photo in a dossier. He asked for a cup of coffee and a cigarette, and took a few minutes to think. His mind had never moved as quickly, even when he was making rapid assessments of animals in full flight. He drained the paper cup, placed the butt in it, and looked at Huntley.

"Would sir like anything else?" enquired the agent.

"No thank you. I'd just like to say my piece and get on my plane, unless of course you have anything to charge me with?"

"Think you're so fucking clever, huh?"

"No, I don't think I'm so fucking clever. I just want to go about my business and get myself out of all this. I'm going to secure deals to retire the horses I bought for my client. That'll conclude my business and, believe me, I've no intention ending up like the guys in those photos. I have never stolen anything from anyone, and I never will. So I really don't see what you want from me."

"What I want is your help . . ."

Oliver put his hands over his ears. "Please, don't."

"Yeah, well, you can either help voluntarily or we'll put you away with your buddies. And we will get you, you can bet on that." Huntley flicked the cup off the table, got up and opened the door. "Take him to the fucking plane," he barked to the guards.

Oliver hesitated in the doorway and spoke over his shoulder. "Good things come to those who wait patiently, Agent Huntley."

"What the fuck?"

Oliver headed down the corridor

* * *

Huntley shook his head as he watched the cocky little shit disappear. "You think you know what you're doing, don't you?" he muttered. Then he closed the door, sat down, swore at himself, pulled the voice recorder out of his pocket, listened to the meeting again and started writing his report.

Huntley felt a little more dismayed every day; race-fixing wasn't exactly what he had in mind for Marco Romano, and even then Huntley would have to hand the case over to another agency – that was not going to happen. The smug Irishman could end up like his brother, for all Huntley cared.

* * *

Oliver fastened his seatbelt and vomited into the sickbag. The stewardess brought him water. He gulped it down and resolved never to tell anyone about the photos, not even Rebecca. He didn't want to worry her. He would have to let Marco know about the meeting, but perhaps he would leave out the details.

He told himself it would all be fine once he got the stallion money. It was, after all, just a business deal. It was just about money. He was beginning to understand that now. He was starting to think more like his brother, though that was a realization that didn't really appeal to Oliver.

Chapter 45

"What the hell? I don't usually get told how to run horses by owners," said Claude, with a measure of false bravado.

Oliver raised his eyebrows. "Yeah, well that may be true when you're dealing with yuppies, tycoons or old widows, but we both know you're going to have to do it with this guy, so stop whining."

They were sitting in Claude's office on the back stretch of Churchill Downs. Oliver had called to see him an hour ago, but had to wait until Claude finished making the arrangements to transfer his operation to Belmont for the summer.

They were the only two people there. It was lunchtime and the grooms had all gone on their break; their charges were quietly munching hay and relaxing after the morning's workouts.

"That means I'll have to work a goddamn miracle to keep Boot sane and ship him alone to Maryland for the Preakness. Jesus, what a mess." He sighed and lit up a smoke. "You can be a cocky fucker," he said half-jokingly.

"Thanks, Claude. You act like this is my idea."

"You sure it isn't?"

"Very droll. Now listen, all we have to do is pull off the Preakness without fucking him up for the Belmont. I had three calls this morning from bloodstock agents. They're all sniffing for a bargain deal for different farms. I told them we'll talk after he wins the Belmont. Then we'll do a deal, take our cut, and part company with Marco. How's that sound?"

"Peachy fucking creamy. You sure it'll be that easy?"

"Well, it has been so far. Right up till last Saturday, that is.

By the way, where's Pablo? I think it's only fair to tell him what the deal is."

"He dives to the bottom of a bottle after he rides out in the morning; does that when things get bad. He'll sort himself out or I'll cut his retainer. It always worked in the past." Claude shook his head and clicked the heels of his cowboy boots together. "I shoulda known better than to take these horses. Guys like that never take the knocks and always get greedy. I got a bad feeling about this."

"Don't make me laugh, Claude. Your eyes lit up when I told you about these horses and how much we paid for them. I bet you'd even seen them at the sales. You just thought you'd have some easy money." Oliver hesitated with his mouth slightly open. "But then again, I suppose I did, too."

Claude looked up at him, surprised.

Oliver tried to be reassuring. "We'll get out of this. Just need that stallion deal."

Pablo leaned on the bar and cradled his head in his hands. The cigarette wedged in his fingers burned so low that it singed his skin, though in his inebriated state, it took a second for the pain to register. He sat up with a jolt, flicking his left arm out in a wild gesture, sending the butt sailing across the bar and down into an ice bucket. His wiry frame wavered on its high perch, and he grabbed the edge of the bar to steady himself.

The exasperated barman looked up from his newspaper. "Do I have to throw you out again, man?" he asked. Though both men knew he didn't mean it.

Rick Brown was the owner of this dank, filthy little bar in a backstreet a few blocks from Churchill Downs. He was used to Pablo's binges and actually enjoyed it when he won big and came in here with a crowd of hangers-on to blow it all on booze and girls. Today was different, though. It was always a darker vibe whenever he found the jockey alone banging on his door straight after morning workouts. But it didn't really matter, as long as he kept drinking vodka and running up a tab.

Since the race, Pablo had hit rock bottom. He normally balanced his drinking with his extraordinary talent in the saddle, but this was the last thing he needed. The public ridicule he had endured that day, coupled with the abuse from angry punters and the mauling he took from the press, had sent him hurtling over the edge. When the champagne wasn't flowing, he had nobody to turn to for help or advice. Claude didn't give a shit, unless he stopped showing up for morning work.

The jockey poured himself another shot of the sharp, clear liquid and wondered how many more he needed before he would pass out.

Rick fished the soggy butt out of the ice and flicked it into the bin. He ambled back to the storeroom, scratching his large belly and muttering to himself.

Pablo's sozzled brain registered a creaking noise behind him, followed by shuffling feet. He turned his head and tried to focus on the two men that approached and sat at the end of the bar. Their cheap tracksuits and chain bracelets rustled as they installed their stocky frames on barstools.

"S'goin'?" said Pablo, raising his glass and throwing the contents down his neck.

The two men nodded and started talking to each other in guttural tones that were just a bit too loud.

"Pity about the Derby, lost my fuckin' ass on that horse."

"Pity? A fuckin' disgrace. Lotta people lost their asses on that race. Concrete Boot? I'd like to fit that jockey up with a pair." He let out a wheezing laugh.

His companion cackled.

Pablo's head swayed as he stared at the four of them. A small warning light flickered at the back of his brain.

Without looking at the jockey, they continued. "If I was that fuckin' idiot, I'd be sure not to fuck up for the, uh Preakness and um, uh, Belmont. I'd be sure to do exactly what I was told to do."

The light started flashing brightly, causing his head to thump.

"Fuck yeah, if I was told to hold back in the Preakness and save the horse for a big win in New York, that's exactly what I'd do."

Both men swiveled their heads in unison and stared at the petrified Brazilian, who was sobering up fast, his heart pounding, adrenaline forcing its way around his system.

The storeroom door swung open and Rick sauntered back in, carrying a crate of sodas. He eyed the newcomers suspiciously. "You guys want a beer?"

"Say, is this Dick's Tavern?"

Rick cocked his head to one side and raised an eyebrow. "Sign outside says Rick's Tavern."

"No, the sign outside says ick's Tavern. You a Rick or a Dick?" He cackled and nudged his friend. As they shuffled past Pablo towards the door, he added, "Must have gone off track somewhere and fucked everything up."

"Assholes," said Rick to the slamming door.

Pablo chain-smoked for half an hour before calling a cab. When he was alone in his apartment, he called Claude. "Are we running in the Preakness, Boss?"

"Has Oliver been talking to you?"

"No, Boss. I, I heard a rumour."

"Sleep it off and get your ass here before evening stables. We've got a change in plan to deal with." The line went dead.

Pablo lit a cigarette and flopped onto his sofa. He wondered if he should just drive straight to the Mexican border after he slept off the booze, then he remembered his car was at the track. The cigarette burned down to his fingers again as he fell into a comatose state.

* * *

Two weeks later, Claude was sitting on a borrowed horse, to give himself a better view of the morning's workouts at Pimlico racetrack in Maryland. Racehorses milled about on the dirt, their rippling bodies throwing long shadows across the track in the sunny spring morning. Some were warming up slowly, trotting or cantering on the outside rail, others breezing down the inside rail straining their riders' arms to the maximum. All the runners were having a final, short blowout before the Preakness tomorrow.

Concrete Boot had worked alone before the sun rose and was now safely back in his stable, but his trainer wanted to observe the opposition. When the spectacle was over and the horses walked to their barns under a fog of sweat, he followed them off the track, dismounted, and threw the reins to the animal's owner.

"Thanks, that was worth it," he said to the rugged, middle-aged Virginian, who made a living using his horse to escort runners to the start.

"Anytime, Claude, I reckon your ole' hoss'll win by a country mile."

"You and half the State," he muttered, walking away, his boots crunching on the gravel.

He checked on Boot, made a call to Oliver, and was about to make his way to the car park, when a golf cart whirred around the corner and stopped in front of him. The security guard driver was accompanied by the Track Manager, Bob Green.

He looked at Claude. "Mr. Duvall," he said, with a serious tone. "Can you accompany me to my office?"

"Why so formal, Bob? What's going on?" said Claude, sliding onto the cart.

Not another word was said until they were alone in Green's office.

"The Kentucky Horseracing Board sent this report. It arrived by courier this morning." He opened an A4 size envelope on his desk and took out two copies of a urine analysis report.

Claude read the horse name on the top of the sheet and instantly knew what was going to follow.

Green allowed Claude to read the report before he said his piece. "Mr. Duvall, I have been instructed to escort you from the premises, and to inform you that pending the outcome of disciplinary action by the KHRB, you are required to relinquish your trainers' licence. Who will you nominate as your replacement?"

"Ricky'll take over. How long will they give me?"

"I'd say it'll be six months. The ban will apply to every State." Green's mask of formality began to slip. "Shit, Claude, it's a damn shame. All you've done for racing the last decade." He chewed his lip. "But I gotta tell you: the powers that be are pissed. I mean really pissed. The fine'll be big and there's talk they'll try to slap you with a lifetime ban . . . Unless you tell them where you get the stuff. There's talk that people are pushing to establish a federal body to deal with this kind of thing. They'll want to make an example of you."

Claude rolled his eyes and shrugged resignedly. "So, I'll have to play ball to keep playing ball? They get one positive after ten years, and they threaten to kick me out? Well fuck, I guess you're only as good as your last winner round here."

"I feel for you, Claude, I really do. God knows, everyone's giving needles to their horses, but they've targeted you. They got a positive and they're freaked out. Results say this is some kind of spider venom. That's some weird shit, Claude. Makes racing look bad."

"That's weird shit, alright. Maybe I had an arachnid problem in Kentucky. I always said those barns are too old and dirty."

Green gave him a deadpan expression. Claude decided not to push his luck. He thanked Green for his candour and retreated. The security guard followed him to the car park and watched him drive through the gates. On the road, Claude called his lawyer and told him everything. Then he made another call.

Chapter 46

Oliver staggered and fell against the kitchen table in Rebecca's apartment. The phone was still pressed to his ear. He wanted to be sick, but he summoned up the willpower to continue the conversation. He lowered himself to the floor and sat cross-legged on the tiles. "How did it happen? I mean, why the fuck would you take such a stupid chance with a good horse?"

"Oliver, I know what I'm doing. I don't take stupid chances. I just want to find out how the hell they knew what to test for. I'm the only one in the world who uses this, you know. It's cutting edge stuff."

"Stop, Claude. I really don't care. I can't believe you doped Painter, especially after what I said to you about steroids."

"What did you think? That you buy three horses and they're all just that good?" He laughed, "Hell, I bet you thought you were that good, huh?" He thought for a second. "To be honest, you are. Boot's the best I've ever trained, Shadow's a speed machine, and Painter's gutsy and game, but they all need a helping hand. Anyway, it's done now. I've got a good lawyer on the job. I guess they'll ban me for six months, then I'll start up with a better chemist."

"Ban you? Ban you? Are you fucking stupid? Marco'll do a lot more than ban you."

There was silence on the line.

"Claude, did you give that stuff to Boot? Are we looking at another positive?"

"Boot's clean. You have my word."

Oliver laughed nervously. "Your word?"

263

"Look, that stuff is basically a cocktail: venom from some South American spider, mixed with stuff from a toad. Don't ask me how I get it. It's very expensive, but it's like a narcotic painkiller on steroids. They just zip along hard and fast if you get the dose right. You only need a tiny shot and it's untraceable, unless you're looking for it specifically. But there's one side effect. In some animals and humans with highly . . ."

"Wait – humans?" Oliver cut in.

"Oh, you don't wanna know. Anyway, it can induce a kind of psychosis, sends them a bit nuts. So naturally, I never gave any to Boot. Besides, there's not a horse in the country to beat him. Pablo's gonna have some fuckin' job to make second look genuine tomorrow."

"Well, he'd better do it. Marco's not going to be happy if we screw this one up. Hey, will they ban Painter, or just strip her of the race?"

"I'd say they'll ban her for a few months. And we'll lose the prize money."

"Shit, I hadn't thought of that. What about the betting money?"

"That usually stands. It's too difficult to know who bet what – the money has all changed hands, and it'd be impossible to get anyone to return their winnings. Besides, nobody who bet against her would have kept a losing ticket."

"Jesus, I hope so. Or else you and I are going to be in a world of shit. In fact, we may be already. Remember what happened to my brother?"

"What the fuck has that got to do with anything?"

Oliver thought he had probably gone too far, so he left the question hanging and ended the call. He sat there on the floor and waited for Rebecca to return from her shift. Five minutes later, he realised what needed to be done. He swallowed hard and punched the numbers.

"How's it going, my friend?" said Marco.

Oliver blurted it all out as quickly as he could without sounding ridiculous. He told Marco everything, including the likely punishments for Claude and Painter. There was silence at the other end.

"I can't believe it. I just can't believe it. He, er, he swears he hasn't given anything to Boot," offered Oliver, purely for the sake of saying something. He needed a response from the boss.

"My friend, we need to talk. Get yourself down here tomorrow morning, OK?"

"Er, what about the Preakness? I was going to fly to Baltimore tomorrow."

"Plans change, I need you here. Besides, we'll watch it together on TV with a bottle of wine."

"OK."

"Call Mike with your flight time, he'll pick you up."

"Will do."

The line went dead.

Marco tossed the phone onto his desk. He had a dark look in his eyes.

"What's up, Boss?" said Mike, standing almost to attention.

Marco studied the bookshelves, then his eyes wandered around to the fireplace. Eventually, he turned his gaze to Mike and told him the story.

"Looks like we're going to change the plan earlier than I thought. I had an idea a while back, now's the time to give it a go. Tomorrow, do the other thing first, but keep the tool in the car. Then pick Oliver up from the airport. Drive him somewhere quiet."

"Then what?"

Marco told him exactly what was to happen.

Mike took it all in. Marco stood. "I'm fuckin' starving. You want a sandwich?"

Mike shrugged and followed Marco into the kitchen. As Marco pulled things out of the fridge, Mike spoke his mind. "And if Oliver fucks it up or goes to the Feds?"

Marco stared at him. "Tidy up. He disappears. I don't give a fuck how you do it, but I don't want a trace of him ever found. Understand?"

Mike smirked. "I get it."

"One more thing," he waved a carving knife at Mike. "You don't do shit till I give the order."

Mike looked confused. "Sure thing, Boss. Like always."

Chapter 47

Rebecca got home to find Oliver stretched out on the sofa, music blaring from the stereo. She kicked off her boots, padded over to the sofa, snuggled up beside him, and caressed his hair. "You still stressed about the race tomorrow, hon?"

Oliver snapped out of his trance. "What? Oh," he looked at her as if he didn't recognize her. "The shit's hit the fan," he mumbled.

She sat up and gave him a worried look. After he told her the latest events and Marco's instructions, the look became etched on her face.

"Holy shit, that's a big deal. The dope test, I mean. Spider and toad venom? Claude's a tricky bastard."

"He wouldn't tell me much about it, or how it works, except that it can make some horses and humans go a bit nuts."

"He actually said that?" She thought for a moment. "The toad venom is basically known as Bufotinine, which contains a by-product of dopamine. That acts in a number of ways, but basically it's like adrenaline. The thing is, it's also a bit like LSD. People lick toads to get high, or they collect the venom, dry it, and smoke the residue."

Oliver sat up, looking puzzled. "Are you serious? Licking toads? I've heard it all now. Imagine if you were stopped by the cops and found in possession of toads!"

Rebecca chuckled nervously. "Bizarre but true. It gets the horses feeling euphoric and hypes them up; no wonder some go psychotic."

Oliver shrugged. "I suppose we've all had an occasional fit

of paranoia after too much indulging. I'd hate to see a horse get like that."

"Yeah, they wouldn't even know it was the effect of a drug, it'd just drive them nuts if they were a bit that way inclined anyway." She shook her head. "But I can't figure what spider venom has to do with it. That's new – must be difficult to harvest. This is serious, hon, they'll nail Claude to the wall for this."

Oliver gave her a funny look; a shiver crept up his spine. "I have to admit, I'm a bit freaked out by this meeting tomorrow. Especially after being hassled by Huntley again."

"Do you think you should call him?"

"Who, Huntley?" Oliver looked aghast. "No fucking way! I'll just have to go and see what Marco wants to do. I'll tell him Huntley approached me again. I have to do that. If he ever found out from someone else, I'd be screwed. That airport was way too packed, somebody might have seen me with the cops. Don't worry, Bec, the horse'll win the Belmont, I'll get that stallion deal and we'll get away from Marco. Then we'll get married."

She smiled. "Seriously, though. You need to get away from this guy."

"I know, I know."

Rebecca got up and grabbed two beers from the fridge, and they lay together sipping away in silence for a few minutes. At last she said, "When this whole thing is over, we should travel. I want to get out of Lexington – for a while, anyway. Would you be up for it?"

Oliver raised his eyebrows. "Would I be up for it? Damn right, Bec! I'd love to, but I thought you couldn't get that kind of time off."

"I'm thinking of taking a sabbatical. I'm tired of all this shit. This season's a bitch. The only break I've had since January was two days for the Oaks and Derby, and nothing but politics and bullshit at work."

"Cool, I'd love to do that, and I could afford to now, after Rich's will." He kissed her and stroked her hair. "I thought you couldn't bear to leave your job?"

"We'll take off and have an adventure! Nothing like it to clear the mind."

"It'd be great to see India. Or New Zealand."

They had a few more beers and talked about far-off places they would go.

* * *

At three am, the door to room 36 of a pleasant roadside motel about three miles from Pimlico racetrack was opened silently with a passkey. The tall lean man, dressed in a cheap crumpled suit, slithered into the room and eased himself into a chair facing the bed. He pulled a pistol from his jacket. His narrow, sunken eyes squinted in the darkness as he slowly screwed a silencer onto the weapon. He let the piece rest on his lap, and lit a cigarette.

* * *

Claude was alone in bed. He rarely had a girlfriend, and his wife had left him four years ago, tired of being a horse widow and frustrated by their inability to have children. His dreams were not always rosy and he rolled in his slumber and imagined that he had left a butt burning in the ashtray. The trainer scratched himself and cursed; he always needed to get up to piss during the night.

He stretched his arm out and turned on the bedside light. He groggily sat up, rubbing his eyes, and only then did it occur to him that there really was fresh smoke in the room. He looked up and saw a man who resembled a tall skinny rodent, staring at him with narrow black eyes. Claude was so startled that he threw himself back against the wooden headboard.

"Who the fuck are you?" he screamed. "What the fuck you think you're doing?"

The man contorted his face into a grimace that was supposed to be a smile. "Chill out, man. Here, help yourself." He tossed Claude the packet of cigarettes and let his hand fall onto the pistol. Claude noticed the silenced weapon. A feeling of panic began to engulf him. With trembling hands, he lit up and inhaled urgently.

The man began stroking the cold steel weapon as he spoke.

"OK, let's not fuck around. You don't know me, but I bet you can guess why I'm here."

"Concrete Boot?" he mumbled. He really hated calling the horse by his full name.

"If that horse fucks up the plan, you can bet your ass you'll be in a world of shit. Understand?"

Claude nodded between drags, ash from his cigarette dropping onto his bare stomach.

"Good." The man's fingers kept caressing the gun. "And you better make sure Concrete Boot doesn't ever test positive. If that happens, you won't just get nailed by the horseracing cops, know what I mean?"

Claude nodded again, far too petrified to even grunt an answer.

The man picked up the gun and made a show of fondling it, before he placed it in his inside pocket. "Keep the cigarettes," he said, getting up to leave. "And don't even think of calling the cops. Go back to sleep and worry about your horses."

Claude watched him slip out and close the door without a sound. He turned out the light, went to the window and peered out of a crack in the curtains to watch the man drive off, but he couldn't see anything. He collapsed on the bed and lay there wondering what had possessed him to agree to train for a man like Marco Romano; after all, he had heard the rumours.

He searched his mind and had to admit to himself that it was probably the same reason he backed up his considerable abilities with whatever cutting-edge illegal drugs he could get his hands on. Like he often said to his closest buddies, "If you're not cheating, you're not trying" – and Claude wanted to win at all costs.

The three horses Oliver had picked out looked to be the best ammunition he would have that year. But this extra shit that came along with them was getting beyond a joke. Things'll have to change after this racing season, he promised himself.

PART III

Chapter 48

Next day – the third Saturday in May 2006 – when he should have been getting himself and Rebecca to Pimlico for the Preakness, Oliver found himself alone on the noon flight to Newark. He prepared a list of the farms that might be in a position to purchase the breeding rights to Boot, and placed stars beside those that had already made enquiries.

He wanted to hold out until after the Belmont before discussing figures, but given the animal's pedigree, ability and the fact that the whole racing world widely regarded him as the real winner of the Kentucky Derby, Oliver was beginning to think ten million dollars would not be unrealistic in the current economic climate. More importantly, it would give Marco a nice profit.

For ten million, the buyers would need to impregnate 130 odd mares every year for the first three years at a fee of thirty thousand dollars to make the money back before the horse ever had progeny running on the track. That way, even if produced bad runners, nobody would lose – except the breeders who sent mares to him, but those were the chances you took in this game. Oliver knew he could seal the deal if he won the Belmont.

Oliver pondered the idea of giving Marco his own share of the money. It was possible that Marco would demand it anyway, but by offering to concede it now, Oliver would appear to be sacrificing to give Marco more in return. It was definitely not something his brother would ever have considered, but a gesture he hoped would help to ease him out of the partnership. After all, if it was just business, then a bonus and a cancellation of all debts would surely be the end of things?

He waited outside the terminal. Out of the corner of his eye, he saw the white Cadillac cut another driver off, steal into a parking space, and stop abruptly. He jumped in.

Mike grunted at him.

Oliver gave him a strange look as he flicked the car into gear and pulled away. "How's it going? I suppose you know we've had a couple of setbacks."

"Shut the fuck up."

"What's up?" said Oliver, staring at him in disbelief. He noticed a few tiny stains on Mike's collar. It looked like he had spilt tomato sauce on his shirt.

Mike turned the radio on and they drove in silence. Oliver stared at the road. His feet touched off something in the footwell, and looking down, he saw a nail gun wrapped in clear plastic. The stains on it were definitely not pasta sauce. Oliver started to sweat.

"Mike, what's going on? Where we going?"

No answer. He eventually pulled the car up on a leafy road in the woods. Oliver recognized it as the same spot where Mike had first told him about the cops and keeping his mouth shut. Panic crept up his spine as Mike turned off the engine but left the radio blaring. *Stealers Wheel: Stuck in the Middle With You* chimed from the speakers. Oliver couldn't help himself but think of some film where a guy gets tortured with this song playing in the background. He took a deep breath and willed himself calm.

Mike turned in his seat to directly face Oliver, and leaned in so close that Oliver could feel breath on his face.

"You remember this place, don't you?"

Oliver nodded.

"There's been a change of plan."

"What kind of change?"

"Nothing much. It's like this. Painter has a new job to do, seeing as how she can't race no more."

"She'll be able to race in a month or two . . ."

Mike jabbed his finger at Oliver's face. "Shut the fuck up and listen. You gotta take her away from the track. Somewhere nice and quiet, then make arrangements to fly her to Ireland."

Oliver frowned. "But . . ."

Mike ignored him. "So, you take her to a quiet place, book the flight, then a day before she goes, someone'll give you a package that you'll put inside her."

Oliver was lost. "What?" He interrupted again. "You want me to put something *inside* her? What the fu–! What's that supposed to mean?"

"Inside her!" Mike roared. "I don't give a fuck if you stick it up her ass or shove it down her throat. Get your little vet chick to help you figure it out. Now let me finish."

Oliver nodded gravely, trying to digest what he was being told.

"You go with her on the plane, and take the package out at the other end – again, somewhere quiet. Someone'll take it off you. That's all you gotta do. You make sure it goes smooth. Then you get your ass back here, go to the sales, and buy more females. Nothing too expensive." He wagged his finger in Oliver's face. "Then we fill 'em up and send 'em over. You'll buy them for a price and you get to make commission at 15%; that'll be your end so it's legit on paper, OK? It'll be cool, simple, and everybody makes money." He smiled at a bewildered Oliver.

"Er, right. So, um, what's in the package?"

"She's a useless fuckin' mule, so now we're going to use her as one."

"Okaay. But what's in the package? Is it big? Heavy? Fragile?"

Mike smiled. "I figured you'd ask that, and I'm gonna fuckin' tell you. The package is that white shit you like to put up your nose at the weekend or whenever I give it to you."

Oliver turned pale.

"You don't like it? Tough shit. You don't have to know what it is, you don't have to handle it or open the package or touch it. Just put it inside her and send her to Ireland. That's all you gotta do."

He could see Oliver's jaw hanging open. "Hey, my friend, don't worry about it. Plans change, is all. This is the new deal, but it'll be OK. Only don't do anything stupid, you know what I'm saying? You remember our little chat a while back? Well, we know you're a guy that's honest, loyal, trustable. That's why you get an important job like this. Just don't freak out." He smiled warmly and clapped a hand on Oliver's shoulder. "Aahh, you'll be fine. Just remember one thing: if she fails *this* dope test, you can kiss your ass goodbye."

Oliver swallowed. The sweat was pouring off him.

"See that gun by your feet?"

"Yeah."

"You could easily get nailed by one like that."

Mike gave him a deadpan stare. Oliver closed his mouth and regained his composure. He thought now would be a good time to mention Huntley.

"Not a problem. I, I'll get it done, but something happened which may cause a problem."

Mike was surprised. "Oh yeah? What's that?"

"Agent Huntley accosted me again. At the airport, last time I was flying back to Kentucky. He pulled me into a room and started asking bullshit questions like, had we fixed the Kentucky Derby. I explained the stupidity of anyone wanting to throw the Derby." He shrugged. "That was it. I think he was just trying to scare the shit out of me to get me talking."

"Get you talking about what?"

"Search me."

"You said nothing?"

"There's nothing to say. But, I did forget to mention the racing plans for today and the Belmont." Oliver forced a smile, in an effort to relieve the tension.

Mike laughed. "You're a smart guy, you know that? C'mon, you gotta tell the boss about that cocksucker Huntley."

As they drove through the leafy New Jersey suburbs, Oliver thought about his new mission. There was something he couldn't figure out.

"Mike, correct me if I'm wrong, but aren't people normally trying to smuggle drugs into America?"

Mike answered in an irritated voice, without taking his eyes off the road. "Don't do too much thinking, OK? Don't try to make sense of things. The fuckin' reasons don't concern you. What concerns you is getting the job done. And if you do it properly, you'll make money, so you got nothing to complain about. So shut the fuck up, already."

Oliver found himself thinking about the drug scandal in his brother's airline and the silent Italian steward. He had been so wrapped up in the racing he hadn't even bothered to check with James Foster what was going on.

These guys never issue direct orders. They use middle men. Richard's words echoed in his brain. Marco had definitely put the guy on Rich's plane, and Rich either let him do it or encouraged him, and he ended up dead. Now Marco wanted pretty much the same thing from the other brother.

Oliver knew he was in deep shit, and if anything went wrong, he would share his brother's fate. He resolved to push the illegality of the matter out of his mind and make calm rational decisions, always keeping the end goal in sight. A bit like he did at the yearling sales. Oliver would dearly have loved to spend more time mulling it over, but before he knew it, the large gates were lumbering open like a hungry mouth to admit them to the lion's den.

Marco greeted them in the hall with warm embraces. Oliver was taken aback by this affability, considering the chat he had had with Mike. As Marco released him, he noticed an almost imperceptible twitch in the big man's right eye. Mike responded with a less-than-subtle nod. The orders had come from the top.

"My man," he said. "I hope that jockey does the right thing today."

"Me too, Marco."

Mike cut in. "Say, Boss, wait till you hear this. Tell him," he said, nudging Oliver.

"Oh yeah. The Feds gave me some abuse again. The same Agent actually: guy named Huntley. He interrogated me at the airport. I think he thought if he could make me shit myself, I'd tell him everything."

Marco cocked his head to one side and looked quizzical. "Everything? What everything?"

The eyes burned into Oliver.

"He reckons we're fixing races. Specifically, that we threw the Derby."

"Can you believe it? If only they knew the shit that caused us." He laughed out loud, but stopped abruptly. "Mike, go change your clothes. Right fuckin' now," he said, staring at him.

"What? Oh. OK, Boss."

Marco nodded.

Mike spun on his heel and marched out of the house. Marco threw his arm around Oliver and guided him into the TV room. "We'll watch it in here."

They found Robert sprawled on the sofa watching a horror film. He was wearing a T-shirt and shorts, his bare feet were on the coffee table. The dazed depression on his face indicated the previous night had been a long one.

"Hi, man," he said to Oliver, without averting his gaze from the screen.

"Turn that shit off. Put the racing on," said Marco, walking behind the bar to grab a bottle of wine and three glasses. He pointed to a platter of sandwiches that stood on the bar.

"Butler's off: self-service today. Sit back, relax, and help yourself," he said, installing himself on a leather recliner.

Oliver looked around the room and saw an elaborate stereo system and enormous TV, but was struck by a bizarre-looking abstract painting above the fireplace. He couldn't help himself but stare at the violent composition of bold colours, which looked as if they had been hurled onto the canvas. The deep-pile white carpet underfoot and the over-varnished wood of the bar combined to give the room a garish feel that was in sharp contrast to the elegant serenity of Marco's office next door.

Oliver sat on a large armchair as Robert hurriedly changed the channel.

"Shit, I totally forgot about the race," said Robert.

"You know, I almost did myself," said Oliver, without thinking.

Marco gave him a sharp look.

"What time's it on?" asked Robert.

"Five-thirty." Oliver looked at his watch. It was nearly four. The next couple of hours would be nerve-wracking. Oliver resolved to get a little tipsy to help time slip by. When Marco poured him a glass, he gulped down the Italian red.

The muted drone of TV racing pundits flooded the room. Oliver rolled his eyes. "These guys talk some awful shit," he said.

Marco chuckled. "I thought I was the only one who thought that."

"Oh no. Jesus, it's boring. There's very little informed comment, and they try to make everything into an emotional human-interest story."

"Yeah, and what about all those guys who write their forecasts in the paper? They're like those goddamn stock market analysts. If they really knew what was going to win, they'd just bet on it, instead of telling everyone else what to do. In fact, Robert, turn the sound off till the race starts."

The young Romano did as he was told. He tossed the remote onto his father's lap and helped himself to sandwiches.

Oliver felt the alcohol begin to soothe his nerves. "So, d'you do anything mad last night?" he said, picking up a sandwich.

Robert perked up. "Working on this hot chick. Smokin' hot. Took her clubbing." A huge grin spread over his face.

"Don't get him started. He's doing nothing but calling her and sending messages. Phone bill's goin' to be huge," said Marco, with a smirk.

"You see what I have to put up with." Robert cast a thumb in his father's direction. "Hey, it's been a while since we did anything. What do you say we go out tonight, after the race? Hopefully, we'll have something to celebrate."

"I don't know . . ."

"C'mon. It'll be fun. We'll stay around Jersey, shoot some pool."

Oliver shrugged. "Yeah, OK."

"Good idea," said Marco. "In fact, book yourselves a hotel, have a blast. I don't want you guys turning up here hammered in the middle of the night."

"Cool, thanks, Dad." He gave a thumbs-up sign to Oliver.

Oliver forced a smile.

Marco found a *Daily Racing Form* and rustled it open to the correct page. Oliver pondered the practicalities of getting any kind of foreign object into an animal in such a way that it could be retrieved again. A thought occurred to him.

Just then, Robert's phone rang. He got up to leave as he answered it. "Hey, babe! S'up? Hold on a sec."

Marco took his nose out of the paper. "Again? You're like a lovesick puppy."

Robert blushed as he padded out of the room and closed the door behind him.

"I tell you, he's gone all soppy," said Marco. "I don't know. Kid's soft like his mother, I guess."

Oliver cocked his ear and could just about make out the soft humming of Robert's voice behind the door.

Marco wore a distant, melancholy expression.

Oliver seized the opportunity to voice his fears.

"Marco, I need to have a serious talk with you."

"What?" The eyes went on full beam. "What about?"

Oliver pursed his lips and spoke in a matter-of-fact tone. "About this new deal, new direction for Painter Girl."

Marco's face darkened.

Oliver averted his eyes and continued, "I'm not sure it's even possible. We can't put the drugs down her throat and expect her to shit them out like people do; a horse's intestines are too complicated, they're prone to blockages and painful spasms. And we can't put it up her ass, because she'll eject it. The only possibility would be to try to insert them into her uterus, but she's never been pregnant. Our only chance is to take some time, let her relax and give her some hormones, but it's risky. Is it really worth it?"

Marco' face was thunderous. He stood up, glanced at the closed door and crooked his finger at Oliver, who stood to face his boss. Marco touched his finger to his lips. Then he reached out with both hands.

Oliver felt a sudden rush of adrenaline but was paralysed like an animal caught in headlights. Marco calmly opened the buttons of Oliver's shirt and looked at his bare chest, before running his hands around the Irishman's back and neck. Then he patted down both legs and suddenly squeezed Oliver by the balls with his right hand.

His eyes bulged as a sharp pain shot up into his guts. He saw nothing but savage anger on Marco's face.

"Who the fuck do you think you are?" Marco's voice started off as a whisper, but ascended into a roar that filled the room within a few syllables. He jabbed his left index finger at Oliver's cheek. "Don't you ever mention product to me again. EVER. You shut the fuck up. Stop asking stupid questions. Do what you're fuckin' told and everything'll be alright. Don't do too much thinking, or things have a habit of getting very fucked up. I mean," he paused momentarily and shrugged. "What happened to your brother was a waste of a good businessman."

Oliver stood staring at the black eyes. He found himself looking at a vicious thug; the kind of guy who would nail somebody to a wall to make a point. Or at least give the order to have it done. Now was not the time to think of such things. Got to stay focused.

"Calm down, Marco. Please. I'm just discussing things, like always. There's no need to get so mad. Whatever happened to relax and enjoy the ride?"

Oliver's straightforward, innocent reply appeared to knock the wind out of Marco's sails. It seemed to throw him; like he wasn't used to people reacting like this. He relaxed his grip on Oliver's testicles. Oliver supposed most guys he intimidated either panicked and began babbling, or caved in and cowered like bullied schoolboys.

"Nothing. The ride has changed, is all. You can still enjoy it, but you gotta stay relaxed. That's important."

Oliver let out a breath. "It really wasn't necessary to open my shirt and grab me," he said, reaching a hand down to cradle his crotch.

"Yeah, well, you can't be too careful in my business. Besides, it wasn't necessary to question me here and now about this. Make it happen. OK."

"Consider it done."

Marco gave him a warm smile and clapped a hand on his shoulder. "Good man. Now do up your shirt."

Oliver shrugged resignedly. "I suppose if I was in your line of work, I'd have done the same thing," he said, closing his buttons.

"You know, they've been trying to get in here for years. Nobody ever has. They can't get a warrant, and thanks to Luigi my security guy, they can't sneak in, either. Assholes," he said with a satisfied grin. He replenished Oliver's glass and sat down.

Oliver took a long swallow of wine and congratulated himself for remaining calm, but he desperately wanted Robert to return and provide a welcome diversion until the runners went to post for the Preakness.

* * *

Robert closed the door and leaned against the wall, whispering sweet nothings into his phone. God, he really liked this one. She was so cute and didn't mind that he was Marco Romano's son — she never asked awkward questions. He was distracted by the roar of his father's voice behind the door.

"Hold on a sec, babe." Jamming the phone against his stomach, he pushed his ear to the keyhole. Robert listened to his father attack Oliver, and somewhere in the back of his mind a deeply repressed memory stirred. A frown creased his forehead as he heard his father growl like a bear. He suddenly felt terribly afraid, but he couldn't fully understand why.

Oliver's matter-of-fact reply further jolted his memory. His father's voice calmed. Robert's stomach churned.

"Babe, I'm really sorry. I gotta go. I . . . I don't feel so well. Call you later?" He wandered into the kitchen, downed a glass of cold water, and sat at the table with his head in his hands, desperately trying to arrange his memories.

After several minutes, he realized the only time he had ever heard his father shout like that was some time before his mother had died. Robert remembered hearing noises from their bedroom. Bewildered, he had trotted down the corridor to investigate.

Peering through the half-open door, he saw his mother lying on the bed, his father loomed over her like an angry bear. He had his arm raised, while his words rained down in a torrent of abuse.

Robert had watched in stunned silence as his mother remained stoic and simply told her husband never to speak to her like she was one of his goons. She had a look of disgust in her eyes. Robert had wanted to go and hug his mother, but was too afraid. He retreated back to his room and took solace in the TV. Later that evening, his mother came and sat with him. She took him in her arms and cried so hard, her body shook.

Robert remained in the kitchen, thinking. Eventually, he summoned up the courage to go and sit in the same room as his father. And when he finally opened the door to the den, he did so for Oliver's sake. Otherwise, he would simply have gone upstairs and played a computer game.

* * *

Oliver was relieved to see Robert, though the young guy looked subdued, not like someone who'd just spend half an hour on a lovey-dovey phone call. Marco had assumed command of the TV and flicked back and forth between some baseball game and the racing. Robert grabbed a cold beer from the bar, shot his father a sideways glance, and sat near Oliver. All three sat in silence, watching sports and counting the minutes until the race.

Two beers later, Robert perked up and talked continuously about where they might go that night. He said he had itchy feet all of a sudden and needed to get out.

"Holy shit, that chick's got a spell on you," said Marco.

Robert glanced at his father.

On the TV, the runners were making their way to the start. Marco clapped his hands together. "Here we go. Let's see what that jockey's made of."

Oliver crossed his fingers and prayed. If ever things needed to go to plan, it was now. He leaned forward in his seat and ogled the television.

Pablo contrived to break slowly from an inside draw and

get Boot completely covered up. He kept him boxed in against the rail, and the other jockeys were only too happy to keep the talented horse stuck in traffic until the last minute. By the time Pablo made a meal of extracting himself and swinging the horse to the wide outside to make his run, there was simply not enough time to finish any better than third. Oliver had to hand it to the Brazilian, it wasn't the most sublime piece of stopping he had ever seen, but it got the job done and didn't look suspicious. Pablo had even avoided hitting or upsetting the animal. He pulled him up shortly after the finish line and managed to look suitably disappointed for the cameras.

"Yes!" shouted Marco, punching the air, much to the surprise of his son.

"Only for a show in third. Everyone else thought he'd piss in. Easy money," said Marco triumphantly.

Oliver called Claude. The banned trainer said Ricky had reported that the horse seemed relatively calm after the race. The crowd and fanfare was nothing compared to Kentucky, and they'd left the earplugs in for the whole race, which worked like a charm.

Claude said it seemed likely he would be banned for one year and ordered to pay a thirty thousand dollar fine. He would know in a couple of weeks.

Marco watched Oliver with beady eyes. "We on for the Belmont?"

"More than likely. We'll know for sure tomorrow when he pulls out for a walk." He told Marco about the ban.

"Pah! He got off light, if you ask me. No jail time and he can still run the business over the phone." Marco waved his hand dismissively. "White-collar criminals getting looked after by the system. He gets caught giving some weird drugs to an animal, and he gets a rap on the knuckles. I know guys who'd get five to seven for less."

Marco's sense of logic didn't necessarily give Oliver any comfort, in light of the new plan.

"Any news on the stallion deal?" asked Marco.

"Nothing concrete. We'll have to wait till he wins the Belmont.

People'll probably blame today's defeat on Pablo, so the horse won't lose any face. But we need an emphatic win in New York to get the big farms interested."

"I'm sure that won't be a problem. You guys aren't going to fuck up again, right?"

"No."

* * *

Robert stared at his father and listened to him speak. He saw the animal that had bullied his mother all those years ago, not the charismatic teddy bear who looked after him and made sure that a driver was always available.

He felt a mixture of fear and anger that he had never experienced before. His life seemed bizarre and false. He needed to get out of here for a while.

"Hey, Oliver, I'm going to my room. Got some things to do. What do you say we leave in like an hour?"

"Ready when you are."

Marco looked quizzically at his son. "What've you gotta do in your room?"

"Things, Dad. Things." He padded out, leaving the door open behind him.

* * *

"He'll be talking to that girl again. Anyway," Marco raised his glass. "Well done today, you got the message across, my friend. Here's to the Belmont and the stallion deal. How much you reckon we'll make on that, anyway?"

"Five to six million – gross." He decided it was better to be conservative.

"Not quite seven-to-ten, is it?" Marco said, nodding.

Oliver forced a smile and gulped down more wine.

A few hours later, Oliver and Robert were playing pool in a quiet bar near Elizabeth. They had travelled in silence in the back seat of one of Marco's Lincolns. Robert told the driver not to wait around.

"We've got a room at a motel round the corner from Shadows," he said to Oliver, as they watched the car pull away from the kerb. "I'm thirsty, c'mon!"

* * *

Mike drove like a lunatic to get back to Marco's place. He had been curtly summoned and he hurried up the steps, burst through the door, and trotted into the office. Marco was sitting by the fireplace with a poker in his hand, jabbing it at the unlit logs in the grate.

"Call that son of mine," he said, without looking up. "Find out where they're staying. Tomorrow morning, when they're all hungover, send round two guys to give our Irish friend a reminder. Make sure they get him on his own. I don't want Robert to see it. And don't send two fuckin' idiots who'll get carried away and cripple him."

Marco stared at Mike and thrust the poker up towards his chin. "He questioned me in my house. In my fuckin' house! I thought you explained it all to him?"

Mike did not flinch, nor did he dare point out that it was Marco who had invited him to the house in the first place. "I did. I thought he took it well. A little too well, as it turns out."

"Yeah well, make sure he gets the point."

Mike nodded. "That all?"

Marco nodded back and withdrew the poker. Mike spun on his heel and left to make arrangements.

* * *

"That horse-guy McMahon's at his house again," said Rosen.

"Good. How're we doing on the listening?" asked Huntley.

"Real backed-up. It takes the guys ages to go through it and file it. There's a lot of interference. Can we get a couple of extra bodies?"

"I'll ask, but don't hold your breath."

Chapter 49

They downed beers and hammered balls around the table, but neither felt like talking very much. Both had other things on their minds. The handful of other drinkers all sat at the bar watching basketball on TV.

Robert found the click of ball-on-ball soothing, and with the steady flow of alcohol he began to relax. He needed someone to talk to, and he realized that Oliver and Rebecca were the closest thing he had to real friends. He liked his new girl, but he couldn't share this kind of information with her.

Oliver took a shot and missed. "Shit. I'm not really into this. Can't focus."

Robert took another swig of beer and decided it was now or never. "Hey, Ollie. Do you mind if I call you Ollie?"

"Er . . . No, it's OK. My brother used to call me Ollie."

"Oh, sorry."

"No, you're grand."

"Cool. It's like this . . . Ollie, be careful with my dad, OK? This afternoon, I remembered something that happened when I was younger. It's like . . . Aw shit, man, this is..." He buried his face in his hands.

Oliver looked surprised at this sudden outburst, and he placed his cue on the table. "Let's sit in a booth."

"That's better," said Robert, sliding himself into a corner seat.

Oliver faced him, looking concerned. "Go on, have another beer, take your time."

Robert finished the bottle. "Thanks, man. Look, I've been doing a lot of thinking today. One time, Rebecca asked me 'what my deal was' and I didn't get it. But I think I do now. I think I'm growing up, beginning to wake up."

Oliver looked despondently at the table as he peeled the label off his beer bottle. "You know, I think I'm doing a bit of waking up myself," he said absent-mindedly.

Robert stared at him.

"Sorry, go on," said Oliver.

"I guess you could say my deal is that I do what my dad says, mostly 'cause I'm afraid of him."

Oliver stopped peeling the label. "But you're his only son. He loves you. Surely you can talk to him?"

The young Romano put up his hand. "I've tried. Trouble is, he doesn't care. That whole California thing was just for show; it's like, even if I'd graduated, he'd have found a way to get me back at his side. This whole horse thing was just a way to get me earlier."

"But you're his son. You could've said no and stayed there, right?"

Robert looked sceptical. "I don't know, man. And the thing is, he'd have made me do it on my own, no more money or help. No more wheels being greased, probably just hassles from the cops. And see, it's like, I don't think I'm ready to be poor and free just yet. It scares me more than he does. I, like, realized about an hour ago, it's difficult to leave a gilded cage when you love the gold more than you hate captivity. And besides, he's never tried to get me to join the business. So all I have to do is stay with him." His voice trailed off and he got up and went to the restroom.

Watching him walk away, Oliver began to think that under all the bravado of youth and money, he was a frightened kid who probably badly needed his mother's affection but got only his father's money. Something in his own brain stirred and reminded him of his childhood.

When Robert returned, Oliver said, "Jesus, you *have* done some thinking. But I don't really know what to say. For me, I went my own way and my dad never really forgave me for it, but I did what I had to do. There was just no way I could have followed in my brother's footsteps." He frowned. "I'm not telling you what to do. You can do what you like, as long as you do the right thing for you and not the wrong thing for his sake." Oliver stopped speaking suddenly.

Why don't I take my own advice? He wondered. He paused for a second to regain his train of thought. "I suppose I just want to do my job and be on my way."

In truth, Oliver was so taken aback by this conversation that he didn't fully know how to react. It was better to play it safe. Robert wouldn't be the first young guy to be upset with his dad, and Marco was still his father. Robert may be afraid of him, but surely he still loved him.

Robert's phone broke the heavy silence.

"Hi, Mike," he said, looking apprehensive.

Oliver looked on, riveted. His heart suddenly beat faster.

"We're staying round the corner from Shads. Why?"

"I, er, nah, it's cool. Might just get shitfaced." He touched his nostril with a finger and looked quizzically at Oliver, who shook his head violently.

"Ollie's cool, too."

"Thanks anyway, man." He stuffed the phone back in his pocket.

Oliver's hackles were raised and he wasn't sure why. The thought of taking a few harmless lines of coke didn't excite him tonight. It wasn't just recreational fun anymore; it wasn't a seductive white powder which gave him the illusion of invincibility. It was the consumer end of a dirty business. Snap out of it, he told himself. Stay focused.

"Fuck it," said Robert. "I need more beer. It's my round. Let's try to enjoy ourselves." He sauntered up to the bar.

The night descended into a state of extreme inebriation and pathetic attempts at sinking pool balls. They were ushered out onto the street at two-thirty in the morning, and when they checked into the motel, they raided the vending machine in the lobby for stale chips and chocolate. Eventually, they passed out on the grubby twin beds and stayed that way until nearly noon.

* * *

The silver Toyota pulled up outside the motel just after nine that morning, and by eleven-thirty its occupants were getting bored. Tomo and Tito were short, heavily-muscled guys who spent every spare second lifting weights, and were ambitious enough to make their collections for Marco on time, every time. They lived spartan lives, kept a low profile, and sent a greater percentage of their take uphill. This tactic ensured that Mike and Marco took notice.

Tito was sure they would be 'made' in a couple of years. Until then, they would have to put up with this kind of shitty job. Still, boring as it was, it beat driving the boss's son around. That mission really made them sour. They didn't want to be childminders.

Tomo studied the motel – an L-shaped building on a corner lot. The access to the central courtyard was from the street perpendicular to them, and meant that any car entering had to pass by the window of the office. For this reason, Tomo elected to park opposite, facing the direction of traffic. They had a prime view of all the rooms and it would be easy to cross the road, do the job, and get the fuck out.

Tito heard his stomach growl and looked at his watch. He sighed. "I hope they make a fuckin' move soon."

"I'm fuckin' starving, too," growled Tomo.

Oliver was sprawled on the bed and had fallen asleep open-mouthed, so his lip was stuck to the pillow. He stirred a little and managed to focus on his watch. Dehydration made his head thump, but numb to thought and emotion. He could hear the drizzle of the shower, and a minute later, Robert appeared with a towel wrapped around him. "Come on man! Grab a shower, we'll get some breakfast."

"Not me," groaned Oliver. "I'm wrecked. Can you get me some water?"

Robert got him a tepid glassful from the tap. Oliver downed it instantly and held the glass out for a refill. He finished three glasses.

"Shit, man, you're in a bad way."

"Dying. Feel like I'm getting old. Need more sleep." He flopped back into the pillow.

"OK, man, I'll go get us coffee and stuff."

"Yeah," mumbled Oliver, already half asleep.

Tomo watched Robert appear, slam the door, and traverse the courtyard. "Tito, heads up." He slapped his partner on the chest with the back of his hand and Tito took his head out of the bodybuilding magazine.

"Thank fuck for that." He reached for the door handle as Robert disappeared round the corner.

"Wait!" said Tomo. "Give him a minute, in case he forgot something. We go in and out fast. He's probably gone to get doughnuts or some shit like that."

Tomo counted the seconds. "OK, let's go," he said, after two minutes. He sprung out of his seat and marched across the tarmac. Tito casually followed him, scanning around.

Oliver heard the loud banging at the door and tried to ignore it. He pulled himself out of bed, cursing Robert for locking himself out. When he turned the handle, the door flew open with such force that he was knocked to the floor. Stunned, he barely saw the two short monsters burst into the room.

"We got a message for you," one of them spat. "Do your fuckin' job."

They stood over him and started kicking. Oliver was too dazed to block the boots.

Robert ambled back towards the motel with a bag full of steaming, microwaved pizza pockets, sodas, and two large paper cups of black sludge which masqueraded as coffee. He got to the corner of the motel, stuffing a pizza into his mouth as he walked. He was just entering the courtyard, when hot molten cheese spilt down his shirt. He stopped, pulled it off in one long string and flicked it onto the ground. Out of the corner of his eye, he noticed movement.

Looking up, he saw two guys come out of his room. He pivoted and shoved his back to the wall, almost spilling the coffee. He peeked round the corner and recognised them as guys who sometimes drove him around. Robert watched them cross the road and slip into a silver car. They pulled out sedately and drove off.

He waited until the car disappeared out of view before he considered moving. He turned the key in the door, and as it opened, he could hear a different type of groan to those Oliver had been making.

Oliver was on the faded carpet, curled up in a foetal position. He was shaking and holding his groin. Tears streamed down his cheeks and he sobbed loudly. He was vaguely aware of Robert standing over him holding the coffees.

Robert tossed the bag on the bed and put down the cups. He knelt down on the floor beside Oliver and put a hand on his shoulder.

"Fuck, man. You OK? What happened?"

Oliver rolled onto his back and slowly unravelled himself. Keeping a hand clamped to his groin, he used the other to wipe the tears, sweat and snot from his face. He took a while to try and compose himself before he could speak.

"I'm pretty damn far from OK. Two fucking thugs – I think there were two of them – burst in here and gave me a reminder to do my job." He looked at Robert suspiciously, but the look of shock and terror on his face told Oliver that he didn't know anything about it, at least as far as he could be sure.

"I-I-I saw two guys leave and drive away," he said lamely. "Here, I got you these."

He offered him a coffee and pizza pocket. Oliver propped himself up against the bed. A grimace contorted his face; his entire torso was on fire and screaming with pain.

"You'll have to help me up."

Robert blinked at his friend.

Oliver raised his eyebrows. "Any time that suits you . . ."

"Oh, sorry." He sprang up, hooked his elbows under Oliver's armpits, and hoisted him onto the bed in an awkward sitting position.

The dark liquid was foul, but Oliver drank it anyway. He took little bites of the soggy pastry and stared at the carpet. A throbbing spread through his ribs.

"Thanks for helping me up. You're stronger than you look."

"Thanks. Runs in the family. Dad's like that, too."

Oliver stared at Robert in an imitation of Marco's gaze. "No. Your father looks as strong as he is. He just has a way of making you forget it . . . Until he wants to remind you."

"I, like, can't believe they did this to you. I'm gonna tell Dad about it."

Oliver looked horrified. "No fucking way!" he said, with a sudden burst of energy. "Don't say a bloody word. You'll only make things worse. The best thing you can do is go home and pretend this never happened. I'll take off to Kentucky and get things done."

"I could say something . . ."

"What? What could you say that wouldn't make things worse?" He thought for a second. "It's occurred to me that they waited for you to leave to give me the message. Specifically so you wouldn't see them. So, as far as you are concerned, you don't know anything. OK?"

Robert twirled his phone between his thumb and index finger for a while. Eventually he said, "Like, now you can see why I'm scared. I don't want to have no money and I definitely don't want a warning like this. I'm really sorry, man. It's no way to treat people. You're a good guy."

"I should be telling you how pissed off and wronged I feel, but it's just business to those guys. As they say: nothing personal. Except, it feels personal when you get a kick in the nuts."

Robert gave him a pathetic look.

"You'd better take off," said Oliver, when he had finished the coffee. "I'll try to take a bath and relax."

"You want some money for the room."

"No, I'll cover it."

Robert asked him again if he would be OK, and Oliver assured him that he would. On his way out, Robert paused at the door.

"I'm starting to wonder if that's why Dad always wants me to take a driver. It's like, if I'm driving myself around, then he has no way to keep tabs on me."

Oliver didn't reply, but thought that Robert had hit the nail on the head. The younger man slammed the door behind him.

Oliver ran himself a bath in the small tub and gingerly eased himself into it. He dearly wanted to hug Rebecca, feel her hands on his skin. He lay there thinking, trying to soak the pain and self-loathing out of his system. After a while, he decided he needed to get lost for a bit before he could face Rebecca and reality.

An hour later, he paid the bill and took a taxi to the train station. He caught the next train for New York and checked himself into the same fleabag hostel he had stayed in all those years before. It was still there, and owned by the same Chinese man. He paid the extra to rent one of only two private rooms. Shutting the door, he flopped onto the bed and squawked as he felt a dart of pain. He was back where it all started.

He turned on his phone and called Rebecca. He told her that something dramatic had happened and that he needed to think.

"My God, hon, what's up? You sound terrible. You OK?"

"I'm fine. I'll tell you everything face-to-face. I just need some time to think." He sighed. "God, Bec, I miss you. I want to be in your arms, I really do. But I've to sort out some stuff first."

"Why can't you come back? We'll sort it together."

"I know, I know. I just need to be lost for a bit."

"Am I losing you?"

"God, no! We're getting married, Bec; I want to grow old with you."

"So you can sort out whatever it is with me. Oliver, we'll do it together. We can get through anything together."

"I know that, too. I really do. It's just . . ."

Then it hit him. He went silent.

"Hello? You still there?" asked Rebecca.

How could I have been so stupid, he thought.

"Yeah, sorry, Bec," he said in a clearer, more direct tone. "Could you look in my things and find the card that Huntley gave me at Belmont?"

"I suppose," she said hesitantly. "Why?"

"I just need to check what's written on it."

She clamped the phone between her ear and shoulder as she went into their bedroom, and began rummaging through the leather folder where Oliver kept his personal things and documents relating to the horses.

"You're sure it's here? You didn't take it to Ireland?"

"I'm positive."

She found it stuffed into an envelope with a number of other business cards.

"You want the numbers, hon? I thought we agreed we weren't going to call him."

"We're not. Just tell me what it says after his name."

"Nothing, just Peter Huntley, Special Agent."

Oliver frowned. "What else does it say on the card?" He was sure it was written there.

"Not much. It lists his numbers, is all. Then there's the Bureau emblem, and DEA printed in bold capitals at the top."

Oliver suddenly felt very sick. And stupid. Very stupid. Drug Enforcement Agency. How could he have missed this?

Through the receiver, Rebecca heard a stifled curse. "Are you thinking about your brother and the planes?"

"Not really. There's more to it than that. Don't worry, Bec. I'll book a flight for tomorrow. Love you."

"Love you, too, hon. You can tell me anything, you know."

"I know. And I will."

Oliver left the hostel in the afternoon and went walking down Broadway. When he got to Times Square, the barrage of lights hit him. He felt repulsed by the vulgarity of it all; the sheer weight of neon advertising no longer left him with a sense of awe. Now it just felt wasteful and unnecessary. Shaking his head, he descended into the subway tunnel.

As he hustled his way through the crowded corridors, he was struck by the dirt of the place. Everywhere was filthy and reeked of decay. Even the old steel support struts were rusty, and looked barely capable of stopping the city from crashing into the tunnels. He took a train for the financial district and wandered around.

An hour later, he found himself crossing the Brooklyn Bridge on foot. He stopped on the walkway and scanned the Brooklyn shoreline, trying to pick out the restaurant where he had first met Marco. It felt like a lifetime ago. He could not locate the long window with the famous view. A group of runners sailed past him on the walkway. They made the floorboards creak as he watched them bound along the long span.

He decided to turn back, retracing his steps with his hands stuffed into his jeans pockets and his eyes following the steel cables. As he passed underneath the enormous pillars, his eyes followed the cables up to their resting places atop the stone structure. The bridge was badly in need of renovation. Out of the corner of his eye, he caught sight of the Manhattan Bridge, trains rattling across its vast expanse of iron. It was looking shook, too. The old beating heart of America was aging and getting a little shabby; the cracks were definitely visible.

Back on the street, he walked aimlessly around Chinatown. After a while, he bought a bowl of noodles and a bottle of Chinese beer, and ate them sitting outside. He watched two teenage boys at a nearby table, chattering and laughing, both eating plates of dumplings. The larger boy wore a high school football shirt and was stealing his friend's food, while vigilantly guarding his own bowl.

Suddenly, and without warning, it all became obvious and Oliver knew exactly what he wanted to do. The plan meshed together in his mind. He had all the pieces in there all along; they suddenly just fitted together. He was euphoric and felt alive. His senses crackled, and he found himself smiling again.

Rebecca would be the judge of it. He knew it would be a lively discussion; the thought of it made him grin. Plus, her veterinary input was vital, but he knew enough about horses to be fairly sure the plan would work.

He got up and marched down the street, buzzing with a sudden energy.

"You're gonna fall, you greedy motherfucker," he said out loud.

An elderly Chinese man sitting on a doorstep gave Oliver a puzzled look as he strode past. The sun had gone down and darkness descended on the city, but not on Oliver. He treated himself to dinner in an up-market restaurant, drank a half bottle of expensive wine, and went back to the hostel. He felt absolutely no desire to go clubbing and get high. He had more important things to do.

Chapter 50

In the Arrivals hall of Lexington's Bluegrass Airport, Oliver grabbed Rebecca like he never wanted to let go again. The pain in his ribs made him wince, but he pushed it out of his mind. He hugged her and smelled her hair. He was glad to be back.

Rebecca wrapped her tanned, toned arms around him. His enthusiasm reassured her.

"God, I love you, Bec. I'm sorry about yesterday," he said, holding her face in his hands.

"You kinda had me worried. Promise me you won't do that again? I'm here for you. You can tell me anything."

"I know, Bec. I won't."

"Better not!" She playfully thumped him on the chest. He grimaced.

"Holy shit! Are you hurt?"

He took a deep breath and put his arm around her, guiding her towards the door. "I've got a lot to tell you. But first I need a shower and a cold beer."

As they got into her SUV, Oliver watched a grey sedan roll past with two men in it. The passenger averted his gaze when his eyes met Oliver's. Oliver felt cold again; grey car, grey men, Bluegrass International Airport carpark. He sat in and closed his eyes.

"Oh, that's just the best," he said, cautiously stretching himself out on the sofa in a large bathrobe, with an ice-cold beer in his hand. Rebecca held a bag of tortilla chips and a beer, and sat cross-legged on the coffee table facing him. "So what happened?" she said.

"I woke up, Bec. I woke up. Till now, I'd been asleep in my own world of horses and races. All this Marco gangster stuff was like a dream. Jesus, it was like comic relief watching other people's reactions to me and him, and to Robert. Not anymore. Reality came knocking, or rather kicking, last weekend."

He took a sip of beer and told her about Marco's change of plan, the nail gun in Mike's car, and how Marco had assaulted him out of the blue. He told her absolutely everything, up to the point that he and Robert took off to get drunk. She sat with a stunned look on her face.

"That's why you wanted Huntley's card."

"Yeah, I couldn't remember for sure if he was DEA."

"So you think he's on to you?"

"There's no way he could know about the new deal. But he must be tracking Marco. I suppose we can assume that Marco deals drugs in a big way. I've no doubt any more about the whole thing with Rich and the planes. It had to be him."

"What I can't figure is, why would anyone want to ship drugs out of America to Ireland?"

Oliver snorted in amusement. "You know, I asked Mike that same question."

"I don't suppose he gave you an explanation?"

"He told me not to ask. But I'm guessing it's one of the usual reasons – supply and demand; growth market; superior product. Money, greed. Blah, blah, blah."

Oliver stopped and pondered. "You know, I could be wrong, but I swear Robert must have heard Marco roar at me when we were in the house."

"What?"

"He was a bit weird for the rest of the afternoon, and later that night he got all emotional and told me to be careful with his dad. I mean, it's possible he was standing right outside the door."

"You're kidding," she said, with arched eyebrows.

"No. He started telling me about how he feels trapped, but doesn't have the willpower to get himself out."

"Or maybe he just doesn't want to."

"I don't know, Bec. I mean, we were pretty well-oiled, but he seems to have copped on a bit."

"What do you mean?" She hadn't heard him use the expression before.

"He's grown up; he's thinking a bit. And it's like what happened to me was the start of it."

She looked sceptical. "I'll take your word for it."

"Oh, you're too kind." He smirked at her and she returned the look.

"You know, he even said that he reckons the reason Marco always wants him to have a driver is so he can keep an eye on him."

"Well, that's a fair assumption," she conceded. "Who knows? Maybe he is growing up. But you still haven't told me why you're acting like you got bucked off a horse."

He froze his face in a deadpan expression. "Two horses, Bec." He told her about Tomo and Tito's visit to the motel room.

The humour disappeared from her face. "Fucking hell."

She reached over and gently opened his robe. The bruises were starting to make him look like a chessboard. He covered himself up.

"There was no fucking need for that, at all, but Marco just couldn't help himself, could he? He had to push the point. Well, now *I'm* pissed off."

Rebecca shook her head despondently. "Part of me is so mad at both of us for getting involved with a gangster. For a while there, you acted like it was a game. We should've seen this coming."

"I didn't think it would go belly up like this. It all seemed like a friendly deal. I was happy; really happy. For the first time in a long time, I felt like I was successful *and* getting recognition for it. I just wanted everything to keep sailing along. Hell, I even looked at Marco like a father figure. But that fantasy isn't really an option anymore." He peeled the label from his bottle.

"Bec, I realised something. All these business guys are the same. They can be nice and throw you scraps from the table when they're making money, or when you're making money for them, but you see their true colours come out as soon as they lose ten bloody cents."

"You can't call him that. Marco's a gangster, they kill people."

"He's just a businessman. Only, his particular ruthlessness is against the law, but they're all the same. They'd all kill to make a buck. You think my brother, or my first boss, would give a shit about hurting someone to make money?" He put up his hand defensively. "I'm not saying they'd shoot anyone or cut their arms off, but it's war to those guys. They don't give a fuck as long as profits go up, up, up." Everything started to flow out of him. It felt good to confide in her.

"My brother wore his callousness like a badge of honour. Marco strives to cover his up, to make him seem more respectable. I mean, I'm trying to forgive Rich for the way he treated me; it's a pity he didn't open up before he got killed. But what really upsets me is that he was my brother. That should have made a difference. Surely that should have given us a greater bond. Shouldn't it?"

She shrugged. "I guess it should. I don't have brothers or sisters, so I can't say for sure, but I suppose you guys should've been friends, at least."

"Right, but we weren't. And even if we had been, that doesn't take away from the fact he treated people like shit to exploit them and make money from them. He was an asshole bullyboy with his employees. So was Gorman to me, and it turns out Marco's the same. They're just thuggish businessmen. So I reckon the best way to take care of Marco is to appeal to his greed."

"You are really angry," she said, shocked.

"Yes, I am. And it usually takes something dramatic to make me focus. Look, Bec, we'll get through this, but I can't do it alone."

"I'm here, you know that. All the way." She looked into his eyes. "I love you."

He returned the gaze. "Me, too, Bec. So, here's what we do."

Oliver laid out his plan. Rebecca took it all in and climbed onto the sofa beside him. She took his hand in hers.

"When you put it like that, I reckon we don't have much choice," she sighed. "And there goes my job, and my licence to practice."

He squeezed her hand tightly. "I know. I know. Look, if you're not in – and you don't have to be – then I'll call Huntley and take my chances and you can walk away . . . The problem is, Marco and Mike told me to use you, so I reckon we'll lose a bit more than our jobs if we don't get this done. But I can still tell Marco I'll do it alone."

She chewed her lip for a moment. "I'm in. I have to be. Like you said, it's the way he wants it and you'd never manage alone. Anyway, I'm not leaving you, so we'll do it together. Screw my job. I'm sick of the place anyway. They're really sticking it to me for that time off I took to go racing with you. I think a few people are jealous. At least, they were until Painter failed the test. When do we start?"

"I'll make the call tomorrow."

"This is going to turn everything upside down, isn't it?"

"I'm afraid so, but better that than a cell or the alternative."

"Another valid point."

Rebecca looked around her apartment. It wouldn't be a big deal to leave. After a while, she said, "So, assuming all goes well with Painter, we still won't be able to fit very much inside her."

"I've thought about that and we'll just have to do our best. We'll have to fit what we're given."

"If we do it all at Pat's farm, he'll get suspicious – he's a nosey bastard and he can't keep his mouth shut."

"We'll have to use his place. We don't have the time to rent our own farm, at least not for the Painter mission. I was just going to tell him that because of her ban, we'll ship her to Europe to visit a certain stallion for covering in September, because we've had an offer from Argentina for her. A confidential deal, no names involved."

"Reckon he'll buy that?"

"Sure, and it'll explain away the hormones and treatment you'll have to give her to expand her uterus. Plus, I'll appeal to his monetary nature."

Rebecca chuckled. "That should do it."

They lay there for a few minutes, both thinking hard. A phone rang in the bedroom.

"Mine or yours?" said Rebecca.

Oliver cocked his ear. "Mine. Could you, please?"

She padded into the bedroom to retrieve it from his jeans pocket.

He looked at the screen with a puzzled expression. "It's a local number."

He was about to answer, when it stopped. Then, before he could toss it onto the cushion beside him, it started again.

"Same number . . . Hello."

"Oliver McMahon?"

"Er, yes."

"Hi, how're you doing? Larry Marshall, Blackbirch. We met once at the sales."

Oliver searched his mind, but was sure he had never met the owner of Blackbirch Farm, though he knew who he was, of course. Everybody knew Blackbirch Farm. They had thirty stallions on the roster, and divisions in Florida and California in addition to their flagship stud near Lexington, which sprawled over a thousand acres.

Larry Marshall was recognized by all in the business as a visionary when it came to stallions. He had the knowledge, funds and business acumen to buy the best prospects before they finished their racing careers. He was an old-fashioned horseman who shot straight and had no time for bull-shitters.

He had bought the father of Concrete Boot for peanuts from his Californian owner-breeder, then took the horse from his small-time trainer and sent him up to New York. There, he blossomed and won two Grade One championship races. Larry made a killing charging breeders a fortune to use the talented but unfashionably-bred horse, and by mating him with nearly two hundred mares a season.

Oliver could smell a deal.

"I've been better, Larry, what can I do for you?"

"I was kinda thinking we could talk about your big colt. He's an unlucky son of a gun. You have any plans for his stud career?"

Oliver smiled at Rebecca, and she raised her eyebrows quizzically.

"The phone's been red hot the last week, mostly agents sniffing for figures. I thought one of them was working for you."

"Hell, no. I like to deal direct. No sense in getting all those middle men involved."

"I quite agree."

"Anyway, like I said, it's a terrible shame you can't market him as a Derby or Preakness winner, so I thought I might make you an offer and take him off you. A bird in the hand, kinda thing."

The wheels turned in Oliver's head: Larry thinks he'll win the Belmont. Otherwise. he'd wait, or not call at all.

"Tell you what. Larry, you can have him lock, stock, the lot, for ten. That'll be a hell of a deal for a Belmont winner, who should arguably be a Triple Crown winner."

Larry whistled down the line. "That's one heck of a figure for an unlucky horse who only won a Grade Two. I was thinking more along the lines of five to six."

"Larry, we both know when he wins the Belmont he'll show them all he was robbed in Kentucky and Pimlico. By the time the next breeding season rolls around, breeders are going to be knocking themselves out to send a mare to him. Then you'll be able to charge . . . Oh, I'm guessing thirty, thirty-five grand a shot. Even if you only get 130 mares pregnant per year for the first three years, you'll have your money back before he ever has a runner. About eleven or twelve million — minimum, off the top of my head, so ten's a fair price."

Larry let out a belly laugh. "Goddamn! Tell you what I'll do. Ten million if he wins the Belmont. Five if he doesn't; even if he loses by a whisker, got it? Either way, he's mine after the race."

"Sounds fair to me."

"And I get 100 percent of him, you guys don't get to keep shares, or lifetime breeding rights, or any other frills. You want to send a mare to him, you have to pay the fee; no special concessions. OK?"

"No problem at all." Oliver punched the air and beamed.

"I'll have contracts drawn up. Where can I send them to?"

Oliver gave him Rebecca's address.

"You're living with the lovely Dr. Liddell?"

Oliver rolled his eyes, "Yes." As if Larry didn't know already.

"Pleasure doing business with you."

"Likewise, Larry."

Oliver flipped the phone shut and shouted, "Yes!" at his gobsmacked fiancé.

"So come on, tell me. How much?"

He told her. Her eyes nearly popped out of her head.

"Holy shit! That was easy." She thought for a moment. "You sure it wasn't too easy?"

"Not with Larry. Wham-bam, thank you, ma'am. The old cowboy doesn't like to mess around. Besides, we both know the horse'll win and he'll make a killing on him. So nobody loses."

"As long as the horse doesn't."

Oliver shrugged. "Even if he loses, we'll still get pretty much what I told Marco we'd get."

"What about your cut?"

"I'm not taking a cent. I haven't told Marco yet. I'm going to surprise him. Put it to him like it's an apology for the Derby loss."

"What? Are you crazy? You're going to voluntarily give up money to him after all the shit he's asking you to do? Asking us to do."

"He's not asking. But anyway, yeah, I am. It'll seem like a grand gesture and make him think that he still owns me. I want him to think I'm a good little soldier."

"You are a good little soldier. My soldier." She kissed him. "I just hope your battle doesn't turn into a war."

* * *

Rebecca turned her mind to the logistics and practicalities of getting a foreign object into a horse's uterus. She went through the scenario in her mind and realized something that made her sit bolt upright.

"Hon, if we can get Painter across in one piece, we're home and dry."

"Hardly."

"No, listen. It'll be tough to get the stuff in her, but if we pull it off, you can tell Marco that we'll buy old, barren mares at the sales for the next shipment."

Oliver pricked his ears. "Of course!"

"They'll be cheaper, so he'll have to pay you less in commission and they'll be physically perfect for our needs – I mean, Marco's needs."

"You're a genius, Bec."

"Some team," she said, kissing him long and hard. Then she opened his robe and let her hands gently wander.

"I'm not sure I'm up to this," winced Oliver. "I got a fair kick in the nuts."

"Let me be the judge of that," she said, peeling off her shirt.

Chapter 51

Two weeks later, Painter Girl was resting at Pat O'Malley's farm. She spent the June morning sweating profusely from the injection of Prostaglandin hormone which Rebecca had given her, after an ultrasound examination revealed that she was not cycling naturally; probably due to the intense training regime and the additives she had been given by her trainer.

Oliver leaned on the paddock railing with Pat. Rebecca had gone back to the clinic to examine another horse. Painter pranced around enjoying herself, with a slightly confused look in her eye. The surge of hormones would soon be powerful enough to bring her into season and completely dominate her behaviour.

Pat watched her intently. "Didn't I tell you those trainers pump them full of all kinds of shite? A terrible shame she had that race taken off her. She was some filly."

"She still is, Pat. But we need her pregnant to close the deal."

"Who was it you said made the offer?"

"I didn't. Nice try, though." Oliver shot him a sideways glance and a smile.

Pat winked. "Ah go on, you can tell me."

"No, Pat, I can't. Not till the deal is done."

"Fair enough, I suppose. So do you reckon the big horse'll win at Belmont this afternoon?"

"He'd better. He'd bloody well better."

"I hear you done a deal with Marshall."

"That's right. It'll be finalized after the Belmont."

"Fair play to you. By the way, I'm sorry for your loss. It was an awful tragedy about your brother."

Oliver looked somber, he hadn't thought about Richard or his mother or the airline at all since the shit hit the fan with Marco.

"It was indeed. Thanks, Pat."

"I heard the news from back home that there was some kind of drug scandal with his company."

Oliver bristled. "Some asshole he employed, trying to be smart and got caught. It was nothing to do with my brother."

"Jaysus, I was only making conversation."

"Conversation or gossip?" Oliver astonished himself that he was defending his brother, and he wondered if he was doing it out of sincerity or because he was about to engage in some serious drug trafficking himself.

"He was some man to do what he did and create a thriving Irish business, taking on the big boys, and all that. You know what? You've done pretty well yourself. I heard about the touch you had at the sales back home with those yearlings. That brother to Wolf Spider was some score. Success must run in your family."

Oliver thanked him, told him he would pay the full rate for Painter's board, and drove back to the apartment. On the way, he decided he didn't want to sit alone waiting for the race, so he stopped into a bar to watch the Belmont on their large TV.

He pushed open the creaky door to the old bar in central Lexington. It was a nice place, with cosy alcoves along one side and a long bar which ran down the other. There were tables and low stools dotted around the room, the lighting was dark, and the place almost felt like an Irish pub. The ex-pat clientele and County Meath-born owner only added to the feel. The place was full with a gang of stud farm workers, all gazing up at the huge screen and having a lively chat about the racing.

"Well, here's the man in to watch The Boot," announced John the owner, whose brother was a well-known jockey in Ireland. "What'll it be, Oliver? A pint? I hope you've better luck today."

"You and me both, John. A pint'd be just the job."

"I thought you'd be in New York today."

"Too busy. Other things to do."

John gave him an uncomprehending look.

Oliver took his beer and slipped into a side booth, hoping nobody would turn round and see him.

Forty-five minutes later, everybody turned around, because Oliver was screaming. He jumped up with such force that he knocked over the table and his empty glass. Faces looked at him as if he was mad. Oliver didn't care: tears were streaming down his cheeks.

Chapter 52

Concrete Boot won the 2006 Belmont Stakes by nine lengths. He simply destroyed the opposition. Pablo guided him through the field and had no choice but to let him go early, but the big horse kept straight as a die. Pablo would later say in an interview that the animal quickened with such speed that he feared he might shoot out from underneath him, or words to that effect, in his thick accent.

Oliver burst out laughing when he saw the jockey perform a flying dismount in the winner's enclosure and leap into the arms of Ricky. The two of them danced around together, both forgetting that there was a tired, sweating horse beside them.

"He's the man!" Ricky roared into the camera, his voice hoarse from shouting. "This is the best damn horse in the country!" He kissed the lens.

Oliver knew how Ricky felt; finally, a result after all the pressure. The stress evaporated from his body.

A couple of guys in the bar offered congratulations to Oliver, which he sheepishly accepted. Then he righted the table, ordered drinks for himself and everyone in the room, and called Rebecca.

She answered with a whoop. "Well done, cowboy! I saw it on TV at the clinic. Things are turning around, I can feel it. We'll get through it all."

"Yeah, Bec, we will."

"Hey, sorry, but I gotta go. I've patients to treat. See you at home? Love you."

The next call was to Claude. The line was engaged, but Oliver smiled as he looked at the screen and caught a glimpse of Ricky talking into his phone with a serious face.

Oliver waited for Ricky to step up to receive the trophy. Then he tried Claude again. The disgraced trainer was half drunk and very relieved that the horse had not only won, but also appeared to be still in one piece mentally and physically. Oliver told him about the stallion deal, and he also told the trainer that his cut would only be one percent. Claude was not best pleased.

"What the fuck is that about? I thought we agreed I'd get five as trainer."

"That was before you fucked it all up by getting caught doping horses. I'm forfeiting my end totally, just to keep Marco happy, so you should be grateful you get anything at all. In fact, Marco may demand you give it to him."

There was silence at the other end.

"By making this gesture, you'll have a better chance of keeping something. Anyway, it's still a hundred grand . . . That'll pay your fine and then some."

"I guess you're right."

"Maybe Marshall will want to keep him with Ricky, I'm not sure."

"Time will tell. I heard you took Painter away last week."

"Yeah, got an offer from Argentina, if we get her in foal to southern hemisphere time immediately."

"Sounds a bit weird to me."

"I don't care as long as we get paid."

"I hear you." He hung up.

Oliver didn't feel very comfortable lying to everyone, but telling the truth was impossible, and the more he told the cover story, the more he started to believe it. He downed his beer and left John the bartender enough money to cover the round of drinks. He drove back to the apartment, stopping on the way to buy expensive fillet steak, fresh vegetables, chocolate ice cream, and a very good bottle of French wine.

He called Marco when he got in, and passed on the news about Marshall. Marco was over the moon at the result, and the stallion deal was the cherry on top.

"I think I told you one time you'd be a genius if you could make me seven figures on a horse deal.

Good going, my friend."

"Don't mention it, Marco. Just doing my job. Also, I've decided to forfeit my cut on this to make up for the Kentucky thing."

"You're fuckin' shitting me. Now that's a first! I've never had anyone voluntarily give up money to me before. You'll go far, my friend. And, like I said, you're with me now."

"Er . . . In light of your new windfall, do you still need to go ahead with Painter?"

There was a stony silence for a few seconds.

"Damn straight. The wheels are in motion, nothings stops now, OK?"

"OK, just checking."

"I'm sure she'll do good in her new career."

"Yeah, me, too."

Marco ended the call. Oliver shrugged; there was no harm in asking, but he would have been amazed if Marco had changed his mind. He probably had all the calculations done and was counting his potential profit from the Painter trip, before it had even happened.

By the time Rebecca got home, she was drained after a long day. When Oliver hugged her, she felt like sleeping right away in his arms. He sat her down, poured two glasses of wine and prepared dinner. She was asleep on the sofa minutes after the meal. Oliver carried her to bed.

Five days later, the contract with Marshall was signed and the money wired to an account in Robert's name.

As he drove away from Blackbirch Farm over to Pat's place, Oliver cracked a smile, which developed into a fit of laughter. Until now, the sum of money had just been a figure on a piece of paper. It hadn't actually sunk in that he had made ten million dollars; it was almost absurd. But it would keep Marco happy – for a while.

Painter was just coming nicely into season. Pat had been letting the pony stallion sniff her every morning to tease her, enhancing the effect of the hormone injection.

"She'll be mad for it in a day or two," he said, with a smutty cackle.

"Rebecca'll come early in the morning to swab and check her. I'll be here, too, so you don't have to bother getting up," said Oliver.

"Grand so."

"We'll tease her through this heat, then by the time she comes around again, we should be good to go with a plane. We'll take the first blood for quarantine tomorrow as well."

"No bother, sure you know this place is certified as a quarantine station. And you're dead lucky I've no yearlings to prep and sell this year and no boarders. I sold everything at the January sales. I only have my own seven mares, so I put them out in the back paddocks for the summer."

"You're a gifted man, Pat."

"Sure I know, I know," he said with a wink.

"She'll be out of your hair in about a month, I reckon."

"Not a bother, and if you're going to be here in the mornings, maybe I can get you to give me a hand?"

Oliver rolled his eyes. "I suppose I can, Pat. What happened to your lads?"

"José went back home for a month, and Ciaran pissed off back to Cork. Couldn't hack it. No bother, sure it'll save me a few bob over the summer."

An hour later, Oliver stopped at a payphone and called Mike. He was told to wait for ten minutes, which he patiently did. Mike called him back exactly on time.

"OK. What's the story, my man?"

"I have to call the shipping agent again tomorrow, Mike, but she says there's a flight in four weeks out of Chicago which can take a crate just for us. No other horses on the flight. That should fit our timetable, so plan on having the stuff here a day before we fly. I'll let you know the exact dates in a few days."

"Why not now? What the fuck are you waiting for?"

"I'm waiting for a horse to ovulate, Mike. Do you guys want this done right or not? It's not going to be amateur night, OK?"

"Don't get cheeky, you little prick. Remember our drive together?"

"Er, yeah. Oh Mike, how big will the package be?"

"Four keys. That's kilos to you."

"Holy shit!"

"What holy fuckin' shit? Like you say, it's not fuckin' amateur night. Deal with it."

The line went dead.

"Holy shit!" said Rebecca.

"That's what I said."

"Are they insane?"

"I didn't ask, but at this rate I'm beginning to think we may have them by the balls later on."

"Huh, assuming we can actually pull it off."

"We'll do it, Bec. We have to."

Chapter 53

It was pitch dark when Rebecca and Oliver arrived at Four Oaks Farm. Her green SUV crunched the gravel as they pulled up beside the barn, which now served as a quarantine station for Painter Girl. The pre-dawn silence reassured them and provided ideal cover for the operation.

Rebecca crossed the yard to the tack room, ran some warm water into a bucket, then returned to her vehicle and began preparing her equipment.

Oliver went to the barn, turned on the lights and led Painter from her stable, down the aisleway in the otherwise empty barn to the examination stocks, which looked like a variation of a starting stall used at a racetrack. It was used to make rectal ultrasound scanning and examinations safer for horse and vet. Painter gave a cursory sniff at the curious structure, then entered willingly behind Oliver. Rebecca placed her gear on the small table and slowly closed the half-door behind the horse's rump.

Oliver let himself out of the front end and closed the door. He stood beside the stocks and, holding the lead rope, made calming noises to reassure Painter.

"I'll take the blood for shipping first, then I'll give her a tiny dose of sedative."

She filled two vacuum tubes of blood from the horse's jugular, then drew a millilitre of a yellow liquid into a syringe and calmly administered it intravenously.

"Easy girl," she said, but Painter did not flinch.

"I'd say she got well used to needles at Claude's," said Oliver with a smirk.

As the horse's head began to droop slightly, and her lower lip hung loosely from her jaw, Rebecca looked at her watch.

"OK, let's go. Grab the tail, hon."

Oliver reached back with his free hand and gently pulled the tail around Painter's rump and along her flank, allowing the vet unimpeded access to the horse's rectum and vagina. Rebecca pulled on an elbow-length plastic glove and squirted a liberal amount of lubricant on it.

"OK, girl. Easy now, this may feel a bit weird."

Rebecca turned on the machine and took the probe in her gloved right hand. Applying more lubricant to the probe head, she went in. Painter flicked her ears a bit and made a groggy effort to look behind her, but decided it was not worth the trouble. Oliver kept his attention on Painter's eyes, ready to anticipate any reaction she might have. All appeared calm in the animal's head.

"OK, there we go." Rebecca's eyes were fixed on an image on the screen which resembled a cross-section of an orange. "Great uterine tone." She moved the probe and the image changed to something that looked like a bunch of grapes. "Clusters of follicles on this ovary, and a huge egg about to burst on the other side. I'd say she'll ovulate in about twenty-four hours."

She withdrew her hand, stripped off the glove and began washing the rectum and vagina with cotton wool and an iodine solution. She pulled on a new glove and opened a sterile packet containing a metre long clear plastic tube. One end she took in her gloved palm and the other she attached to a four litre bag of physiological saline. With yet more lubricant, she slowly entered Painter's vagina. With her index finger, Rebecca could feel the horse's cervix. It was open. Very carefully, she inserted her finger through the cervix, along with the plastic tube. When this was done, she raised the bag of saline above her head with her left hand.

"So that's how you tone your arms."

"It's a cheap workout." She had a dazzling smile, even at this hour of the morning. "I'm not sure if she'll take the whole four litres in the first go, but we'll try. It's basically like we're treating an infection, but now we're using the fluid to develop the elasticity of the uterus. I want to get it used to stretching. We need it to accommodate something big and foreign in three weeks' time."

The bag of fluid was nearly empty when she gave up.

"That's most of it. It's full to the brim in there, starting to come back at me. If we hadn't given her the sedative, she'd be trying to contract now. The last thing we want her to do is push this out. In fact, we should keep her a bit sedated for another hour. I'll give her another little shot."

She gave the horse another small amount of the sedative, then took a uterine swab from her pocket, opened the packet, and wiped it in the vagina. Then she dropped it on the ground for good measure, before sealing it into its tube.

"A dirty swab should keep the lab busy and justify me coming out here to flush her through this heat and during the next one," she giggled. "Shit, they'll wonder how a maiden could be dirty. They'll say I botched the swab, of course, but I'll tell them she was rotten with fluid and infection, probably a side effect of whatever shit Claude was giving her."

Oliver nodded. "OK, Painter, back to bed."

He undid the latch and swung the front door open. Painter took a wobbly step forward, then another. Oliver coaxed the drunken animal back to her stall.

Rebecca already had her things cleaned up when he came back.

"I'm off. Busy day today. We'll meet back here at seven tonight," she said.

"Cool. I'll hang around till Pat surfaces. I'll need to spin him a yarn."

"Good idea." She kissed him and jumped into her SUV.

He watched her drive away and promised himself that he would do everything to keep her safe.

He went to the tack room, made himself a cup of coffee, and sat flicking through old stallion brochures. Just as the sun was sneaking over the treetops, Pat appeared.

"Jaysus, you're at it early. How's the filly?"

"Rank with fluid, would you believe? We flushed her. Can you leave her in till this afternoon, then turn her out for an hour or so."

"I can indeed, but how in the name of God could she be dirty?"

"Probably all the shit Claude pumped into her."

Pat considered this for a second. "You could be right there. Still, you're lucky she's cycling at all. Some of them come back from training so full o' juice, they think they've got a dick and balls."

Oliver rolled his eyes.

"I don't need to remind you that all this is top secret until we get the deal done, do I?"

"What? Oh, not at all. My lips are sealed."

"Good man, Pat. And there'll be something in it for you as long as they stay sealed."

Pats eyes lit up. "I always said you were a decent fella. You don't have to worry about a thing with me."

Oliver watched the grin spread across the horse dealer's round face. He could see Pat trying to work out how much he might get for letting them use his farm and simply keeping his big mouth shut. Another greedy fucker.

"Can I get a lift into Lexington when you've a minute?"

"You can indeed. As long as you make yourself useful and give me a hand to feed and muck out."

Oliver rolled up his sleeves. A bit of hard labour would be just the job right now to clear the head and get a good sweat up.

He realised as he tossed fork-loads of steaming manure out of Painter's stable into the trailer, that he had forgotten to call his mother to tell her about Painter being shipped to Limerick, or the stallion deal for Concrete Boot. When he had finished and set a nice fresh bed of clean straw for Painter, he called her.

"Hello?" His mother sounded frail and tired, her voice nearly a whisper.

"Hi, Mum." There was no longer any need to specify which son was speaking. "Sorry I haven't called in a while," he said, wandering into a paddock away from Pat's cocked ears.

"Oh, it's so good to hear you! And how's Rebecca?"

"Bec's great, Mum. In fact, I've a surprise for you."

"I could do with a bit of good news."

Oliver felt bad. His mother must be lonely, after all that she'd been through, and here he was on the other side of the world pursuing his own life.

"Mum, we're coming to Ireland in a month or so. Rebecca can only stay for a day or two, but I'll be around for a few months, until the Breeding Stock sales start in November."

"That is a wonderful surprise! I can't wait. How are the horses going?"

He recounted the whole saga of Concrete Boot's bad luck in running, the eventual stallion deal, and Painter's disqualification and her impending Irish trip. He didn't mention Marco's name once.

"I'm absolutely delighted for you. You must be so proud of your horses – what a pity your trainer is such a crook."

Oliver shuddered. Not just the trainer.

"He's not *that* bad. To be honest, I think most of them are at it in some way."

"What about the other one, Shadows of Guernsey?"

"Jersey, Mum, Shadows of Jersey."

"I knew it was one of the Channel Islands."

"Er, yeah. Well, he almost got lost in all the scandal and gossip about the other two. He won two sprint races last month, but we're going to keep him for Saratoga in August. He'll have some opportunities there. Should win a Grade One."

"That's nice. I really can't wait to see you. It'll be nice to have a horse around the place again. How long will you keep her here?"

He really hadn't thought of that. "Oh, er, until she gets pregnant. Then she'll ship to Argentina."

"How exciting!" Her voice was filled with hope and optimism. "Oliver?"

"Yes, Mum."

"I know I don't really follow the racing or what you do, but I am very proud of you."

"I know, Mum, thanks. I wish Dad could have . . ." he cut himself off.

"He would be proud of you, too, Oliver. So would Richard."

"I'm sure you're right. Thanks, Mum. I'd better go, things to organize."

"Let me know when you have your tickets booked."

"Will do. Bye, Mum." He flipped the phone shut.

That evening, they flushed another two litres into Painter. The scan revealed that her uterus was starting to sag and retain a certain amount of fluid.

"Good," said Rebecca. "Progress already."

The filly accepted it all easily, and Rebecca decided that they would try the procedure without sedatives the following morning.

The next day Painter was treated twice more.

"OK, she's ovulated. So if she cycles normally, twenty-odd days from now she should be spot on for the mission."

"I'll talk to the shipping agent tomorrow. Then I'll call Mike and arrange delivery."

"I suppose they'll hardly Fed-Ex it," she said, drily.

"Why use a courier when you have your very own pony express?"

"Do we need some kind of insurance for the trip? I mean, if we get caught before you call Huntley, we're basically fucked," said Rebecca.

The grey sedan flashed through his mind. So did the hammer. "We won't, Bec. We'll get away with it because nobody'll see it coming: nobody would think it possible. The stress'll keep us sharp."

Chapter 54

Two days later, they finished work on Painter and let her out in a small paddock to de-stress and enjoy herself.

The same afternoon, Oliver finalized everything with the shipping agent. Painter would be sent to Chicago O'Hare Airport and put on a direct cargo flight to Shannon. As she was the only animal on the plane, her sky-stall crate would be loaded last and unloaded first. All the paperwork was taken care of by a small bloodstock agency in Lexington, which specialized in sending horses across the Atlantic. They would also arrange the tickets and passes for Oliver and Rebecca to accompany the horse. Oliver stressed that he did not want to use a professional flying groom; as Rebecca was a vet, there was no need to provide one.

"Oh, having a vet on board isn't compulsory any more, but it is advisable," said the matronly woman, called Darla, who dealt with Oliver's enquiry.

She tried to persuade him to wait until after the summer sales, so Painter could be placed on a horse specific flight and save considerably on costs.

"We don't have the luxury of time," Oliver explained.

"Shucks, that's a pity," she drawled.

"But we'll probably have a big shipment of mares after the November sales."

"Oh, that's no problem. We always have plenty going to Europe at that time of year."

"Good, then book me ten places provisionally."

"Can do. They'll be stalls, mind. No crates on those flights; they all fly economy, except for the stallions."

"That'll do nicely."

"That's all great. I'll call you with exact dates and times in a week or so, then book the truck to collect you. We'll have someone meet you at the airport to make sure it all goes off smoothly."

"Excellent," said Oliver, relieved.

After he hung up, he realized that he wasn't quite so relieved after all. In fact, his nerves were jangling. It was getting very real now.

Rebecca got home that evening to find her fiancé sprawled on the sofa, sound asleep in the dark. She kicked off her boots and settled beside him.

Oliver woke with a smile as she ran her fingers through his hair.

"I was dreaming about you," he said, still drunk with sleep. "Us, actually."

"Oh yeah?"

"Yeah," he kissed her. "I don't know about you, but I'm glad we're getting out of here. I know it's been forced on us, and what we're doing is risky, but . . ."

"It doesn't feel wrong," she interrupted.

"Exactly. I want us to start a new life in a new place."

"Away from all the shit."

"That would be nice, but . . ." he looked doubtful. "There's always shit. It just depends on how much."

She sighed. "Ain't that the truth."

Chapter 55

Three weeks later, Oliver waited in the car park of Lexington's Fayette Mall in Rebecca's SUV. It was sweltering outside and the air-conditioning was blasting cold air from the vents, but he was stressed and stuck to the leather seat. He looked at his watch: three-twenty. They were late.

It was a Sunday afternoon, and he passed the time looking at the multitudes of people; young couples, families, and giggling gangs of teenagers, as they all made their way into the vast shrine to consumerism.

A police car rolled past the entrance doors, once, twice, three times. Oliver sweated profusely and craned his neck for a grey sedan; the spectre of Huntley perched like a monkey on his back. On the fourth pass, the car stopped as a cop appeared from the mall clutching take-out drinks and a bag of cookies.

A tap on the door jolted him. He nearly vomited when he saw Tomo standing there with a lopsided smile breaking up his pitted skin and hard features.

Oliver lowered the window a crack. "Do you have it?"

"Yeah," he said, lifting a duffel bag he had in his right hand.

Oliver let the window fully down to take the bag, but Tomo strolled round to the other side and jumped in, casually looking about. He tossed the bag onto Oliver's lap. "It's all there: four keys, four cans."

"Cans?"

"Yeah, canisters. And no hard feelings, eh? I was just doin' a job. Business. Fuck, you could be a nice guy, for all I know."

Oliver looked at him sideways. "I understand. We're all just

323

trying to do our jobs and get on."

Tomo opened the bag fully, and Oliver gazed at the four transparent plastic tubes stuffed with white powder. Each was about three inches wide and about a foot long. They were sealed perfectly: vacuum-packed with a thin film of plastic.

"I was told they had to be watertight," said Tomo.

"Yeah, yeah. Looks good to me. Shut the bag." Oliver glanced around.

Tomo laughed. "See ya later." He slipped out, gently closed the door, and got into a blue Ford Taurus that passed by.

Oliver drove to the apartment, picked up Rebecca, and they set off for Four Oaks Farm.

She opened the bag to check the canisters.

"They're a good shape and size, we shouldn't even hurt her inserting them, but that's the least of our worries." She paused for a moment, deliberating. "I won't be able to sterilize them at the clinic, it's too risky."

"So what do you want to do?"

"I'll have to soak them in a bucket of iodine solution, rinse them with saline, then immediately insert them." She cursed under her breath. "I wish we didn't have to do this in daylight."

"Me, too, but the truck's coming at seven pm. It'll take most of the night to get to O'Hare for the morning flight."

"Are you sure Pat won't interfere?"

"It's Sunday afternoon, he'll be safely planted on a bar stool, talking horses to whoever'll listen."

They got to the barn and Rebecca set the four canisters to soak in a bucket of warm water and iodine. She then set two bags of saline in another bucket.

Oliver led Painter into the stocks and Rebecca administered a larger dose of sedative. Then she started the filly on a course of intravenous antibiotics and painkillers.

"We'll start her now and give her another shot at the airport. Probably need more sedative as well."

Painter's head drooped and she almost wobbled on her feet. Rebecca bandaged her tail with a roll of clean gauze, so every hair was tucked away and would not touch off the package during insertion.

Rebecca cleared the table and laid a sterile drop sheet on it. Then she placed another drop sheet on a bale of hay, on which she put all her equipment.

"OK, here goes. Fingers crossed," she said.

Oliver winked at her. "No problem, Dr. Liddell."

Rebecca looked momentarily sceptical, then she pulled on a set of long gloves, grabbed the tube and a bag of saline, and flushed all three litres into Painter. When the bag was empty, she let it drop to the ground and the liquid began to flow back like fuel siphoned from a car.

"That should stretch her out another bit. Now for the hard part."

She changed her gloves, putting on clean long polythene gloves and short latex ones over them, to give her hands a better grip on the slippery canisters. She took one out of the iodine, placed it on the table, rinsed it with saline from the second bag, applied lubricant, cradled the canister in her right hand and very carefully entered Painter's vagina. She felt the open cervix with her fingers.

"Hold tight, grab an ear in case." She looked at Oliver.

He closed his hand around the animal's left ear and prepared to squeeze hard in case she struggled, but Painter was in another world. Her eyes were partially closed.

Rebecca put her fingers into the cervix and opened them out. With her left hand, she reached in and pushed the canister up inside Painter. She met with resistance – it wasn't exactly a camel through the eye of a needle, but it wasn't a perfect fit either. After some coaxing, the cervix stretched and the canister slid inside. She withdrew her right hand and used it to push the object all the way in. It was a kilo in weight and so dropped over the pelvic brim and caused the uterus to sag downwards slightly. Painter opened her eyes for a second, vaguely registering the strange sensation, before drifting off again.

Fifteen minutes later, the other three packages were in place.

"Jesus, it'll take ages when we have ten mares," said Oliver.

"It won't be too bad. They'll all be old and saggy inside."

Rebecca then quickly examined Painter.

"It's tight as a drum in there. We can't let her wake up too much or she'll start to contract. It'll be a miracle if she doesn't start to panic and show distress during the flight," she said, removing her arm.

Oliver led the groggy beast back to her stable. Time was ticking by, so Rebecca hastily started clearing everything up. Oliver helped her, and within a few minutes they had the place looking clean. They packed everything into Rebecca's SUV and threw a blanket over all the equipment. She parked it beside Pat's house and locked it.

They assembled their bags, with a bale of hay and large drum of water for Painter, along with Rebecca's small bag of veterinary medicines. She took sterile gloves, lubricant, a bag of saline, needles and syringes, more antibiotics, painkillers, oxytocin, sedative, and a bottle of liquid for a lethal injection.

"We're not going to be needing this," said Oliver, handling the bottle of T-61 barbiturate and potassium mixture.

"I know, hon, but if she freaks out mid-flight, and starts kicking all around her, we may have to euthanise her for the safety of the plane."

Oliver looked flabbergasted. "Jesus, she's doped up to the gills."

"I know, it's just in case."

Oliver felt like throwing the bottle out, to remove temptation, but if she really did damage the plane, another beating from Tomo would be the least of their worries. He made two cups of coffee and they waited in the tack room for the truck to arrive.

It rattled up the driveway at seven and pulled up to the loading ramp. Oliver coaxed the drunken horse into the truck. As she gingerly walked up the ramp, he could have sworn he heard a clunk from her insides.

* * *

The young agent ripped off the headphones, rubbed his eyes, and yawned. He went downstairs with the device in his hand, poured a coffee, and sat at the kitchen table opposite agent Rosen. "Shit, I'm tired. This is getting long." He yawned. "Anyway, there's something you should listen to."

Rosen looked up from the reams of paper scattered on the table.

"What's up, Mitch?"

"See what you think." He played the excerpt from the disc. "What the fuck is that about?"

Rosen shrugged, then he flicked open his notepad and scanned the pages. "Hmm . . . I have a feeling, Mitch. Yesterday, I got word that McMahon's booked on a cargo flight out of O'Hare today. With a horse. Better check it out. Do me a favour. Call Kimble, tell her to get over there ASAP. Nothing obvious, just get it checked."

Mitch yawned again and picked up the phone.

* * *

On the way to Chicago, Rebecca gave the horse more injections and offered her some water.

It wasn't until they parked in a loading bay and let down the ramp that the full roar of a modern airport hit Painter. She whinnied and pawed the ground with a front leg. Oliver spoke softly to her as she flicked her ears about and tried to rid herself of the fog of sedative.

"We need to load her quickly," Oliver bellowed at the cargo attendant, who seemed utterly bewildered by the spectacle. He sprung into action and opened the door of the sky-stall crate. It was a large shiny aluminium container that had the back end removed. It had a small sliding door at each side, to allow the handlers access, and was big enough to accommodate two horses, but the partition had been removed to allow Painter the full area to herself. It was on the back of a flatbed lorry, and the driver backed it up to the ramp of the horse truck to make the changeover almost seamless.

Oliver turned Painter round in the truck and encouraged her to take a few steps. She ambled onto the ramp, sniffed the curious object, and snorted a jet of air from her nostrils onto the clean wood-shavings that covered the floor of the sky-stall, causing some to flutter about. Once inside, she took a mouthful of hay from the net hanging at the front of the container, but had no interest in chewing. She let it fall from her mouth and pawed the ground again.

As soon as the door was fitted and Painter enclosed with him, Oliver pulled a syringe from his pocket and deftly delivered the contents into her jugular vein. She instantly stopped pawing the ground and picked another morsel of hay from the net.

He looked at the empty syringe and wondered if he should take a shot, too. This was going to be a long trip.

The container was driven to the loading elevator and hoisted up to meet the lip of the hold on the Boeing 757 cargo plane.

Soon the whole crate was inside, strapped, and bolted to the floor. Take off in forty minutes.

Rebecca poked her head in the front door. "I'll take over, you go clear Customs and Immigration."

He took his small bag with him and trotted down the stairway to the tarmac, where a stern-looking female Immigration official waited to escort him to the terminal building. Ten minutes later, he bounded back up the steps brandishing a stamped passport. Then Rebecca grabbed her bag and did the same.

"Did Customs comment on your bag of tricks?" Oliver asked her, when she returned.

"I had to show them my licence, but apart from that, no."

They heard a succession of clanging noises as the large hold doors and smaller passenger door were sealed.

Oliver kissed Rebecca and crossed his fingers. "Here we go."

She tried not to think about the prison sentences for smuggling four kilograms of pure cocaine into Europe.

* * *

Monica flashed her ID at the gate and asked to be taken to the flight bound for Shannon. The guard made a call. He shook his head as he cradled the receiver. "Too late, honey. Took off a half-hour ago."

"I'm not your honey," she spat. "Fucking last minute shit." She got back into the car and called Mitch.

Chapter 56

Six hours flying through the night, and another injection later, they touched down at Shannon Airport in the early morning drizzle. Oliver and Rebecca were close to jubilation. The plane taxied to a halt beside the hangar which served as a cargo terminal. Customs officials boarded and circled the hold, examining crates. Rebecca and Oliver were gazing out of the hold into the fresh Irish air. The drizzle had abated and the thick low clouds were blowing away, allowing shafts of sunlight through.

"Looks like our truck," said Oliver, pointing to a lorry in the bright red livery of a local equine transportation firm. It was backed up to the loading ramp beside the hangar, ready and waiting.

"Discreet getaway car," said Rebecca dryly.

"Morning to you," mumbled the official. "Passports and papers, please."

Oliver jumped, startled. Then handed them over.

"Grand job," said the ruddy-skinned official, flicking through the documents and checking his clipboard. "Your transport company lodged the import certs with us already, so you're all set."

"Thanks," said Oliver.

Two hours later, Painter was mooching about in her new Irish stable. Evelyn watched in amusement as the groggy animal pawed the ground and flopped herself down to roll.

"She's getting to know her new house," said Evelyn, smiling.

Oliver and Rebecca shot each other nervous glances. She had given Painter a shot of oxytocin on the journey from Shannon, to start the contractions.

"I think she's a bit colicky after the trip," Rebecca announced helpfully.

"What on earth do you mean?"

"Horses' intestines are complicated, it's almost like they're made by committee," continued the vet. "They're prone to gut pains in times of stress, and they can't tolerate that kind of discomfort at all. Hence the continuous rolling: we call that colic."

"Oh dear, poor thing."

"Oliver, why don't you take your mother inside? I'll see to Painter."

"Good idea, Bec. Come on, Mum, I'm dying for a proper cup of tea."

He guided his mother across the yard towards the house.

Rebecca watched them disappear inside, then set to work with lightning speed. While Painter got down to roll again, she reached for her bag and pulled a small amount of ketamine into a syringe. When Painter was looking around at her own flank, the nimble vet squatted on the straw, found the jugular, and carefully administered the anaesthetic. Within seconds Painter drifted off into a deep sleep. Rebecca looked at her watch.

She darted across the yard to the tack room. She filled a bucket and rummaged in a cupboard to find cotton wool and iodine solution. Racing back to the stable, she glanced at the kitchen window long enough to see Oliver had positioned his mother at the table with her back to the yard.

Back inside the box, she peeled off her jumper and, pulling on a pair of long gloves, she got to work. Rebecca found one of the packages already lodged in the cervix; it was slippery, but she managed to coax it out slowly. She rinsed her glove in the bucket and went in again. She eased her wrist through the cervix and groped for another tube. Cupping her hand around the narrow end, she slowly withdrew and the tube slipped out.

Painter whinnied in a dream-like state.

"Easy, girl. Two down, two to go."

Mercifully, after a bit of careful manipulation, the other two came out. Rebecca tossed the last one into the corner with the others, and sat back, exhausted. She stripped off the gloves and wiped the sweat from her brow. It had taken forty minutes. Painter should be waking up soon.

She crawled over to the horse's head and cradled it in her lap.

"I'm sorry, girl. That must've been weird, but you'll be OK. And you're free now; lucky for you." She sighed, placed Painter's head back on the soft bed, went to her bag, drew up shots of antibiotics and painkillers, and gave them to the recovering beast. She rinsed the four cocaine-filled tubes, patted them dry and stowed them in her bag. Job done. She checked the patient's heart rate and left the poor animal alone to recover.

Oliver gave her a concerned look when she entered the kitchen.

"She's fine, just a little upset tummy." She winked at her man.

Oliver relaxed his shoulders and finished his cup of tea. "You know what, Mum, I think we could both do with a proper drink, after all that." He stood up.

"But it's not even noon yet," said Evelyn.

"It must be five o'clock somewhere in the world," he said with a chuckle.

"I could use a drink, too, I'm afraid," said Rebecca apologetically. "Join us, Evelyn. C'mon, it's time to celebrate your son's success." She sat beside the older woman and gave her a playful nudge.

Evelyn was slightly taken aback, but eventually a smile broke out.

"Oh, go on then. It's been too long since I had something to celebrate. I suppose I could have a little sherry. Oliver, you know where I keep the drink."

"That's the spirit," said Rebecca, smiling.

Oliver disappeared into the dining room and found a bottle of red wine that remained since the funeral. They toasted their success around the large oak kitchen table, and Oliver was delighted to see his mother really smile for the first time in as long as he could remember.

Evelyn volunteered to cook lunch, and she shooed her son and his fiancée into the sitting room and insisted they relax after their long flight. They detoured out to check Painter, who was on her feet but still groggy. Her head and neck were droopy, and her bottom lip hung limply from her jaw, making her look ridiculous. Oliver smiled and rubbed her forehead.

"You're a lifesaver, you know that?" he said. "Did the removal go smoothly, Bec?"

"She was great. Slept like a baby. I decided to sedate her and do it manually. But I tell you one thing. I'm glad I won't have to go through that with ten horses next time. That'd be a total pain, that's even if we could manage that many."

Oliver chewed his lip for a second. "Bec, as a vet, are you OK with the plan?"

She shrugged her shoulders. "Like you say, we don't have a choice. Anyway, I've heard of worse being done. How 'bout you?"

"I don't like having to use some poor old mares as our pawns in our game, but I suppose compared to everything else we're doing . . ." He shrugged. "Like you say, we don't have a choice."

He kissed her forehead, shut the stable door, and led her inside.

"Any news yet?" Marco barked into the receiver.

"No, Boss," said Mike. "Phone's off."

"Well keep fuckin' trying. Some fuckin' Fed bitch turned up at the airport, but the plane had already gone. I need a delivery confirmation. Now."

"Yes, Boss."

Mike hung up, got out of his car, walked across the street to the payphone, and tried Oliver's number again. Same message: customer unavailable.

He lit a cigarette. "I'll kill you, you little fucker."

Oliver woke with a start, and panic crept up his spine. He could hear the muffled sizzling of lamb chops being prepared by his mother, who was humming to herself. Rebecca was snoring softly, her head on his lap. He carefully extricated himself and trotted up to his room. Turning on his phone, he took a deep breath and called Mike, who picked up instantly.

"Bout fuckin' time. I'll call you back."

Oliver paced the floor for five gruelling minutes before the call came.

"Well?" said Mike.

"Job done. No problems. We got it out."

"See, I told you not to worry."

"You were right, Mike . . . Er, what happens now? I don't want to be holding on to this stuff for long."

"A guy'll call you. Do what he says."

"No problem."

"Atta boy."

The line went dead.

Oliver threw off his clothes, took a quick shower, and went down to the kitchen. Rebecca was already seated, looking as groggy as Painter had. Oliver placed his phone on the table and kept looking at it as he ate. Evelyn was in good form and talked of this and that; mostly local gossip. Rebecca ate mechanically and nodded politely, but was too tired to speak.

When the call came, Oliver grabbed the phone and stood up with such speed, it startled his mother.

"Call from the States, got to take it," he said, leaving the room.

In the sitting room, he answered with a cautious hello.

"I look for Oliver," said the rough accent that could have been eastern European.

"This is Oliver."

"OK, we meet Harlequin Shop Centre, Limerick City. Six pm. Go to café. Wait. I call," he growled.

The call ended before Oliver could even say yes.

He rejoined the others.

"Is there petrol in my car?" he asked his mother.

"Yes, why? You're not going off already, are you?"

"Got to do a bit of er, shopping, this evening." He could see Rebecca staring at him out of the corner of his eye.

At ten to six that evening, Oliver parked his car in the vast lot that surrounded Limerick's largest shopping mall. It was a sprawling complex in the suburbs of the city, not far from his mother's house. Oliver supposed that it had once been farmland, too, but now it had been transformed into another consumer paradise.

He slung the bag over his shoulder and nonchalantly pushed through the revolving doors into the mass of humanity. Throngs of people crowded the shops, like magpies eyeing shiny trinkets. He forged a path through the masses to the food court, and found an empty stool at the counter of the only café amidst the glut of fast-food joints. He ordered a coffee and his phone chimed. The message read: *Turn around. Italian football shirt.* He swiveled on his stool to scan the customers.

Amidst the tables of giggly teenagers and gossiping housewives, Oliver spotted the blue of the Italian strip on a man sitting alone, hunched over a table. He had a shaved head and his nicotine-stained fingers gripped an empty teacup. The man had a tattoo creeping up his neck like a dark tendril. He stared at Oliver. When their eyes met, he nodded to the doorway.

Oliver took a cursory sip from his cup, left some coins on the counter, and slipped away. When he got out the door, the guy followed. He grunted and tossed his head as he passed Oliver.

They slowly walked to an exit and, as they shuffled through the revolving doors together, the guy took the bag from Oliver.

"Next time, you have big amount?"

Oliver could just about tell it was a question. "Er, yes." Apparently four kilos wasn't a big amount.

"Not possible meet like this. I call you, tell you where." He walked off into the rain, which had begun streaming out of the heavens.

* * *

Back at home, he let himself through the front door and could hear Rebecca and Evelyn talking in the sitting room. Rebecca was drinking wine and Oliver could tell the glass of sherry in his mother's hand was not her first.

"Oh, there you are. We've been having a great chat. I've been hearing more about all your trials and tribulations with Concrete Boot. What a saga! But at least it had a happy ending."

Oliver plonked himself into an armchair and tried to look delighted.

"What about the airline, Mum? Any news from James?"

His mother looked surprised. "Don't tell me you haven't heard!"

"No, Mum, I really haven't given it a thought since I went to America,'" he said with a sigh.

"That awful Italian will stand trial, though all the papers say he won't say a word to the police. I mean *not a single word*, can you imagine? Very strange."

She glanced at them for approval. Rebecca gazed into her glass, Oliver nodded blankly.

"Anyway," she continued, "the company *still* hasn't found a permanent successor to your brother, which is causing mayhem. Apparently the Board is continuously arguing about it and nobody seems to be able to take control."

"You know what Rich was like; he controlled everything, ran it like a dictatorship. Of course they're lost now he's gone."

Evelyn looked puzzled. Rebecca was surprised at Oliver's insight.

"A bit like Dad was with you, really," said Oliver, flippantly.

He saw the hurt look on his mother's face. The insensitivity of his remark dawned on him. Rebecca gave him a withering look.

"Sorry, Mum, really. I didn't mean . . . I'm just a bit tired after everything."

"Not too tired to go out shopping though, are we?" said his mother.

Oliver chewed his lip, pondering for a moment then said, "Mum, I, we, are doing some things that are . . . well, a bit unorthodox."

"Are you sure about this?" Rebecca cut in.

He put up a hand in her direction. "Don't worry, Bec."

Evelyn immediately became concerned. "Unorthodox? What on earth are you talking about? You sound like one of our politicians."

"Mum, I can't tell you more at the moment, but I just want

you to know, that if anything, er . . . dramatic, should happen in the next few months, don't worry. It's all part of the plan."

"Oliver, you're not going to do anything stupid, are you?"

"Stupid, no. Tricky, yes. But I don't want you to worry."

She looked as though she was sobering up fast. "When my only surviving son says something like that to me, of course I'll worry."

Oliver rubbed his temples with his hands. He knew he shouldn't have said anything, but he couldn't help himself.

"Mum, I just want you to know that it's part of a plan and that we're covered, OK?"

"If you really want me to relax, you should tell me everything, or else you shouldn't have said anything at all."

"Maybe I shouldn't, but if I hadn't, then you'd only think the worst later on. Can we change the subject now?"

"You brought it up," she said in an irate voice.

"Evelyn, it'll be alright, I'll make sure of it," said Rebecca, putting an arm around her.

"Thank you, my dear." She looked at her son. "You're a lucky man, Oliver, I hope you realise that."

"Lucky? I suppose I am." He winked at Rebecca. "You know what they say, Mum. Better lucky than rich."

Rebecca managed to get another sherry into Evelyn and regale her with more racing stories. Oliver knew how lucky he was, but he needed that luck to hold out.

The next day, he treated them to lunch in an upmarket restaurant. They all put thoughts of the future out of their minds, and enjoyed the day like a normal family. The following morning Rebecca hugged a teary-eyed Evelyn goodbye, and Oliver dropped her to Shannon Airport.

"This time, I really don't give a shit about going back," she said, as they embraced at the security gates. "Except without my man."

"It'll go quick. See you in a few weeks."

"I know. But you'll call me when you've talked to him?"

"Of course."

She gave him one last kiss, then turned to give the guard her passport and boarding card. Oliver watched her go through the checks, then walked to his car and made the call.

"You see, it's easier to do what you're fuckin' told," said Mike. "Plan worked a treat. Everyone's happy."

"I'll be back in a month, but you can tell him that we'll buy the next batch at the November sales."

"Attaboy."

He spent the next four weeks doing up his mother's house, and fitted new locks for all the doors. He tried his best to persuade her to go on a sunny holiday with a friend, but to no avail. Neither of them referred to the future.

Every now and then, he would pull Agent Huntley's card out of his wallet and just hold it. The time was getting close. Two days before he left for the States, he made the call.

Chapter 57

It was a hot, sticky August evening when Oliver sat in the office at Shadows nightclub. He looked down over the floor. It was early and the place was still deserted, except for a handful of wiseguys sitting at the bar and talking shit over the music.

Marco and Mike walked in and the guys stood to attention like soldiers. Marco greeted them with a large smile and warm embraces. They watched him go up to the office with looks of reverence.

"My man!" he said, barging through the doorway with open arms. "Didn't I tell you there was nothing to worry about? Didn't I?"

"You did indeed," Oliver replied, as Marco gave him a bear hug.

Marco took his place behind the desk and turned up the music. Mike went to the desk and took out the scanner. He yanked his thumb at Oliver. "You know the drill." He ran the device over him.

"Is that necessary?" asked Oliver, his head pounding.

Mike finished. "I guess not," he said, and sat beside Oliver

"So, my friend. What's the go for next time?" said Marco.

Oliver leaned forward in his seat. "It's like this. I'll buy ten mares at the November sales in Kentucky. They'll be cheap, but not total heaps of shit. They have to be mares that would look legit travelling to Europe."

Marco nodded.

"So we buy older barren mares."

"Barren?" interrupted Mike.

339

Oliver glanced at Mike. "Not pregnant. Anyway, the older they are, the saggier they are. That means we'll be able to get things in and out easier – it was a bit too tough with Painter, and there's no way we can be fucking around like that with ten mares to pack. So I reckon we could get five in each horse. Is that doable?"

Marco's eyes lit up, and he let out a huge belly laugh. "You're some piece of work. Sure, it's doable. No problem. But we'll have to time things to a fuckin' T. This farm in Kentucky you're using, no problem there? You going to be able to take care of a deal that big without anyone asking questions?"

"I'll go to see the guy when I'm done here. We'll have to rent the whole place from him the rest of the year. That'll stop him taking on other clients. Don't worry, he'll buy into it."

"So how much to buy the horses?"

"Should be able to get away with five to seven grand per mare."

Marco was doing calculations in his head, smiling.

"Tell you what, I'll give you a hundred grand, you buy for whatever you like and keep the change. How's that?"

Oliver didn't care about the money, but made a show of thinking about it for a moment.

"Sounds fine, but you'll have to pay the shipping costs on top of that."

"Naturally." Marco nodded. He stood and they shook on the deal.

"It's better if we don't see each other for a while. Mike, you sort out the deliveries. And make sure those fuckin' lunatics at the other end have their shit together, and remind them not to cut the goods more than twenty percent. Keep it fuckin' quality."

"Sure thing, Boss."

"OK, I gotta go to Vegas. You relax and enjoy that girl of yours till November. By the way, when's Shadows goin' to run again?"

"Ricky has him in Saratoga. He might run next week. Should be on for a touch in the sprints. Then, all going well, the Breeder's Cup."

"Good. Call Mike when it's on."

"Will do."

He swept out the door.

Mike ordered them two beers, and a tired-looking waitress brought it up. Oliver gulped it down as quickly as he could to escape listening to Mike's vulgar bullshit. All he could think about was meeting Huntley in the usual room at Newark Airport in a couple of hours.

* * *

Oliver slid onto the chair opposite Huntley. The agent looked tired – his skin was almost translucent – but he was visibly excited. He tapped a folder with his pen and shook Oliver's hand vigorously.

"You finally saw sense," he said. "I just hope it's not too late. Look, we can give you immunity if you help us. Tell me everything you know about Marco Romano's business activities, including race-fixing and the incident in Ireland with your brother's airplane, and why you took that horse to Ireland last month."

Oliver had to stifle a smirk. "I'm glad you're sitting down for this."

Huntley narrowed his eyes. "Get on with it."

"Well, all that other shit about race fixing is now irrelevant, and I didn't want to discuss it with you before, because I still believed that I had a fair deal with Marco, and I thought I could just wrap it up and walk away." He paused. "Anyway, things have changed. As you know, last month we took Painter Girl to Ireland. Supposedly, we took her there to get her pregnant, before selling her to Argentina. The real reason was to use her as a drug mule. We flew her to Ireland, carrying four kilos of what I imagine was pure cocaine."

Huntley dropped his pen and his jaw on the table.

"Jesus H. Christ. You . . ."

Oliver put up his hand. "Please, let me finish – there's more." He swallowed. "Could I get some water, please?"

Huntley sighed and asked the guard outside to fetch two bottles.

"OK, I assume that you suspect Marco of drug dealing or trafficking, or whatever, otherwise the DEA wouldn't be watching him. I feel stupid, really, for not realising it earlier. Anyway, it's like this: we – that is me – are going to buy ten horses at the November sales in Kentucky, then we plan to fill them with a total of fifty kilos of coke and send them on their merry way to Shannon. This is where you come in, Agent Huntley."

Oliver carefully outlined his plan. Huntley was astounded both at the plan and at Oliver's calm, matter-of-fact demeanour.

The agent took it all in and sat in silence for a minute. Oliver drank from the water bottle and waited for him to say something.

Eventually, he leaned in close to Oliver and said in a dark voice, "I could have you put away now for smuggling. Who do you think you are?"

Oliver kept his cool. "Agent Huntley, I'm sorry if I was a smart-ass with you before. I assure you, I'm not trying the same thing now. I had no choice but to do the last job, and I needed it to go smoothly so I could suck Marco in for the big shipment. I consciously decided not to call you to keep it real and keep me sharp. I was worried that I might get a bit blasé and Mike and Marco would smell a rat, or you guys would step in and ruin it. Anyway, if you want to get Marco Romano, then this is it."

Huntley regarded him with narrow eyes. "And you're sure you can pull it off?"

"As sure as I can be. Rebecca thinks it'll work, too."

Huntley stared at the table for a moment. "Alright, I'll give you the chance, but I can't do anything if it happens in Ireland. You'll have to do it on American soil. Is that something you can work into the plan?"

Oliver considered the adjustments, then after a second he shrugged. "I'll have to run it past Rebecca, see how we'll work the timing of it, but I reckon it's possible."

Huntley gave him an amused look. "It'd better be."

"So, is that it then?"

"We'll proceed like this: I'll keep the whole thing between you, me, and my partner, Karl Rosen. You just go about your business, tell me when you've booked the plane, and when the shit hits the fan I'll make sure Rosen is at the airport to meet you."

Oliver nodded. "Will I have to testify against him?"

"That depends on how much evidence we have, but you can assume the DA will want to go with a witness. Besides, having looked into the legalities of your little business, it seems that the horses are officially the property of his son, and the money used to start the venture was clean, or well-laundered. So, as I say, testimony will be the cherry on top."

"I figured as much. What kind of protection will we get in return? I'm going to need some kind of guarantee."

"We?"

"Rebecca and I. And my mother."

"I'll have to see what I can do about your fiancée, but there's no way any deal can stretch to your mother."

Oliver hadn't really thought of this. "Deal's off then," he said rashly.

"Oh really? How's about I just toss you in jail now and round up Marco tonight?" He wagged his finger at Oliver. "Don't get fucking smart all over again. I'll see if I can arrange something for your mother, but guys like Marco don't bother about women or family members. She's not a priority."

"She's a priority to me."

"No, your priority is not to fuck this up, or I'll put you away for twenty. Got it?"

Oliver swallowed. "Got it. So can I go now?"

"Yes."

Oliver stood and turned for the door, then stopped with his hand on the knob.

"By the way, I told Marco about our last two meetings. Nothing specific, just that you hassled me and I told you to piss off, but I'll have to tell him much the same thing about today. Just in case."

"I suppose that's smart."

"Thanks."

He let himself out and dashed to the gate for his flight.

* * *

Huntley flipped open his phone and called Rosen.

"Get me all the transcripts and recordings from The Gent's

house. I'll have to go through it personally. The game has changed; we got an ace in the hole. He's going down this time – real soon."

"You've got a real hard-on for this guy, haven't you?" said Rosen.

"Guys like The Gent think the rules don't apply to them. That cocky little Irish shit needs a lesson, too. He'll end up in jail, too, if I've anything to do with it."

He ended the call and allowed himself the pleasure of a smile.

* * *

Mike answered his phone. "He did? Again? Keep an eye on the little prick. Yeah, in Kentucky, too. I don't give a fuck. Do it."

Chapter 58

Oliver fell into Rebecca's arms at Bluegrass Airport.

"Marco bought it," he whispered in her ear. "And Huntley likes the plan."

She squeezed him tight.

When they were on the road she said, "You think they'll be watching us?"

"Who, the Feds? Or Marco?"

"Both, either."

"Huntley says he'll keep his distance, but something tells me that Marco will want some kind of insurance, so I'm guessing he'll have somebody keep tabs on us, if he hasn't already. Or maybe that was Huntley. Or paranoia."

"What?"

He told her about the grey cars.

"If it was Huntley, he'd have busted us at Pat's with Painter."

Oliver shook his head. "Shit, I don't know. Anyway, Huntley says we'll have to do it on American soil. That means, before the plane takes off."

Rebecca pondered this for a second, as if considering a course of treatment for a patient.

Keeping her gaze on the traffic she said, "It might even be easier logistically. I'll just hold off on the painkillers and antibiotics, but we'll have to be quick. I mean, like, seriously quick." She shrugged. "I reckon we can do it and all . . . Hang on a second, there'll be flying grooms for the other horses on that flight . . ." She started to speak rapidly, and blurted out her idea to Oliver.

"Holy shit, Bec, you're a genius."

"I wonder if Huntley's given much thought to the timing of it all," she said. "I mean, he'll have to get him before word leaks from the airport, or else he'll have time to vanish."

"And if they get him before it goes down, he'll know we ratted on him."

They sat in silence, neither one wanting to say what they were both thinking.

Eventually, Rebecca changed the subject. "Come to think of it, what'll we tell Pat? Ten mares for treatment is going to look a bit strange."

Oliver smiled. "Oh, I'll seduce Pat. He'll ignore anything we do if he's getting paid, and we only have to load the horses up and get them onto the plane. After that, he can talk as much shit as he likes – or dares."

Taking out his phone, he made the call to Mike and reported the official version of the latest encounter with Huntley, adding a touch of nervousness for dramatic effect. Mike again told him to relax and keep his head down, before abruptly ending the call.

Oliver breathed a sigh of relief. "He bought it. Greed and overconfidence are like blinkers on a racehorse – tunnel vision only."

Rebecca shot him a lopsided smile. "The overconfidence thing can apply to us as well, you know."

They drove the rest of the way home in silence.

* * *

Huntley shut himself in his house for three days, going through all the files and some of the footage from the three devices that Agent "Sherry" Wilkins had placed in Marco's house. At the time, he had congratulated himself on a masterstroke, and his partner – the long-suffering Karl Rosen – had assigned a hand-picked team of two ambitious young agents to rent a house about a kilometre from the wall of Marco's compound to intercept the fragmented transmissions.

The sound-activated devices would store six hours of audio in their tiny chips, and send that information automatically to the receiving unit whenever capacity was reached. The signal would then need to be processed by the receiving computer, using a code key, in order to render the information usable and to prevent interception by another system. If anyone did pick up the signal, it would simply look like a locked wi-fi internet band.

The listening team endeavoured to sort the wheat from the chaff and wrote transcripts. These transcripts were indexed, and any subject thought to be a code was noted. Copies of the audio footage were made to correspond to the key parts of the transcripts, and the files were burned onto CD. It was a laborious, meticulous job, which lacked satisfaction. The two single, male, junior agents assigned to the task for the past year were on the brink of insanity, and to make matters worse, nobody had ever asked them for a briefing or given them any idea if they were working towards anything specific. Every week, they compiled their reports and send them to Rosen. That was it.

Huntley found out to his annoyance, that not one single piece of relevant information had been gleaned from the device in the toilet. The device in the den yielded mundane conversations, and appeared to have stopped working after three months. The one in the office had plenty of interesting information on it, but the conversations were somewhat muffled.

Huntley swore and called his partner.

"Rosen, what the hell is this? One tells me more than I need to know about the shitting habits of a criminal. The second gives a little useless information before it stops working. Only the third gives me anything to go on, and even that's thin. What the fuck was Wilkins thinking? Get hold of her, will you?"

"I'd love to, but she handed in her resignation two months after we pulled her from that job."

"You're kidding. Why wasn't I made aware of this?"

"You were. I told you she signed up for psychotherapy. When she requested a transfer back to D.C., I had no choice but to agree. Shortly after that, she quit, citing stress as the reason. I think the undercover work kind of messed her up."

"Really? I don't remember that. Shit, if she couldn't handle it, she's better off out of the Agency. Anyway, we're going to need testimony of some kind. We're also going to need good timing when the shit goes down, how's it going with your team selection?"

"I'll use Kimble for the airport. The two poor saps who got stuck listening to him can go with you to The Gent's place; they deserve it. I'll get ten others from D.C. and lock them in a hotel in NYC. You can brief them at the last minute." He paused, searching for the right words. "Don't you think we should break it to the local PD, in case it turns into a shoot-out?"

"No. It won't. The Gent won't go out guns blazing, it's not his style. All that security isn't to keep us out, it's to combat a mob war, or attempted hit. The only ones who might give you any shit are the guards, and even they'll give up if he tells them to. I want you to get a construction team in the area; double check there's no tunnel or way out we don't know about."

"Will do."

"And for fuck's sake, keep it low-key."

"I have done this before, you know."

Huntley ended the call, fondled his phone, and grinned. He hadn't felt this good in a long time. At last, The Gent within his grasp, and for extra satisfaction, the arrogant little Irish shit was going to have to take the stand to send his sugar daddy away for life. Then we'll see how cocky he is under witness protection, stuck in some shithole in the Midwest waiting for the day a Romano goon knocks on his door.

Chapter 59

The weather was unseasonably warm for Kentucky in the first week of November. Oliver found himself sweating under his thick jacket, but wasn't sure if it was the humidity or his nerves.

The twenty-two-year-old mare he bid on had a long shaggy coat and a dipped back, from long years of carrying foals inside her for eleven months at a time.

Oliver's bid got her without much opposition. She was the tenth and final addition to the team of trafficking mules. Each one had cost less than eight thousand dollars. He signed the sales slip and made arrangements to send the mare to Four Oaks Farm.

His throat was dry so he ambled over to the bar and ordered himself a congratulatory drink. In an instant, Pat materialized at his shoulder.

"I'll say it again, that's a quare bunch of mares you bought. Old as the hills, every one of them," he said, staring at Oliver's cold beer.

"True, Pat, but like I said, Marco and I want to try something different. They've all produced decent winners on turf in the past, if we can get them in foal to a good Irish stallion, we'll be laughing."

"That's a big if. Sure, God was a boy the last time any of them gave birth."

"We can only hope, Pat."

"Ah sure, fools and their money."

"I was about to offer you a drink, but if you're going to take the piss . . ."

Pat's eyes lit up. "Oh er, sorry. I didn't mean it."

Oliver rolled his eyes. "Yeah, yeah, Pat. Bottle or draught?"

"Bottle."

He shook his head in amusement as Pat guzzled the beer. It would be too easy to let Pat see us and call the cops, Oliver thought. But that would be a death sentence and, as annoying as he was, he didn't deserve to be nailed to the door.

Oliver's phone rang, and he used it as an excuse to extricate himself from Pat.

"What's up, Bec?" he said, weaving through the bar.

"Got the last one?"

"Sure have."

"Good. They'll need a hormone shot tonight. Then we'll get started treating in a week. I'll keep them filled with hormones till we load up."

"Sounds perfect. I talked to the shipping agent earlier. Three weeks from tomorrow. There'll be twenty-five horses on the flight," he paused for effect. "Two flying grooms. And you're the only vet."

"Good. When are you going home?"

"In a few minutes. I'll cook, if you give the injections at the farm."

"Deal."

Oliver made a final tour of the sales complex. He wandered about and took the place in one last time. In his early twenties, he had always imagined that he would spend a lifetime in places like this, buying and selling horses for large sums. But now everything was different. He bid goodbye to Keeneland and drove home.

He rang Mike, who called back ten minutes later as Oliver was peeling onions, weeping.

"What the fuck's wrong with you?" asked Mike, as Oliver sniffled on the line.

"Onions. We'll be good to go in three weeks. How do you want to do this?"

"Couriers. They'll call you. Then you bring 'em wherever you want."

"The same place. It'll be early morning, before anyone shows up."

"OK, call me again the day before you need it."

"OK."

"Good luck." The line went dead.

"I'll bloody well need it," Oliver muttered, as the knife nicked his thumb and blood stained the chopping board.

* * *

Oliver waited in the car park of a popular restaurant near Fayette Mall. Looking at his watch, he swore at them for their tardiness. It was nearly one am and the place was closing up; the lot was emptying of cars, but there were no grey sedans around.

Ten minutes later, a green Chevrolet station-wagon pulled up opposite him, and the driver lit a cigarette and let his arm dangle out of the window between drags. Oliver recognised the man and the signal. He started up the SUV and inched out of his place towards the new arrival.

"You looking for a horse farm?" he said to Tomo.

The hard features broke into a sarcastic smile, then Tomo flicked his smoke onto the ground and started up the engine. They crossed Lexington in convoy and slid up the avenue of Four Oaks.

Rebecca opened the barn doors, and Tomo reversed into the barn. Oliver parked the SUV and jumped out to help Rebecca close the large wooden doors. In the barn, one or two of the mares made snorting sounds and stuck their heads over their doors, curious, eyes blinking in the bright glare from the headlights.

Oliver could see the two little thugs checking out Rebecca as she walked through the headlight beam towards the rear of the car. "Turn the lights out," he ordered. "You'll frighten the horses."

They did so without a word, but the looks on their faces told another story. Rebecca opened the trunk and flicked back the blanket covering the merchandise, whistling when she saw the fifty canisters.

"That's a lot of coke," she said to nobody in particular.

Oliver appeared beside her, equally impressed and dismayed. The delivery men stayed in their seats.

"Can you give us a hand to unload?" said Oliver.

Tomo shrugged and punched his accomplice on the shoulder. Grumbling, Tito got out to lend a hand.

"OK, we're going to need them all over there, on that large sheet of plastic." Rebecca indicated to the work station she had laid out near the stocks. It was a larger, more elaborate version of what she had set up to impregnate Painter. To the delivery men, it looked like a field hospital in a war zone. Green sheets and plastic were draped everywhere, in addition to four open containers of iodine solution.

Oliver and his reluctant helper unloaded the car, while Rebecca began dipping the canisters in the iodine solution. She put five into each container and let them soak. Then she emptied five gallons of lubricant into a large tub.

When the car was empty, Tomo nodded at Oliver and started up the engine. Oliver ran to the doors and threw them open. The car eased out into the brisk night air and Oliver watched it disappear down the avenue.

"Assholes," he said.

He closed the doors and got the first mare from her stable. It was going to be a long night.

It was nearly seven and dawn was creeping over central Kentucky when Rebecca finally finished the last mare. All ten were now loaded up with cocaine, and all on antibiotics. She had not bothered with any sedatives. Instead Oliver had restrained the old horses by squeezing an ear if any of them objected to the impregnation procedure. Most of these old girls had been around the block and seen it all before. To them, this was just another desperate veterinary procedure to try to coax one last pregnancy out of them. It was only when they were filled up that symptoms of discomfort became visible on some of them.

Oliver rubbed the forehead of the mare nearest him. "I'm sorry, old girl. You've done nothing to anybody," he whispered.

"Don't beat yourself up, hon," said Rebecca. "They've had a long life and the end'll be quick and painless, I promise."

He let his hand drop and glanced at another mare. "Hmm.

Will they hold out?" he asked, watching the horse paw the ground.

"Should do. I gave them all a large shot of painkiller. Enough to get us there and loaded. Then we'll hit 'em with the cocktail. Then we let the flying grooms panic," she said, winking.

Oliver nodded thoughtfully. "Like I said, not just a pretty face."

She punched him on the arm playfully, then they set about tidying up the evidence.

A few minutes later, Pat poked his head into the barn. "How're you? Jaysus, but you're at it early."

"No rest for the wicked, Pat," said Oliver, rolling his eyes.

Pat scanned the barn and the stocks, looking for something to question them about, but the sound of the lorry pulling into to the yard provided a welcome distraction.

Oliver tapped Pat on the shoulder. "Help them back up to the ramp, will you? We'll get the bags ready."

"Yes, Boss, right you be," he said, with just a touch of sarcasm.

They loaded the old mares onto the truck and were trundling up the interstate highway half an hour later. Rebecca passed out into a deep sleep.

Having triple-checked that all the mares were now the registered property of Robert Romano in their passports, he stowed the documents in his bag, tried to settle his mind, and eventually closed his eyes. When he woke with a start several hours later, he looked out the window and saw they were stopped at the cargo entrance of O'Hare Airport. The driver showed his shipping papers to the guards and was ushered inside. Oliver nudged Rebecca awake.

"Oh boy, did I sleep the whole way?" she said, stretching her arms.

"We both did."

She smiled groggily.

"Back to business, I'm afraid," he said.

Rebecca rubbed her eyes. "Right, a shot of oxytocin to the first two mares now. Intramuscular – two ccs. We want a delay before it starts to work."

"Sure thing," he said, drawing up the injections.

Rebecca rummaged in the bag and drew two large fifty cc syringes of a clear liquid. "Keep that with the big shots of oxy. When I give you the signal, get it done fast and clean."

Oliver grimaced, his heart was thumping against his chest. He placed the four syringes in the inside pocket of his jacket and zipped it up.

"I mean it," she said sternly. "You have to be quick."

He stared at the floor, like he hadn't heard her.

"You OK, hon?"

"Up till now, this was all words: a plan. Now I've actually got to put a horse down. I haven't had to do that since Gorman's place. And back then, I didn't have much choice." He slumped onto the seat.

She took his face in her hands. "We don't have much choice now. I'm not thrilled about this either, but they're all old and, well, if someone else had bought them at that sale and got them pregnant again, they'd probably suffer in some other way from the stress of it all. This way, they won't feel a thing and the ones you give oxy to will just think they're in labour. It'll be OK, hon."

Oliver hugged her.

"I'll do it if you want."

"No, Bec. My idea, my job. I'll be OK." He chewed his lip. "Marco's going down for this; the fucker."

She kissed him on the cheek.

He squeezed through the partitions and gave the first injections.

The plane was a horses-only flight. Inside, it was divided up into twenty-five individual stalls and there was a long ramp extending from the rear cargo doors to the ground. The truck was allowed to pull up to just a few yards outside the wingspan of the 757. Oliver leapt out and let the ramp down directly onto the tarmac.

Two figures approached, one carrying a large sack of wood shavings.

The taller man spoke to Oliver with a thick Irish accent. "Well, Oliver McMahon, is it? How're ya doin'? Tom Callaghan, a fellow Limerick man." He extended a large hand.

"Hi, Tom." Oliver shook his hand vigorously. "Your reputation precedes you."

Tom was one of a community of professional flying grooms who spent their lives escorting horses around the world on planes. He was a sprightly, teetotal man in his early fifties, and was known for being the best there was.

"Cathal." He clicked his fingers at his short, pimply sidekick. "Look lively, scatter a bit o' shavings on the ramp." He shook his head at Oliver. "Young fellas. I'm trying to show him the ropes, but God love him, he's wicked dopey."

Oliver eyed the plane. "Are yours already loaded?"

"They are. I always like to get here in plenty of time." He looked at his watch. "You're cuttin' it fine. We'd better kick on. Cathal, get back on the plane and watch the horses. I'll help this lot load up."

The young guy scurried up the ramp and disappeared into the belly of the plane.

Tom took a look inside the plane and was surprised to see Rebecca. "Oh, are you the vet?"

"Sure am."

"Grand, well you wait here and we'll start loading."

Oliver tossed him a lead rope, they grabbed a horse each and the driver opened the partitions.

"Fockin' hell, this lot've seen better days," said Tom. "They look shooker than my auld mother."

Oliver didn't reply.

The two old mares clambered stiffly up the ramp into the plane, without even so much as a snort or whinny.

When Tom returned to the truck ahead of Oliver, he cast an appraising eye over the remaining horses and was not best pleased. "Jaysus," he said. "There's a couple there don't look too fockin' happy at all."

"Don't worry about it," said Oliver dismissively. "They'll be grand. They're just old, is all."

Tom crouched down and shuffled up through the partitions, inspecting each horse individually. Oliver watched him in silence.

Rebecca hopped down from the truck and arranged their bags on the tarmac.

Tom called after her. "Listen, young one, I don't know what you're like as a vet, but you want to get back in here and have a look at these last few. One looks sweaty and the other colicky. In fact, if I didn't know better, I'd swear she was having contractions."

"I'll deal with it," she said, climbing back into the truck. "You guys get the next two loaded."

They led the next two off, and Rebecca stood watching the mares.

When Tom returned, he looked quizzically at the vet.

"They're fine. Just a bit upset by the road. Heart rates are normal, but I gave one a shot of fenadine just in case."

She could see Tom wondering where her stethoscope was. "Look, I've been at this for donkey's years, and I'm telling you, those two don't look right."

"They're fine," she said again, in a stern voice.

He shook his head. "Well, you're the vet, but I'm not happy about this. If those mares start to colic or thrash about when we're up over the Atlantic, then we're focked, you know that?"

Oliver appeared behind him and clapped a hand on his shoulder. "They'll be fine, Tom, chill out. You worry about your own horses, we'll take care of ours, OK?"

The man led the next mare into the plane, muttering to himself disapprovingly about young people and standards of work.

They finished loading, then the Customs officers conducted a final check of the plane and the passports. Tom grumbled to them about Rebecca, but they simply stated that, as a groom, he should listen to her veterinary opinion and leave it at that.

Shortly afterwards, the doors were closed. Tom and Cathal stood at strategic positions between the partitions of the fifteen horses they were officially escorting. Rebecca watched the first few of theirs, obstructing Tom's view of Oliver, who stood at the rear of the plane, beside the second last horse. The two filled with oxytocin were near Rebecca. They were looking confused and uncomfortable.

The engines fired up and, as they began taxiing, the cabin attendant informed them they were second in line for take-off.

Oliver produced the two large syringes from his jacket and gripped them in his left hand, then inched down to stand beside the head of the last horse. The plane ambled along the taxiway. Rebecca nodded and mouthed, "Go, go."

They felt the plane swing onto the runway. Oliver jabbed the syringe into the neck of the animal beside him, pulled back to confirm he was in the vein and swiftly pushed the contents into the horse's jugular. The effect was instantaneous: the animal dropped to the ground. Dead.

The massive dose of potassium had been enough to induce instant cardiac arrest, but wouldn't show up on any autopsy. Rebecca had been adamant that they could not use normal T61 humane killer, because it had to look like an accident.

The plane was gathering speed at an alarming rate; the noise was deafening. Rebecca shouted to Tom, "We've got a problem! Tell the pilot!"

The older man swore. "I fockin' knew it! Cathal, sprint, tell them to abort. NOW!"

The young guy went deathly pale. The plane was starting to climb. In his panic to move, Cathal was thrown back, and he crashed to the floor banging his head.

Rebecca braced herself and swore. "Fuck, fuck. We have to land."

"Mother of God," Tom said to her. "You fockin' stupid yoke, you're not cut out for this job."

Oliver euthanised the second horse and pulled himself towards the next two, whom he gave more oxytocin. Then he bound all four syringes together with a rubber band and slipped them into his pocket. Only then did he realize, through the fog of adrenaline coursing through his veins, that they were airborne. He braced himself against the partition and shot a panicked look at Rebecca.

"What the fuck?" he shouted above the engines.

The plane climbed steadily, and he inched along the aisleway to Rebecca and made a show of telling her that two were dead and two looking dodgy.

Tom swore again. "McMahon, get your fockin' hole up there and tell the crew we're turning back. You come with me, Missy, I want to see what kinda shit you've got us into."

Rebecca remained silent, and they groped their way rearwards. Oliver pulled himself towards Cathal, who sat on the floor rubbing his head. He was in tears. "Jesus, I'm awful sorry. T'was too late when Tom shouted."

"Don't worry about it. Your head OK?"

"Bit sore, but I'll be grand."

Oliver stepped over him until he reached the jumpseat. Tapping the dozing shipping agency representative on his shoulder, he roared into his ear, "Tell the captain we have to abort. A horse has died, and another looks pretty sick."

The man's eyes flicked open. "Goddamn!" He reached for the intercom and repeated it all for the cockpit crew.

In a minute, Oliver could feel the plane even out and slow down. The cockpit door opened and a concerned-looking pilot stepped out.

"What's going on?" asked the Captain.

"Some of the horses are down. One's dead, I think. It looks like we'll have to turn back."

The pilot took in what he said, then walked to the rear.

Tom took delight in informing him that, due to Rebecca's neglect, they had put everyone at risk.

"And that's not all. Get a load of this." He grabbed the Captain by the elbow and made him look over the partition.

The mare was thrown down awkwardly in the stall, wedged in the bottom of it, straining like she was giving birth. But the only thing emerging from her vagina was a tubular object.

The Captain said nothing, but returned to the cockpit and locked the door.

Tom was livid. He took stock of the situation and bellowed at Rebecca and Oliver. "I don't know what the fock you lot are trying to get away with, but you're in some deep shit now. There's two dead ones, another colicking, and this one." He jabbed his finger at the animal nearest him. "She's fockin' spitting some kind of contraption out of her, and all you two can do is stand there looking stupid."

He poked Oliver in the chest. "I expected more of you, McMahon. I thought you were a proper horseman. I shoulda known when I heard those rumours about your boss, and then that whole thing with your brother. Oh, yeah. It all comes out in the end."

Oliver rolled his eyes at Rebecca. They let him rant and rave. There was nothing to be gained from saying anything.

Agents Rosen and Kimble were waiting patiently in the artificial light of a windowless office in the bowels of O'Hare Airport, under the pretext of doing a special inspection of a flight due in from Istanbul in an hour.

The only other occupant of the pokey office space was a portly Customs officer, who sat at his desk trying to pass off computer solitaire as engrossing paperwork, and sipping a coke from the can.

Rosen tried not to look at his watch too often, but he was sure the call should have come by now. Had something gone wrong?

Eventually, the desk phone throbbed and buzzed. The officer minimized his game and sighed as he picked up.

"Yeah?" he said, in a thick local accent.

The voice barked an order at him. He kept the receiver wedged under his chin, ended the call, and dialled for help. "Yeah, it's Johnson. We got flight aborted after take-off. Tower requests Customs and local PD. Can you call up a car?" He listened to the reply. "I'm on my way." He dropped the receiver into its cradle with a bang.

Agent Rosen pricked up his ears. "What's going on?"

"A plane's doubling back five minutes after take-off. Some kind of emergency. They want us and the cops to meet it."

"Terrorists?" said Monica.

The officer shrugged. "Nah, if they thought that, the plane'd be diverted and all hell'd break loose." He got up and strapped on his gun belt.

Rosen looked at his watch. "Mind if we tag along? Nothing else to do."

He shrugged again. "If you want." He shuffled his bulk towards the door. "Say, you any good with animals?"

"What?" asked Monica.

"Animals. They've got 'em on board."

Outside the terminal, they waited by an airport police car for the plane to land. Passenger jets roared overhead and all around them. Monica asked a cop for earplugs, which produced a loud cackle and a bit of mocking. She walked away from the group and flicked the finger to a cop who wolf-whistled.

Rosen turned his back and made a call.

"It's me. The plane took off. OK, OK, don't have a shit; it turned around. We're waiting on the ground. You should go now."

"Let me know how it goes down," said Huntley. "And don't forget, you'll have to take the syringes from our guy before PD finds them."

"Won't he dump them on board?"

"No, if he does that, they'll be found when they tear the plane apart. He knows he has to give them to you. If PD does find them, pull rank and take over, citing drugs as the cause."

"Leave it to me."

* * *

Huntley got out of his blacked-out SUV. The stress lines on his face were deeper and craggier than usual, and his skin was almost transparent from lack of sleep. He scanned the thickly wooded area where the team was parked up waiting. The squad consisted of Mitch and Jerry from the listening post, and ten other agents brought in from Washington DC and briefed on the mission just two hours ago. They would drive the ten miles to Marco's fortress, in a convoy consisting of Huntley's SUV, a blacked-out minivan, and two unmarked prisoner transportation wagons.

Huntley checked his gun and patted his pocket for the warrant. The other agents followed his lead, checking their weapons; some tapped their kevlar vests for good luck and zipped up their

DEA jackets. Mitch and Jerry as team leaders were excited at the prospect of taking down a crime boss and getting credit for their months of confinement in a rented house.

"Saddle up," said Huntley, in an ominous voice. "You three, with me. We drive hard and fast, but no sirens. Understand?" The other men nodded. Huntley got behind the wheel and the convoy pulled out of the woods. They stuck to the quiet roads for as long as possible, before swinging out into suburbia.

Chapter 60

The plane taxied away from the runway and ground to a halt on an empty piece of tarmac near the cargo terminal. The Customs officers waiting in the cars had been given direct radio contact with the Captain, who informed them two horses were dead and others appeared to be sick. He also did his best to describe the strange object he had seen protruding from one distressed animal.

The cargo doors were kept locked, while the ground staff drove a sky-stair up to the smaller front door. The Customs officers rattled their way into the plane without delay, the two cops following them. Agents Rosen and Kimble climbed up last, as if only vaguely interested in the situation.

Rosen poked his head into the plane and took stock of the situation. Customs officer Johnson was standing in the cockpit doorway, talking in hushed tones to the pilots. Another was leading the two cops back through the aircraft toward the rear, where Oliver, Rebecca and one very angry, red-faced man were standing. The flight steward was attending to a young guy plonked on the jumpseat with a cut on his forehead and a frightened look on his face.

The horses in the forward part of the plane were snorting curiously at the visitors, while a number of those towards the rear were whinnying nervously and pawing the ground.

Rosen moved into the aisle and motioned for Kimble to remain in the doorway. She was visibly pleased to do so, and shot a horrified look at the nearest horse, who snorted sharply at her.

Rosen took in the emotional babbling and finger-pointing of the red-faced man, and saw the expression on the cops' faces when

362

they looked over the partition. The Customs officer called for his partner, who pushed his considerable bulk past Rosen and joined the others.

Oliver and Rebecca were boxed in at the rear of the plane, doing their best to look nervous. The cops drew their guns and the Customs officers cuffed them. The red-faced man was also cuffed, much to his disgust. He started complaining even louder. "What the fock are you doing? Tis them, tis all them," he kept repeating.

Officer Johnson beckoned for Rosen to join them.

"It's all fun and games today," said the DEA agent in a relaxed voice. "What's the deal?"

"You'd better look in there," said Johnson, cocking his thumb at the nearest stall.

Rosen peered at the stricken horse and carefully looked at the tubular object now almost all the way out of the horse's vagina. Immediately, his demeanour changed.

"Holy fucking shit!" he said. "I've got a good idea what that is. I've got to insist that DEA take over the situation." He whipped out his badge for all to see.

Johnson gave him a blank look. "You *what?*"

Rosen turned his head. "Kimble, get your ass back here."

Monica trotted up to her boss, while avoiding to touch off any of the stalls. She listened intently with a calm expression while Rosen barked orders at her.

"Take these three off the plane; the police officers will help you. Stash them in a holding room and keep them restrained. Do not, repeat, *do not* let anyone question or search them until I join you. I'll stay here with Customs and search the plane."

Then he turned to Johnson. "Get me a vet and get the horse trucks back for the animals. They can't have gone that far. We're also going to need dogs and more men to go through the plane. Get on it."

Johnson still had the blank look on his round face.

"Now!" barked Rosen.

Johnson pulled his radio to his face and repeated Rosen's requirements.

Rosen shot Monica a look, which said: what are you still doing here?

"What about the plane we're waiting for?" she said.

"I'll get another team for that, it's not due in for an hour."

She nodded and drew her weapon. "Let's go." She waved the muzzle at Oliver and a cop grabbed him by the elbow and moved him out. The second took Tom, and Monica escorted Rebecca off the aircraft.

Nobody said a word until they were seated on the floor in a small room.

* * *

Mike answered his phone. "Yeah?"

The voice spoke in a whisper. "The plane came back. There were cops crawling all over it. They took everyone away and now they're hauling dead horses off."

"Oh fuck." Mike hung up and ran to a payphone.

"This is a fockin' total joke altogether," Tom said to Monica and the cops.

He was met with stony gazes from the three chairs at the other side of the room.

Tom's eyes were wild with rage. He leaned closer to Oliver and strained his hands in their cuffs. "You fockin' asshole."

One cop stood and pushed Tom's shoulder with his baton. "Easy, now. Back to the wall and calm down, OK?"

Tom took a deep breath. "You know his brother was caught smuggling stuff on his planes in Ireland?" he said to Monica. "I'm telling you, it runs in the family. By all accounts, he was a prizewinning asshole, too."

Monica looked a bit unsure of herself. In, truth she was as much in the dark as the poor man spitting fire opposite her.

Rebecca broke the tension by asking for water and telling Tom to shut his ass, which made the young agent smirk. She dispatched a cop to get a large bottle and six cups.

Four-and-a-half hours later, Tom was still seething with rage, but Oliver and Rebecca were fast asleep on each other's shoulders.

Monica figured this was the best textbook indication of guilt that she had seen in the field.

An hour after that, Rosen burst into the room with four more DEA agents and dismissed the cops, who vacated their chairs hastily in case he changed his mind. Monica stood upright as if at attention.

"We take them all to local CPD station for questioning. They ride in separate cars." He pointed at Oliver. "Kimble, he comes with us."

Oliver was bundled into the backseat of Rosen's car. He found it difficult to sit properly wearing handcuffs and had to sit sideways, facing Monica, who looked at him like he was a piece of garbage.

When they were underway, the senior agent addressed his partner. "Kimble, check his jacket and remove any syringes you might find."

Her jaw dropped open as if she was about to ask a question, but she remained silent and went through Oliver's pockets, avoiding eye contact with him. She found the bundle in his pocket and held it up.

"This what you want?"

Rosen glanced in the mirror. "Yeah, throw it on the front seat. Are there any more?"

"No," answered Oliver.

"Nobody's talking to you," spat Monica.

"It's alright, Monica. Go easy on him, there's a few things you don't know. Are you OK, man?"

"Yes, thanks. Except for all the abuse I've had to put up with – that Tom Callaghan could be your star witness. At least, he could keep me and Rebecca from getting nailed."

Rosen glanced back pensively at him in the mirror.

Glancing from Oliver to her boss, Monica said, "You going to fill me in?"

Rosen told her the whole story.

"So the other team's busting Marco Romano as we speak?" she said.

* * *

Marco was sitting in the kitchen sipping a coffee and watching the trees rustle in the mid-morning breeze. His terrier was snuggled on his lap and snoring lightly. Marco stroked him, grinning as he considered the profit he would make from the shipment. He would be the first to flood Celtic Tiger Ireland with proper high quality product. They would go mad for it, and they had cash to burn.

The intercom on the kitchen wall buzzed urgently. Marco sighed and got up, depositing the disgruntled dog onto the floor.

He could barely understand the old man's garbled gibberish at the other end.

"Luigi, slow down. What the fuck's wrong?"

Luigi took a deep breath and got a grip of himself. "Sorry, Marco, but there's a bunch of blacked-out cars and vans at the gate, and a goddamn Fed waving a badge and a piece of paper."

"Jesus fuckin' . . ." Marco gripped the cordless handset in his fist and hurried into the den, where he found his son sprawled on the sofa watching a romantic comedy.

"Gimme that thing," he said, snatching the remote from Robert's hand.

The young Romano's surprise turned to shock when he saw the image from the gate camera plastered onto the enormous screen.

Marco's face darkened, and he clenched his other fist so hard, the knuckles turned white. There was a tinny voice coming from the phone.

"What?" he said, bringing it up to his ear.

"Do I let them in?"

"If that's a warrant, you'll have to. Tell the guards to stand down. All their weapons are licenced, right?"

"Yeah, Marco. To the gun club out west."

"Will they find the heavy weapons?"

"Not a chance, unless they cut the tree down."

"Good. Open the gate a crack and check the warrant. If it's good, let them in. I don't want a fuckin' shoot out, so make sure all three guards are standing in front of the house with their guns on the ground and their hands in the air. Got it?"

"Got it."

"And tell everyone to be polite, no matter what, OK?"

"OK, Marco."

The Mafia boss threw the phone hard against the wall, shattering it. His son jumped. It only took a second for the wheels to turn in Marco's head. That little Irish prick must have fucked something up at the airport. The only question was: by accident, or on purpose? If they had a warrant ready, they must've known something. He considered the options.

"Robert, get your ass upstairs. Shit's hit the fan, we gotta talk," he said, in a voice that was pure, rough, street menace. "You stay here, little buddy," he said affectionately to the dog, which looked at him as if he understood. "When those assholes come in, you bite 'em. OK?" The dog barked. Marco grinned again and began trotting up the stairway.

Robert was too bewildered to protest, so he followed his father meekly up to the small room at the top of the house. They sat on the window seat and watched Luigi open the gate and talk to the agent.

"Dad, am I going to lose you?"

Marco looked at his frightened son with an expression that was a mixture of disappointment and steely resolve. His phone rang. "Boss, the plane turned back. There's cops all over it. There's dead horses, too."

"I got Feds here, too. You take off. Now. Find the terriers. You said they'd do anything for me; now's the time. They gotta step up, just like we said. Or else you gotta tidy up. Understand?"

"Sure thing. I'm on it."

"You don't have time to fuck around. Use the Weasel."

"It's done, Boss."

"Good luck." He flipped the device shut and checked the front gate. It was opening slowly, and Luigi was standing just inside it with his three guys. Three shotguns and a pistol were lying on the ground. Marco looked at his watch. He took the SIM card out of his phone and bit it in two, then he dropped the handset and stood on it.

"What's going on, Dad?"

"Robert, listen to me very carefully," he said, jabbing a finger at his son. "I got some business going with Oliver and the horses. We've been using horses to ship product to Ireland."

"Product?"

Marco had an exasperated look in his eyes. "Don't play dumb with me. That fuckin' South American powder you like so much. Now shut up and let me finish."

Robert was visibly shocked.

"Here's the thing: those fuckin' assholes outside are Feds with a warrant, so I know something's gone wrong. I want you to give a statement saying that the operation had nothing to do with me. You say the terriers, Tomo and Tito, came to you with a deal. You wanted to prove yourself to me, so you used your horses – they're yours on paper, remember – to ship the stuff to Ireland. You knew there was demand there and a shortage of quality product. Those two little fuckers wanted to make extra money and they heard that shit about Oliver's brother, so they figured he'd be an easy touch for the transport. You guys all wanted to make good business to get rich and impress me."

"But, Dad . . . I . . ."

"Shut up. Tell the Feds it was them, and you and the Irishman. They'll believe you, 'cause the terriers'll back up your story and, after all, you are my son." He slapped Robert playfully on the face. "They don't know you're soft, like your mother. It's time to man up and do this one thing for me. Don't worry, I'll get you all kinds of lawyers and shit. You'll probably get eight to ten. Shit, you'll still be young when you get out. A man, ready to go into business with me: set for life. I mean it."

"Eight to ten years? You'd sent me to jail for eight years just to save yourself?" Robert sobbed.

"It's not a simple as that. Yeah, I know I'm getting old," he said, waving his hand dismissively. "But I gotta stay out here to run the business. If I go away, the fuckers'll start a war and they'll probably even come after you. So you see, I gotta stay out here. And don't worry, you'll be safe inside. Nobody'll put a finger on you. That's a guarantee."

"So you'd send me to jail *just to keep your business running?*"

"Hey, this fuckin' business pays for the clothes on your back and your lifestyle. I don't see you complaining 'bout that. You're my son; I'd *never* ask you to make your bones, but you gotta do this for the family."

"But I never wanted to be a part of it."

"You like the fuckin' money, though, and the wheels I grease for you."

"Well, I . . ."

"Well, you what? You could've told me to fuck off, and stayed in California being a poor artist."

"But you forced me to come back. You bribed me!"

"Yeah, and you took it. So don't be a pussy when it's payback. Come on, think of it as a deal. You do this for me and you're made."

Robert could feel tears welling up. He switched his gaze from his father to the window, and could see Luigi and the others being handcuffed and loaded into a van. Other agents cocked their weapons in the direction of the house. One saw the figures in the top window and pointed directly at Robert.

"And what if I don't do it? What if I just keep my mouth shut?"

Marco flew into a rage. He grabbed his son by the neck. "You don't say no to me!" he roared. "This is not a fuckin' request, understand?"

Robert was so stunned by his father that, for a moment, his fear shut down and the distant memory of his mother being attacked came flooding back.

"So now you're going to bully me, like you did Mom."

Marco's eyes were as black as coal, but he faltered for a second, relaxing his grip. "I loved your mother; I still do. Her death was the worst thing ever happened to me, but she was weak." He uttered the last few words in a tone of sheer contempt.

"Maybe she wasn't weak, maybe she just wasn't like you."

The big man's resolve returned, and he darted his fist into his son's jaw with lightning speed, knocking him off the window seat into a heap on the floor.

"Fuck you!" he bellowed like a wild animal. "Your mother was weak; she took her own life." Even as he said the words, he could not believe he had uttered them.

His son looked up at him with glazed eyes. "Dad? What?"

There was a banging sound from below, as a battering ram was used on the front door.

Marco shut his eyes, pinched the bridge of his nose, then clasped his hands together. "Your mother took the easy way out – she took an overdose. I found her, but it was too late. I got the doctor and coroner to say it was a heart attack, and I greased palms to cover it up." He paused and looked at his son. "For what it's worth, I'm sorry it happened."

Robert held his head in his hands. "But why, Dad? *Why?*" His brain spun back to the day she had held him, crying. He started to think he could guess the answer.

"She did it because she couldn't face the truth, but she didn't want to leave, either."

"Didn't want to, or couldn't?"

Marco stared coldly at his son.

"Which was it, Dad?"

The right fist shot out again and caught Robert on the temple. He let out a cry, put his arms over his head, and curled up into a little ball. The tears were flowing freely now.

Marco sighed and searched his mind for something to say. "I'm sorry," in an aggressive tone, was all he could manage.

He put his hand out to touch his son, but the cries of the Feds and careful footsteps on the creaky wooden stairs stopped him. He withdrew it.

"We're clear, right?" he said. "You plead guilty, we'll get you a deal, you'll be out in eight-to-ten."

Robert just kept crying.

Marco stood up, took a deep breath, straightened his tie, and opened the door. He put his hands in the air when he saw the first agent.

"We're in here and unarmed," he said softly to the barrel of a gun.

Four agents poured into the room brandishing assault weapons, followed by a thin, unhealthy-looking man in a grey suit.

"Marco Romano?" he said.

Marco nodded. "You must be Huntley. What can I do for you?"

"I have warrants here for your arrest and the arrest of your son. I also have a warrant for the complete search of the premises. Do I need to read you your rights?"

"That'd be nice. Thank you."

* * *

Huntley could barely suppress a smile as he watched his prisoners being driven away in the fading light of evening. He stayed behind with one agent to organise forensics and a thorough search of the whole compound. Huntley would give them orders to scour the place all night and into the next day like busy ants – for as long as it took. He had waited a long time to get access to Marco Romano's house. After the preliminary interviews tonight, he thought he might treat himself to a beer.

The tall skinny guy known as Jimmy the Weasel got into the car. Mike grimaced from the foul smell which followed him. This was part of the reason he earned his moniker; his breath was so bad, everybody was convinced he ate raw chicken. Coupled with his lean frame, sharp features and darting eyes, he was almost a rodent in human form.

Mike looked at his cheap crumpled suit. "Jesus, Jimmy, you gotta change that shit sometime. You're letting the fuckin' side down. The boss has shot people for less, you know."

"He goin' pay for it?"

"What do you think?"

"Fuck you, Mike."

They both burst into fits of laughter. After a few minutes, the smiles disappeared from their faces.

"So what's the deal?" asked Jimmy.

"You got your rifle?"

Jimmy patted the bag on his lap.

Mike looked at his watch, then the amber sky. "We don't got much time. Fuckin' light's going."

"Long as I can see, I can shoot."

"Good. I got some shit to tell the terriers at the landfill near the shore in ten minutes. I'll drop you round the back. Find a spot to watch, and if they try any fuckin' shit, take care of it. You get one down, I'll do the other up close."

"No fuckin' problem, Mikey." Jimmy narrowed his eyes and scratched his chin. "Only thing is, they're good fuckin' guys. You sure about this?"

"I gotta ask them to do a shitty job. If they do it, they get made; if not, we tidy up."

"Must be a fuckin' shitty job."

"Enough with the questions. It comes from the top."

"Say no more."

"Keep an eye on me. I'll smoke. If I flick the butt away, you shoot. If I drop it and stand on it, you do nothing. Got it?"

Jimmy nodded. "Piece o' cake."

They arrived at a giant landfill site, which received a constant stream of barges from New York City and State. It was a vast, sprawling mess of rubbish and scavengers. Seagulls, rats and homeless people competed for the things that other people considered out of sight, out of mind.

Marco and Mike used the place from time to time for meetings that had the potential to get messy. They had a share in the waste business, and the union workers on site had a convenient habit of forgetting anything they saw.

Mike dropped Jimmy off near the rear entrance, and he scurried off behind a giant digger that lay idle now it was past five. Jimmy crouched, clicked open his case, and assembled his pride and joy – a small calibre, military issue, sniper rifle with a telescopic sight.

Mike drove on and parked near the prefabricated units that served as offices. He sat on the bonnet of his car, lit a smoke and called Jimmy.

"You see me?"

"Yeah."

"Can you make the shot?"

"Jesus, Mikey, the light's not great, but there's no wind. I could put a slug up your japs eye if I wanted."

Mike left the cigarette in his mouth and grabbed his crotch. "Fuckin' try it, you cocksucker."

They cackled at each other briefly. Five minutes and another cigarette later, the silver Toyota appeared and parked beside Mike's Cadillac. Tomo and Tito embraced Mike in turn. Mike gave them a warm smile.

"Hey, guys, how you doin'?"

The terriers shrugged. They were men of few words.

"I got a job for you. If you do it and keep your heads down and mouths shut, you'll get made. OK?"

Their faces lit up.

"So what's the job?" asked Tomo.

"The horse shipment went bad, there's Feds at the boss's place. He wants you and his son to take the rap. He'll get you out later, and you'll be set up for life if you own up and keep quiet. Capiche? All you gotta do when they come for you is say it was you, the Irishman and Robert. You did it for extra cash and points with the boss, OK?"

It took a few seconds for the order to sink in. Tomo looked dismayed, but he forced a smile.

Tito opened his mouth before engaging his small brain. "Gee, Mike, it's a big one. I got a body building comp comin' up next month. Can't you get someone else?"

Mike gave him a thunderous stare. "You're not goin' to be asked twice. Make up your fuckin' mind. Now." He took a final drag on the cigarette and held it between his thumb and index finger.

Tomo put a hand on Tito's shoulder. "Sure thing, Mike, we'd be honoured. One for the team. No problem."

Mike was about to let the butt drop when Tito piped up.

"Nah man, fuck that. I been training too fuckin' hard for this comp. Fuck, Mike, get someone else. I can't do this, not now."

The thunderous stare remained as he flicked the butt towards them.

Tito's chest exploded an instant before they heard the crack of the bullet breaking the sound barrier. His body fell against Tomo, who screamed in shock and lost his balance. Mike had enough time to draw his pistol and empty three rounds into Tomo's head and chest. Then he put another in Tito's skull, just to make sure. He wiped the gun, dropped it, and drove off leisurely.

He picked up Jimmy where he had dropped him off.

"Let's get the fuck outta here. By the way, nice shooting for an ugly prick," he said. "Jesus, you stink. You roll around in that shit, or what?"

"Yeah, with your mother when she blew me."

They continued like this as they took the interstate and headed for Wisconsin.

Chapter 61

Sitting in a small, dank interview room in a Jersey police station was not Rebecca's idea of fun. She almost wished that she was back in the drudgery of life as a junior vet, up to her neck in blood and guts all night and taking shit from her boss. The fluorescent light on the ceiling was depressing, and as she sat alone nursing a plastic cup of tepid water, she wondered if they really were going to get away with it. The sparkle was gone from her eyes. She wanted to be with Oliver. Like Dorothy in the film, she wanted to click her heels and return to Kansas, or at least, Lexington.

Every now and then, she shot a quizzical look at the two way mirror on the wall, wondering if anyone was watching.

Eventually, Agent Rosen came in, slamming the door behind him. He had two cups of steaming coffee and a doughnut from a vending machine.

He set a coffee and the doughnut down in front of Rebecca. She sipped the brown liquid and inspected the doughnut warily.

"Sorry, it's all I could rustle up."

"Thanks, but I'll pass. You have it."

He tossed it into the bin with a smile. "You must be tired."

"That ain't the word."

He leaned in close to her conspiratorially and whispered, "OK, this won't take long. I'm going to turn on the tapes and ask you questions. During the interview, neither you nor I will reference the fact that my colleague may have had prior knowledge of the events. You just answer the questions I ask." He winked.

Rebecca nodded slowly and thoughtfully. She glanced at the mirror.

"Don't worry, there's nobody out there except my team."

Relief began to spread across her face. Rosen waved at the glass, then recited the date and time for the record. Rebecca stated her name, date of birth and address.

After the initial questions establishing that she would waive her right to counsel for this interview, and that it was indeed her who inserted the foreign objects into the mares, Rosen produced a piece of paper, on which he had scribbled extensive notes.

"Dr. Liddell, according to the preliminary findings of the Government veterinary surgeon who examined the ten horses after removal to a local clinic, a total of fifty tube-like containers of a substance that appears to be pure cocaine, were removed from the animals in question. Each tube weighed approximately one kilogram. That's a lot of coke. Where'd you get it?"

Rebecca looked at him sideways. "You said *appears to be cocaine*. What does that mean?"

"We all know what it is, but we'll have it confirmed through proper laboratory analysis. Then we won't have to say *appears* any more. I say again, where did you get it?"

"I don't know, two guys brought it last night."

"And who were they?"

"I didn't ask."

"Surely they didn't appear out of thin air."

"Oliver arranged everything. I just did what I was told, no questions asked. It could have been cash or diamonds in those tubes, for all I knew."

They went around in circles for half an hour before Rosen, appearing to believe her story, finally said, "That will be all – for now, Dr. Liddell. You will be provided with a lawyer, unless you wish to procure one of your own. The DA will take your limited co-operation into account."

"Thanks. By the way, how are the horses doing?"

Rosen looked at his notes. "The Government vet said they're all stable and showing no ill effects after removal. They're on antibiotics and stuff, but he says they'll recover from their ordeal." He paused before reading the last bit to her. "It is his opinion that whoever performed the insertion procedures was a very skilled vet, though perhaps of questionable morality."

She shrugged and gave him a lopsided smile.

Rosen nodded at the glass and left the room.

Huntley found Oliver slumped on the table, his head cradled in his arms. The agent had to prod him to wake him up.

"You don't exactly make yourself look very innocent, sleeping like a baby the last couple hours."

Oliver grunted. He was past caring. The stress had flooded out of his body; he felt desperately tired.

"Do you ever stop being a cocky little shit?"

"Agent Huntley, this may surprise you, but I'm really not the cocky little shit I pretended to be. It was a combination of bravado and fear. Right now, I'm just exhausted."

Huntley was taken aback for an instant, but he cleared his mind and came straight to the point.

"OK, it's like this. We'll keep your girlfriend out of it, but you'll have to testify that Marco personally told you to put the drugs in the horses."

"Can you guarantee Rebecca and I protection – and my mother in Ireland?"

"That old chestnut again. Like I said, I can't do shit for your mother."

"Then you'll have to make do without a testimony."

Huntley had had enough. "Oliver, do you think it was skill, or just blind luck that we left you alone the last year or so?"

He looked at the agent, puzzled.

"Wake up, boy. We've been trying to find a way to get Marco Romano for years, and you showed me the way in. You may think that giving me a tip-off gives you a free pass, but you're wrong. I could put you away for smuggling. Like that." He clicked his fingers for dramatic effect.

"So if you know everything, then you don't need me."

"It's not that easy, smartass. It's like this. We have some audio footage of Marco telling Mike the Nail to organise the Painter and send her away, which I can now assume was the first shipment."

Oliver nodded.

"He goes on to instruct him to buy some more horses – cheap ones – and to instruct you to acquire them. We also have him at a later date, giving an order to have you beaten as a reminder to do your job. We didn't fully appreciate the significance of these matters until you came to me, but you're still the key. Without testimony, there's not enough clear verbal evidence to convict him, his lawyers would have a field day."

Oliver pricked up his ears. "Hold on a second, are you saying you bugged his house?"

"Thanks to you." Huntley spread a satisfied smile on his gaunt face. "It was only when we realised he let you in his house and appeared to trust you, that we got an idea for infiltration."

Oliver was astounded. "You're shitting me?"

"I never joke about my work."

"Why didn't you tap his mobile?""

"What?"

"Sorry – cell phone."

Huntley shook his head gravely. "We're not the NSA or CIA. Besides, he's usually careful and uses codes. We thought he'd be more relaxed in his house. Anyway, we need you to testify that he gave you the order directly."

"Except he didn't. He told Mike to tell me." Oliver cast his mind back to the day of the Preakness and the attack. "But he did assault me in the den, and there's a direct mention of drugs in that conversation. Did you get that on tape?"

"No," said Huntley, with a grimace.

"Pity," muttered Oliver in a tone of resignation. "So I'll have to take the stand, then?"

Huntley heard him, but did not answer. He was thinking. After a minute, he said, "Did he mention drugs himself?"

Oliver frowned. "Err no, wait . . . I said drugs . . . and told him I thought his idea wouldn't work, then he went nuts, ripped my shirt off, and patted me down. Then he told me never to mention product to him ever again and to just shut up and do my job."

He looked at the wall and continued, nodding, "That's right, he said product, but he was definitely talking about drugs, because of what I said."

The agent took it all in, nodding slowly, and scribbling notes on his legal pad. "Product. Hmm, I like that," he said. "Product," he repeated the word over and over to himself. "You're going to be our star witness."

Oliver had a puzzled look on his face. "Do you mean to tell me that you need testimony to figure out that Marco's code for drugs is *product?*" He chuckled. "Come on, Agent Huntley, it's not brain surgery."

"It doesn't matter what we might know or assume. It matters what we can convince a jury of, and if we don't have a point of reference for his use of the word product, his lawyers will have a fucking field day. Now shut the fuck up and start getting used to the idea that you're going to stand up in court and be a witness for the prosecution."

"I thought Tom was going to be the star witness. I mean, he's the one who raised the alarm. Officially, anyway."

"No, he'll be *your* star witness, to convince them you didn't inform us about the shipment."

Oliver looked sceptically at him. "Please don't tell me that's your idea of protection. Marco won't give a fuck how it happened. If I take the stand, then he'll kill me. And I don't want to end up like my brother."

"Relax, we'll get you new identities, but your living allowance won't be much and you'll have to stay where we put you." He gave Oliver an insincere grin. "But you'll be safe."

"You make it sound so good . . . I was thinking that you could provide two passports for me, two for Rebecca, and two for my mother, and a plane to take us wherever we want to go, then you cut us loose. We'd be less of a burden on the US taxpayer that way and you could wash your hands of us. It makes sense, you know it does. Besides, it'll save you money on the annual budget."

Huntley narrowed his eyes. He hated being told what to do by Oliver, but he did like the idea of cutting the little shit loose and letting him take his chances.

"I'll think about it," was all he said.

* * *

The three agents sat in an empty office, while others guarded the interview rooms and the cells containing their prize catches.

Huntley sat at a desk. He was deep in thought, which gave his wrinkled face a strained grimace. Rosen lolled in a chair and sipped cold coffee. Kimble was going through her notes.

"Can I have permission to release Callaghan, or tape his mouth shut? He's a pain in the ass," she said.

Rosen smiled into his coffee. Huntley looked at her, unsure if she was making a joke.

"We'll process him in the morning and get him a lawyer. He'll have to go into custody somewhere. That kid Cathal can go – Monica, find him a hotel and a flight home, but make sure they both sign a gag order or they can stay in jail till the end of the goddamn trial."

A smile cracked the young agent's face.

"Oliver and the girl will have to stay locked up. We'll move them to a secure location in a few hours and assign a team to guard them. The others can sweat for the rest of the night; we'll get to them at our leisure tomorrow." He paused and took a deep breath. "Rosen, we'll start with the guards. They'll probably be useless, but we'll take one each, then I'll interview old Luigi after that."

Rosen and Monica nodded in unison.

"Then we'll take our time on the other two. Rosen and I will double-team on the Gent. Monica, you'll take Junior. Smile at him, be nice, and wear something revealing."

Monica gave her boss a suspicious look.

"Oh, come on, you *know* you're young and pretty. Use that; put him at ease, dazzle him a bit."

"If you insist," she said acidly.

Huntley threw his eyes to heaven. "Jesus, I'm not asking you to show him your tits or suck his dick. Just . . . Flirt with him a bit.

He may have nothing of any use, but on the other hand, he may give us something without realising. Get it?"

"Oh, I get it alright." She had always thought there was more to her selection than met the eye. It was something about the way Rosen kept eyeing her up and down when they had first met.

Huntley could see she wasn't happy. "Monica, be professional. What do you want me to say? We've got a rich kid in his early twenties to coax information out of. I need someone who looks like you do. It's not discrimination, it's nothing personal. It's putting the best man or woman on the job. It's business. So, appreciate the fact that you've been given a chance to be part of a massive bust, and take that sour look off your face."

She did her best, but wanted to tape another mouth shut.

Huntley and his colleagues simultaneously spent about half an hour trying to get Luigi's three men to say anything apart from *can I have a cigarette?* and *fuck you, cocksucker.* Huntley was the first to abandon the effort. He left his room and called the others to do the same. The guards were taken back to the cells, and Luigi, Marco and Robert were placed in the interview rooms.

Huntley began with Luigi, as planned. The old man sat opposite the agent for forty minutes without uttering a single word. He let Huntley bounce questions and abuse off him as if he were a stone pillar. He was not abusive or demanding, he neither smiled nor frowned. He just sat there.

Huntley gave up and joined Rosen behind the two-way mirror to observe Marco before they went in for the kill.

The Mafia man sat in his chair with a straight back; his hands were clasped in his lap and he had a pleasant expression on his face. His chin was showing greying stubble, but he had managed to comb and slick back his hair. His shirt collar was crumpled, but his jacket still looked freshly pressed. He had the air of a deposed President awaiting judgment, convinced that it was all a terrible mistake.

Rosen shook his head. "Usually gangsters like him threaten all round them and try to intimidate the cops. By all accounts, this guy's been no trouble at all. Got the cops here eating out of his hand already. One of them even called him Sir when he brought him coffee and a sandwich."

"Sneaky fucker. The Gent, remember? Come on, here goes."

They went into the next room, and Marco stood as they entered.

"Sit down," said Huntley curtly.

Marco did so with a smile. Rosen eyed him with intense curiosity. Huntley made a show of letting the thick file under his arm crash onto the table.

Marco give it a darting glance.

Huntley cleared his throat. "The suspect will state his name for the record."

Marco nodded politely. "Marco Giuseppe Romano."

"How many racehorses do you own, Romano?"

"Actually, I don't own any. My son has some in partnership with an Irish guy, Oliver McMahon. I take a passing interest in them, having given my son the initial investment money from the profits of one of my businesses."

Huntley and Rosen glanced at each other.

"You're telling me you don't own them?"

"That's correct."

"So how come you gave an order to use the horses as drug mules?"

Marco wore a perplexed expression, as if Huntley had spoken in Chinese. "I'm sorry, what did you say?"

Huntley repeated the question. Marco sat still, then after a few moments, he said, "Let's dispense with the formalities here. You and I both know that I have nothing to do with narcotics, I despise them. So your allegations . . . They're false. I'll say one thing, though." He paused, momentarily opened his mouth as if to continue, then closed it again.

"Go on," said Huntley.

"No, it's nothing. Forget it." He attempted to make a dismissive gesture, but was impeded by his handcuffs.

"Spit it out, or I'll take you back to your cell and powerhose you down."

"OK, OK. There's no need to issue threats. I was going to say that I cannot speak for whatever my son might have chosen to do with his horses. I believe he despises drugs as much as I do, but the young can be stupid. I hope he hasn't done anything stupid." He looked at his hands briefly. "Has he done anything stupid, Officer?"

Huntley discreetly scribbled on his pad and passed it to his partner.

Rosen took the pad. *He's trying to finger his own son for this.* Rosen wrote *unfuckingbelievable* and returned it.

Marco took in the exchange, but kept his affable demeanour.

"Romano, we have a recording of you giving a direct order to Michelangelo Cassoto, outlining a business plan to use your – excuse me – your son's horses as drug mules, and to instruct one Oliver McMahon to make sure the job got done. Do you deny this?"

Marco's brain processed the information and calculated the possibilities in an instant. "Gentleman, I'm sorry, but your line of questioning is so bizarre that I'm going to have to decline to answer. I will not give further comment until I have consulted with my lawyers and have them present."

"We'll get to all that. But first, why don't you tell us about your suppliers and the chain of command. If you give us the structure of the organisation, we can guarantee you a deal."

"Chain of command? I don't know what you're talking about." He shrugged. "But if you want to find out about the drug trade, why don't you call your buddies in Langley?"

Huntley began to turn red.

"I'm really sorry." Marco stifled a grin and continued. "But if you're going to make these kind of wild allegations, then clearly, I need legal counsel. Otherwise, the situation is unacceptable. I'm so sorry." Marco had a soft look in his eyes and a tight smile.

Rosen put a hand on Huntley's shoulder to steady him. "You will be taken back to your cell now, Mr. Romano. Thank you for your co-operation," he said.

Huntley kept his mouth shut, for fear he would not be so rational.

Rosen summoned the cop from the hallway and Marco was escorted out, leaving them sitting there in frustration.

"You must have expected that?" said Rosen.

"I thought we'd get more. I can't believe he's trying to finger his son. Where does he think this'll go?"

Chapter 62

Robert hadn't said a word since his incarceration, not that he was following family etiquette, he was simply unable to get himself together. He spent the first few hours pacing back and forth, fighting back the tears. He desperately wanted to break down and hold onto someone, but at first he steeled himself and refused to let the cops see him shed a tear.

Over the course of the night and the next day, his mind boiled like a pressure cooker. He went through a short stage of denial, refusing to believe the last conversation with his father was real. He punched the wall until his knuckles were raw, hoping the pain would wake him from the nightmare. In the end, the sobbing started and the tears flowed out of him in torrents. He stopped caring what anybody thought of him. The only important thing was to get away from his father once and for all; something he wished he had been strong enough to do a few years before.

After he was served a sandwich for lunch, he composed himself and, for the first time in his life, he said a prayer and asked his mother for inspiration.

An hour later, he knew what had to be done. Eventually, a cop came, cuffed him, and led him to an interview room. He sat in the chair and took deep breaths. When the door opened and he saw the pretty, flame-haired agent walk in and take off her jacket with a flourish, his concentration simply lapsed.

* * *

Monica slung her navy suit jacket over the chair and sat opposite Robert with her pad and a thin file on the table in front of her. Her low-cut, fitted white T-shirt revealed her athletic frame. Robert couldn't stop staring at her. He sat up in his chair and flicked his fringe out of his eyes with his cuffed hands.

He managed to pry his eyes away from her cleavage when she subconsciously folded her arms across her chest.

"Please state your name for the record," said Monica.

"Robert Giuseppe Romano."

"How many racehorses do you own?"

"Er . . . None."

"So these horses which run in your name . . ." She flipped open the file and tossed him a sheet with the details of Painter Girl, Shadows of Jersey and Concrete Boot. "They're not yours?"

"Er, no. Well, they're in my name but they're my dad's."

She gave him a warm smile, not the icy stare she wanted to. "So why are they in your name?"

"It's like, normal in horseracing for guys to run the horses in their wives' or sons' names, or something like that. According to Oliver, anyway."

"So . . ."

"Look," he interrupted. "Save your questions. I'm going to tell you the whole thing from beginning to end."

Monica dropped her pen and stared at him in surprise. Maybe Huntley was right, after all.

Robert started from the beginning. The very beginning, from that day when he saw his father stand over his mother. The tears flowed freely; he was past caring what anybody thought of him.

When he had finished, she couldn't think of anything to say. She stood and darted out of the room to find Rosen and Huntley.

They were still fuming over Marco's little act when Monica burst in looking flustered.

"What the fuck? We could be conducting an interview here," said Huntley.

"I checked first," she said, pointing at the glass.

"What's so important?" asked Rosen, in a softer voice.

"Junior Romano's just spilled a whole truckload of beans."

Chapter 63

The atmosphere in the small grey room began to crackle.

"What did he say?" said Huntley.

"Basically, he said his father would try to pin all this on him. And he's willing to testify that his father told him to take the rap, along with two others he knows as the terriers. But you should really watch the tape."

Huntley and Rosen looked at each other, before leaping to their feet.

"See, Monica, I knew your charm would work," said Huntley, moving for the door.

"My 'charm' had nothing to do with it."

Huntley could barely contain himself as he watched the footage, keeping one eye on Robert through the glass. He nudged Rosen with his elbow. "This is fucking brilliant. With the bug transcript and his testimony, and the Irish guy, we'll get the fucker."

"You think he's on the level? This could be a game."

"I doubt it. Jesus, look at him – he's falling to bits."

They both looked from the small screen to the large glass. Robert was slumped in his chair, staring blankly at the table. The tears had dried onto his face.

* * *

Robert watched the two men sit opposite him.

"I'm Huntley, this is Rosen," the thin one said.

Robert nodded.

"So, tell us what you told our colleague,'" said Huntley.

"Why? You must have it on tape," said Robert, cocking his head towards the glass.

"We'd like to hear you say it all again. Come on, humour us,''" said Rosen, in a jovial tone.

Robert shrugged. "Like I said, when you guys came to bust him, he told me to go up to the top of the house with him."

"Why the top of the house?" said Huntley.

"To buy time, I guess. Anyway, he like, told me that he had done some business with Oliver, using the horses to ship 'product' to Ireland."

"Product?" said Huntley.

"That's what I said, too. He told me product was the white powder, no, the South American powder that I liked so much . . . that kind of shocked me to actually hear him say it."

"You use cocaine?" asked Huntley.

Robert looked ashamed. "I do a line or two sometimes."

"And where do you get it?"

"Mike usually throws me a bag whenever I want."

"Who's Mike?"

"Mike is Mike. My father's assistant."

"And it didn't occur to you that your father was a trafficker?"

"No. Fuck, man, there's coke *everywhere*. I just always figured Mike had a contact or something."

"Oh, he had a contact alright." Huntley let out a chuckle.

Robert looked hurt. Rosen shot a dirty look at his partner. "Please go on," he said to Robert.

"Anyway, it was like, a total shock to hear him admit he was a drug dealer. Then he hits me with the bomb that I have to take the rap. He told me to say I'd done it with two guys called Tomo and Tito, but he used to call them the terriers. They used to drive me around sometimes. Anyway, that was fucking it for me. I mean, he totally expected me to go to jail for him, just so he could stay out here and keep the business running. He said he'd have me out in eight-to-ten. So I figure I'd tell you all this, then he goes inside where he deserves, and I go free."

"Who said anything about going free?" snapped Huntley.

A look of horror and panic contorted Robert's face. "What? It's him you want. You can't lock me up. You can't. We have a deal."

"What deal? You told us a bunch of things, we have the information now. You have nothing to bargain with."

Robert looked from Huntley to Rosen; he was terrified. "Fuck you. F-U-C-K you! You're just like he is. You don't give a fuck about me. Well, here's the deal: I testify, then I go free. I disappear into my own world. You get to put my father away and I get to live my own life. I don't want your protection, I'll take my chances on my own, but I'm not going to prison just for being a gangster's son." He looked indignant.

Huntley and Rosen were astounded. They froze for a moment.

"OK, so supposing we do use your testimony – and we can back it up. Then, with the tapes and your buddy Oliver's testimony, we should have enough to put your dad away. If that were the case, we would be willing to . . ."

"What the..? What tapes? What would Oliver say?"

Huntley stifled a chuckle. "We have your father on tape. We also have a guarantee from Oliver that he'll say your father told him to put the drugs in the horses, and that he assaulted him in your house." He consulted his notes for dramatic effect. "In the den, I believe."

Robert's mind turned over quickly, just like his father's. "I can testify about that, too. I was listening at the door that day. That's when I first had the flashback of my mother being attacked by him. You can use me and the tapes, I don't want Oliver or Rebecca to give evidence."

Huntley actually burst out laughing. "You arrogant little shit, you're like your Irish buddy – think you can call the fucking shots?"

Robert stared at the agent in his best attempt to mimic his father's icy gaze. "Look, it's a long story, but I owe Oliver my life. I'm doing this for him, too. So, like, make up your goddamn mind, 'cause I'm not going to say shit unless you guarantee they don't testify."

Rosen scribbled a note in his pad.

"Aren't you worried your dad will have you killed for ratting him out?" asked Huntley.

"You know what? I'm not, I'll take my chances. I don't give a fuck anymore." Robert liked to think that his father wouldn't be able to bring himself to do it. At least, he hoped so.

"Is there anything else we can do for you?" said Huntley sarcastically.

"No, that's all thanks."

"Oh, *that's all*? Hah! You don't expect much for your story, do you? We'll have to see what we can do. In the meantime, tell me more about listening at doors."

He looked at the ceiling and gathered his thoughts. Then he told them about that afternoon and the memories it had brought back. His throat went dry.

"So, what's the deal about your mother's death?" said Rosen.

"I always figured she had a heart attack, until yesterday when he told me that I was weak like her. She took an overdose . . . He faked the . . . Does it really matter?"

"We'll get to it later," said Rosen. Huntley shot him a surprised look.

Rosen tapped his pad with his pen. "So tell me why you owe your life to Oliver McMahon."

Robert cast his mind back and told them what he could remember about that day in New York.

The two agents were fascinated, unaware exactly how Oliver had got involved with someone like Marco.

"That's a hell of a story," said Rosen.

"Yeah. So I don't want him to give evidence that will cost him his life."

"Even if it costs you yours?" asked Rosen.

"Look, I'm still his only son. I know, in his world, sending me to jail is no big deal 'cause he thinks he's doing me a favour, but I don't think he could give the order to kill me."

"I hope you're right," said Huntley, though he really didn't give a shit if Marco succeeded in killing his son. As long as they got the testimony first.

"Now tell us more about your mother's death," said Rosen.

Robert told them what he remembered, what he had been led to believe, and what his father had finally confessed to.

Huntley concluded the session after that. Robert was led back to his cell.

* * *

As the agents ate take-out in an empty office, they went over the interview tapes again and formulated a plan of attack to present to the District Attorney.

Huntley considered what they had. He was of the opinion that a written statement from Oliver could be prepared and introduced, only if necessary. The testimony of Robert would confirm that Marco was behind it all, and his confirmation that product was Marco's codeword for cocaine should make the information on the CD decipherable and admissible.

Robert's evidence about his mother was anecdotal, at best. Huntley also decided they would make no mention in court of the previous successful shipment. There seemed no point in bringing up a crime that had gone undetected and making themselves look inept. Besides, that would mean having to alert, and co-operate with, the Irish Government, and that was a chore he had no interest in. Rosen knew better than to argue with him. Monica kept her mouth shut, to prevent her contempt from spilling out and ruining her career.

The three of them kept at it until dawn. After a fitful few hours sleep, Huntley called one of his team and ordered the young agent to go to his house and fetch the transcripts and discs from the bug in Marco's office, and bring them to the station. He dragged a bleary-eyed Rosen and Monica from their rooms and back to the office.

"You guys haven't heard this before," he said, sipping his fourth coffee and feeling jittery with caffeine and excitement.

Rosen and Monica looked at him, puzzled. Huntley tossed the transcript on the table.

"This is the tape of Marco giving the order to Mike to put

the drugs into the horses. He speaks in code, but with his son's testimony, we can convince the DA and a jury that he was talking about drugs." His hand was shaking as he pressed play.

The machine started to whirr as the disc spun and Marco's voice bellowed from the speaker.

"Looks like we're goin' to have to change plans earlier than I thought. I had an idea a while back, now's the time to give it a try. Tomorrow, do the other thing first, but keep the tool in the car. Then pick Oliver up from the airport. Drive him somewhere quiet."

"Then what?"

"Then you tell him we're goin' to fill Painter up with product and send her to Ireland. Like that thing I told you about – the Mexican bitch with the dead baby, and the other one with the dog. Know what I mean?"

"Yeah, I got you."

"Good. Get the terriers to make a delivery to him. For starters, capiche?"

"Good. Then tell him if it goes well, he can buy me more horses. I'll give him a wedge for himself on top of the purchase fees. Everyone stays happy as long as everyone makes money."

"I hear you."

"Good. Get it done."

He tapped the pause button. "That's it."

"I don't get it," said Monica. "I thought you said we wouldn't refer to this crime, that there was no need."

"I did, but it came to me when I slept: this is the key order. We have to use it. Shit, we'll just tell them we didn't appreciate the full significance of it until we interviewed Robert. And fuck the Irish authorities – it's my bust."

"What if the DA wants heads to roll for this?" asked Rosen.

"Then we feed him Oliver and the vet," he snorted. "Little shit should have come to us about it, anyway."

Chapter 64

"Geez, I think he did the right thing," said Monica.

Huntley shot her a look which said: *I don't care what you think.*

She continued regardless. "If he *had* come to you, that would have been the end of that and you'd have got Marco Romano for four kilos of blow. Now you have him for fifty, and whatever you think of him, it's mostly down to that Irishman."

Rosen cracked a wry smile. He was really pleased he had chosen Monica.

"What are you grinning about?" snapped Huntley.

"I hate to rain on your parade, but she's right."

Huntley glared at Monica. "Find out anything you can about a Mexican woman smuggling coke inside a dead baby, or – what else did he say? A dog? Anyway, we'll need the info to explain the conversation and give more credence to the 'product' code. Get on it now."

She was already furiously scribbling notes, delighted to be given something to do that didn't require filling a coffee cup.

When she had hurried out of the office and closed the door, Huntley spoke. "As I see it, we'll proceed like this: Keep Marco in the dark; McMahon has to give a written statement; Robert will testify, *before* the jury hears the tapes; then we put Marco on the stand and hit him with everything."

Rosen raised his hand. "Hold it right there. Isn't that for the DA to decide?"

"It's for me to tell the DA."

Rosen raised his eyebrows." And what if Marco's lawyer fucks up your plan?"

"*That's* the DA's problem, but we have to keep Marco in the dark as long as possible. I bet you he's not expecting this. He'll be sitting in there thinking all we have is an Irishman, a bunch of guards who won't talk, and a son who says it was all him, the Irishman and two others, the . . . the . . . er . . ." He clicked his fingers, trying to remember.

"The terriers," Rosen prompted.

"Right. Shit, that reminds me." He picked up his phone and called Monica. "Yeah, get information on associates or members of the Family known as Tomo and Tito, *the terriers*. What? Yes, that's all we have to go on." He ended the call.

"You reckon we'll find them?" said Rosen.

Huntley shrugged. "If they're willing to take the fall, then yes. If not, we never will."

"That's a no, then."

"Hey, this kind of thing happened before. Remember? That Italian guy in Ireland."

Rosen looked lost.

"You know, the guy caught on the Irishman's brother's plane – I sent you the file. Anyway, he'll get fifteen years, and he hasn't said a word to the cops. I mean, not a fucking *word*. That's loyalty."

"Or bribery."

"Whatever, whichever. Who cares? It works." He scratched under his chin.

"What about the race fixing?"

"Fuck race fixing. Your little broad Monica's right; we got him for fifty kilos of pure coke. Who gives a shit about fixing a fucking race? So maybe some rich Kentucky asshole lost a few bucks. Let the NTRA or the Jockey Club, or whoever hands out the discipline, sort it out; like they sort out those crooked trainers and their doping and all that shit."

"What about the deals for Oliver, Rebecca and the kid?"

"Fuck, I guess we'll have to do something," he said grudgingly. "Give them new passports and cut them loose. It'll be cheaper *and* less of a headache. And we won't give a shit if they get hit."

"I'll get on to a guy in Langley or Homeland Sec," said Rosen, making a note.

"Fuck that. Use Immigration."

"No, it's too leaky."

"What do you care?"

"I want to do it properly. Jesus, we owe them that much."

Huntley shrugged. "If you want that kind of headache, you take care of it all yourself."

"Don't worry, I will," Rosen muttered. He resolved to get it done personally and quietly. He reckoned they were entitled to a fair go at a new life. They weren't the first people to be sucked in and used by the Mafia, and they wouldn't be the last. Rosen was content to let his partner hog all the glory for this; for him the important thing was the result – and to do things in a fair and decent way. That was something Huntley always forgot about in the thrill of the chase.

* * *

Oliver and Rebecca slept on the government jet from Newark. They touched down in Atlanta and were taken from the plane by a stern, tired-looking agent, who introduced himself as Mitch.

"I'm in charge of your protection detail," he said, driving them through the city in a brown Ford. "You'll be in a safe house. Four of us'll mind you. Two teams of two on rotation. No going outside. No phones, no e-mail. No complaining."

They got to the house in an affluent, leafy suburb, and Mitch showed his charges to their rooms and asked them to make a list of food and other things they would need. Nothing expensive. Basics only. The house was large, with six bedrooms and a huge living room, but sparsely furnished.

"Where'd you guys get this place?" asked Rebecca.

"Drug bust. Seized asset," said Mitch. "Your room's at the top of the stairs. Put your bags in it and write out your list. I'll send someone to the store."

Rebecca decided they should start to change their appearances, to be ready for their new identities. Oliver smiled. "I've always wanted to shave my head and grow a goatee."

"Now's your chance, hon. You'll look like a badass biker. I'm going strawberry blonde."

They wrote out their list and handed it to Mitch.

The next morning, Oliver woke feeling troubled. He sat on the floor in their bare room. "Even if we get a new passport for Mum, I'm pretty sure she'd never leave Limerick. That means she'll be alone. I'll have to go to Ireland to see her before we take off."

Rebecca sat up in the bed, wearing a concerned look. "Wherever you go, I'm coming, too."

He smiled. "Thanks, Bec. There's also Rich's inheritance, we have to do something with that, I mean, we *could* sort Mum out and just take the rest – I'm sure Foster can figure out ways to hide the money for us – but I'm not sure I *want* all his money."

"Are you crazy? He gave it to you."

"I know, but he made most of it by exploiting people or situations for massive profit. I don't want to just sit around living off it."

"Then what do we do? We have to have some cash to start a new life eventually. We can't just keep wandering for ever. It'd be nice to start a family someday, but I don't think I'll be able to work as a vet under an assumed identity. I'll never be able to practice again."

He looked deep into her eyes. "I want a family, too. I want to do better by my own kids than was done to me." He rubbed his temples. "I'm not sure what to do yet, but taking all the money just doesn't sit right in my head."

"So what do you want to do? Give it to charity?"

He shrugged. "I'm not sure, we'll both have to think about it, but I just know it's the right thing to do. We have to give something back."

* * *

Two weeks later, their boredom was broken by a visitor. Oliver padded into the kitchen to see the young female agent having a heated discussion with Mitch. She stopped abruptly when she saw him. "Holy shit, you look different."

Oliver smiled and ran his hand over his smooth head. "Time for a new look. Bec's gone all blonde."

"Yeah, they think it's Hallowe'en," said Mitch.

Oliver ignored him. "Last time I saw you, you were waving a gun at me on a plane full of drugs," he said. "Agent Kimble, wasn't it?"

"You can call me Monica, if you like. Sorry if I was a bit rough on you back then, I didn't know all the facts."

"And now you do?"

"Where's Rebecca? Is there some place we can talk?" she said, glancing at Mitch.

Up in their room, Rebecca and Oliver sat on the bed and Monica leaned on the window sill. "At the moment, we have a strong case and the DA wants to press on immediately," she announced. "Marco's arraignment will take place tomorrow. The DA will ask for bail to be denied and for a trial in two months, tops. At the moment it looks like you will not be required to testify. I'll have to take a written statement from you now, but we don't anticipate we'll have to use it. You guys will get passports, drivers' licences, and a plane to wherever you want to go. That's it. No protection."

"Jesus, what happened? I thought you needed me. I thought that was the whole idea."

Monica put up her hand. "I can't say any more at this time." She paused for a second, before changing the subject. "Anyway, I also have to take photos of you for your new passports, and get you to make signatures."

"Great," said Oliver. "Did Huntley say anything about my mother?"

Monica chewed her lip. "No."

Oliver and Rebecca exchanged looks.

Monica took a deep breath and said, "Look, I wouldn't put much faith in Huntley, if I were you. He doesn't care about you. He's got his man, and he'll get a conviction. He says he doesn't even need you, he's done the deal with the DA without you, says you're lucky he doesn't send you down for smuggling. He only wants the statement as a back-up and to keep you scared. I'm afraid the best you can hope for is a new identity and a fresh start."

"Charming," said Oliver. "Pawns in another business deal." He flopped back on the bed and stared at the ceiling.

"But don't worry," she continued, "that'll be done properly. He put Rosen and I on it."

"Can we choose our nationalities?" Oliver asked.

"No. Canadian only."

"Beggars can't be choosers, I suppose. Let's get on with it, then," said Rebecca.

Monica stood them against the bare white wall and took their photos. "OK, that was simple. Now I'm going to need you to write out and sign your account of things with Marco."

Oliver sighed. "Not again."

"Fraid so."

Oliver went to work. An hour later, he was satisfied and signed the three page statement. Monica tucked it into her case. "That's everything. If all goes well, I'll see you guys after the trial. Don't let Mitch and his crew drive you crazy." She strode to the door and paused with her hand on the knob. "Say, I um, I know how you first met Marco and this is how it all ended up . . . So I gotta ask: if you could go back in time, would you still have done it and got involved?"

"Would I still have saved Robert? Of course. What kind of a question is that? I probably wouldn't have asked Marco to invest in horses, though, but there's no point in dwelling on that. What's done is done."

"Hey, Monica. Before you go, can you ask Mitch if I can use his phone?"

"I guess so. Follow me."

After repeated drilling from Mitch about what she could and could not say, Rebecca was granted the use of a satellite cellphone for a few minutes under strict supervision. During the brief call, she learned that Watson and Hollenbach had terminated her position to avoid a scandal and media frenzy. Doug Hollenbach was pushing to have her struck off for malpractice; the matter was to be decided at a board meeting next week. Damage limitation, she was told.

Chapter 65

Marco sat in the small interview room, fuming. He was feeling like a Death Row criminal in his yellow jumpsuit, though he had shaved his face and immaculately slicked his hair back. This strange attention to detail, along with his prison garb, made him look more intimidating – a bit like Hannibal Lecter – and he was certainly angry enough to consider eating his lawyers.

He drummed his fingers on the plastic table and stared at his companion. The grizzled guard had seen it all before, but still looked quite honoured to be assigned to Marco Romano today.

Marco composed himself by counting silently to ten, then asked in a calm voice, "I thought you said my lawyers were here?"

"Looks like they're late, Sir."

Marco kept drumming his fingers.

"They're probably getting searched, and a glove up their assholes." said the guard, in an attempt at humour.

"Huh," said Marco, with a smirk. "Now *that* I'd pay to see." He stopped himself from calling them useless fucking pricks in front of the guard, but he wanted to roar it from the rooftops. None of the deals they oversaw, the money they hid and re-routed for him, counted for shit now, as far as he was concerned. If they couldn't make this go away, well . . .

Moments later, there was a rattle of keys in the door and two men in thousand-dollar suits slithered into the room. They were twin brothers – both in navy, with white shirts and fine silk ties; both had their blond hair slicked back, not unlike Marco's; and both were a little plump from middle-age spread and comfortable living. Todd and Hal Bristow had grown up on the Upper East side of Manhattan, in a world of moneyed entitlement that had taken a huge hit in the stock market crash of the mid-eighties.

Fear of ordinary, middle-class living had motivated them to graduate law school and pass the bar within a year of each other. Pedigree and connections had guaranteed them positions in major New York practices. Both were intelligent and could have been accomplished attorneys, but they soon got sick of the anti-social hours and the interminable drudgery necessary to become a partner. They felt they should reap the rewards without having to put in the effort.

A chance meeting with Marco over a planning dispute for a nightclub, had led them to quit their jobs and set up a small practice. They had some other clients, but Marco was the one who financed their lifestyle and kept them in champagne and tailored suits. For the most part, it was easy money.

Marco had always felt that he was not only retaining the services of lawyers, but purchasing a glimpse of the upper-class respectability that he craved. He sometimes pressured them into wangling him an invitation to a society event, despite the fact that whenever he attended most guests politely ignored him out of fear or shock. Todd and Hal always tried to avoid being seen with him. Secretly, however, they loved the aura of mystery being Marco's lawyers gave them. It made them sexier, and gave them an illusion of power above their station.

Now, they looked cornered and out of their depth. The social stigma and very public ordeal of going down on the good ship Romano did not appeal to them, but then again, neither did the prospect of a terminal meeting with Mike the Nail.

They stood there, rooted to the spot. Eventually, one swallowed and clicked his fingers at the guard, who dragged his feet out of the room and fondled his baton as if he wanted to crack it over the man's head.

"Tweedle-Dumb and Tweedle-fuckin-Dee. Bout time. How's the upper east side? Life easy in your big fuckin' townhouses? You better have good news for me."

They squirmed in unison.

They inspected the two plastic chairs with distaste, and gingerly sat on them.

Marco stared at them in astonishment. "Whenever you're ready, I mean, don't let me rush you."

"See, it's um, like this, Marco," said Hal, clearing his throat as if the words disgusted him. "It's um, not looking good. You're in some deep shit this time. They have you for fifty kilos of *absolutely* pure cocaine and . . ."

"*Absolutely* pure?" Marco cut in, mockingly. "Oh, you mean like the shit you put up your noses at your Long Island beach houses? 'Cause I can assure you, gentlemen, it came from the same source."

The two lawyers exchanged embarrassed looks.

"Um, they also have testimony against you *and* audio tapes," Hal continued.

"What fucking testimony? That goddamn Irishman? He's up to his neck in this." Marco's eyes burned through his counsel, as he jabbed his index finger on the table. "They don't have shit on me. Your fuckin' job is to see to it that the Irishman, the terriers, and my son, get the rap for this. Then you work on reducing my son's sentence. Capiche?"

"Marco, calm down. Please," said Hal, producing a cigarillo and offering it to Marco.

He snatched it and inhaled fully.

"OK, Marco, it's like this: we spoke to the DA this morning and he outlined the case against you. There are two key pieces of evidence, which appear to dovetail nicely. First, they have extensive audio footage of you obtained from devices planted in your house."

He nearly dropped the cigarillo. "What? Say that again? In my house? *In my fuckin' house?* How the fuck..?" He banged his fist on the table and set his brain into overdrive. "Hold on a second. Whatever they got in there would be in code. Have you listened to the footage?"

"Our team is on it now, but that's not the problem," continued Hal. "The problem is the testimony: we've seen video footage. It's not good. Not good at all."

"We would advise you to make a plea and take a deal. We're not saying you should give anyone up, but if you were to cooperate, the DA will advise the Judge to dramatically reduce your sentence," said Todd.

Marco did not dignify that with a reply.

"Look, the DA wants you put away quickly, but he knows the public soon move on, so if you were to help him get somebody else – your suppliers, say – then he could have you quietly released after a respectable period of years."

"You make it sound so appealing," said Marco. He flicked the butt on the ground and leaned in close to Todd, the eyes on full beam, full of thunder. "What the fuck do I pay you for?" he said in a very calm voice.

Todd swallowed hard. "We wouldn't be acting in your best interests if we didn't advise you to make a plea."

"Fuck you," said Marco, without taking his eyes off Todd. "You listen to me: you were happy to take a fat retainer when times were easy. Now you gotta earn it. That Irishman is not in a position to give evidence against me. You can discredit him easy enough. Get off your fuckin' ass and build me a defence. And if you can't do it, find a criminal lawyer who can. But you'll pay his fees, not me."

"We already thought of that. Nobody'll touch you. Not for any money. Not once they look at the evidence."

"Find Mike, I want to talk to him. Tell him to send someone."

The Bristow brothers looked at each other nervously.

"Marco," said Todd, with a quiver in his voice. "Mike disappeared the day you were arrested; nobody has seen Jimmy or the terriers either. Half the Federal Agents on duty are looking for them." His voice trailed off.

Hal picked up the conversation. "There is one other major point. Er . . . The testimony is not from Oliver McMahon. It's from . . ." He cleared his throat again. "It's from your son. Robert."

"What the fu–" Marco paused and fell back in his chair like he had been punched in the chest. He was speechless.

After what seemed like an age, he took a deep breath and ran his hands over his hair, smoothing it down. Then he locked his dark eyes onto his lawyers, switching from one to the other, cutting right through them.

The Bristows sat as if turned to stone by the Medusa.

"Get the fuck out of here and find Mike."

"We'll put the word out," mumbled Hal.

"Do that. And build me *a fucking defence*," he bellowed. Then he shut his eyes.

After a minute, the Bristows stood and knocked on the door. When they were let out, the guard appeared and motioned for Marco to get on his feet. He waited until he was back in his cell before he started to think about Robert and what this all meant. Part of him wanted to scream and shed a tear, but the other part held sway. He needed to contact Mike more than ever.

Chapter 66

The DA had his way and the case was rushed to trial, after Marco – as expected – refused to plead guilty or no contest.

Huntley actually danced a jig alone in his office when he heard the news.

The case was hurried before a judge in just three months; the mid-term elections were approaching and the Governor of New Jersey wanted a high-profile conviction to give weight to his apparent tough stance on crime.

Oliver and Rebecca spent a white Christmas playing cards in the safe house with the four bored agents who were dying to get back to their own lives. Oliver did manage to persuade them to stretch the Federal budget to a few bottles of wine to ease the burden on the long, cold festive nights. He even managed to gain permission from Mitch, via Rosen, to be able to speak to his mother for exactly two minutes on Christmas Day.

Evelyn talked quickly through relieved tears upon hearing her son's voice, and asked him how he was. The trial had been in the news briefly, she said, though she had never heard Oliver's name mentioned. James Foster had been kind enough to call her up from time to time and see how she was, and to report how her finances were doing.

"He says Richard's company has a new boss and seems to be stable and doing well again. Apparently, the little Italian was sentenced. It said in the papers that he never did say a word to the police, or his lawyer, or in court. Very strange chap indeed," she said.

"Yeah. Very strange."

"When are you coming home?" she pleaded.

"It might not be that simple, Mum," Oliver told her, with a lump in his throat. "I, I . . ."

He was cut short by the sight of Mitch across the kitchen table, violently shaking his head and dragging a finger across his throat.

"Er, Mum, I'll tell you more when I can. I, I . . ." He was about to tell her he loved her, but the connection had been severed. Mitch had the grace to offer him an apologetic glance.

* * *

Though the trial itself lasted only three weeks, it was a dramatic start to 2007. When the prosecution presented its evidence, Marco remained stoic. He was not permitted to sit with his lawyers; instead, he was led into a witness box and forced to endure the proceedings alone.

The majority of the column inches focused on the emotional impact of Robert's testimony. It took him a whole day to get through it, carefully guided by the DA and given time to compose himself when he was on the verge of tears. The jurors were spellbound.

Marco stared at his son the whole time, but the look on his face was not the usual dark, piercing gaze. It was tinged with disappointment and sadness. He did his best to conceal it from those present in court, but the more he listened to his son, the more he slumped in his chair and dropped his hands between his legs, as if the handcuffs weighed ten kilos.

The final drama, and the one that hit all the headlines, was when Robert was being led out of court, past his father. He was already sobbing from the strain of taking the stand, when he suddenly broke down and uttered the perfect media soundbite, "I'm sorry, Dad. You woke me up. I can't keep lying to myself."

The press went into a frenzy. The Judge tried to instruct the jurors to dismiss the remark, but she might as well have told them to forget their own names. It was better than Gotti. Every network news broadcast led with the story: mobster turned in by his own son.

Any earlier visible lack of strength on Marco's part was obliterated when he saw that his own lawyers gave what could, at best, be described as a feeble attempt at cross-examining Robert. In later sessions – clearly rebriefed – Hal and Todd went on to try to dismiss the rantings of a bitter young man as explanation for the codes used on the recordings, but even they looked as if they didn't really buy what they were selling. Marco was helpless, though he occasionally looked as if he was considering lunging out of his box and garrotting his lawyers with his handcuff chain.

It all went according to plan for Huntley and the DA. The jury took just over an hour to deliberate and find Marco guilty on all counts. He was sentenced to twenty-five years for the supply and smuggling of narcotics worth tens of millions of dollars on the street. In an almost comical aside, the Judge imposed a fine of $100,000 for cruelty to horses resulting in death, the money to be donated to the Kentucky Horse Park.

All his assets were to be seized: Shadows nightclub, the shooting club, his house, the horses. They would be sold at the earliest opportunity. The proceeds of the sale of Shadows – the Judge instructed – would be held in an account for Robert, until his twenty-seventh birthday. The proceeds from the shooting club and the house would be split between various charities in the State of New Jersey. The Judge warned the Governor's office that every cent would have to be accounted for after the fine was paid. Painter Girl was not specifically mentioned. However, the Judge ordered that the DA investigate all of Marco's assets, including a ten million dollar sum he had received for the sale of a racehorse named Concrete Boot. The Bristows squirmed in their seats when they heard this, and Marco cut them into small pieces with a dark gaze across the courtroom.

Several members of the press laughed openly at the mention of the horse's name, and used it in their headlines the next day. Claude Duvall laughed until tears streamed down his cheeks when he read them; Larry Marshall hired lawyers to make sure that his new purchase couldn't be repossessed by the Government.

The Judge gave a personal address to Robert, applauding his

courage and sense of justice. "Mr. Romano, you are a very brave young man. I expect you to use the money I have set aside for you, wisely and positively. I instruct you to spend the next few years thinking about this, so that you will be ready when the funds become available to you."

She then turned to Marco and said in an icy voice, "In a final note to the convicted, I must warn you that if any unfortunate accident should befall your son in the coming years, the possibility of parole will never, ever be discussed."

Robert broke down in the courtroom and had to be comforted by the bailiff and the social services worker assigned to him.

Oliver and Rebecca read the details in a stack of newspapers Mitch dropped on the kitchen table, and listened to his gossip about the trial, which he got from a courtroom reporter.

The following morning, almost absentmindedly, he told them that they should pack and be ready to leave for the airport by ten o'clock. A plane was being sent, along with their passports. Just like that.

Mitch showed ID at the gates of the cargo terminal and the brown Ford was ushered into a hangar, where a Government Gulfstream jet was parked.

Monica paced around outside the steps and looked relieved when she saw the vehicle.

Rebecca and Oliver got out with their bags, and Monica greeted them with a warm smile and two fat brown envelopes.

Oliver laughed when he fondled his. "Jesus, it's like something our politicians get under the table, stuffed with cash."

"Fraid there's no money in it, but you do have a passport and a driver's licence each. Don't open them until we're in the air."

"We?" said Rebecca.

"I'm coming with you. I've been instructed to escort you to your destination, wherever that may be."

"Cool, and we get to travel in style. Any champagne on board?" asked Oliver.

"I doubt that. There might be a beer, though."

"Then beer it is! After you, Agent Monica," he said, sweeping his arm towards the steps.

She told Mitch to wait and led them onto the plane.

When Oliver stepped in and flung his bag on a seat, he was stunned to see Robert, looking thin and pale, but with a huge smile on his face.

"Jesus, I thought they'd have you stuck in some remote spot by now," said Oliver.

Robert stood and threw his arms around Oliver. "Good to see you again, man." Then he embraced Rebecca. "And you."

"What the hell are you doing here?" she asked.

"Part of my deal. I told them I wanted to meet you guys before we go our separate ways. I'm flavour of the month right now, so they agreed."

"Yeah, we've heard. The press is loving it," said Rebecca.

Robert chewed his lip, searching for the right words. "Anyway, I told them before the trial that if they got you to testify, or presented your evidence in court, then they could forget about me. So officially, you're in the clear."

"Hmm, you sure about that?" said Rebecca.

"I had a lot of time alone in a cell to think about shit and, like, I reckon my dad'll let it go, long as he never has proof you gave evidence."

Oliver looked sceptical, but hoped Robert was right.

"What about you?" said Rebecca, sliding into a seat. "You sure he'll leave you alone?"

He flopped down heavily into a seat. "Rebecca, a long time ago, you asked me what my deal was. I didn't get what you meant, but when the shit hit the fan, it got me thinking." He took a deep breath. "Being trapped with my dad probably killed my mom. I get that now. I don't want that to happen to me. You guys," he pointed at them with both index fingers, "made me face up to him. And the weird thing is, I'm not scared of him any more." He chuckled, "Even though I just put him away. I have a feeling he's not going to do anything to me, and even if he tries . . . Well, fuck him, let him do it. At least I'll be with Mom again, and he'll still be all alone . . ."

Oliver wanted to speak, but the words choked in his throat.

Rebecca smiled. "You're a man now."

"Where'll you go? What'll you do?" said Oliver.

"They'll stash me somewhere secret until they can get me a new ID and stuff. After that, I don't know. Nebraska, Canada, somewhere I can be anonymous and try to paint. Shit, maybe Australia, I've heard the chicks there love an American accent!"

"I guess some things never change," said Rebecca, rolling her eyes.

Mitch appeared in the door hatch. "Enough of the kiss-and-make-up. Romano, we've got to move."

"That's my cue." Robert stood up and took his bag.

Oliver reached out his hand and grabbed Robert by the shoulder. "Take care of . . ."

"Please, no goodbyes. Let's just say we'll meet up again in some pool hall in a sunny place." He looked at them both and plastered on his best smile. "Thanks for everything, guys, I owe you one. Shit, two or three, more like."

They watched him disappear through the hatch. Both Rebecca and Oliver were unable to speak until the plane was in the air. Even Monica looked a bit downcast.

"You think he'll be alright?" said Rebecca at last, when they were cruising at altitude and the whine of the engines had faded to a quiet drone.

"We'll keep an eye on him," said Monica.

Oliver suddenly snapped out of his daze. "I just realised, we didn't say where to go."

"We're bound for Newfoundland. We'll take on fuel there and plot a course. Where you want to go?"

"Ireland. Dublin."

"You sure about that?"

"I have to sort things out and see my mother, or at least say goodbye to her."

"You know I have orders to, and I quote: cut you loose on

arrival," she said with raised eyebrows.

"Charming. Still, I did suggest it to him, I suppose," said Oliver.

"So you're not worried someone'll be waiting at your mother's house?"

"Who said I was going home? But anyway, even if Marco wants to punish me, he won't touch my mother; it's not his style. Rebecca and I'll get lost for a while, then hopefully I can get my mother out to see us at some stage." He rubbed his forehead with his hand. "Anyway, it doesn't concern you. What about that beer?"

"Fuck it, I'll have one, too," said Monica, getting up and darting for the cabinet. "You, too?" she said to Rebecca.

"No. I'll have a soda."

"Oh, come on. They're on the Federal Government."

"Well, in that case . . ."

Monica smiled.

* * *

Mike spoke Italian into the receiver. "Yeah, it's me. Get on to Ireland. Get someone to watch that little prick's mother. He's dumb enough to go see her before he takes off."

"What the fuck? You know how much time that'll waste?"

"I don't give a fuck. You do it," he bellowed.

There was a pause. "If he turns up, then what?"

"I'll let you know. Keep an eye on him." He hung up and swore. He needed to contact Marco.

Chapter 67

Oliver woke and looked out of the tiny window. He could see the sun on the horizon and knew they were approaching Ireland when he saw the thick, low clouds in the distance. Ninety minutes later, the plane dipped through them and plunged into the damp, grey air above Dublin. The crosswind buffeted the small plane and stopped conversation until they were safely at a standstill.

Monica was the first to her feet. She pulled a card out of her pocket and thrust it at Oliver.

"Hmm, business cards," he said with a grin.

"I'm sorry, what?" said Monica.

"Never mind."

Monica looked puzzled, but shook it off. "Anyway, this is Rosen's card; it has his numbers and a secure email on it." She turned the card over. "I wrote my own details here. It'd be great if you could check in with us from time to time. Let us know you're OK."

Oliver was genuinely taken aback. "Thanks, Monica, really. I, er . . . thanks."

"Look, I know Huntley would like to just forget about you, but Rosen told me to make sure you were looked after. You can call anytime."

Rebecca gave Monica a hug and Oliver awkwardly shook her hand as they alighted.

"Bec, the last time somebody told me they'd look after me, or words to that effect, it was Marco," he said, as they stepped on solid ground.

"Hon, she's nice. Take it from me. Woman's intuition."

412

"Well, how's it going?" said a cheery voice behind them.

Oliver turned his head and saw the redhaired and redfaced young Customs officer, who told them he would escort them to Passport Control.

"Aren't you going to inspect the plane?" said Oliver, winking at Rebecca.

"No point, sure it's not stopping. Anyway, it's a US Government plane. What were you two doing on it?"

"You could say we got a present of the flight."

"Jaysus, not so bad. Better than going with Freefly, I'd say."

Oliver shot him a sideways glance as the three of them splashed across the tarmac to the busy terminal. "Why'd you say that?"

"Stingy fuckers. Treat you like shite, and herd you in like cattle. Still, it's cheap, I s'pose. But a free flight on an American private jet – now that's beat all!" he chuckled to himself.

"Do Freefly still do the private jets?"

"No, they had to knock that on the head after the drug scandal and yer man's death. They locked up some flight attendant for it, I think. The new man in charge said the company made a mistake, and would concentrate on what it did best. They can talk some shite, them suits. What he didn't say was that the Minister for Transport and Aviation took away their licence to operate private jets."

"Really, why's that?" asked Oliver.

"Sure, they were shitting themselves somebody else in Ireland'd try it. Imagine: some gangster trying, like that fella in America, the Mafia lad. Unbelievable!"

"Oh yeah, I think I heard about that. Unbelievable is right."

"He got done with a planeload of donkeys full of dope. Ha, talk about drug mules! That's beat all. They reckon that plane was coming to Ireland, too!"

Rebecca and Oliver exchanged glances and tried to stifle nervous chuckles, to no avail. All three of them laughed like school kids as they entered the terminal and found their way to Customs and Passport Control.

They flashed their Canadian passports at the Duty Officer,

who gave them a cursory look and scanned them into the system. Rebecca felt slightly uneasy when she heard the machine beep, but their passports were handed back without comment.

On the way out, while Rebecca dashed to the toilet, Oliver's eye was caught by a national newspaper headline: *MORE COCAINE DEATH.* He bought the paper and stood bolt still as he read the article.

Four people overdosed on cocaine in Limerick city in twenty-four hours last weekend. Add this to the six that died from overdoses last autumn, and Limerick is becoming a graveyard of drug tragedy, the journalist clumsily commented. One of the victims last weekend was a well-known, pretty, 20-year-old classical violinist. She was celebrating having won a scholarship to the Julliard in New York.

Gardai found a small amount of the drug in her pockets, which they sent for analysis. It is believed that the recent deaths are due to the purity of the drug. According to Gardai, cocaine of this purity has never been dispensed on the streets in Ireland.

The article contained a lengthy quote from a senior Garda officer in Limerick. *"Usually the drug arrives in Ireland in relatively small quantities, so the gangs water it down, so to speak, to maximise profit. In this case, the drug was distributed in an almost pure form. The user would have a better high and keep coming back for more of the same product. It would follow that whoever brought this batch may well be planning on bringing in sufficient quantity so as to reduce the need to cut it down, thereby flooding the streets with a highly addictive and dangerous narcotic. Ireland could be on the cusp of a cocaine epidemic."*

Oliver felt himself weaken and his stomach start to churn. He really hadn't given much thought to what might have happened to the drugs he brought over inside Painter.

Rebecca saw the look on his face as she walked towards him. He offered her the paper and slumped against the wall.

"Holy shit!" she said. "Are you thinking what I'm thinking?"

"That we may have killed those people?"

"I, well, not exactly that. I mean, we didn't force them to take it. But it was here because of us."

Oliver looked uncomfortable and conflicted. He tore off the front page and folded it into his pocket. "Come on, let's get to a hotel."

They said nothing as they caught a taxi to the city centre and booked into a generic, plain hotel near Temple Bar. Oliver bought a pre-paid mobile and used it to call his mother.

Evelyn answered, sounding frail.

"Hi, Mum. How are you?"

"Oliver! How are you? I saw in the papers they put that awful man in jail for life. They didn't say much about you, though, apart from something about you and a vet being forced to work for him. There was some sordid gossip about you and Richard being drug smuggling brothers, but I declined to read the details. Anyway, enough of that. Where are you? Is Rebecca with you?"

"We're both fine and we're in Ireland. Er, Mum, can you catch the train to Dublin tomorrow?"

"Of course, but why don't you come here?"

"I'll explain it all to you tomorrow. Call me on this number with the times, OK?"

"What's it all about?"

"I'll explain everything tomorrow . . . And, Mum?"

"Yes?"

"You know I love you, right?"

"Of course I do. Why are you saying that? I'll see you tomorrow."

"Thanks, Mum."

He ended the call and immediately dialled Foster's office. After being kept on hold for ten minutes by the sourly efficient secretary, he eventually got through to Foster.

"James. It's Oliver McMahon."

"Oliver, God, how are you? You, er, just vanished for a while. Your mother's very worried. I've been keeping her up-to-date on everything. I carried out those instructions you left me. They, er, mentioned you in the papers a bit. The horse world papers, I mean. My wife showed me the articles. Quite the scandal in the horse business, it seems. Some flying groom is planning a tell-all article in next week's *Horse's Mouth* magazine."

"Hmm, I don't suppose I'll be returning to my former line of work, James. Look, I know this is a bit out of the blue, but I'm under pressure and I have to disappear for a bit. So I was wondering, can you meet me tomorrow morning in Temple Bar?"

"Tomorrow? Well, I'm not sure. Can I get back to you?"

"No, I'm only here for a day or so and I've got a lot to sort out. Please, James, meet me in the Quality Night Hotel in Temple Bar at eleven. I'll explain everything to you then. There's a lot of stuff you don't know. Oh, and James?"

"Yes?" he said gingerly.

"Don't tell anyone where you're going to be."

"What?"

"And before we meet, please go to the safety deposit box you opened for me. Open it, read the letter that Rich wrote, and bring me fifty grand in cash, please."

"I don't understand all this cloak-and-dagger stuff, Oliver."

"Look, I haven't asked you for much up to now. I'd give you more time if I had it, but I don't. So cancel what you have to, and do what I ask. Please, James, it's very important."

The lawyer remembered the last time a McMahon had asked him for help in such a tone, and told Oliver he would cancel his meetings and be there for eleven the next day.

At six-thirty that evening, Oliver sat himself in a corner booth in the hotel lounge. He ordered a pint of Guinness and a gin and tonic, and waited for Rebecca.

She slid in beside him and took a sip of her gin. "Hmm, that's not much of a drink."

"All style and no substance here. The Guinness isn't great, either."

She looked him up and down. "Why the long face, hon?"

"I've made a proper bollocks of things. Family-wise, I mean. It's funny, it occurred to me that Mum'll end up a bit like Marco: separated from her remaining family, except in her case it's no fault of her own. And all I can do is see that she's set up financially, just like Rich used to do."

"Don't be so hard on yourself, there's not much you can do about it. For the moment, anyway."

He had a pained expression on his face. "We crossed the line when we brought that shit here inside Painter. I can't believe I never considered that before. That shipment was a part of our game also, and the stuff got onto the street to mess up kids and families. We allowed it to happen to serve our own ends."

She wagged her finger at him. "Hold on a minute. We, yes *we*, are responsible for putting Marco Romano away for a very long time. If we'd called Huntley for the Painter bust, Marco'd have barely got a rap on the knuckles. Then how long before it was business as usual for him, huh? How many people dead then? No, we did the right thing. And let's face it, we didn't have a whole lot of options."

"Hmm, I suppose you're right." He pushed his glass away and glanced around. "Let's go somewhere for a quiet dinner. I don't want to keep talking here."

Chapter 68

The next day the rain hammered down out of the thick, grey winter sky as Oliver collected his mother off the noon train at Heuston Station. She had put on a little weight and looked almost sprightly as she wheeled her case along the platform. Oliver ran to her and hugged her tight, kissing her cheek. Her skin was icy cold. She barely recognised him.

"Mum, you're freezing."

"And you look strange with no hair and that dirty-looking stubble."

He rubbed his shiny scalp. "Oh, er, a new image – and Bec's gone blonde. You look well, though."

"Thank you, I think," she said jokingly. "I've been keeping myself busy, feeding that nice horse you left on the place. She really is a sweetheart."

Oliver forced a smile. "I'm glad she's keeping you company."

"It's not the same as having you and Rebecca, but I'll manage."

The smile disappeared. "I know, Mum, I know."

They walked off the platform onto the street and took a cab for the hotel.

* * *

Neither of them noticed the burly man wearing the bomber jacket who followed Evelyn off the train and got into the next cab. He made a call on the way. "Yeah, I'm in Dublin. The old woman, she met a guy at the station."

"Was it him?"

"I never saw him before. This guy has shaved head and beard, but he embraced her, kissed her on both cheeks. So I think we have our man. I am following them now. What I do next?"

"Wait there. I have to talk to the Italians. I'll get back to you."

* * *

When they arrived, Oliver took his mother for tea in the lounge. Evelyn threw off her coat and gloves, sank into an armchair, and sipped the hot drink with a look of relief.

Oliver took a deep breath and spelled it all out for her. "Mum, I'll get straight to the point. Rebecca and I have to go away for a while. It's just a precaution, after all the stuff with Marco Romano and the horses, but it's for the best. The Americans got us new passports and we're going to keep travelling around, stay on the hop, and use the time to see the world."

She put her cup down and looked at her son with a mixture of sadness and resolve. "I was expecting this. I can't say it's thrilling to hear it for definite, but . . ." Her voice began to crack and a tear slipped down her cheek. She brushed it away sharply.

Evelyn reached across the table and took his hand in hers. "You just take care of that girl of yours and start a family, that's all I want. We'll see each other soon enough." She took a deep breath. "I don't want you to end up like your brother," she said, letting Oliver off the hook.

"What?" He looked puzzled.

"Foster and the papers kept me informed of the news here. The Gardai are sure that organised crime was involved in the drug scandal and your brother's death. Can you believe that Italian chap still hasn't said a word?"

Oliver could believe it only too well.

She sighed in exasperation. "So they locked him up. The airline looked ruined, but a chap called Martin Forrester got Freefly off the hook somehow. Wasn't he the thin chap who came to the house after the funeral?"

"Yes, he was."

"Anyway, they never did explain it fully." She shrugged. "Then it all blew over." She looked straight at him. "Two brothers, drugs, and a Mafia boss. I can't imagine what persuaded you both to get mixed up with him. Anyway, what's done is done. I've already lost one son to that awful man, I don't want to lose another, so go on, take off and look after yourselves." Another tear welled up in her eye and threatened to stream down her thin face. She fumbled in her handbag for a tissue.

Oliver was in shock. He knew she was selflessly saying this to make it easier for him, but he still felt like he was deserting her. Hell, he was deserting her. He rubbed his temples, to stop his brain spinning. "Mum, you can't make it that easy for me. I'm doing exactly what I promised not to do."

She looked at him sharply. "I can make it as easy as I like. I'm an old woman, and you're now my only son. You're in the prime of your life; now I want you to enjoy it. This is my gift to you." She paused. "Consider it compensation for your father's neglect. He was too hard on you, but try to understand that he didn't mean it. He just wanted you to be as tough as your brother. What's done is done; I've learnt that since Richard died. Don't dwell on the past and don't let it eat away at you."

Oliver was stunned, and flopped back in the chair. He had never seen his mother look so steely, and he was starting to realise that she was tougher than he gave her credit for. She took everything life threw at her without complaining.

"You sound like Rebecca," he said, smiling. "But the only way I can try to put this behind me is to do something good with Richard's money. And with Painter."

She raised her eyebrows. "What did you have in mind?"

"Well, I met James Foster this morning. We discussed everything. First of all: he sold Rich's apartment for 600,000. The money will go to you, along with another million."

Evelyn nearly dropped her teacup. "600,000 for a flat? In Clontarf? That's ridiculous!"

Oliver chuckled. "I agree, but there you are. James says property's worth a fortune in Dublin, and still going up in value."

"Huh, the country's gone mad."

"Hmm . . . Anyway, we'll set up a charity that will provide

legal advice and representation for people who have been treated unfairly by their employers, dismissed without just cause, or who have been victims of lies and deceit by corporations."

Evelyn looked stunned.

"James will run it. I appealed to his humanitarian streak – you know what he did in the Philippines when he was young – and you'll be a trustee. So will I; the Americans haven't killed me off, just given me a new ID. I gave James my real passport and driver's licence."

He gulped down a glass of water. "Anyway, the service will be free of charge, but if litigation fees soar, which they might do if the case is against a large corporation, then we'll have to work it like those so-called *ambulance-chasers*: take a percentage of any settlement to cover costs. We can't do any good if we go broke defending a case against a multi-national, or if we lose a case and get wiped out. Far better we take a percentage of a generous settlement and live to fight another day."

"Is it always all about money, these days?" asked Evelyn.

Oliver sighed. "Yes, Mum, unfortunately it is. I wish it wasn't. I'd love to do all the work for free, but there's no point in going out of business. Who'll fight for the little man, then? And like I said, I can't take Rich's cash and run off into the sunset. I just can't."

"Why on earth not? You've certainly earned it, with all you've endured."

"I haven't, Mum. I haven't earned *seventy-five million* Euro. And neither did he. He just figured out a way to make it. So I've got to take that and use it to help people. James will take care of it and set it up; he'll be in touch with the details. I'll communicate via email. Claude's brother will set me up an untraceable account."

"It's all very cloak and dagger."

Oliver shrugged. "Better safe than sorry . . . Um, I also need you to auction Painter at a horse sale and give the proceeds to the Limerick Drug Treatment Centre. Specifically, I want to find a way of educating school kids and students about the link between their occasional joint and organised crime."

"I don't know how to do that."

"Sean'll help you get her ready and enter her for the sales, but call James first. He has to get permission from the Americans." Oliver slid Monica Kimble's card onto the table. "He'll use this agent as a contact to put pressure on the justice system to get Painter released from Marco's assets. If she has any trouble, James will contact this reporter for *Trackspeed* magazine." He placed Emmy Harris's card beside Monica's. "She'll go public about the Feds denying an addiction centre a windfall. That should do the trick."

"How much is Painter worth?" she said, putting the cards in her purse.

"Maybe half a million. More, if the right people do battle for her. She was a hell of a racehorse."

Evelyn was about to speak, but instead she glanced over Oliver's shoulder, smiled broadly, and stood. Rebecca had arrived from the room. The two women embraced.

"You look different with blonde hair. I hear you're off travelling," said Evelyn.

Rebecca gave her a lopsided smile.

"Stay safe, both of you." She gripped both their hands. The silence was deafening.

Suddenly, Evelyn released them and started to put on her coat. "I'm going to dash and catch the evening train."

"But, Mum . . ."

"Not a word, Oliver. Just let me know you're alright, wherever you end up." She nudged Rebecca. "I'll be relying on you for that. He's been hopeless about keeping in touch since this whole episode started." With that, she buttoned up her coat. "Onwards and upwards."

"Mum, please stay the night, I got you a room."

"I'll get back to Painter. You get on a plane and stay safe." She held out her arms. "But I would like a hug, before I leave."

Oliver gripped his mother tight and kissed her on both cheeks. "I'll take you to the station."

"That would be nice." She hugged Rebecca and whispered in

her ear, "Look after him for me." Tears were welling up in her eyes, but she hastily wiped them with a tissue.

Oliver hailed a cab and dropped his mother to the platform just in time for the express train back to Limerick. He hugged her tightly before she boarded.

"We'll see each other again before you know it," she said, though neither of them believed it.

He stood on the platform until the train was long out of view.

When he got back to the hotel, Rebecca had already packed their bags. "That was some job today. Hell of a plan you came up with."

"Thanks, Bec. I'm glad we'll be able to do something with all that money."

"There's no point staying here any more, hon. Let's go to the airport." She arched her eyebrows quizzically.

He grabbed her and kissed her passionately. "You read my mind. Let's go right now."

They paid the bill and hopped in a taxi for the airport. An hour later, they stood in the check-in area, gazing up at the departures board amidst a seething mass of humanity.

"Holy shit, it's pretty busy for a Tuesday evening in winter," said Rebecca, jostling for space to stand in the crowds.

"The celtic cubs never stop. For now, anyway. Where to, Bec?"

"Paris. Definitely Paris – I've never been. Then on to Bombay."

Oliver pulled a plastic bag out of his holdall and handed it to Rebecca.

She opened it. "What the–! Are these all five-hundreds?"

"Yep! There's fifty grand in there. I got it from the bank. James slipped it to me this morning."

"Crafty devil."

He smiled.

They walked hand-in-hand to the Aer Lingus ticket desk, where Oliver asked for two economy tickets for the next flight to Paris. "No, hang on a second," he said to the girl as she typed details into her computer. "Make that two *business* class seats." He winked at Rebecca and they both burst out laughing.

Chapter 69

Marco strode purposefully down the dreary corridor, ignoring the faceless shouts which echoed around the walls, and made his way to the electric door. The burly guard followed him at a respectful distance of three paces, contrary to procedure.

"How's the wife and kids, Bruce?" Marco said over his shoulder.

"They're good, Mr. Romano. And thanks again."

"Anytime, Bruce."

The door buzzed and snapped open, letting the Mafia boss through to the holding area. He stood tall, and smiled and nodded at the door guard behind the glass, who jerked his finger towards the interview rooms. Marco ran his hands over his slicked-back hair and tugged on the collar of his prison jumpsuit to reveal the immaculate white T-shirt underneath.

He passed the entrance to the row of cubicles for normal visitors, linked to the other side by telephone handsets, all conversations eavesdropped on by the door guard and his assistant. There was no such lack of privacy for Marco when he had a lawyer visit.

"Which one?" he asked.

"Number three, Mr. Romano," said Bruce, scurrying around to open the door.

The heavy steel door swung open to reveal Hal Bristow, sitting alone on a plastic chair with his back to the door. He swivelled at the sound. There was sweat running from his hairline and trickling down the side of his face to form a dark stain on his collar. His neck bulged as if his purple silk tie was cutting into him like a noose. He began to stand.

"Don't bother," spat Marco.

Bruce pulled out Marco's chair and let him sit comfortably. "Will that be all, Mr. Romano?"

"Yeah. Thanks."

Bruce shot a curious look at the perspiring attorney and closed the door behind him.

Marco stared stony-faced at his lawyer. "Where's Tweedle-Dee?"

Hal looked terrified. "Todd got, um, hit by a car. He's in hospital – ICU."

"He gonna pull through?"

Hal swallowed. "Doctors aren't sure."

"Huh. Got a cigarette?"

Hal fumbled in his pocket and produced a pack. Marco tore the whole thing from his hand and lit one. He inhaled deeply and savoured the moment, leaving the cigarette in his mouth while his hands drummed the table rhythmically.

Hal waited.

"So, what do you got for me?" said Marco, drumming continuously.

Hal glanced over his shoulder and leaned in conspiratorially. "I spoke to The Nail. He got in contact." He paused.

"And?" The fingers kept tapping the table.

Another bead of sweat fell down the lawyer's face. Marco followed it, and found it hard to suppress a grin.

"Well, he uh, he told me to ask you if you wanted any tidying up done. Specifically in relation to the uh, young Rat and the, um, Irish situation." Hal could imagine what tidying up referred to, but was not inclined to give it much thought, lest he might start wondering if he would find himself on the garbage list. Mike had assured him that he and Todd were on very thin ice and no further fuck-ups would be tolerated.

Marco's hands stopped moving and he slumped back in his chair. He discarded his cigarette and pondered the tasks. A wave of sadness passed over him, one that he did his best to push out of his mind during the normal prison routine. But here, alone with Hal in the room, it bore down on him like a vise.

"Forget the young one. He's not to be touched. Ever. Make sure word gets out. I don't want some eager asshole trying to make a name for himself trying to impress me. Understand?"

Hal nodded. "And the Irishman?"

Marco stuffed another cigarette in his mouth and started drumming the table again.

After a couple of minutes, Hal cleared his throat.

Marco glanced at him momentarily through the smoke and took another deep drag of nicotine. The fingers kept drumming.

ABOUT E.H. WARD

E.H. Ward was born in England in 1973 to a racehorse trainer father and a mother who studied speech and drama at the Royal Academy in London. He moved to his mother's native Limerick in Ireland at the age of nine and grew up riding, pony clubbing, fox-hunting, and working for local racehorse trainers and stud farms.

After school and a brief stint in the British army, he returned to England to start full-time work with racehorses. He spent the '90s travelling the world working with horses and in the bloodstock industry. From England, he moved back to Ireland then down to the Hunter Valley in Australia where he worked on a large stud farm and travelled and spent time on a cattle farm, breaking-in wild horses.

From Australia it was on to Kentucky the home of American horse racing and breeding, where he began working for the US arm of Ireland's renowned Coolmore Stud. He spent the next ten years working at Coolmore and was put in charge of their China/Mongolia project, spending six months creating a stud on the plains of Inner Mongolia and a year training racehorses on the outskirts of Beijing.

He was seconded to the Turkish Jockey Club for a year to upgrade and run the Turkish National Stud, before returning full-time to Ireland in 2001, as an area manager at Coolmore's Tipperary headquarters.

In 2006 he went back to Turkey to build and manage a racing/breeding operation on the Aegean coast working with a local businessman who wanted an international standard manager/advisor.

He is married to a Frenchwoman, and they have one son aged

five. He currently divides his time between the stud farm near Izmir and southern France. He writes analytical articles and horseracing and sale reviews for The Irish Field newspaper and James Underwood's Racing and Breeding Digest in the UK.

• • •

Find E.H. Ward online

Facebook
www.facebook.com/eric.ward.3760

Tirgearr Publishing
www.tirgearrpublishing.com/authors/Ward_EH

• • •

Thank you for reading A Sure Thing.

If you liked this story, watch for other releases from E.H. Ward at Tirgearr Publishing.

Lightning Source UK Ltd.
Milton Keynes UK
UKOW07f2144061114

241196UK00001B/42/P